THE DUKE

THE DUKE

Catherine Coulter

WHEELER
PUBLISHING, INC.
ROCKLAND, MA

★ AN AMERICAN COMPANY ★

Published in Large Print by arrangement with Penguin Books USA Inc. in the U.S. and Canada.

Wheeler Large Print Book Series.

Set in 16 pt. Plantin.

Library of Congress Cataloging-in-Publication Data

Coulter, Catherine.
    The Duke / Catherine Coulter.
      p.   cm. — (Wheeler large print book series)
    ISBN 1-56895-416-6
    1. Large type books. I. Title. II. Series.
[PS3553.0843D8   1997b]
813'.54—dc21   97 714
                                                            CIP

To my husband, who's the sexiest, smartest and the most entertaining man in the world. Second time around, babe, for The Generous Earl. *Thanks for the first time and all the other times.*

THE SCOTTISH ROBERTSONS

ANGUS ROBERTSON—Earl of Penderleigh, now deceased

LADY ADELLA—Dowager countess of Penderleigh

Lady Adella's sons:

DAVONAN—deceased
CLIVE—deceased

Lady Adella's granddaughters:

BRANDY
CONSTANCE } Clive's daughters
FIONA

Lady Adella's grandson:

PERCIVAL—Davonan's bastard son

DOUGLAS ROBERTSON—Angus's elder brother, deceased; disinherited and his line severed

Douglass's son:

CLAUDE

Douglass's grandson:

BERTRAND

1

Lady Felicity Trammerley, eldest daughter of the Earl of Braecourt, had been taught from her cradle by her devoted mama what was due to her. Certainly a lot was due to her, she reasoned, from her betrothed, the Duke of Portmaine. After all, she had consented to marry him. Certainly it was an achievement for him to have won her consent. She knew he believed her docile and malleable, very probably like a sheep, and those qualities were what he desired. She did her best to convince him she possessed them. Diligence and hard work. Her mama had patted her beautiful black hair and told her diligence would always get her what she wanted. Ah, but sometimes it was trying, particularly now, after the duke had told her why he'd come to visit her. She held her tongue. She let him talk. She knew she still had to tread lightly, even though their engagement had been formally announced in the *Gazette* the previous week. Yes, she had to be careful not to scream at him when he told her in that clipped, arrogant way of his why he'd come, the selfish clod.

The charm came swimming through her voice as she said, "My dear Ian, you know I'm pleased about the inheritance, even though it's just a Scottish title and estate. But I fail to understand the urgency of your traveling now, in the middle of the Season, to inspect some moldering old castle that has probably been close to ruin for the past hundred years. Surely, the turrets won't crumble if you postpone your trip until the summer. Oh, dear, it doesn't still have a moat, does it? They're dreadfully unhealthy. Now, no one could expect you to give up all the pleasures of the Season just for this."

She didn't add that her own pleasures were very much intertwined with his, for the umbrella of his consequence as a wealthy and powerful peer made everyone treat her just as they ought now that they were affianced and she was recognized as the future Duchess of Portmaine. There were still a couple of old biddies who still hadn't accepted the fact, but when she finally married him, she'd fix them but good.

Ian Charles Curlew Carmichael, fifth Duke of Portmaine, regarded the dainty, altogether delicious specimen of womanhood seated before him with an indulgent look in his dark eyes. He smiled at her, for it was impossible not to, for it pleased him simply to look at her. She was very beautiful. She spoke softly, as a duchess should. She moved gracefully as a duchess should. Yes, he'd done the right thing.

"No," he said finally, "you're right about that, Felicity. No one would expect such an excess of landlordly zeal—no one save myself and, of course, my late uncle Richard. He taught me to care for what was mine because if I didn't, someone else would, and that would leave me nothing more than a fool. I must go. If I leave within the week, I should be back within the month. I know you'll understand, my dear. I can't simply turn my back on my obligations, no matter if they must intrude upon other, more interesting pursuits." Actually, he thought, it was more to the point that he would seize on any possible excuse to save him from all the flash and dash of the Season. The endless parties and balls bored him to his eyebrows and completely deadened his mind.

Ah, but he knew that ladies enjoyed that sort of thing, and he was, after all, a gentleman. But now he could remain a gentleman and escape as well. He was enjoying exquisite relief with virtually no guilt.

Lady Felicity went stiff as a board at his despotic dismissal of her objections. He preferred going to the backwater of the world rather than remain in London with her, damn him. She carefully swallowed an acid reply and managed to say with reasonable good humor, "But, Ian, you have told me yourself that you don't even know these people. And you know the Scots—nasty barbarians, all of them. I can't believe they'd welcome an Englishman. Why don't you just send your solicitor, Jerkin, to see to things?"

The duke gazed into the soft leaf green eyes, slightly slanted at the corners, eyes that reminded him so much of his first wife's. No, he wouldn't think about Marianne, not now. It wasn't right. He had to forget Marianne. Surely once Felicity was his duchess, she would take Marianne's place. She would make him release his hold on his long dead wife.

He said, "You just might be right, my dear,

but nonetheless, it is my duty to at least visit Penderleigh Castle and determine what I'm going to do with the place. After all, these offensive barbarians, as you call them, are related to me, though somewhat removed in bloodlines."

"I said they were nasty, not offensive."

"Forgive me, the two words seem remarkably akin to me. Now, the title comes to me through my great aunt, whom, I understand, still lives at Penderleigh through some sort of bizarre Scottish legal ruling made some years ago. I regret to leave you alone during the height of the social whirl"— at least he had the grace to avoid looking at her directly as he spoke—"but you know you can always depend on Giles to take you wherever you want to go. You like him, he's witty and lighthearted. He dances well. He knows every scrap of gossip in London. I have no idea how he does it."

The duke looked perplexed, then shook his head and grinned. "Can you bear that he wraps himself in a yellow-striped waistcoat with a row of huge silver buttons and plants a hunter green coat over all of it?"

He pictured Giles preening in that ensemble. He'd called him a peacock with his tail feathers all plumed out, but his cousin had only punched his arm and told him he was too stolid in his dress, an absolute bore, as a matter of fact.

It would have come as a drop-dead shock to the duke to learn that Lady Felicity held Giles in fashionable esteem and believed his mode of dress far more elegant than the overly simple styles the duke wore. And he would have laughed

4

in denial had he known that she considered Giles, with his slender, far slighter frame, less intimidating than the duke. He didn't know that right at this moment Lady Felicity felt a cramp in her belly, remembering her brother, Lord Sayer, coarsely teasing her about the duke when he'd been told by their ecstatic father about her betrothal. He had tweaked her chin in that hearty, loathsome way of his, all the while allowing his laughing gaze to flit over her petite body.

"Well, little puss, the duke is a man mountain. I bravely took him on in the ring the other day, saw him stripped to his hide, you know. All hard muscle, my dear, not a patch of fat on him. Most *noble* proportions even in rest, if you glean my meaning, which I hope you don't, since you're a virgin and a ninny. I vow you'll have a lusty wedding night with him. You'll probably not walk straight for days."

Felicity quickly looked away from the duke, realizing that she'd been eyeing him with something akin to horror. She repeated to herself that Ian was, after all, a duke. One didn't look at dukes with horror. One admired dukes. When she became his duchess, she would be compensated for what she would have to endure in his bedchamber. She would give him an heir—she knew that was expected by everyone, including her fond mama, who profoundly regretted that her little treasure would have to be violated by a husband—but then, surely, he would leave her alone and be content to dally with his mistresses.

Lady Felicity managed to smile up at him. She knew it wouldn't be wise to protest his decision further. She had seen often enough how he would withdraw from her at any hint of opposition. She drew herself up confidently. When she became the Duchess of Portmaine, ah, then things would change.

She managed to keep her smile firmly in place. "You know I'll miss you dreadfully, Ian."

The duke rose from the pale blue brocade settee and clasped her small hands between his large ones. "I'll miss you too, my dear. I'm delighted that you understand my reasons. I shan't be gone long, you'll see."

Lady Felicity didn't understand his reasons at all, but she held her tongue. She allowed the duke to kiss her cheek. His mouth was warm. She didn't mind it. If only a husband would stop with a kiss, then it would be perfect, but her mama had told her that she would have to endure much more than just simple kisses. It was something all ladies had to endure, including her poor little precious, and she'd patted her head.

She said as the butler helped the duke into his cloak, "August seems a lifetime away, Ian. A full six months until our wedding. It will be the largest wedding of the year and at St. George's. Everyone who matters will be there."

A vivid image of his first wife, Marianne, rose uninvited to his mind. They'd been married at St. George's. Everyone of any importance had begged to come. It had been the happiest day of his life. Marianne, his beautiful Marianne. She was indeed a lifetime away from him, an eternity.

He looked down at Felicity, in whose company he'd rediscovered pleasures that had long since been missing from his life. She bore a striking resemblance to Marianne, and as he had come to know her better, he had seen more and more the same gentleness and modesty, the same softness and kindness.

He could not deny that it was time for him to marry again. He was twenty-eight, life was always uncertain, and everyone expected it of him simply because he had to sire an heir. He reminded himself how lucky he was to have a Marianne and a Felicity come into his life.

He looked down at her a moment longer, then took his leave.

Later that day, in the drawing room of the Portmaine town house, Mr. Giles Braidston twirled the delicate stem of his brandy snifter between his slender fingers, remarking as he did so to his cousin, the Duke of Portmaine, "Felicity informs me that you've determined to travel to Scotland. Rather a troublesome adventure, I should say, but you like that sort of thing, don't you? All that endless hectic travel, never knowing if the bed at the next inn will have more fleas than the owner's dogs. Of course, you realize that Felicity is, shall we say, rather agitated by your decision. Actually, I'd call it a good old-fashioned snit, but what do I know? Felicity does a snit very well—nose in the air, lips all thinned out, eyes turning dark with meanness. Yes, she's quite good at the art of the snit. I fancy her mama taught her how to do it before she was out of the schoolroom."

Ian was leaning over a large oak desk, scrutinizing a map of Scotland. "Bedamned, Giles, as far as I can tell, it will take me at least five days to reach Penderleigh Castle. And from what I understand, the roads are rutted paths, more suited for sheep than for carriages. It's near to Berwick-on-Tweed, on the eastern coast. I'm sorry, old fellow, what did you say?"

"Your betrothed, Ian, and her snit."

Ian said easily, "If Felicity has sent you to me to change my mind, you can forget it. I have to go. It's my duty. You'll see to her, of course."

"Certainly I'll take very good care of her and enjoy myself as well, since everyone treats me very nicely when I'm in your place. Being your nominal heir has its benefits, and I do enjoy them all, thank you, cousin."

The duke thought of the pile of bills he'd told Pabbson to pay to Giles's creditors only a month ago. He was fond of his fashionable cousin, and didn't begrudge Giles's occasional dipping into his much larger till. Thank God Giles wasn't addicted to the gaming tables, but only to silver buttons and outlandish waistcoats.

He said, "Do just as you please when you're in my place, Giles. The only favor I ask of you is to see to Felicity's comfort. You will do that, won't you, Giles?"

"Oh, yes, trust me to soothe her troubled brow, if she even has one. Her mama taught her never to frown. It would make her forehead wrinkle at too early an age. Have you ever thought that Felicity much resembles her mama?"

The duke didn't even pause but said, "Since you are my cousin, the gossips can't fault you as her escort. Felicity dearly loves town life, just as did Mari—well, damn." The duke looked away, drew a deep breath, and added, "If Felicity wishes her routs and balls, I don't want her to be disappointed."

Giles was swinging the black velvet ribbon that held his watch back and forth, back and forth. "It seems to me, Ian, that your trip to Scotland is exquisitely timed. A rather drastic measure, I should say, to avoid the Season and all its gadding about."

"Gadding? What a nonsensical word. The Season is a bloody bore and you know it. Well, perhaps you don't, but I do."

"I pray you won't say that quite the same way you just said it to me to your betrothed. You just might be treated to an earl's daughter's rendition of 'You're a bloody bugger and I'll make you pay.'"

The duke just waved him away, but he did look thoughtful for a moment. He carefully rolled up his map of Scotland and fastened it with a short length of ribbon. "Perhaps, Giles, you see too much. I know you say too much. If you want to know the truth, I'll tell you. Going to Penderleigh Castle is more a release from gaol than it is a duty. I do have some curiosity about my Robertson relatives and obviously I've got to see the place, but the thought of squiring another betrothed about for the length of the Season makes me want to draw my bedcovers over my head and howl. Indeed, if I was never again in London for the Season, I wouldn't give a good damn. Indeed, I would consider myself the luckiest of men."

"How wise of you, cousin, not to tell Felicity as much. As I said before, I knew you wouldn't like her response. Lord, she would be hard pressed to keep up that submissive facade she's adopted for you. It is a facade, Ian, a mask, if you will. I can't believe you don't see it."

"She would be disappointed, Giles, but she is kind and understanding and very giving."

Giles gave him an incredulous look. "Good God, Ian, I grant you that Felicity bears a striking physical resemblance to Marianne, but all similarity ends there.

"Incidentaly, Felicity has told me that you utterly refuse to talk about your first wife to her. It is natural, I think, for her to have some curiosity about Marianne."

"Felicity will know exactly what I wish to tell her, Giles, and I have told her that I have a great fondness for girls of her general coloring."

"Lord, Ian, isn't it enough that most of your mistresses over the last five years have been endowed with black hair and green eyes? If Felicity ever discovers that fact, you will soon learn the bounds of her gentle nature."

He threw up his hands as Ian's eyes darkened. "Acquit me of mischief, Ian, I will say no more on the matter. If you wish to marry Felicity, for whatever reason, who am I to talk you out of it?"

2

"Thank you for all your keen opinions. As for Felicity's character, I daresay that she will become whatever I wish her to be—if, that is, she isn't already exactly what I require in a wife."

No sooner were the pompous, utterly arrogant words out of his mouth than he regretted them. He meant them, but he knew he shouldn't. He didn't want to mean them, yet they were there. What was he to do? Keep his mouth shut, obviously. He had the wit to change the subject.

"You must know, Giles, that poor old Mabley hasn't stopped his predictions of doom and gloom. I told him that if he didn't wish to accompany me, being an older man and perhaps not quite up to it, I would take Japper. That shut him up fast enough. Told me, he did in that hang-jaw way of his, that I'd like as not forget my waistcoat and cravat if he wasn't there to remind me. He still can't think of me as a man grown despite my twenty-eight years."

Mr. Braidston unconsciously fingered his own flawlessly tied cravat. Although nature had not seen fit to endow him with his cousin's grand height or broad shoulders or athletic build, he believed that he presented a far more elegant picture. He was civilized. He was a hostess's dream. He always knew exactly what to say, what to do. In his view, Ian was a dull dog, much too

11

serious and set in his ways, and his clothes proved his point.

"Mabley is an old man, Ian. Valet to your father, wasn't he? Time to put him out to pasture, pension him off." Giles yawned.

How very like Giles, the duke thought, to think only of the benefits of a title and wealth without any concern for the responsibilities.

He said only, "No, I think not, Giles. I daresay that I should be as lost without him as he would be without a dozen pair of hessians to polish. But enough of my time-honored valet. Did Felicity tell you of the round-about manner in which I have succeeded the Earl of Penderleigh?"

"She said something about a great aunt, an Englishwoman and the absurd Scottish courts. I'm loath to say that she quite lost interest in the subject when a new ball gown arrived from Madame Flauquet. She wanted my opinion of the gown, of course."

"Of course. Well, I have no waistcoats that cry out for your opinion, so you have no choice but to listen to me."

Mr. Braidston waved his monocle and settled back against the settee, a look of gentle suffering setting comically on his face. "My heart is a-pounding, my soul awaits your poetry."

Ian didn't have time to get beyond the name of Robertson before his butler gently opened the double library doors. "Your pardon, your grace. A Dr. Edward Mulhouse is here to see you."

"Edward! Good God, it's been months. Show him in, James. You remember Edward Mulhouse, don't you, Giles? You met him on

12

your last visit to Carmichael Hall. I fancy that with him I'll have a more attentive audience."

Edward Mulhouse strode into the duke's darkly elegant library, his tanned, lean face alight with pleasure. He was a huge bear of a man with large hands and large feet. But he was nattily dressed, though not as elegantly turned out as Mr. Braidston, a fact that Giles quickly noted. He and the duke had become fast friends as boys.

The two gentlemen shook hands, and Ian clapped his friend's shoulders. "However did all your patients allow you to escape from Suffolk?"

"There was only one lame horse when I left, Ian. Not even a single boil. I couldn't even scare up a sprained ankle. I was unneeded and unwanted. I was downcast. What could I do but come to the fleshpots of London and visit my father? I thought I would give you a marvelous treat and visit you. So here I am."

"Excellent. Edward, you remember, of course, my cousin, Giles Braidston?"

"Indeed, I do. A pleasure to see you again."

Giles suffered having his hand gripped by a man built like an oak tree, who could likely take a broken leg and pull it back into place without even a huff.

He said with a sigh, "Do sit down, Edward. There are now two of us that Ian can bore to the devil."

"If you must know, Edward, I have just come into an earldom in Scotland and was in the process of telling Giles here how it all came about." He handed Edward a glass of sherry. "But

13

first, my friend, does all go well at Carmichael Hall? Is Danvers still his same stiff, arthritic self?"

Without a trace of envy Edward pictured the duke's Suffolk estate, Carmichael Hall, and its many inhabitants. "Danvers is just as you describe him. I swear, Ian, your butler frequently makes me feel as though he's the master. His dignity tends to be overwhelming."

"Ian keeps him on to bolster his importance."

"Untrue, Giles, you're the one who likes bolstering."

"You do too, Ian. You're just used to it, thus you don't ever remark upon it."

Could that possibly be true? the duke wondered. Conversation continued in this vein for some minutes before Edward cocked his head to one side and said, "Enough of Carmichael Hall, London, the king, and everyone's importance. What is all of this about a Scottish earldom, Ian?"

"Oh," Giles moaned, "and here I'd thought we'd distracted him."

"Not a chance, Giles. I'm just sorry that I have so few facts, for I would like to string out the telling for your benefit."

Giles rolled his eyes heavenward, but the duke ignored him, and for a moment he appeared lost in his thoughts, his long fingers stroking the firm line of his jaw.

"It's curious, really," he said finally. "I come to the estate and title through my great aunt, my grandmother's only sister, who, as I understand it, married Angus Robertson soon after Bonnie Prince Charlie's final bid for the throne. There was some sort of legal debacle, God knows what, but the courts ruled that the title and estate would come to me. There are no other male relatives." He paused a moment and cast a twinkling eye toward his cousin. "The lowland Robertsons are not, of course, to be confused with the highland Robertsons."

"Indeed not," Giles said, nodding and looking as wise as the Bishop of York. "Never would I have put the two together. At least not in this lifetime or the next, for that matter."

"All that I know from my English solicitor is that there are no Scottish male relatives to inherit, the only son remaining to the earl having died in seventeen ninety-five, leaving three daughters."

Mr. Braidston yawned delicately behind his very white hand. "Ancient history is such a bore, don't you agree, Edward?" At his grin, Giles added, "Thank God, Ian, that you have brought us quickly to the present. I don't suppose you told Felicity about this multitude of females? Three of them? That would bring a wrinkle to her brow sure to displease her mama."

"As to Felicity's displeasure, Giles, from my understanding, all the females in question are children. At least that is what I inferred from my great aunt's letter."

Edward Mulhouse looked startled. "The old woman is still alive? Good God, she must be a relic, someone old enough to have seen the flood in the Bible."

"Very much alive. She must be at least seventy years old now, or eighty or one hundred. Who knows?"

Mr. Braidston rose, allowing a look of commiseration to darken his face. "Poor Ian, playing a nursemaid to an old harridan and guardian to a gaggle of brats. Well, I must be off, old fellow. I'll leave poor Edward here as you contemplate your fate."

"A new waistcoat awaits your inspection, Giles?"

"Indeed it does. I must decide if the puce stripes will be best contemplated by gold or silver buttons. Naturally the shape of the buttons and the size are also prime considerations. This sort of thing takes time."

Giles turned to Edward. "Do call on me in Brook Street. Ian, here, is journeying to Scotland before the end of the week. Ian, I'll see you before you leave. I hope your reception in Scotland won't be unpleasant."

After Giles had been shown from the drawing room, Edward said, "Even though it's been fifty years or so since Culloden, I understand that the Scots don't in general look favorably upon their English neighbors."

The duke said quietly, "I have thought about that, Edward. I have decided to take only Mabley with me. Whatever their attitude toward the English, I have no wish for them to despise me because I come armed with ten servants and pack mules carrying all my belongings. Damn Giles anyway. Trust him to think only of an old relic and a gaggle of girls.

"Now, enough of my affairs, Edward. Tell me, which of London's more infamous fleshpots would you like to frequent during your visit?"

Actually, Edward had composed a quite impressive list, since his visits to London were few and far between.

"Good God, Edward," the duke said in some amazement when his friend had finished, "You'll have me driving out of London with a head hung so low from brandy that it will take me the entire journey to recover."

That, Edward hoped, smiling, was just what he wanted. Suffolk was a fine place, but a fleshpot, now that was just the thing he needed.

"All the way to Scotland then, Ian," Edward said, and clicked his glass to his host's.

"Damn, but this will be fun. Perhaps the pain will be worth it. You're a doctor. Can't you make the days after less painful?"

"Nary a bit, sorry," Edward said cheerfully. "It's nearly four o'clock in the afternoon. Don't we need to make plans for the evening?"

Ian thought of his mistress, the lovely Cherry Bright—he'd always prayed it was a stage name—and sighed. "Perhaps this doesn't include visiting a place like Madame Trevalier's?"

"Oh, yes. I'm ready," said Edward. "More than ready. I've been immured in the country for six months. There are only virtuous squires' daughters and married women. All the daughters giggle and give me sloe-eyed looks and make me nervous. The wives look at me with the kind of interest that scares the hell out of me. There's nothing else but sheep. What's a poor doctor to do?"

"All right," said the duke. "We'll visit every fleshpot until you're sated."

"Then look at my list, Ian. Yes, read it all the way down. Have I missed some of the best places?"

"Where did you get this bloody list?"

"From the ostler at the Gaggle Goose Inn, where I'm staying. He has a lovely daughter, but I won't get near her."

The duke sighed. "Come back here at six o'clock and bring your gear. I can't abide the thought of you staying at the Gaggle Goose Inn. You'll stay with me. And you'll stay as long as you like. Then we'll eat at my club and begin on your list."

One didn't let down one's friends, particularly when one had hunted, fished, and committed uncounted mischief with that friend, beginning at the tender age of six.

3

Lady Adella Wycliff Robertson, dowager countess of Penderleigh, lifted her worn ebony cane and waved its blunted tip toward her granddaughter. "Come, child, I won't have ye slouching about, looking just like Morag before she itches herself. Though ye carry the Robertson name, there's still English blood in yer veins and that makes ye a lady. Ladies don't slouch, do ye hear?"

"Aye, Grandmama," Brandy said, and squared her shoulders. There were chilling drafts wafting through the dowager's large, circular sitting room that always made her want to huddle into a round ball for warmth.

Even though the stone walls were covered with ancient thick wool tapestries, they had long ago been soaked to their fibers by the damp cold from the North Sea. Occasionally Brandy saw the frayed edges of the tapestries billow forward as the harsh sea winds whistled through the craggy castle stones. She inched closer to the fire in the age-blackened hearth.

"Is it true, Grandmama, what cousin Bertrand told me? The new earl is really an English duke? He's really to be our new master?"

"That he is, child. As I've told ye, his grandmother was my only sister." She snorted. "She was weak, had pap for blood and water for spirit. Lord, what separate paths we traveled . . ."

Lady Adella's voice trailed off, and Brandy realized that her grandmother's mind had traveled far away from her, many misty years in the past. She waited patiently for a few moments, then leaned forward and shook her grandmother's black satin sleeve.

"Grandmama, do ye think he will come to Penderleigh, this English duke?"

"He?" Lady Adella straightened and focused her faded blue eyes upon her granddaughter. "Och, the duke. Come here, ye say?" She curled thin lips that hadn't been kissed by a man in thirty years. "It's not likely, child. I would imagine, if anything, he will send one of those horse-faced

19

men of business in their shiny black suits to poke about. An absent English master is what we'll have, Brandy, who will care only to increase our rents. Aye, he'll take and take until there's nothing left. He just might take the old rusted cannon."

Brandy's expressive face turned red. "But we don't have any rents. We don't have hardly anything. Why, our crofters would starve if it weren't for the fishing. Grandmama, ye must be wrong—the blood in my veins that makes me a lady, it can't be English. If no English lady would do such a thing, then why would an English gentleman?"

Lady Adella sat back and drummed her arthritic fingers on the curved handle of her cane. She couldn't hate the English, for she was one of them. Still, she couldn't forget Culloden, the years of vicious English reprisals, the devastation of crofts and manors alike, the destruction of the once proud clans. She'd managed to save the Robertsons, not the highland branch, to be sure, for the Duke of Cumberland had sworn to crush them beneath the heel of his boot, and he had. They'd been slaughtered, the men, the women, the children. So little left in the highlands, except hopeless rage and the bone-deep desire for revenge.

Until nearly ten years ago even the innocent bagpipes were forbidden, the English masters reasoning that the sad, harsh sounds might reunite the clans, calling back their now far distant glory. Aye, she thought, she was still English to her bones, despite the more than fifty years spent in this isolated, forbidding castle on the North Sea.

She drew a deep sigh and said slowly, "No, Brandy, I was wrong to speak like that of the English duke. He is of my blood and thus also of yours. Time will show what kind of man he is. Maybe he won't be that bad."

She watched Brandy's strange amber eyes narrow and her nostrils flare. That was very English of her, Lady Adella thought. No one had even had to teach her how to do it properly. The girl had pride and she hadn't gotten it from the weak, willful Robertsons, but from her.

If only she had been born a boy, how very different everything would be now. There would be no Englishman to lay claim to a Scottish title and estate.

Brandy suddenly uncoiled her arms and legs and came up to rest upon her knees, never losing her balance on the small square pillow at her grandmother's feet. She stretched languidly, pulled her arms above her head, and arched her back.

Lady Adella blinked, seeing her with new eyes. Although she couldn't be certain, her eyesight not all that exceptional now, it seemed to her that the girl's breasts were straining against the bodice of her old blue muslin gowns, breasts that appeared much more exceptional than her eyesight. Her narrow waist was unmistakable against the arch of her back. Somehow the years had escaped her. Brandy must have long since begun her monthly cycle. Lady Adella frowned. "How old are ye, child?"

21

Brandy swung around at her grandmother's words, the two heavy blond braids falling forward to touch the faded carpet. "I'll be nineteen, Grandmama, on Michaelmas. You don't remember?"

"Watch your impertinent mouth, girl. You're eighteen, then. Don't mince words with me. Michaelmas bedammed, you're just into your eighteenth year. Naturally, I remember very well every birthday of every Robertson in this benighted family. Do ye think me a senile old woman?"

"Not at all, Grandmama. Stubborn and imperious, but never senile. Mayhap a bit autocratic even, but not more than you should be."

"See that ye don't, miss," Lady Adella said, leaving Brandy to wonder what she was referring to. Lady Adella closed her eyes and settled back into the soft cushions of her favorite chair. Eighteen, nearly nineteen, come next Michaelmas. Marriageable age she was. More than marriageable age. And there was Constance. Lord, she must be all of sixteen now. And little Fiona, not so very small now. Lady Adella ticked off years in her mind. Sniveling little Emily, dying in childbed with Fiona—why, that was all of six years ago, the same year the ridiculous French had been busily slaughtering each other. Amiable and weak Clive, her second son, left to himself with three daughters. How disconsolate he had been before he too had died when his boat had gone down in a storm not a hundred yards from shore.

Brandy pulled her tartan shawl more closely over her shoulders, tying it in its usual sturdy knot

22

between her breasts. It would be her constant companion until the end of April, when the heather burst into purple bloom. Then she didn't know quite what she'd do. The shawl would be too warm. She would have to think of something.

She smiled in anticipation of the warm, breezy spring weather, though even then the sea currents sometimes chilled the winds as they swept across the rocky cliffs. Perhaps she would be lucky enough to find a patch of white heather this year, said to bring good fortune.

She wriggled her cramped toes in slippers that had just recently grown too small, and shifted her position. She knew not to interrupt Grandmama while she was in one of her reminiscing moods. She thought of her grandfather and felt a twinge of sadness that he was gone, yet she was forced to admit to herself, she hadn't been particularly fond of him. He was even crustier and bawdier than the rest of the family, delighting, she sometimes thought, at making her squirm as if she had to go to the convenience at his unending coarse jests. What a pity it was that he had died refusing to reconsider Uncle Claude's disinheritance. If only Uncle Claude could have been the next Earl of Penderleigh, there would be no English stranger coming to take their lands.

Brandy glanced up at the ancient clock, set at an angle like a drunken sailor on the mantelpiece. Nearly four o'clock and time for tea, a tradition that Lady Adella had firmly established over her husband's grumbling some fifty years ago. She listened for Crabbe's familiar heavy wooden step.

A knock sounded on the oaken door. The

glazed look fell slowly from Lady Adella's eyes. "Och, tea time, is it?" She raised her voice. "Well, come in, Crabbe, don't dawdle, damn yer dim eyes."

The tall, stout Crabbe, a silver tea service held gently in his large hands, strode into the sitting room. Cousin Percival waited behind him.

"Master Percival be here to see yer ladyship," Crabbe said, quite unnecessarily.

Brandy watched with sinking heart as Lady Adella's parchment features cracked into a wide smile. It was always so. Brandy shivered and rose slowly to her feet, retreating to stand behind her grandmother's highbacked chair. She disliked Percy intensely, not only because he flattered Lady Adella so shamelessly but also because she had begun to fear him.

Last Michaelmas, at her birthday, he had begun to stare at her oddly, his hooded green eyes intent with a look she didn't understand but somehow recognized deep inside her. She'd figured over the winter what that look meant. It scared her to her toes.

Lady Adella said, "Come, Crabbe, don't stand there like a flabby dolt. The tea tray sets on the table as it has for the past fifty years. That's right. Now ye may take yerself off—and tell Cook that I've no wish to see another tureen of lentil and rice soup this evening. I've had enough of that swill to burn my belly to the ground. Tell her to prepare something special—my grandson is here."

Lady Adella turned to Percival and waved her

cane in the direction of a faded green velvet settee opposite her.

"Well, my boy, it's about time ye present yerself. Sit down, sit down. Brandy child, pour the tea. My fingers are stiff as my cane today."

Brandy slithered self-consciously from behind her grandmother's chair. She had reached down to clutch the silver handle of the teapot when Percy's hand covered her wrist.

"Good day to ye, little cousin. You're looking remarkably fit." His hand tightened about her wrist, and she felt his fingers gently stroke the palm of her hand.

She wanted to hit him on the head with the teapot, but it was so old, so fragile, she was afraid she'd give it even more dents—that, or it would just burst apart. She jerked her hand free, managing to keep her mouth shut. She wanted no scene in front of Lady Adella. She wiped her palm on her skirt.

He laughed softly even as he said, "My dear grandmother, how do ye contrive to grow more deliciously lovely by the year?" He bowed low and planted a light kiss on her blue-veined hand.

"Ye're a dog, Percy, my boy, but a dog of my liking. Now, why didn't ye come when I bade ye? Three months late to offer yer condolences. Were the truth to be told, it surprises me even now that ye would forgo all yer dissipations in Edinburgh."

"I'm not a hypocrite, lady. Ye must know that Lord Angus's passing must bring all his saddened relations sooner or later back to his heap of damp stone to pay their respects. Some of us just take longer than others."

"Yer tea, cousin Percy."

"Ah, a bright light amid the dismal shadows. My thanks, little cousin. Ye grow more and more like the fair anemones waiting to be plucked."

"Yer attempt at simile sets wrong with the child, Percy," Lady Adella said, all sharp now because she'd realized that Percy's experienced male eye had observed the changes in Brandy before she had.

"Grandmama, may I be excused? I promised to go for a walk with Constance and Fiona."

"Aye, child, ye may, but mind ye not to be late. Ye know I don't like my soup cold."

Brandy dipped an awkward curtsy toward her cousin, picked up her skirts, and was out the door in a flash. She thought she heard a chuckle as she slipped from the room, curse him.

"Not so much a child anymore, lady," Percy said with sufficient loudness that Brandy caught his words from the corridor.

"Don't flirt with the girl, Percy. She's far too young yet and inexperienced to glean yer meaning." She locked her stiff fingers about the cup handle and took a noisy sip of the scalding tea through her remaining teeth. She saw his hooded green eyes narrow, as if in a challenge, and smiled to herself. Aye, all Robertson males were the same. Flamboyant and weak, the lot of them. Always believed themselves to be gods to women. Ha, rutting stoats who whined when they didn't get what they wanted, which was usually another woman.

"To yer continued immortality, lady," Percy said, raising his cup.

Lady Adella gave a parchment laugh. "Aye, indeed. I swore that I would cling to this world longer than Angus. He was exceedingly furious when the doctor told him that he was dying. If there had been any money left, I swear he would have burned it rather than leave it in my hands, poor old gouty bastard."

"I do wonder how he feels now, roasting in Hades, knowing that you're here and I'm here." Percy smoothed the bitter sarcasm from his voice as he added, "At least now I can visit Penderleigh whenever I wish to."

Lady Adella looked at her hands, at the teacup on the small table beside her, then grinned at Percy. "What would ye say, my boy, if I were to make ye legitimate?"

Percy felt his blood suddenly pounding at his temples, but there was wariness in his voice. "Ye think to make up for years upon years of slights, lady? Old Angus would rise up from his grave and strangle ye."

"A fond thought, I can't deny, seeing his shrouded old bones heaving out of that deep hole I buried him in. But ye can't be blind to the advantages it would bring ye. What do ye say, Percy?"

"Advantages? Mayhap it would bring me a better chance of wedding an heiress, but it would gain me nothing of anything here. The English duke would still have claim to Penderleigh and the title, would he not?"

"Perhaps, my boy, but ye then would also have

27

full claim to the Robertson name. I haven't liked Davonan's son called the Robertson bastard. It's turned my innards. Come, Percy, don't give me your devil's stare. Ye know that I've never been one to mince matters or deny a truth. Who can know what may happen if ye become legitimized? Well, do ye want it or not?"

Percy thought of the rather squat, myopic Joanna MacDonald, daughter and heiress of a wealthy merchant in Edinburgh. Unless his instincts had grossly misled him—which they hadn't, he was sure of that—she was much enamored of him. Her priggish father wouldn't be able to deny him. He smiled at lady Adella, his full, sensuous lips curving into a boyish grin that had brought many an unheeding female to heel and then to his bed. "Aye, Grandmama, I should very much like to be legitimate. I suspect even my creditors would be properly impressed. I do wonder what would happen to my claim to Penderleigh if my name were secured."

"Mayhap ye should wonder what would happen were the English duke not to produce an heir?"

"Or if the English duke were to fall ill, say, and not survive?"

Lady Adella regarded her grandson with a malicious eye. "Och, my boy, the English duke is, I believe, a young man, not above twenty-eight years old—too young to depart this world without some outside assistance. As to heirs, the duke may already be wed and have a nursery full of hopeful brats. If not, there's always the hopeful uncle or cousin. There's always an heir some-where in the woodwork."

"Acquit me of murderous designs, lady. I have raised a question of speculative interest, nothing more. It's but a game we're playing. A game you started."

Lady Adella snorted in disgust. "Aye, and a question our dear Claude's son, Bertrand, would ask were he not so lily-livered. One illegitimate grandson and one disinherited grand nephew. Angus be damned. He was always a fool and stubborn as a donkey leashed to a hay cart. I will tell ye, Percy, if I make ye legitimate and reinherit Claude and Bertrand, the English duke might very well find his soup poisoned even if he doesn't budge from London."

He still felt the shock of surprise to hear this old woman speak so ruthlessly, with such spite, and the good lord knew he should be used to it by now. "Ye speak nonsense, Grandmama. Angus would never have reinherited Claude and Bertrand. Ye make me legitimate, and I will be the one to have claim after the English duke."

"It brings bile to your throat to think about Claude and Bertrand, eh, lad? It's nothing more than dust in the wind yer claim would be were I to reinherit Douglass's son." She shrugged her thin shoulders, all the while watching him closely. "Time will tell, Percy, about yer claim—time and me, of course."

For a moment Percy gazed at Lady Adella in dumb surprise. Why, the old woman is like a great bloated spider, he thought, weaving her web and taunting me to come into it. Does she want

29

all of us at each other's throats? Rather, he quickly corrected himself, does she want me at their throats? He consciously pulled himself away. For the moment, he hoped that she would make him legitimate.

He rose and clasped Lady Adella's hand.

"I will stay, if ye don't mind, until all this business is straightened out. When I return to Edinburgh, I have a fancy to carry my legitimate name with me."

"As ye will, Percy," Lady Adella said. "Tell Crabbe to have MacPherson fetch here on the morrow, and I shall tell the old buzzard what to do."

"Aye, Grandmama," Percy said, and turned to take his leave.

"Percy."

He turned.

"Brandy will have nothing to do with ye. She's much too much the child yet and doesn't know what use to make of men."

She saw the suppressed gleam in his eyes as she nodded dismissal, and wondered if he knew how much he was like the grandfather he hated so much.

Alone, Lady Adella parted her lips in a smug grin that showed most of her upper teeth. She knew something of the law, and now that Angus had finally left the world to take up residence with the devil, she fully intended to stir the legal pot to boiling.

Old MacPherson would do her bidding, no fear about that, and the courts would fall in line. The Robertson name still wielded power. She would legitimize Percy and, aye, perhaps even reinherit Claude and Bertrand. As to what the English duke would think about her machinations, she shrugged her meager shoulders. He was, after all, safely stored away in faraway London. She was certain he would stay there.

She gazed down at the small square pillow at her feet, Brandy's pillow. Her granddaughter, with the curves and hollows of a woman's body. Lady Adella thwacked her cane in annoyance. Three granddaughters, none of them with any prospects of marriage and even less dowry. Absurd to believe that the unknown English duke, although now the girls' nominal guardian, would freely part with some of his guineas for some unknown Scottish relatives. Even though she admitted to herself that it was an outlandish idea, she did not relinquish it. Time would tell, and she would be there to help in the telling.

At least Percy would be able to fend for himself once she had seen to legitimizing him. Handsome and carefree he was—exactly as she had been once, many a long year ago. Drat Davonan anyway for not at least giving Percy's mother his name. But then Davonan had always been odd. She remembered how delighted she'd been to hear that Davonan had even lain with a woman. But it hadn't lasted, of course. Not a year later, he'd gone off with a brawny Irishman, leaving her to care for his small, helpless son. She wondered idly, with no pain now, if Davonan had really gone willingly to the guillotine with his French lover, a dissolute *comte* who had deserved to have his worthless head severed from his decadent body. At least Percy had not inherited *that* tendency from his father.

Lady Adella slewed her head about toward the clock. Time to call Old Marta to assist her to dress for dinner. She gave a sudden cackle of laughter. Old Marta indeed. A saucy slut that one had been.

Thank the Lord Angus had never gotten *her* with child.

4

Bertrand Robertson was chewing thoughtfully on the end of his quill as he sat hunched over a thick ledger. His only servant, the sharp-eared Fraser, had just told him that Percy had returned. Damned blighter. What the hell did he want this time? Stupid question. Money, of course. Well, there was no money for him, not a bloody *sou*, so let him flatter Lady Adella's beautiful eyebrows and sharp wit. It made no difference. Of course, he wouldn't be surprised if the old woman lied to him and made him all sorts of promises. He wouldn't put anything past her.

He forced himself back to the column of numbers, neatly entered row upon row in the account book. Stark numbers. Very bad numbers, their sums leaving his belly cramping.

Penderleigh had lost ground this year, what with Angus dying bringing his creditors demanding payment, and the black-faced sheep's wool bringing much less than expected at Sterling market. The English duke wasn't going to like it one bit.

He ran ink-stained fingers through the shock of dark red hair that fell habitually over his forehead. A disinherited grand nephew he might be, but old Angus had known his worth and trusted him to eke out every possible groat from the estate. His eyes burned as he gazed down at the scraggly numbers, little useless numbers, and he felt again a stab of real fear. Angus was dead and now he might very well find both himself and his gouty father tossed unceremoniously off Penderleigh land. How would he be able to convince the man of business the English duke would send that he had tried to force economics, indeed, that the castle and dower house were in a fair way of crumbling about their ears because he'd not allowed funds to make repairs? That was in a fair way to being a good jest. What funds? It hadn't been all that difficult.

He glanced up as Fraser, his step soundless despite his stout body, poked his round face into the small, sunny room and coughed discreetly. Bertrand looked up and nodded.

"Master Bertrand, yer father's just heard tell of Master Percival's a-comin' to the castle. He be in a tither, if ye ken me meanin'."

"Aye, Fraser, I ken all too well. Tell him I shall join him presently. Tell him not to worry about Percy. Tell him that Percy is the least of our problems. Wait, I'll tell him all that. Don't you worry, Fraser."

"Och, no matter what ye say, it's still a bad

time, wi' Master Percival bein' aboot." Fraser shook his grizzled head, his enduring smile fading a bit.

"Don't worry, Fraser," Bertrand said again. "Percival is naught but a buzzing, bothersome fly. It's the English duke, our new master, who will tighten the collars about our necks. It just might be the killing blow. Then all of us will be looking about for a way to feed ourselves. Do you know how to fish, Fraser?"

"A bit. I love abalone, but I can't catch it. Ye're right, Master Bertrand, we would be in a bad way if what ye say comes true. Ye really believe that the dook be like the Black Cumberland?"

Bertrand laughed humorlessly as he rose from his chair. "This isn't seventeen forty-six, Fraser, and the English duke wasn't born yet. Doubtless, though, he's a proud man and, like all the English, disdainful of the Scots. Ye know, of course, that it's likely he'll dispatch one of his London men here to grub about and accuse us of stealing from him."

Fraser's intelligent, close-set brown eyes, as round as his face, narrowed, but he remained silent. He said finally, "Not a blithering thing we can do about it now, master. Ye'd best go on to yer father's room. I canna be sure, but my ears tell me he's a-pokin' his stick on the floor. I'll hae some tea brewin' fer ye an' bring it."

Bertrand left the book room with a lagging step. As he mounted the decrepit stairs to the upper floor of the dower house and his father's stuffy bedchamber, he continued to ponder his

34

problems, and with each step he became more depressed.

"Well, don't just stand there, Bertie, come in, come in. By the time it takes Fraser to fetch ye, I am near to forgetting what I wanted. Come in, boy, come in. So what can ye tell me? Have we more money now than we did in the morning?"

"How are ye feeling, Father? Ye're looking well. No, we haven't a groat more. This afternoon looks just as bad as this morning did." Bertrand crossed the bare floor to where his father, Claude, sat wrapped from head to toe in a heavy tartan blanket next to a roaring peat fire. The room was surely hotter than the fires of Hades. Bertrand wiped his brow. In another ten minutes he'd want to dip his head in a bowl of cold water. In another twenty minutes he'd have a headache that would send him to the cliffs to stare over the sea and gather himself back together again in the stiff cool breezes. His father was a trial. He couldn't seem to remember when his father hadn't been a trial.

"Ye have eyes in yer head, Bertie. Look ye. My foot's the size of a bloated, rotting dung heap, no thanks to ye. And it's cold in this bloody room. Ye're to speak to Fraser, tell him that the cold pains me something terrible. We need more peat. Have him fetch more peat."

"I'll speak to Fraser, Father." Bertrand sat back in the chair, which smelled of long ago clothes and pipes, and waited patiently for his father to get to the point. He prayed what his father wanted would be said before his headache arrived in full force.

"Move yer head a bit to the left, Bertie, ye're

35

blocking out my sunlight. Not that I like sunlight all that much, but it warms my bones, and the good Lord knows that bones need to be kept warm or they'll buckle and that's the end to a man."

Bertrand shifted himself in the cracked leather wing chair across from his father. He ran his hand over his forehead, for the blast of heat from the fireplace was already making him sweat. The headache was coming soon. A man shouldn't have headaches, but what could he do? He hated this bloody room that was like a furnace.

Claude said, "Ye know, of course, that Percy is come back. The vulture swooping to gnaw the bones afore old Angus is worm-picked in his grave."

Bertrand sighed. "Father, it makes no difference what Percy does. There's naught but bones for him to gnaw, so much the worse for us. Ye may believe me that Percy is the least of our worries."

Claude yelled, "Don't ye treat me like a dim-witted chirper, my fine young man. Did ye know that Adella plans to legitimize yer fine bastard cousin?"

"That's ridiculous, Father. I'll thank ye not to weave tales like that. Whoever told ye such a buffoonish story? It's bloody nonsense, nothing more, just nonsense. Forget about it." Bertrand realized that his hands were fisted around the arms of the chair. Damn, he forced himself to relax. He flexed his hands.

His father hunched himself forward. A

momentary spasm of pain deepened the myriad wrinkles in his cheeks.

"Crabbe told me, Master Prim an' Prissy." He enjoyed the whitening of his son's face. "Crabbe is a good man—minds others' business and keeps his ears to the ground. He's owed me for years, but that's another story. Ye know what that means, don't ye, lad?"

He'd kill the old woman, he'd kill her. Bertrand shrugged and managed a show of indifference. "It simply means that my esteemed great aunt is growing more eccentric."

"Ha! She's as mean as that pug she used to shove in all our faces."

"You mean the one that pissed on your feet, Father?"

"That's the one, the little bitch. Lady Adella is that crazy and she gets crazier as each day passes. She's mean-spirited and petty and a bloody witch. Have I covered it all?"

So that's where you got it, Bertrand thought, but he didn't say it aloud, just shrugged. "Well, she's entitled, since she's older than death. And, aye, you covered it well.

"Did I tell you that when Angus was near the end, he tried to pay me to kill her so she'd be dead before he was? I told him he didn't have any money. He told me I should want to do it for free since she was such a harpy. I'm forced to say that I laughed, Father. I was afraid that he was going to breathe his last right then, but he didn't, of course. He did hang on longer than I thought he would."

"Ye never told me that before, damn yer eyes,

Bertie, not that it makes one whit of difference. But a son is supposed to tell his father everything, do ye hear me? Everything. Did he really try to get you to kill the old bitch? Aye, I know ye never lie, Bertie, more's the pity. But that was then and this is now. Take off yer blinders, Bertie. Yer cousin will now be next in line to Penderleigh if the English duke doesn't yet have heirs. Ye must know what that means."

Claude achieved the result he'd perversely desired. His calm, reasonable son—he'd finally pushed him over the edge. Bertrand said between gritted teeth, his voice heavy with age-old bitterness, "That bloody bastard. He's taken so much money already from Penderleigh for his own frivolous amusements in Edinburgh. Damn him and damn Lady Adella, it's not just. Maybe I should have strangled the old witch, damn her eyes. Old Angus was right. The world would be a better place without her and her damned machinations."

Claude leaned back with a crooked grin and tapped his fingertips together. "It's good to see that ye've got red blood in yer veins, Bertie. Sometimes I've wondered if yer mother didn't play me false."

Bertrand just stared at his father, baffled at the way he thought, the way he reasoned, the casual cruelty that came out of his mouth.

"And just what would ye say if I told ye Lady Adella also intends to reverse my father's disinheritance?"

For an instant Bertrand's eyes blazed as brightly as his father's. Penderleigh. God, how he loved every crumbling, damp turret, every damp stone that had been soaked for centuries with the heavy air from the North Sea. He'd give his soul for Penderleigh. Hell, he'd already given a good portion of it. Aye, he'd already given everything he could, and it wasn't enough. Ah, but if his father were reinherited, perhaps someday he, Bertrand Douglass Robertson, would be the Earl of Penderleigh. He, Bertrand Robertson, would be the master. He would do what pleased him. He wouldn't have to play games with that old witch. Aye, all the pleasure as well as the responsibility would be his. The joy of it took his breath away.

Painfully he brought himself back to the grim present, to hear his father say, "Nay, Lady Adella is a deep old witch, and she'll play and keep us both dangling in the wind and laugh as she does it. For the first time I don't want the old woman to die. I'm glad Angus couldn't convince ye to kill her. If she does die before she sees that we're reinherited, then it's all over for us, Bertie, all over. I think it highly likely, though, that she will do it. If she lifts dishonor off one Robertson head, she might as well lift it from ours as well. Surely she values us more than she does that blackguard Percy."

God, sometimes it hurt to be logical, to be practical, but Bertrand managed to say in his even, calm voice, "One can't make plans with suppositions, Father. Even if she were to reinherit us, it's likely not to gain us a thing. The English duke is bound to have heirs."

"Ye talk like a man who's a miser with his

optimism, Bertie. First we must lift the curse of our disinheritance, then we shall see." The old man gave him a near-toothless smile. Odd that Lady Adella had more teeth than Claude, who was twenty-five years her junior.

"Ye know as well as I do that she loves her games and her tricks. She's just stirring the pot like MacBeth's witches. I don't want you to dream about something that won't ever happen, Father."

"Mayhap ye're right, and it is foolish to trust her. But there is heavy guilt upon her soul. Methinks she must make amends afore she dies. I would not doubt that she helped old Angus to his eternal reward, for she could do naught about either us or Percy as long as the old bastard lived."

Now his father was accusing his own aunt of murder? "*Her* guilt, ye say, Father? Will ye not tell me now why our line was severed? Why did Great-grandfather disinherit Grandfather Douglass?" Bertrand realized he was holding his breath and forced himself to exhale slowly, very slowly. He'd wondered for so very long, wondered and wondered, but his father had always told him it was none of his business, and usually added, "Ye nosy little blighter."

Claude stared for the longest time into the roaring fire. "Nay, boy, I can't tell ye. Mayhap afore I die ye will know the truth of the matter."

"I asked her once, ye know," Bertrand said, sitting forward, his hands crossed between his knees.

"Ye do sometimes surprise me, Bertie. What did Adella say to that?"

"She threw her cane at me and screamed for me to get out. I was afraid she was going to croak on the spot, but naturally, she didn't."

"Perhaps," Claude said slowly, staring at his son now, "jest perhaps ye haven't yer mother's spun-cotton brain. Ye've shown spirit, Bertie. Now, fetch me that damned smiling Fraser. I believe we shall dine tonight at the castle. There's much to learn here. I don't want to leave that sod Percy alone with my aunt. Ye never know what Lady Adella will say or do if ye're not around to stick yer oar in."

5

"Cousin Percy is so very handsome, don't ye think so, Brandy? Did ye see his beautiful waistcoat, all lovely flowers on a yellow background? And his trousers, all knitted and tight, and he has such fine legs. He's so manly, I can't take my eyes off him when he walks. I think he looks delicious."

Connie had noticed Percy's legs? She'd watched him walk? He was manly? Good God, this was beyond what she'd imagined. What did Connie—only sixteen—know about men's legs? But Brandy knew the answer to that. She'd known that her sister practiced in front of her mirror—smiles, slight frowns, little turn-ups of her lips. Things to entice a man. Things to entice a philanderer like Percy. Oh, Lord.

She smiled and shrugged. "Nay, I don't think Percy is handsome. Food is delicious, not some trollop man."

"Only women are trollops, Brandy, not men."

"Percy's a trollop. Trust me. What he is isn't all that good, Connie. He doesn't care for any of us, he cares only for himself. He isn't a nice man, Connie, please believe me." Brandy paused a moment, realizing she'd never before spoken in such a clean-to-the-bone way before. Please, God, let her see him for what he is. "Connie, please, promise me ye'll stay away from Percy. He isn't worthy. Besides, he's our cousin. Shake his hand but don't think about his legs in knit trousers. Don't think he's manly. Just look at him and know he's a trollop." Why couldn't Connie see that Percy wasn't to be trusted, that he was a miserable libertine who cared for nobody but himself?

Constance fluttered thick, dark lashes, beautiful lashes, and on this particular girl of sixteen those beautiful lashes were unfortunate. She'd even learned how to look up through her lashes to achieve the greatest effect. Who had taught her that?

"Why, Brandy? Why don't you want me to get near Percy? He's lovely, lovelier than any man we'll ever meet in these parts. Do ye want him for yerself? Is that the reason? Aye, that's it, I know it."

Brandy's hand itched to slap her sister. No, she thought, she had to reason with her, gain her belief in what she was being told.

"Connie," she said very slowly, "I wouldn't

want Percy even if the only other man available was the devil himself." She saw that Connie didn't believe her, that her sister probably didn't care what came out of her mouth. "Ye know, Connie, Percy is really quite old. Why, he must be nearly thirty." She tried for a convincing shudder. "And he drinks so much—it's likely he'll have gout just like Uncle Claude. He'll probably have a red, veiny nose like Uncle Claude too. He'll probably lose most of his teeth, just like Uncle Claude. Och, I shouldn't want to be married to a man like that."

"What a pack of nonsense. Those long braids of yers, Brandy, I think they've tugged yer brain too tight. Percy, old? That's ridiculous. He's perfect and he'll remain that way."

Brandy was depressed. She walked to the edge of the grassy cliff and gazed out to sea. The size of the white caps on the waves, the tide level, and the darkening horizon surely meant a violent early spring storm was close. She tried to remember if she had tied her small boat firmly to its moorings, for the storm that was brewing would send crashing waves even into the small inlet.

"It's going to blow up strong tonight," she said more to herself than to her sister. She kicked a pebble off the edge of the cliff and watched it bounce down the narrow, rocky path and land in the sand on the beach below.

She turned back toward her sister and sank slowly to her knees amid the thick carpet of blue-bells and wild anemones that grew in great abundance nearly to the cliff edge. She breathed in the sweet fragrance of the purple-blue flowers and for a moment forgot Percy and her too-grown-up little sister.

"Brandy, it's time to go back now. Ye'll get yer skirt stained, and Old Marta will complain to Grandmama."

Brandy sighed and slowly rose to her feet. The wind was rising, whipping her skirt about her ankles. She tightened her thick tartan shawl about her shoulders. "I suppose since Percy is here that we'll have to change for dinner."

She wished she hadn't said Percy's name aloud again, for Constance's very lovely eyes took on a sultry cast. Oh, dear, where had she learned that?

Brandy tried another track. "Well, you just might think him handsome, but ye're but sixteen years old, a mere child to him. I've heard Grandmama say that he likes his women round and soft and experienced in the art of love. When I asked her what kind of art that was, she threw a pillow at me and started choking. But that's not important. What's important is Percy is not only our cousin, he's too old for you. He's too old for me as well, and I've two years on ye. Forget him, Connie." She paused then laughed. "Don't forget he hasn't a groat. What would one do with a man who hasn't a groat?"

Well, she had tried. She watched Constance gather together her bile. She actually seemed to puff up with it. "Me, a child? Ye're just jealous, that's what you are. It's ye who wear the child's dresses. And yer ratty braids and that snaggled old shawl. Ye look ridiculous. Well, I have no intention of shriveling into an old spinster, alone and poor in this beastly place. Stay if ye wish among all the crumbling stone and pick yer stupid wildflowers. I, for one, am going to be a rich and fine lady. Just maybe Percy will become rich. He's very smart. You'll see, he'll be rich soon."

Constance whipped about, her dark hair swirling about her shoulders, and flounced away from the promontory back toward the castle. Even her walk was enticing, Brandy thought. Where had she learned that? She wanted to tell her sister that she didn't want to stay here and rot either, that she too wanted to have a husband and a family. That she wanted to be a lady.

She started to call after her sister, but Connie's back was so righteously stiff that she didn't bother. They'd just fight some more. That's all they seemed to do recently—fight and snipe at each other. It had been different just two years before. How could she believe that Percy would ever earn any money on his own?

She finally called out, nearly shouting over the rising wind, "Connie, wait for me on the path. I've got to find Fiona."

She saw her sister pause and turn about. She looked impatient, even to her tapping toe.

Brandy hurried to the edge of the cliff and started down the winding, rocky path, careful to watch her footing on the treacherous rocks and pebbles. "Fiona." She cupped her hands around her mouth and called her sister three more times. "Fiona!" She looked up and down the desolate beach below, searching for the bright red thatch of hair that topped Fiona's head. There was no movement among the coarse marram grass that grew thick and sturdy amongst the rocks on the beach, and the only sound above the waves was the hoarse squawking of barnacle geese and redshanks, intent upon finding their dinner. Her attention was caught a moment by a large, bobbing porpoise, alternately skimming and floating on the white-tipped waves, oyster-catchers dipping low over him.

"Brandy, Brandy, here I am. Just look!"

She turned about to see Fiona scurrying toward her up the path, her once neat braids hanging about her small shoulders in a fiery red, wet tangle. Her woolen gown was damp and clung to her skinny legs. Brandy didn't doubt that the gown was thick with gritty sand.

She forgot about scolding Fiona for getting so dirty when Fiona grabbed her arm and cried, "Did ye see him, Brandy? The porpoise? He's been lying on his back ever so long. I called to him and I promise that he twitched his nose at me. Isn't he lovely?"

What was a sister to do? "Yes, love, I saw him. But he is gone now, searching for some abalone for his dinner. And that, little poppet, is what we must do. It is growing late and we must go back." She ruffled the flying red hair and resolutely turned the child about.

Constance was standing in the protection of a beech hedge, combing her black hair with her fingers. She gave an ugh of distaste at Fiona's appearance. "Really, Fiona, ye look like a crofter's brat. Don't ye look at me like that, for I have no intention of brushing the tangles out of that rat's nest of hair."

"I can remember when both of us looked just like Fiona," Brandy said. "Don't you remember, Connie, how we used to swim and gather driftwood and built sand castles? We used to sing all the old songs?"

Constance looked at her as if she'd lost her mind.

"We were children," Constance said flatly. "Now we're grown up, at least I am. I never want to be dirty again."

Fiona gave a secret smile to Brandy, a smile filled with wonder at the gray porpoise. Brandy doubted Connie had even heard her.

"Ye won't have to worry about her, Connie. I shall make her presentable. Come, it is growing late."

They rounded a curve in the path that led onto the rhododendron-lined avenue. Penderleigh Castle rose before them like a giant gray monolith, its ancient stone gleaming in the dull gold of the setting sun. Constance paused and picked a soft magenta blossom and tucked it over her left ear. "I would offer ye one, Brandy, but it would fall out of yer skinny braids."

That was probably true, but Brandy held her tongue. She looked at the fluted turret, once the housing for the now rusted cannons that lay in a heap, forgotten, in the grass-filled moat. She fancied she could hear the strident call of the bagpipes, daring the enemy to approach. She remembered the oft-repeated ballad of the Earl of Huntly, whispered by Marta in her blurred singsong voice:

Wae be tae ye, Huntly
And whaur hae ye been?
They hae slain the Earl o'Moray
And laid him on the green.

She hummed softly, lost for a moment in a strangely romantic past. But it was, she thought, a past plundered and lost forever after Bonnie Prince Charlie's bloody defeat. She remembered tales of the hated Duke of Cumberland, the Englishman's avenging devil. She stared hard at the proud old castle and a knot of anger grew in her stomach. Penderleigh Castle, her birthplace, her home, now belonged to another duke, another Englishman.

"Do you hear the roar of the sea battering the rocks just behind the castle, Connie? All right, so you don't. Did you say something?"

"I said I saw Bertrand and Uncle Claude crossing from the dower house to the castle. Bertrand is such an old stick. Odd that he is so prissy prim when Uncle Claude is reputed to have tumbled many a young maid when he was young."

Brandy couldn't imagine Uncle Claude tossing a rock, much less a maid. Surely she should try to convince her younger sister not to talk that way, but she knew it wouldn't work.

"Ha, Brandy, ye don't have to say anything. I know what ye're thinking. Ye're as prissy prim as Bertrand. What a perfect match ye two would make—both old, stuffy sticks. Why, in one winter ye'd bore each other to death."

There were some things a person just couldn't

48

let pass. She grinned at her sister, and even she had to admit to the touch of malice in her voice. "Bertrand old? He's younger than Percy, ye know, Connie, by at least four years."

That brought a blink and a thankful pause, but it didn't last. "Old is as old does," Constance said, and tossed her lovely black hair.

"Well, that certainly put Bertrand and me in our place," Brandy said. She kept her head down, Fiona's small, dirty hand held in hers. She struggled to understand her sister. It was as if Constance wanted to hurl herself into womanhood, to scoff at all the pursuits Brandy still held pleasurable and dear. She refused to go out in Brandy's small boat to fish, turning up her nose at the strong fishy smell and deploring the sticky, damp sea spray on her gown. If attaining womanhood meant spending all one's time on how one looked and openly flirting with the likes of Percy, she wanted none of it. She didn't want it for Connie either. Perhaps it was just a phase she was going through. Maybe Brandy had gone through it too. Maybe it had been so short that she just didn't remember it.

She hunched her shoulders forward, pulling her shawl more closely about her. At least Constance didn't have to worry about going through life with the deformity Brandy had to endure. She couldn't even take deep breaths for fear of popping the buttons on her gowns. What a dreadful jest nature had played upon her—a skinny body supporting a cow-like bosom.

She thought again of Percy, and found herself wondering why he looked at her with that

49

disgusting, knowing look in his hooded eyes. There was certainly nothing about her appearance or her behavior to give him any encouragement. He was probably just bored here, and could find naught else to do but torment her in that loathsome way of his.

Brandy looked up to see Fiona astride one of the old cannons, yelling at the top of her lungs, which had always been healthy, "Giddyup, ye old nag, giddyup, or I'll whip yer rump."

Brandy hadn't even realized that the child had pulled free of her. "Oh, Fiona, but look at yer gown now." Brandy rushed forward, saw the rust flecks on the child's face and hands, and lifted her bodily from the cannon. "Oh, dear, if Old Marta sees ye like that, she'll tell Grandmama for certain. Hold still, little wriggler, let me try to clean ye off."

"Brandy, look, someone is coming up the drive. It looks like one of those gentlemen's sporting vehicles." Constance shaded her eyes from the dying sun, still bright through the scattered storm clouds.

Brandy straightened, holding Fiona's grubby hand, her own face now covered with copper flecks of rust. She gazed at the oncoming curricle with only mild curiosity. Surely the man was driving too fast, for great whirls of dust whipped around the wheels.

"Great horses," Fiona shouted, jumping up and down with excitement.

"Aye, that they are, poppet. Very big horses and the man driving them is an idiot."

"They're much better than these stupid old cannons."

With those words Fiona broke free of her sister's hold and ran as fast as her skinny legs would carry her toward the curricle.

6

"Dear God, Fiona, come back right this instant or I'll take my hairbrush to your bottom!"

Brandy yanked her skirts to her knees and dashed after the child. "Fiona!" She screamed, fear suddenly clogging her throat. She saw the steaming stallions, their eyes flaming with surprise, rearing and plunging, and heard the blurred shout of a man's voice. With a hoarse cry Brandy leaped forward, grabbed Fiona's arm and, with all her strength, hurled the child backward. She heard the frightened whinnying and snorting of the stallions as she rolled upon her back beside Fiona in a tuft of yellow anemones. She gulped down two heaving breaths and turned frantic eyes to her sister.

"Poppet, are ye all right?" She was running her hands over her little sister's arms, her legs, feeling her head through her tangled braids.

"Of course, Brandy, but ye hurt my arm. I just wanted to play with the big horses."

Brandy cursed, not overly vulgar words because Grandmama had had Old Marta wash her mouth out with lye soap once when she'd tried out something Tommy in the stables had said when he'd been kicked by Uncle Claude's old mule. She wanted to shake Fiona for her stupidity.

She saw Constance standing but a few feet away from them, her eyes widened upon a gentleman who was jumping gracefully down from the curricle.

"Pull yer skirt down, Brandy," Constance said out of the side of her mouth, her eyes never leaving the man's face.

Brandy jerked her skirt over her old woolen stockings and jumped to her feet. The gentleman was striding toward them, his dark eyes narrowed and his swarthy face red with anger. He was wearing the most elegant driving coat she'd ever seen. What right did he have to drive his horses as if the devil were after him? What right did he have to look angry? He was the one at fault here. He was the idiot who'd been driving too fast.

She forgot his elegance when his voice, cold as ice crackling in a glass bowl, cut through the air. "Just what the devil do you mean letting that child run in front of my horses?"

Fiona stared up at the huge gentleman, her eyes wide with excitement. "They're so grand. I just wanted to see them up close. I hoped they'd stop and let me pet them."

"So close that they could have broken every bone in your body. As for you," he continued, turning toward Brandy, "your bravery was quite unnecessary. I always have quite good control over my cattle. You could have killed yourself with that lame-brained stunt."

Connie, all lovely and pale with the shock of the near accident, her black hair waving beautifully down her back and over her shoulders, smiled her lovely budding woman's smile. "Sir, ye must forgive my sister, sometimes she acts without thinking. Though I must admit that Fiona scared me too." Then she gave him a formal curtsy. A curtsy? thought Brandy. This was absurd. So he looked elegant. Who cared? He was rude and he was in the wrong.

Brandy looked at him straight in his very handsome face, but she wouldn't think about that, just about his bloody stupidity.

"You, sir, were driving like a madman. How could anyone begin to guess that ye would have such wonderful control over yer cattle, as ye put it? Should I perhaps just have waited to see if the madman avoided trampling my little sister? Go away, sir, and take your lovely horse with ye. If I had a gun I'd be tempted to shoot ye. Ye're a bloody menace. What's more, ye've no right to be angry with us. This is our land, not yers. Ye were driving recklessly and ye shouldn't even be here."

A very clipped English voice said, cold with anger, "Now that I see that you are unhurt, I have no desire to cross swords with a rowdy, thoughtless pack of children. I suggest that you remove yourselves quickly before I am sorely tempted to take my hand to your backsides. Not have control over my horses? Indeed!"

It was obvious that the stranger believed them to be peasants' brats, beneath his exalted voice.

Brandy's cup was filled to overflowing. "And

53

I suggest to ye, ye pompous sod, that ye remove yerself from Penderleigh land. Now that I realize ye're English, I should have guessed that ye'd have not one smidgen of manners and even less breeding. In short, sir, take yerself to the devil, though I doubt he'd have ye, at least if ye got anywhere near him driving like that."

The Duke of Portmaine, his nerves frayed and his temper already sorely tried from his long journey, took an unmeasured step toward the repulsive brat who dared criticize him. He stared hard into rather large and passionate amber eyes and halted in his tracks. Damnation, the girl didn't even flinch.

He drew a tired breath and said with finality, "I'm sorry I frightened you, children. It wasn't well done of me. You're right. How could you have known that I could easily control my horses?"

He looked at the two grubby faces, ignored the other young girl, who was on the verge of womanhood and was obviously delighted to have a male specimen around for her to practice her budding wiles on, and thought to himself that he could make them, as well as their probably very poor parents, quite satisfied. He quickly drew several guineas from his waistcoat pocket and tossed them to the youngest child. "Here, this should cleanse your wounds and salve your feelings. Do see to the little girl in the future. You shouldn't be so careless with her safety."

Brandy was so stunned, her mouth stood open. In the next instant he had turned away from them and climbed gracefully into the curricle.

She was still trying to dredge up long ago curses that the man would appreciate when he whipped up his horses and was gone from them.

"Ye look like a fish," Connie said. "Ye look stupid with yer mouth standing open like a door."

"I thought you said fish."

"Look, Brandy, they're gold. Big gold pieces, the man gave us gold." Fiona held out the two guineas in her grubby hand and proudly displayed her fortune.

"Give me those." Brandy grabbed the coins. "I can't believe he actually gave us money." Fiona began to sob.

Constance punched Brandy's arm. "How could ye be so nasty to that gentleman? I was never so mortified in all my life. He was lovely and young and you made him really angry. As for you, Fiona, you should be beaten." She added her Parthian shot as she turned away, "Don't expect me to take any of the blame when Grandmama finds out—and you know she will, she has more spies than England. If Papa were alive or Grandpapa Angus, ye'd get the whip."

Brandy raised her fist to Constance's back, then lowered it. She turned on her sister. "Quit yer sniffling, Fiona, and yer nose is running. Here, wipe it. That's better. No, stop whining. Ye sound like a brat. The man gave us the guineas because he thought we were poor crofters' children. It would be wrong for us to keep them, don't ye see?"

Fiona sobbed all the harder, and Brandy, at the end of her patience, grabbed her sister's arm and hauled her to the small wooden door at the side of the castle. She put the man out of her mind, and concerned herself with how to escape Old Marta's sharp eyes. Oh, Lord, she had to hurry.

"Please hush, poppet," she said, her voice gentle. "I'll scrub ye down myself and no one need know. I even promise to throw myself over yer little body if Grandmama raises her cane at ye."

It was close to an hour later before a well-scrubbed Fiona was tucked into her bed, her small stomach filled with cold chicken and buttered scones. Luckily, Morag had brought up Fiona's dinner.

"I canna stay, lassie," Morag said. "Cook be all a-flutter wi' so many mouths to feed." She cast a disinterested rheumy eye over Brandy. "Ye best to ready yerself, lassie. Yer lady grandmother be already wi' the family downstairs."

Brandy carried a candle across the hall to her own small bedchamber. No fire burned in her room this time of year. *Dear* Cousin Percival in all likelihood had a roaring fire in *his* room. Given the way he flattered Old Marta, he probably had buckets of hot water for his bath.

She stripped off her filthy gown and shift, and with cold fingers pulled away the tight lacings of her chemise. She gritted her teeth and splashed cold water over her body. The myriad flecks of rust clung stubbornly, and she was covered with gooseflesh before the harsh lye soap had done its job.

She toweled herself dry and grabbed a clean shift and chemise. She thought of Percy and that

56

repulsive way he'd stared at her this afternoon. She looked down at her excessive bosom, and wondered if he had been staring at that part of her. She jerked the strings painfully tight over her breasts. She gazed into her mirror and saw that the effect was not as flattering as she'd hoped. Well, there was nothing more she could do about it. She pulled a pale blue muslin gown from the old armoire, a young girl's dress, high-necked and sashed at the waist. The buttons over her bosom gaped apart. In desperation Brandy unearthed from her mother's chest a dark green and yellow shawl. She quickly brushed out her long, thick hair, the habitual braids causing deep ripples that fell to her waist. Her hair, she thought, was her only fine feature, and remembering Percy's roving eyes, she rebraided her hair more tightly than usual and wound the long rope into a tight bun at the nape of her neck. There, she looked like a very boring young girl who had not a single bit of taste.

Pulling the shawl tightly about her, she blew out her candle and slipped from her room.

One smoky flambeau lit the long expanse of corridor, and its acrid smell made Brandy's eyes water. She gingerly made her way down the wide oak staircase, for the carpet was threadbare on several of the steps, making the descent hazardous to the unwary.

Crabbe was nowhere to be seen, and Brandy thought again of Percy and how his presence had placed a burden on the servants. She heard voices coming from the drawing room, and mindful that she was late—goodness, more than late now—

hurried across the worn flagstone entrance hall. With the greatest care, she eased open the drawing room door and slithered inside, hoping no one would notice her.

A rush of warm air from the great roaring fire at the opposite side of the room nearly smothered her. She wanted to cough, but she didn't. She saw her grandmother dominating the family, holding court from her faded, high-backed chair, smoke-blackened from its years of proximity to the fireplace. Scores of candle branches illuminated the cozy scene.

She heard a rich, deep laugh. In an instant her eyes sought out the owner, and she found herself staring, mouth agape, at the gentleman from the curricle. She felt color rush to her cheeks, and stood rooted to the spot. Oh, my God, was all she could think.

Oh, my God. What had she done?

He laughed again at something Grandmama said. Even though she was across the room from him, she saw his strong white teeth when he laughed. She realized that he was even larger than she remembered, his swarthy countenance heightened by the snowy white ruffled shirt that reminded her of a pure expanse of clean snow. In the glowing candlelight his eyes seemed as dark as his black satin evening coat. A very elegant gentleman he appeared, and certainly many pegs above any of Grandmama's friends from Edinburgh.

Oh, my God.

"Brandy, there ye are, child. Come here at

once and make yer curtsy. Ye'll not believe what the bowels of England have coughed up."

Brandy's eyes flew to her grandmama's face, and with the lagging step of a person bound for the guillotine, she bowed her head and forced herself to walk forward. It was the longest walk of her life. At the very least, she'd get the whip.

"Ye're quite late, miss, but no matter, all understandable. His grace has just been telling us of yer interesting meeting and how you trimmed his sails but good. I told him ye were my granddaughter and I'd taught you everything ye knew."

Oh, my God. What was going on here?

She fully expected to be taken apart by every verbal apparatus known to her grandmother, but she sounded amused and pleased. Something wasn't right. She forced her eyes to her grandmama's face and indeed saw amusement. *His grace.* The truth struck her with such force that she nearly collapsed with shock. He was the English duke—their new master.

"Miss Brandella," he said in a rich, lazy voice.

Without thought, she said, "Brandy, my name is Brandy."

"Very well, Brandy."

"Make yer curtsy, child."

Awkwardly Brandy bent her knee. She didn't want to look at him. She just wanted to turn around and leave the room. She'd be pleased with cold porridge for supper. Perhaps the floor would open up and she could fall through to Hades, where Grandpa Angus probably was. She bet he'd be glad to see her. He'd always loved to scream at her.

Lady Adella yelled at her, "I've never seen ye tongue-tied before, miss. Now, what is the matter with ye? He too handsome for ye to even look at? He's handsome, I'll grant ye that, but I can look on him. And if I can look at him, then ye can because ye don't know anything about men in any case. Now, stop yer bloody nonsense and bid hello to our kinsman, the Duke of Portmaine."

She'd gotten her scolding after all, but maybe she wouldn't get the whip. "Good evening, sir, I mean, yer grace."

"Ian, my name is Ian." He strode to her and, with the grace of long practice, detached her hand from the folds of her skirt and kissed it lightly. "I am most delighted to see you again, cousin. Your older sister, Constance, has already regaled your family with our small misunderstanding of this afternoon. You appear none the worse for it, my child. I trust that now you will most sincerely accept my apology."

He grinned down at her. "I was driving like a madman, wasn't I?"

"No, not really. It was just when I saw Fiona run toward you that you became quite mad quite quickly. I was terrified for her. I should have realized who you were when you opened your mouth and spoke like such a—"

"Let's just say that I spoke like an Englishman, all right?"

"That's exactly right," Brandy said.

Uncle Claude cackled from his place beside

Lady Adella's chair. "Yer grace mistakes the matter. Our Brandy here is the eldest. It's near to nineteen she is."

Percy said, "Appearances are sometimes deceptive, don't ye agree, Brandy?"

She wanted to kick him, but she couldn't, not in front of Grandmama and an English duke who was related to them. She raised her chin and stared at him.

"Do leave the girl alone, Percy," Lady Adella said, and tapped his arm with her fan. "I told ye that she doesn't yet ken what to do with your sort. Give her time, give her time. I try to teach her a bit each day."

"Well, I for one do agree with Percy," Constance said. "Most gentlemen do think I'm the eldest." She patted several soft black tendrils into place and gazed at the duke with the melting look she'd been practicing in front of her mirror. He looked disconcerted. It was obvious she'd have to practice some more.

"Where could that old sot Crabbe be?" Lady Adella wondered aloud. "I swear we would all starve to death if he had his way in the matter. He becomes slower by the year. I wonder what he's drinking in the kitchen?"

"Good evening, Brandy," said Bertrand in his calm, cultured voice. "Ye're looking fit, but then ye always do."

"Good evening, cousin Bertrand, Uncle Claude. How are ye feeling, sir?"

"As fit as can be expected with this damned gout. Bertie here gives me little sympathy, just stares down at his ledgers and does naught of anything else at all.''

He gazed over at the duke, who stood in conversation with Lady Adella, and added with barely veiled malice, ''The duke's much more the thing than poor Bertrand here, I vow. I'll wager he's a man who tells ye exactly what's on his mind. Of course, Bertie here is much too timid a fellow to tell us how he feels.''

''Father,'' Bertrand said in a low voice.

''Look ye at Percy,'' Claude continued, disregarding his son. ''It's an oily viper's tongue he has, but at least he doesn't chew his cud in silence like a stupid cow.''

''He's a bull, Uncle Claude,'' Brandy said in a loud voice, ''if you must use that simile.''

To Bertrand she said quickly in a low voice, ''Why did the duke come here? Grandmama said he would have no interest in us. She said he'd send a man of business. I don't understand. Isn't he rich? Isn't he a peer of the realm? Why the devil is he here?''

''All of those things, I should imagine. I don't know why he came, Brandy. Mayhap he was visiting some friends in Scotland and thought to deign to visit his poor relations. Time will tell.''

Brandy frowned, thinking of their crofters. Her jaw tightened. The English were always taking. He was here to see for himself how much he could squeeze from the land. He might be elegant, even a bit on the handsome side, but he was still greedy for all that.

Crabbe flung open the doors and announced in his wheezy voice, ''Dinner be ready.''

Brandy, for the first time in her life, felt embarrassed. The duke would think them backward. He would think they weren't civilized. Why could Crabbe not say that dinner *was* served, like a well-trained English servant?

"It's about time, ye old sot," said Lady Adella, planting her cane and rising slowly. Percy slipped his hand under her arm.

"Brandy, ye're the eldest. Let his grace lead ye to dinner, and mind you don't bore him with how ye caught the biggest sea bass last month."

"But, Grandmama," Constance said. "I might not be the eldest, but I looked older than Brandy. Don't you think that I should be the one to escort the duke to dinner?"

"No, little pet, you take Bertrand's arm. It's a solid arm, a strong arm. Be a good girl now and don't argue with me or else I'll have to say things to ye that ye won't like at all."

Brandy stood awkwardly, unconsciously pulling her shawl more closely over the gaping buttons. Without turning, she reached out her arm. She felt soft satin beneath her fingers and sent a quick look at the duke.

7

He was smiling down at her with all the obnoxious tolerance of a kindly uncle. As she walked beside him through the entrance hall and across to the dining room, she felt the two guineas click together in her pocket. She had thought to give them to Lady Adella. Now she wasn't quite certain what to do with them.

"The past seems disturbingly alive," the duke said thoughtfully, eyeing the rows of bagpipes strung from nails about the walls. Indeed, he thought, he felt like he'd chanced to walk into another world in another time. A huge battle ax hung from the mailed hand of an empty suit of armor. What he assumed was the Robertson colors, a plaid of red, yellow, and green, were draped in dusty folds about a red coat of arms in the shape of a shield above an empty, cavernous fireplace.

"Yes," she said, "particularly during a winter storm blowing from the sea. The winds whistle down the chimney and make the tartans quiver and billow out, as if they were alive." She shut her mouth. Talk about boring him with talk of her halibut that all of them had eaten for two days. This kind of talk would send him right off to sleep.

Ian looked down at the girl beside him and saw that her arched brows had drawn together in a frown. He said with all the regret in his repertoire, which, truth be told, wasn't all that large, "If you're remembering my behavior of this afternoon, Brandy, I would ask again that you forgive me. I was tired and had suffered nearly two days of delay. But that's an unpersuasive excuse, isn't it? Actually, it scared the very devil out of me when Fiona ran in front of my horses, then you were dashing after her. I think I lost a good ten years off my life. I think by tomorrow morning I'll have a gray hair in my head. Forgive me?"

She felt churlish. She felt stupid and backward. He was splendid, everything a duke should be. He was kind and sincere. He was possibly noble. But he thought she was a bloody child. Well, damnation. "Of course, ye're forgiven. Do you ever yell?"

"Yell?"

"Yes, ye were very angry, yer face all red, the veins in yer neck throbbing hard, but ye didn't yell. Yer voice just got real hard and cold. Very clipped."

"Yes, I yell. But not at—" He broke off. He'd nearly said, "not at children." But that wasn't right. She was eighteen. She was a woman. It was amazing. He wondered if she had a headache, wearing her hair plastered back so tightly. And the old gown she was wearing was more suited to a fifteen-year-old. Where the blazes did that ridiculous shawl come from? It looked older than Lady Adella, which was saying something. Then he felt more guilt than he could accept. There was no money, that was it. Certainly there was no money for a girl child's clothes. He felt like a clod.

He forced a calm smile and directed her attention to the fireplace. "The three wolves' heads in your coat of arms—when you were a child, did you sometimes fancy they snarled at the thought of invaders?"

"Even now sometimes when I think about them I wonder. Aye, I sometimes fancy that they were once proud and fiercely alive, defending the

65

castle. It's as though they are under some sort of evil spell, holding them lifeless for all time. It's a pleasing and romantic notion."

He saw the glow of Scotland's rich, fanciful past in those amber eyes of hers—he'd never seen quite that color before. He felt something curious, something that felt really quite warm and very real, something he wasn't at all used to. He said, "Are those the Robertson colors?"

"Aye. Once they were a rich bright crimson, and yellow, and green. Old Marta takes no care of them now."

"Old Marta?"

"Grandmama's maid. I think she must be as old as the castle and just as strong. I heard Grandmama once scream at her that the only reason she let her stay here was because Grandpapa wanted her. Oh, dear, I suppose I shouldn't have said that."

"That's quite all right," the duke said, fascinated. He suddenly realized that the others had passed into the dining room. "Come, Brandy, we do not wish the others to wait." But he didn't really care if the others waited. He felt the warmth fade, felt the chill of reality, until she said in that candid, lilting voice, "I wondered why I had no hot water for my bath. I blamed it on Percy's being here. He always makes demands of the servants."

He raised a black brow and felt the warmth again, like smooth honey.

She lightly patted his sleeve. "Oh, it's not yer fault, yer grace. Strange, though, that Morag did not tell me of yer being here."

"The rather slovenly woman who keeps scratching her head?"

"She doesn't scratch her head *all* the time, just perhaps half the time, and that's just because she doesn't take baths."

"That would explain things." He looked down again at Brandy, at the proud, straight nose, and the firm chin, a stubborn chin. A precocious girl, he thought, and not without intelligence and charm. Perhaps someday, with proper nurturing, she would become a lovely woman. Damn, she was a woman, not a womanly woman but a beginning woman. He realized with something of a start that he was now her nominal guardian.

"Come, yer grace," Lady Adella called, "it's the earl's chair for ye. We'll have to rechristen it the duke's chair. Brandy, ye will be seated in yer usual place."

The duke looked about the long dining room. How very medieval it looked, with the long table flanked by rigid lines of carved chairs. The high wainscotting was as dark as the heavy furniture, and the firelight and the branches of candles couldn't begin to pierce into the corners. All that was needed to complete the scene, he thought, was a rush-strewn floor and giant mastiffs gnawing bones on the hearth. He helped Brandy into her seat and crossed to the head of the table. The ornately carved earl's chair stood nearly as tall as his shoulders, exuding a kind of crude power. The three Robertson wolves' heads were carved into its back and pressed against his shoulder blades when he seated himself.

67

He thought of the quiet elegance of Carmichael Hall and shifted his position.

"Ye old sot, pour the wine. I trust ye didn't slurp it all down while ye polished the silver." Lady Adella's strident voice reached him from the other end of the table, and he winced, wondering if all Penderleigh servants were meted out similar insults. The impassive Crabbe filled his goblet.

Lady Adella thwacked her glass upon the wooden table. "All of ye, let us toast the new Earl of Penderleigh." There was a liberal lacing of mockery in her voice, and Ian saw that she raised her glass first to Percival, then to Claude and Bertrand, before turning to him.

So much for a friendly welcome. The old woman was baiting the men. "I thank you all," he said in his calm ducal voice, and sipped the heavy wine.

Morag set a steaming bowl in front of him. He assumed it was soup, but it looked like no soup he'd ever seen before. He was at a loss to determine its origins. He wasn't certain he wanted to know.

Claude cackled. "Ye're in Scotland now, yer grace. Partan bree it is and not yer usual English fare."

"It's a crab soup," Bertrand said in a friendly voice. "I hope ye'll find it tasty."

"It's a lucky happenstance that we poor Scots still have the sea," Percy said. "Even the English could not destroy that."

"Or the Danes or the Vikings or the Picts or the Britons or other unfriendly Scottish clans either,

68

I suspect," Ian said and saluted Percy with his spoon.

"Percy, mind yer tongue," Lady Adella sang out, "or it appears that Ian may very well nip it off. Ye're quick-witted, yer grace, and that pleases me. So few quick wits around these days."

Ian lowered his head to look more closely at the partan bree. Percy had been introduced to him as Lady Adella's grandson. Why the devil wasn't the fellow the heir to the earldom? Perhaps that fact went a good distance in explaining his snide comments on the English in general, and himself in particular. He lifted a spoonful of the crab soup to his mouth and found the meat smooth and rich, the cream tangy. At least as yet he hadn't any complaint to make of Scottish food.

"Cousin Ian," Constance said in a soft woman's voice, "where are yer servants? I always thought that English gentleman had simply hundreds of servants, and since ye are a duke, why ye should barely be able to move from one room to another without someone attending ye?"

"I had the misfortune of breaking an axle on the carriage. My valet, Mabley, is, I hope, successfully negotiating with a blacksmith in Galashiels. I came alone in my curricle, as you know."

"Ye brought only one servant?"

He'd clearly disappointed her, this woman-girl. He said with a grin, "I'm but one man, not an entire household." He thought of his gently sighing valet and grinned to himself. Whatever would Mabley think of the scratchy Morag?

"Ye came from London, yer grace?" Brandy asked.

"Yes, a long journey. Nearly six days. Many poorly appointed inns and a swarm of thieves lurking about everywhere we stayed."

"But why?" Brandy said.

Ian paused with his last spoonful of the crab soup suspended over the bowl, and cocked his head to one side. "Why did I come here, you mean?"

Brandy sat forward, looking at him straightly. "Aye, yer grace. We didn't believe ye would ever come to Penderleigh, being an English duke and all. We believed ye'd sent a man of business to force more rents out of us. But ye're here. Why?"

She didn't realize she was being excessively rude. He did, though, and found himself again charmed by her candor. Lady Adella said to her granddaughter, "Ye pry into matters none of yer concern, child," but Ian saw, as did everyone else at that long medieval table, that the old lady's faded eyes were fair to burning with curiosity.

"I suppose it's natural for you to wonder. But did you really believe that I would ignore my Scottish kinsmen?"

Percy said, a sneer twisting his fine mouth, "What my little cousin means, yer grace, is that we didn't mind at all being ignored. It's the land and rents we feared would gain yer attention."

"Percy, that is not at all what I meant. I'll thank ye to let me put my own words in my own mouth. Well, perhaps I did mean a bit of it, but not all."

The duke was forced to laugh. "From outward appearances, I would venture to say that the lands

70

and the castle are much in need of my attention. The rents appear to be excessive already."

Lady Adella said, "Ye're my sister's grandson, Ian, and part of my blood. I'm heartened that ye visit yer holdings. At least so far I'm heartened. Things change."

The duke would have been pleased by Lady Adella's sudden pleasant words had he not seen the look of malice she gave Percy, followed by a big smile.

Bertrand said quietly, but he was leaning forward, energy radiating from him, "I have seen to the estate for many years now, yer grace. I myself am much concerned. At yer leisure, I will show ye the account books and all I've tried to do. We have such an abundance of raw materials, but we're lacking funds to get us started up again."

"Yes, I see that. I will be at your mercy tomorrow, Bertrand." The duke looked up as Morag removed his empty soup bowl and placed a large platter before him, heaped with something he couldn't and didn't want to identify.

"Haggis," Claude said and smacked his lips.

"Haggis?" the duke repeated, eyeing the atrocious-looking mess heaped up on that huge, dented silver platter not six inches from his plate.

Constance leaned toward the duke and said brightly, "A mixture of oatmeal, liver, beef suet, and the like. Cook always serves it with potatoes and rutabagas. It's quite tasty. Just give it a chance, yer grace."

Ian raised a tentative forkful to his mouth.

Percy tossed in, "The whole mess is boiled in a sheep stomach."

The duke swallowed convulsively, hoping he wouldn't throw up. A damned sheep's stomach? Good Lord, what were these people? He tried another bite. He tasted strong black pepper. He quickly drank more of the heavy sweet wine to avoid sneezing.

He tried several more bites. He chewed. He swallowed. He tried not to think about the sheep's stomach. He looked up to see various pairs of eyes gazing at him expectantly, some smiling, some malicious, some just curious.

"It's delicious. My compliments to Cook and to the sheep." Oh, damn, not the sheep. He almost gagged.

Brandy found herself grinning at Percy's disappointment. She hadn't realized before that he wasn't very talented at hiding his feelings. He looked thwarted, his mouth sullen. But he was her cousin and for just a moment, a very brief moment, she felt a stab of pity for him.

Ian looked around the table as everyone ate. Lady Adella, his great aunt, sat like royalty at the foot of the table, attacking the haggis as if she hadn't eaten in a month. She must be at least seventy, he thought, maybe a hundred, trying to remember his grandmother, her sister. All he could recall was a vague, wispy wraith of a stooped old lady who seemed to have spent most of her remaining days reclining on a comfortable sofa with his own mother in constant attendance. Surely, she couldn't have had the iron personality Lady Adella appeared to enjoy in abundance.

Lady Adella had welcomed him graciously enough, yet had seemed to derive pleasure in pitting him against Percy and Bertrand.

He glanced at Claude, who sat on Lady Adella's left, seemingly quite content to noisily chew his dinner with his few remaining teeth. He had been introduced as a nephew, and Bertrand, his son, as a grandnephew. Why the devil hadn't one of these men inherited Penderleigh? He disliked mysteries and determined to unravel these confusing relationships on the morrow.

He looked at Constance, so lovely and trying so hard to make herself noticed and admired, then quickly at Brandy, and back again at Constance. He found it difficult to believe that the two girls were sisters. The one with the unattractive braided hair, and the other with lush, thick black hair that curled provocatively over her rounded shoulders. Brandy wore a shapeless muslin gown, far outdated, and topped with a pale yellow shawl, and Constance a daringly low-cut violet silk gown that showed the promise of a maturing bosom. And Fiona, the redheaded little urchin who had almost dashed herself under his horses' hooves, in coloring at least was very different from both of her sisters. He looked back down the long expanse of table toward Lady Adella and decided that he had never before seen such a ragtag collection of gentry.

Lady Adella met his eyes and said, "No string of endless courses here, yer grace. When ye are finished with the haggis, we'll have the trifle served up."

The duke smiled easily. "Trifle, my lady. That is a dish I've enjoyed many times."

"Not the way Cook prepares it, ye haven't." Claude cackled, a grating sound that made one to punch him except there was also just a hint of pain in that cackle as well. Lady Adella had said he suffered from gout.

"At least it isn't made in a sheep stomach, I trust," Ian said. "It isn't, is it?" he said directly to Brandy.

"No sheep involved," Brandy said, but she was grinning like a thief accidentally given a collection plate. He discovered after several mouthfuls what Claude meant. The sherry was sour and the cake soggy. Good manners required him to finish the bulk of the noble portion that Morag had spooned onto a plate for him. He downed a large draught of wine to soothe his irritated palate. He gazed toward Lady Adella after some moments, wondering if in Scotland the ladies retired to the drawing room and left the gentlemen to their port, as was the custom in England.

"We'll take our port in the drawing room," she said presently, as if reading his thoughts. He raised his eyebrow fleetingly and rose with the rest of the company.

As he passed Brandy, she whispered, "That was very polite of ye. I was wrong. Ye do have breeding and good manners to survive a dinner with all of us. The trifle was terrible, but Cook was only trying to impress ye." She giggled behind her hand.

He was enchanted, he couldn't help it. "It was a noble effort. I could do nothing else but eat all

74

eleven bitefuls." He lowered his voice. "Doesn't poor Crabbe resent being called an old sot?"

Brandy bit her lower lip. "Nay, yer grace, I assure ye, it's one of her more gentle ways of addressing him. I had hoped that she would refrain from being so colorful in yer presence, but I should have known better." She added under her breath, "Ye mustn't pay any attention to Percy. He is ever hateful and, I think, most jealous of yer position as new master here."

Lady Adella's omnipresent eye prevented him from questioning Brandy further.

"Come, Brandy, Constance. We must show the duke that Scotland is not an uncivilized land. His grace is in need of entertainment."

She turned to the duke, who at the moment wanted nothing more than his bed and a long night's sleep. "Ye'll find the girls not without ladies' accomplishments. Constance, since ye're the younger and it is growing late, ye may perform for his grace first."

Although Constance presented a quite attractive picture seated at the old pianoforte, her rendition of a French ballad in a small, deadened voice made the duke pray that the song had not many verses. When she rose from the pianoforte and curtsied demurely, he forced himself to hearty applause.

"Ye still sound like a rusty wood pipe, girl," Lady Adella said. "After all the advice I've given ye, ye still sound atrocious. I even sang for ye to show ye how it's done. Well, at least ye looked a picture whilst ye were killing his grace's ears."

The duke spoke his lie without hesitation. "I

75

enjoyed your performance, Constance. I look forward to hearing you again."

The petulant child's look vanished, replaced by an almost successful sultry smile. Her eyes darted to Percy in search of a similar accolade. To her chagrin, Percy was staring hard at Brandy.

"The duke is kind, child. Now it's off to bed with ye. Say yer good-nights and then it's yer sister's turn."

Constance saw there was no hope for it, and with as much good grace as she could muster, she curtsied and left the drawing room with a lagging step.

"Grandmama," Brandy said, "it is rather late and the duke must be tired from his long journey. Perhaps he would prefer not to hear—"

Lady Adella snorted and pointed her bony finger toward the pianoforte.

"I should enjoy hearing your performance," Ian added, wishing for the moment at least that he were back in London, in his own home, doing precisely what he pleased.

"I will turn the pages for ye, Brandy." Percy rose and drew close to her. Brandy quickly revised her selection. "Ye need not bother, Percy, I have no pages to turn."

"Then I will stand next to the pianoforte and ye may sing to me." She kept her hands in her lap until he gave her a caressing, mocking smile, sketched a slight bow, and turned to seat himself next to Lady Adella.

Ian watched this exchange with some irritation. He heard Lady Adella hiss to Percy in a low voice,

"I told ye to leave the child alone, Percy. She doesn't ken yer meaning."

In a pig's eye she doesn't, the duke thought. He did not hear Percival's reply, for Brandy touched her fingers to the key board. Three soft, sad chords filled the room and in a low, rich voice she sang,

> "Oh, my luve is like a red, red rose,
> —That's newly sprung in June:
> Oh, my luve is like the melodie,—That's
>   sweetly play'd in tune.
>
> Till a'the seas gang dry, my dear,
> —And the rocks melt wi' the sun;
> And I will luve thee still, my dear,
> —While the stands o'life shall run.
>
> And fare thee weel, my only luve!—And
>   fare thee weel a while!
> And I will come again, my luve,
> —Tho' it were ten thousand mile!"

The duke was held in silence for a moment by the haunting words and the deep minor chords that added to their beauty. He had not understood all of them, for she had sung with a lilting Scottish brogue.

He heard Lady Adella snort in what he assumed was her form of applause. He said, "It's a lovely ballad, Brandy. Who is the writer?"

She turned on the stool. "Robert Burns— Rabbie Burns, as we call him. He died but four years ago, quite near to here, in Dumfries."

"Ye might add, my dear," Percy said with that sneer that made Ian want to plant his fist in his mouth, "that yer beloved Rabbie was a drunk and a womanizer. Peopled these parts with brats."

Lady Adella said, her look more lewd than her grandson's, "I for one wish that our dear Rabbie had been born some forty years earlier. I wouldn't have minded a-takin' a tumble with that one. I ask ye, Percy, 'How can ye doe ocht when ye've nocht tae dae ocht wi'?' Aye, that makes ye calm up yer mouth."

Percy's face tightened in anger. Had the old woman insulted his manhood? Evidently so.

Ian turned to see Brandy quickly rise from the piano bench. "I will go to bed now, Grandmama, if ye don't mind." Evidently Lady Adella had lost interest and she waved her off. Brandy kept her head down and walked quickly from the room. Why in heaven's name was Grandmama speaking in such an outrageous manner? It was as if she was being purposefully vulgar in the duke's presence.

The duke rose slowly. "I fear that I am much in need of my bed. If you will all excuse me, I bid you good night."

Lady Adella said, "If all isn't to yer liking, yer grace, lay yer hand across Morag's back. She's a lazy trollop, that one."

The duke nodded and left the room. He heard Claude's cackle sound behind him.

Crabbe awaited him outside to escort him to his bedchamber. It was scarcely likely that the duke would have lost his way, as he had been accorded the old earl's bedchamber. It lay at the end of the long, drafty west corridor in splendid isolation.

Crabbe opened the dark doors with a flourish and bowed the duke in. The furnishings were as dark and cumbersome as the pieces in the dining room, and the corners of the room just as gloomy. The duke wished he had more than one branch of candles to make the room less austere.

Crabbe gazed impassively at the pitiful fire that lay smoldering in the grate. "Morag laid the peat fer ye, no doubt about that. I took the liberty to lay oot yer things, yer grace."

After the old man had left, the duke bent down to build up the pathetic fire. Some of the peat clumps were damp to the touch, in all likelihood brought in from outside at the height of the storm this evening. No wonder the result was wispy fingers of gray smoke.

He hurriedly undressed and eased between the cold sheets. The covers smelled faintly musty. He fell asleep to the sound of pattering rain against the windowpanes and the roar of the waves breaking against the rocks at the foot of the cliff behind the castle.

8

"Tell me more about the new earl, Brandy," Fiona said, the porridge dripping off the end of her spoon.

"Have a care, poppet. Ye know how Old Marta

hates to scrub porridge out of yer gowns. She complains so much that I do it and I don't like it either." Fiona swiped her hand across her chin; then, her blue eyes on her sister, she very neatly rubbed a napkin over her palm.

"Well done," Brandy said, trying not to laugh. "Now, I know little more than do ye about the earl. First of all, he's a duke, at least he is in England, and that's more important than an earl."

"Aye," Fiona said, nodding. "Maybe that's why he smells good and his clothes are clean. Grandpa Angus used to hug me sometimes, and I'd see food stains on his coat. And his breath was horrid, Brandy."

"Well, yes, that's true," Brandy said. "Now, ye must remember to call him 'yer grace' and not just 'my lord.'"

"He's got a girl's name?"

Brandy laughed. "Nay. That's just a manner of speaking. The way one addresses a duke. We do the same here in Scotland."

"Maybe he'll let me pet that wonderful horse of his."

Brandy doubted that very much, but her smile didn't slip. "Ye must promise me not to make a nuisance of yerself, poppet. The duke probably isn't at all used to children. Besides that, he won't be here that long. What do we have to interest him, after all?"

"But why did he come if he only wants to leave us?"

"I don't know, Fiona. Come, poppet, finish yer breakfast. It grows late." It wasn't really late at all, but Brandy wanted to take no chances of seeing Percy if she could avoid it. She listened to Fiona scrape the bottom of her porridge bowl as she looked out the window at the overgrown moat. The storm of the night before had blown itself out, and it promised to be a glorious spring day, with just a nip of chill in the air and a light breeze to ruffle the bluebells.

"This is a pleasant surprise."

Brandy jerked about in her chair, expecting to see Percy's unwelcome face. "Oh, it's ye, yer grace." Relief so flooded her voice that the duke cocked a black brow.

"Ye're the man with the grand horses," Fiona said, and slipped out of her chair. She looked up at the huge man. "Are ye really a yer grace and not just a lordship like Grandpa Angus was?"

Ian surveyed the skinny little girl, standing arms akimbo before him, her face tilted up. Her hair was thick and bright as crimson velvet. Beautiful hair and eyes as blue as a summer sky. "Yes," he said. "I am indeed a grace. Do I take it you're Fiona, my youngest cousin?"

"Aye, but Brandy calls me poppet. Do I have to call ye by yer girl's name?"

One forgot that children spoke whatever popped into their heads. He touched the bright red curls. "No, not a lady's name, if you please, Fiona. Let me think. I know. I want you to call me something more manly. How about Ian?"

"Ian," she repeated, "it's better than grace. Would ye like some porridge, Ian? It's not nearly so watery this morning, although some of it still ran down my chin. But I didn't get any on my gown."

"These things sometimes happen," he said. "The porridge should be nice and hard by now. How long has this big bowl sat here?"

"Not more than ten minutes," Brandy said. "Aye," she added, lightly stirring the porridge, "still a bit on the watery side, but not bad, really."

"Ah, it should be perfect if it's only a bit. Come on back to the table, Fiona. I'm sorry to have disturbed you."

"Did ye sleep in Grandpa Angus's bed, Ian? He died in that bed, ye know. We had to tiptoe about fer more than a month. I heard him coughing and cursing at Grandmama."

"Fiona, that's quite enough. Grandpapa Angus cursed at everybody. And you know very well that every Penderleigh earl has died in that bed. Here, have a scone. Aye, that's right, spread some butter on it."

"There wasn't a single spirit from the past to disturb me," the duke said. He eyed the porridge, then gave himself a liberal helping. He took his first bite. What a relief, he thought. The porridge was delicious, hardly watery at all. He looked up to see Fiona frowning at him.

"Is there porridge in danger of dripping on my coat?"

"Oh, nay, Ian. I asked Brandy why ye came here if ye only wanted to leave us. She said there wasn't anything here to interest ye, so she thought ye'd be gone soon enough."

Brandy studied her scone. Butter dripped off

one edge. If Fiona had been closer, she would have clouted her.

"And why did Brandy think I'd come?" the duke asked, his dark eyes resting for a moment on Brandy's profile. She had a lovely nose, he thought, nice arched brows that were the same dark blond as her hair, and a nice firm chin. Was she stubborn? Her hair was in its tight braids, the same worn tartan shawl around her shoulders.

"She said she didn't know. Will ye tell me?"

He couldn't very well tell a little girl that he, an adult man, had felt trapped, indeed nearly comatose with boredom, at the thought of spending another Season in London, that it wouldn't have mattered if he'd been given an excuse to go anywhere—to Turkey or to Scotland—it wouldn't have mattered. He'd just wanted to escape. No, he couldn't very well say any of that. He said without hesitation, "I came because you are my cousins and I wanted to meet you."

Brandy's eye flew to his face. She knew he was lying, knew it as clearly as she knew her own name.

The duke arched an elegant black brow and tried to look as innocent as Fiona, who was knotting her napkin in the shape of a doll.

"Well, Fiona, does that answer your question?"

"Aye, but when may I see the grand horses, Ian?"

"When you give me your solemn promise that you won't go dashing in front of them. I'm much too young to have any gray hair."

"Oh, I promise, I surely do."

That was a well-done lie, unlike his, the duke thought.

"Poppet," Brandy said, her tone as motherly as Ian's great-aunt's, who had seven children, "ye must realize that his grace has much to do. We mustn't press him for attention."

An ineffectual mother, he added to himself as he smiled at her. She was trying to look stern and not succeeding.

He felt a tug of liking for her. Well, why not? She was his cousin, of sorts, and she was very young, if not in years, well then, in character, in experience.

"Ye know," she said now, "it truly isn't yer fault that ye've inherited Penderleigh. Nor is it yer fault that ye're not Scottish. Someone must be English, I suppose, and ye had no say in that." She poured him some tea.

"Thank you," he said, and gave her a small salute with his teacup. "You're right. I had no say at all."

He turned to Fiona again, and Brandy felt free to look at him as much as she liked. He was a big man, very big, bigger than any man she'd ever known, and she liked that. And he dressed so beautifully, he surely must think they were all savages. Her own dress was at least five years old. His breeches were knit and very well fitted to his legs. His shirt was as white as the snow that had fallen for just one special night the previous February. It had melted before it could become dirty. His coat fit him perfectly. Everything about him was elegant, including his beautiful black boots. She tugged at her skirt. He was all that she was not. He was all that none of them were. They were the poor relations, nothing more.

The duke watched the changing expression on her face. To his surprise, she suddenly seemed to be ill at ease. He'd done nothing. He said, "What I would like most on my first day here is a tour. The storm has blown itself out, and I would much like to walk along the cliffs and look out over the sea and see anything else you want to show me."

"That's what Brandy and I were going to do," Fiona said, unknotting the napkin. "Do ye like to build things in the sand, Ian?"

He thought of his buff riding habit, his last daytime clean clothes. He couldn't take the chance that Mabley would arrive today with the rest of his luggage. "What I would most like," he said, "that is, if you would not mind, Fiona, is to stay out of the wet sand. Otherwise I'll have to wash my own clothes. That wouldn't be good since I haven't the foggiest notion of how to do it."

"I don't either," Fiona said.

How superbly polite he is, Brandy thought, and gave him a dazzling smile. "Poppet, go fetch yer shawl."

Fiona slipped from the dining room, calling over her shoulder, laughter in her young voice, "I'll be back afore the mouse gets caught in the trap."

The duke said, "Aren't you warm wearing that shawl all the time?"

To his surprise, she looked as if he'd told her

she had a dozen spots on her face. "Nay," she said, "I'm always cold, aye, that's it. Cold. Until August I wear my shawl, sometimes even all the way through the summer and then it's nearly winter again, so my shawl stays with me nearly all year around." She hunched her shoulders forward. One long braid fell over her shoulder, dipping its tip into the warm cream at the bottom of her porridge bowl.

"Your braid, Brandy," Ian said, and leaning over, grasped the long rope of hair.

Startled, she jerked away from him so quickly that he didn't have time to release her hair. She gritted her teeth at the stab of pain in her scalp.

He handed her a glass of water. "Here, dip the braid in the water. I didn't mean to hurt or frighten you."

"I know," she said, not looking at him. She swished the cream from the braid and dried it on a napkin. "I hear Fiona. Are ye ready, Ian?"

"Aye," he replied, savoring the lilting Scottish word that sounded so strange on his tongue, yet satisfying as well.

"Ye wouldn't be mocking me, now would ye, yer grace?"

"His grace never mocks his cousins. He is far too polite. Besides, he very much likes his cousins. Shall we go?"

The three of them walked out to the castle, across the gravel path that cut over the grassy moat, and along the rhododendron-lined walk that led finally to the cliff and the sea.

They soon gained the edge of the grassy cliff, and Ian gazed out to sea, now placid and calm.

Close to shore, the shallowness of the water made it appear a translucent turquoise. Farther out the water shimmered with varying hues of darker blue. He looked up at the cloud-tossed blue sky. He felt the fresh breeze cool on his face, felt it ruffle his hair, and drew a long breath.

"Be careful, poppet, and don't get too dirty." That quickly drew him out of his reverie. He looked to see Fiona running as fast as her skinny legs would go down a well-worn path to the beach below.

He turned to her. "I hope Fiona doesn't break her leg. That path looks a bit treacherous."

"She's a little goat. Don't worry."

"You've a magnificent home, Brandy."

"It's yer home now as well, Ian," she said, shading her eyes after Fiona until she was certain the child had gained the safety of the beach.

"Do you mind? he asked quietly.

She was silent for a moment. She said finally, a touch of sadness in her voice, "Nay, it's not for me to mind. Many years have passed, and although many Scots don't like to admit it, change must come. Ye're a big dose of change. Ye can't help the fact that ye're English, I already told ye that. Ye must remember that I am but a female, and thus of very little worth. My opinion doesn't matter to anyone, nor can I dictate how ye'll be treated or accepted here."

"You're of great worth to me, and I care very much about your opinion of me. I don't want you to speak like that of yourself ever again."

She laughed, her hands over the knot of her shawl. What a stern voice he'd used with that little speech. "Ye should hear how Grandmama speaks to me. If Crabbe is an old sot, why, I'm a feckless idiot with less worth than a cellar of salt. She talks of marrying me off and rolls her rheumy old eyes." She shrugged her shoulders. "I don't mind that ye inherited. Some male relative had to, else our line would die out."

He'd never heard a young girl speak so plainly, with such stark heed to what was real. He supposed that females really weren't worth all that much, and he thought it wasn't all that fair, but on the other hand, he was a man and it was his duty to protect her, to take care of her, to see that she knew no want. But still, to speak of herself as having no worth, it galled him.

The breeze was stiffening, pulling hairs loose from her tight braid, blowing them over her cheeks, thick strands of honey-colored hair.

"I see, then, that it's my duty to marry soon and father a brood of future heirs. If I didn't have a son and fell off my hunter and broke my neck, why then, the Earl of Penderleigh would be my cousin, Giles, of no blood tie whatsoever to you."

"Nay, please don't break yer neck."

"No, I won't. But life isn't all that certain. One never knows. And I'm of an age to beget an heir."

"Oh, I don't know ye weren't yet married. I don't think Grandmama knows either, else she would have trumpeted it all over Penderleigh. Aye, this is something ye must consider."

"I'm twenty-eight, a great age, I suppose, to one of your youth."

"Not at all. Ye see, I am to be nineteen come Michaelmas, so ye are not at all old."

88

It was true. She was scarcely younger than Felicity, the lady he would marry in August. Felicity was so very different from this girl. And Marianne. He welcomed the familiar deep ache, for it nourished her fading image in his mind. She would have been twenty-six now and probably the mother of several children. He wondered yet again what their children would have looked like. Certainly their daughters would have been delicate like her, their eyes a luminous green. Ah, and their sons—his sons—proud and strong, all strong and big as he was. He smiled down at her, saying nothing, and let his attention be drawn to seagulls squawking shrilly overhead.

He heard Brandy say, "Ye see, Ian, Fiona is forever trying to build a sand castle just like Penderleigh. Poor child, the fluted turrets are always collapsing on her."

He pushed Marianne away and looked down at Fiona. He imagined that her fiery hair must already be gritty with wet sand. "None of you appear to resemble each other. Who does Fiona take after, Brandy?"

"From what Grandmama says, Fiona is the only one of us who really looks like anybody. Her hair and eyes are the exact color of my mother's sister, Aunt Antonia. As for Constance, she has somewhat the look of our mother. And I, well, Grandmama calls me her changeling."

"Just as long as she doesn't call you an old sot."

"Poor Crabbe. She used to do horrid things with his real name, very fishy things, insults I didn't understand. Thank God he isn't related, else she would show him no mercy."

"You mean call him a feckless idiot?"

"That's it."

"Speaking of relations, who exactly is Percival?"

"He's a bastard."

"I wasn't referring to his character, rather his relationship to us."

"He's a bastard."

He saw then that she was perfectly serious. Ah, but her eyes were alight with laughter. He grinned back at her. "For a bastard he certainly seems to have the run of the castle."

"Aye, Grandmama is very fond of him, more's the pity. He flatters her, ye see, and I must admit that he does it well."

He gave her a sharp look that she didn't notice, for she had slipped down to her knees and was busily gathering yellow anemones on her spread skirt.

He dropped to his knees beside her, forgetting his last pair of buff breeches. He began to absently pluck the flowers with her. "Just what exactly are his antecedents?"

She raised her eyes to his face and said matter-of-factly, "His father, Davonan, was my uncle, one of Grandmama's sons. When Uncle Davonan was quite young, he seduced a rich merchant's daughter in Edinburgh. When she discovered she was pregnant, he refused to marry her. From what I have been able to glean from Old Marta's gossiping and Grandmama's occasional spurts of anger, Uncle Davonan left

Penderleigh and went to Paris. He died there some ten years ago, with one of his lovers."

"Lovers? He had many?"

"Aye, he did, but it's not what ye think. Uncle Davonan did not prefer women, ye see. Although I must say," she continued with ill-concealed bitterness, "that Percy is continually endeavoring to make amends for that fact."

"To the point of making himself a nuisance where you are concerned, Brandy?"

"Aye."

He thought about her calm acceptance of her Uncle Davonan's preference for men, a subject that no young English lady would speak about even if she chanced to know that such a thing existed. Ah, but this openness of hers reflected only a childlike candor. She was innocent. He said without thought, "I think Percy should direct his attention to women and not children. Perhaps he is unnatural in his own way."

9

She threw the anemones at him and jumped to her feet. "I told ye, yer grace, that I was eighteen, nearly nineteen. Hardly a child. Do I look like a child? Do I?"

"No, not at all. I misspoke. What I meant was that he should direct his attentions toward women of experience and not toward his innocent cousin. You are innocent, aren't you, Brandy?"

"Ye mean, am I still a virgin?"

"Well, that's a sort of innocence."

"Of course I'm a virgin. Who around here would relieve me of my virginity? Except for Percy, of course, and ye can be certain that I avoid him whenever he's about."

"Good. Perhaps I'll avoid him too. He sneers. Sneering annoys me. It makes me want to send my fist into the man's face. What do you think?"

"Smash him," she said and stooped down to pick up the anemones she'd thrown at him.

"That's a thought. Tell me, though, why does he resent me so much? I understand that he could very well hate the English. Is that it? Surely he knows that a bastard could never hold claim to either the earldom or Penderleigh Castle."

Brandy was silent for several moments, struggling with the fact that although Percy was, in her opinion, a rotter, he was nonetheless a Scot, whereas the duke was English. Her liking for him won the day. "There's more to it than that. Constance overheard Grandmama tell Percy that she planned to legitimize him. She wants him to marry an heiress and repair his fortunes."

"Ah."

"What does 'ah' mean?"

"It means that once he's legitimized, he may try to overturn my inheritance. Don't you agree?"

She nodded. "He's a rotter and I don't trust him. If Lady Adella does get him legitimized, I'd be worried what he'd try to do. He isn't to be trusted."

"No, I wouldn't imagine that he is. How do Claude and Bertrand stand in all this? You see, my solicitors really knew nothing about the interesting relationships that seem to abound here. All these male relatives have come as a surprise to me."

"Ye didn't know that Uncle Claude as well as Bertrand are disinherited?"

He stared down at her. "Disinherited? Good Lord, this grows more tangled than a melodrama on Drury Lane."

"What's Drury Lane?"

"That's where all the theaters are in London."

He watched her think about this for a moment, but then she surprised him by saying, "Actually, I don't know the real reason why my Great-uncle Douglass was disinherited. He was Grandpapa Angus's older brother and heir to the title. From what Old Marta says, Grandpapa Angus's father, the old earl, literally threw him off the estate and made Angus his heir. After Douglass died, Grandpapa Angus allowed Uncle Claude and Bertrand to come and live in the dower house. Bertrand has been the estate manager for the past six or seven years." She added, a glint in her eyes, "Bertrand is a good man, regardless of what ye might be thinking of Penderleigh. It's not easy to keep us all fed and pander to Grandmama's whims at the same time. There's so little for Bertrand to work with."

Did she expect him to throw Bertrand off the estate? Or was she in love with him? Oddly, he didn't like that thought. She was too young— well, not that, but too innocent for the seemingly unworldly Bertrand. What she was, he thought, was wonderfully complex. What she needed was a man who would understand this wonderful innocence of hers, this complexity, and at the same time not think her any less innocent when she happened to speak matter-of-factly about her great uncle Davanon preferring men. "I see," he said.

"I also heard that Lady Adella has plans to reinherit Claude and Bertrand, just as she plans to legitimize Percy."

"A wily old woman, your grandmother. Does she want everyone at everyone else's throat? Does she want murder most foul committed at her very feet?"

"She would find that amusing. I love her, but there is a wickedness in her as well. But legitimizing Percy and reinheriting Uncle Claude and Bertrand, I think she does it to right the wrongs of the past. What happened so long ago, I don't know. It must have been something terrible for Uncle Douglass to be disinherited. Also, as I'm sure ye've already guessed, she prides herself on being eccentric."

That was interesting, he thought. "And you, Brandy, what do you pride yourself on being?"

She gave him a charming smile and a shrug. "I, yer grace? I suppose that from yer point of view I'm just a provincial female with no dowry, just a poor relation."

Her matter-of-factness took him off his guard this time, and made him angry. He realized that he was now her guardian and had it in his power to alter her future, a future that indeed seemed rather bleak from his perspective. He mentally dressed her in a fashionable gown. She would be nineteen, marriageable age. It occurred to him that Felicity could take Brandy under her wing and bring her out in society. He said, "I am now your guardian, Brandy, and you are in no way a provincial female to me. I'm to be married in August to a charming lady who, I'm certain, would be delighted to teach you how to get on in society. Would you like to visit London?"

Visit London? Stay with him and his new bride? And this new bride would show her how to behave in their exalted English society? She felt herself turning red with anger. She threw the anemones at him again, shouting, "No, I shouldn't like it at all, any of it. How dare ye offer me up like a country bumpkin? Would ye lead me about on a leash to show all yer fancy friends? Would ye scold me if I didn't curtsy deeply enough to one of yer fine friends? Ye may take yer guardianship, yer grace, and stuff it in yer boot."

He was stunned. He didn't say a word.

Well, that was something, to have reduced the powerful English duke to absolute silence. "I'm going to see to Fiona. Ye may find yer own way back, yer grace." She raced to the cliff path and soon disappeared.

He got back the use of his tongue, but it was swelled with outrage. No words could get out. The damned chit. How dare she treat his generous offer with such scorn? How dare she deliberately misunderstand him? Put her on a leash? Damn her, what she needed was to be shaken hard, perhaps thrown over his legs and thrashed.

Well, damn. He walked to the cliff edge. He saw her finally running toward Fiona on the beach below. Felicity and Giles were right. The Scots were close to savage.

He yelled, his hands cupping his mouth, "You want manners, my girl. You need to be whipped. You need to come back here and let me tell you exactly why I want to whip you."

To his surprise, she turned away from Fiona and marched back up the path. His anger didn't calm much on her return journey. When she got to the cliff top, she walked straight up to him, reached in the pocket of her skirt, and flung something at him.

He stared down to see the two guineas sparkling in the sunlight at his feet. The guineas he'd given to Fiona the day he'd arrived at Penderleigh and nearly run the child down.

"Do ye really think I'm in want of manners, yer grace? Ha!" She turned and raced away from him, back down the path to the beach.

"Damn you, Brandy, that was unfair. That wasn't my fault. It was yours." He closed his mouth. She was long gone. Besides, what he was saying was ridiculous. She'd dished him up quite well. She'd laid him out like Gentleman Jackson occasionally laid him out in the boxing ring. Damnation.

He kicked the guineas with the toe of his boot, then bent down and picked them up. He tossed them in the air, caught them, tossed them again. He couldn't remember the last time he'd mucked something up so badly. She was a damned girl, and he'd been left standing here feeling a fool.

He saw Brandy with Fiona on the beach, both of them on their knees, slapping wet sand in a pile that he supposed was Penderleigh Castle. He brushed off his breeches and turned away. Why, he wondered, was she so against coming to London? He went through what he'd said. No, everything had been straightforward, nothing he could remember to bring on her fury. Put her on a leash? Rubbish.

He walked back toward the castle. His first morning here with the Robertson inmates hadn't turned out very well.

"Yer grace."

The duke saw Bertrand, his hair as darkly bright as a cock's comb under the brilliant morning light, striding toward him.

"Good morning, Bertrand," he called, planting a smile of welcome on his lips. He dismissed one particular female from his mind, curse her hide.

"Ye've been enjoying our bright spring morning, I see," Bertrand said.

The two men shook hands, and the duke looked down at his grass-stained breeches. "I hope my baggage arrives soon, else I'll have to beg a pair of breeches off you."

"Or perhaps one of my father's kilts."

The duke tried and failed to picture himself in a Scotsman's traditional short skirts.

"I know it's a daunting thought, but ye've the legs for the kilt. As for myself, I can't imagine striding about in one, the wind whipping up from beneath. Aye, ye've got it right. There's not a stitch beneath a kilt. It's supposed to be healthy,

97

keeping the air moving about everything." Bertrand laughed. He'd never seen a man look as horrified as the duke did. "All right, no kilt as yet."

"I'll stick to my breeches, grass stains and all, for the moment. As for my legs, they thank you for the compliment."

Bertrand smiled at the duke's reply, then said, "I daresay ye would wish to see the Penderleigh ledgers, and perhaps visit some of our crofters to get the feel of life here."

"I should like that very much," the duke said, thinking that Bertrand, at least, seemed open and intelligent and not at all perturbed that he was a hated Englishman descending on them. "Brandy told me you've run the estate for many years now."

"Aye, I do all my work at the dower house. If ye would like to come with me, we won't be disturbed. My father is at the castle with Lady Adella."

They were in all likelihood discussing his earldom, the duke thought. Well, there was no hope for it. "Let's get on with it, Bertrand, and please, call me Ian. We're cousins."

The Penderleigh dower house proved to be very little more than a two-story, weathered stone cottage, with heavy green vines looping in and out of the crevices. A neat, well-tended garden was planted on the east side of the cottage, in startling contrast to the wild, unkept castle grounds. "You look as if you get along quite well here."

"Fraser takes good care of us. We are very

nearly self-sufficient, what with all the vegetables he coaxes out of his arid ground. We are fortunate to be protected from the sea by all the beech hedges." Bertrand unlatched the narrow front door and motioned to the duke to duke his head.

"Incidentally," Bertrand said under his breath, "please don't mention Morag in Fraser's presence. They're married, ye see, but hold each other in truly remarkable dislike. I believe they lived together for exactly one week."

"Morag is the woman who scratches."

"Aye, the result of not bathing, a behavior that helped to quickly sour their happy union. I've always wondered why Fraser didn't notice this lack in his chosen mate before the wedding. Perhaps she bathed then. Who knows? But Father and I try not to ever bring her up in a conversation with Fraser."

The duke looked up to see a plump, balding man coming toward him, a gardening tool in his hand. "Och, Master Bertrand, yer father's up at the castle. Hied himself off just an hour ago after one of the boys came to tell him Lady Adella wanted to speak to him."

"Aye, Fraser, I know. This is my kinsman, his grace, the Duke of Portmaine and now also the Earl of Penderleigh."

"Yer grace." Fraser gave him a smile and a bow.

"Fraser, be so kind as to fetch us tea. His grace and I will be in the study."

"Aye, Master Bertrand." He gave the duke a salute with the trowel he was carrying and, with a sprightly step, retreated in the direction he had come.

"Good man," Bertrand said as he led the duke into a small sunlit room whose furnishings, although old and time-faded, were distinctly respectable. Piles of papers and large velum ledgers were stacked neatly atop a large oak desk.

Bertrand looked at those ledgers, then down at his feet. He tugged the thick shock of red hair that lay over his left temple. "Well, damn, there's no way to say it. Ye haven't inherited Holyrood House, Ian."

"It matters not," the duke said calmly. "Let's get on with it."

Bertrand seated himself beside the duke and opened the ledger to the most recent page. He began to painstakingly read aloud the entries.

Ian, after some minutes of this recital, grinned and shook his head. "Words I understand better than numbers. Tell me this, Bertrand, can Penderleigh maintain itself?"

Bertrand said readily, closing the book, "Aye, it could if our crofters could be brought into this new century. Ye see, we have rich farmland in the lowlands to our east and south that is admirably suited for growing corn. But our crofters have not the tools nor the experience to sow the land. What happens most of the time is that they join with the fishermen from the small villages to our north whilst their wives and bairns shepherd a few black-faced sheep."

There came a knock on the door and Fraser entered, balancing a sparkling silver tray on his arm. "Yer tea, Master Bertrand, yer grace," he said. With a nod, he pulled the trowel from his pocket and left the room, whistling.

"Cream, Ian?"

"Yes, please," the duke said, his forehead furrowed in thought. "Could the land support more sheep?" He took a long drink of the tea, Chinese tea that was superb. Fraser had depths, he thought.

"Aye, it could, but stocking with more sheep is very costly. Another thing. The black-faced sheep are noted for their coarse wool, good really only for making sturdy carpets and the like; thus it takes a very long time to make them pay for themselves. It's the Cheviot sheep whose wool makes fine clothing."

"Sheep require shearing. Have we enough crofters skilled at shearing?"

"Nay, but we could hire some of the roving workers at shearing time. That's what most large sheep owners do."

"And the wool would go to Glasgow? To the mills?"

"Aye, but not even as far as Glasgow. Mills have just started springing up in the past decade. There are several near us." The duke fell silent. Bertrand sat forward, dangling his hands between his legs. He eyed the new Earl of Penderleigh uncertainly, wondering miserably if he thought him a sorry steward.

The duke set down his teacup and rose. He paced about the room, then sat down, again facing Bertrand. "I think, Bertrand, that you and I should pay a visit to some manufacturers in Stirlingshire. Sheep or corn: we must assess which is the more profitable for Penderleigh's future."

Bertrand blinked. "Ye know of Stirlingshire?"

"Yes, and Clackmannanshire as well," the duke added with a grin. "I didn't come up here totally ignorant, you know, though unfortunately what I did discover about Scottish industry gives me about as much knowledge as you have on the tip of your thumb. You must teach me the basics, Bertrand. I have never been an uncaring master of my lands in England. I will do no differently here. Ah, I see that you're wondering what to say to me. You didn't believe an English duke would want to concern himself with a Scottish estate, did you?"

"That's about it," Bertrand admitted.

"Come, Bertrand," the duke said briskly. "As I told you, I have no intention of becoming like many English absentee landlords. With a little capital and your management, Penderleigh will come to maintain itself with none of the fruits of your labor flowing out of Scotland. Now, if you think it worthwhile, I should like to spend the afternoon visiting the crofters and making out a list for their needs as well as repairs for the castle."

Bertrand simply couldn't believe it. Never in his wildest dreams had he considered that the duke would actually take an interest in Penderleigh, actually want to invest money in the estate, actually leave the profits in Scotland. It boggled his brain. He couldn't think of a word to say. "I feel like a fool," he finally managed. "But know this, Ian, I'll not let ye down. Penderleigh was once a great estate, but of course time and politics and greedy and stupid men, the last being my uncle Angus, brought disastrous results."

"The past is in the past, Bertrand, and there's nothing we can do about it. But the future is in our control. Brandy has told me what an able master you are. You need never fear the future. I hope that you will trust me in this."

Actually, at that moment Bertrand would have trusted the duke to lead him blindfolded through Hades himself.

"I don't blame you for holding silent. Time will tell. Perhaps one of these days you will believe me."

Bertrand gulped. "I've thought time was my biggest enemy," he said. "Time and the future. I'm here to do whatever needs to be done."

The duke's thoughts went to Brandy and her sisters. Their futures were far more uncertain than Bertrand's. He said, "I was speaking with Brandy this morning about a number of things, including her future. Brandy is of marriageable age. Constance is lacking but a couple of years. Penderleigh is rather isolated, and I gathered there is little social exchange. As the girls' guardian, I will, of course, provide dowries, which should help in some measure."

"That is very generous of you, Ian, at least for Brandy. But Constance is young yet, not in need of society or a dowry. Do what ye feel is best for Brandy, though."

Ah, the duke thought, the woman-child with the long black hair and the provocative sloe-eyed looks, the sister who should have been the eldest. Bertrand was smitten. Interesting. He was hard pressed to keep an amused smile from his lips. "I agree with you, Bertrand. Let's leave Constance alone. It's Brandy I'll take care of." Despite her ridiculous anger, he thought.

"Fraser is an excellent cook," Bertrand said, rising. "If ye would have luncheon with me, we could continue our discussion."

"An excellent idea. You will be dining at the castle this evening, will you not?"

"I should be delighted," Bertrand said.

The duke made his way back to the castle late in the afternoon. The visit to the crofters had had to be postponed, for the duke discovered very quickly that there was much for him to learn about the relative merits of sheep and crops. Bertrand's enthusiasm had been catching, and Ian found himself quite pleased with the progress they'd made. Brandy was right. Bertrand was a fine man who cared mightily for Penderleigh. But more than that, he had a fine brain and the discipline to handle details.

The duke strode into the front entrance hall, dim in the late afternoon light, and wondered how a great chandelier would fit with the medieval tapestries and rusty suits of armor. There was no one about. He found his bedchamber and realized he wanted a hot bath very much. He was beginning to believe himself alone in the castle when he opened the bedchamber door to see an elderly woman laying out his evening clothes. Her gray hair was tucked neatly under a large mobcap, and her voluminous black wool dress encased a rather scrawny figure. She turned and straightened at the sound of his footsteps.

"Yer grace?" she asked in a deep voice, and curtsied before he replied.

"Yes. And you are?"

"Marta, yer grace, her ladyship's maid. Said she did that ye didna fancy that scratchy trollop, Morag, aboot yer clothes an' such. Be there anythin' else ye be needin' yer grace?"

"Yes, a bath. Are there boys to fetch up the water?"

"Aye, I'll get Wee Albie out of the kitchen. 'Tis strong he be, but fuzzy in the head, if ye ken my meanin'."

"I ken," the duke said.

As soon as Marta left the huge master bedchamber, the duke stripped off his clothes. He found a towel and wrapped it about his waist.

Wee Albie, the duke soon discovered, was a huge raw-boned lad who looked like a prizefighter. He had large, vacant blue eyes and wore a wide grin, showing a gap between his front teeth.

"Yer water, sir," he said, all that business about graces and bows having long since fled from his mind.

"Thank you, Albie."

Albie unearthed a well-used bar of soap and clumsily dumped the buckets of hot water into a large wooden tub. Small rivulets of the water began to seep from the bottom of the tub and trickle across the floor. The duke stared at the crooked lines of water with a fascinated eye. Albie, however, appeared to take no notice of such a trifling matter. He straightened and beamed at the duke. "Ye'll call if ye need aught else, sir?"

"You may rest assured that I shall call immediately," the duke said, wanting to laugh, but not wanting to make the boy feel as if the laughter was directed at him. He was smiling as he shut the bedchamber door on Albie's retreating hulk.

He lowered himself into the wooden tub, wondering if he was likely to impale himself with splinters. He began to lather himself when he realized that the soap was scented. Damnation, he'd smell like a Soho trollop. No, the soap smelled expensive. He'd smell like a Parisian trollop. He wondered if Marta had filched the soap from Lady Adella.

He was leisurely in his scrubbing and stepped out of the tub only after the water had turned uncomfortably cool. He stood in front of the fireplace, naked and dripping.

At the sound of the door opening, he turned about to see Brandy standing in the entrance, panting as if she'd been running.

He stared at her, wondering just where the devil he had put the damned towel.

She stared back at him, pointedly.

She said with all the wonder in the world, "Ye're not at all like me—ye're beautiful."

10

He just stared at her. No display of maidenly embarrassment. No outraged shriek. No fleeing the scene of the naked man. She just kept looking at him, and he couldn't seem to move.

She said calmly, "Please forgive me for disturbing ye, yer grace. I didn't think ye had yet returned. I'm trying to find Fiona, ye see. We play this game. She hides and I find her. She loves it, particularly when it's time for her to go to bed."

"She's not here," he said, feeling like he'd been dropped into the middle of a play and he didn't know what his lines were. He just knew that he was an idiot, a naked idiot.

Brandy nodded politely, turned after one more very long, pointed look, and walked from the bedchamber, closing the door quietly behind her.

The duke suddenly regained command over his body. He grabbed the towel and wrapped it about his waist, only to realize the next moment how foolish his action was, since Brandy wasn't about to come back.

Brandy ran a few steps down the corridor, Fiona forgotten, and leaned against the wall, closing her eyes tightly. The duke's naked body remained vivid in her mind. She ran her tongue over suddenly dry lips. She had never before seen a naked man. He was nothing she could have imagined, not that she'd spent much time thinking about how naked men looked, but she had a bit, perhaps. Didn't every girl? But the duke was incredible, beautiful. Goodness, she'd run into his bedchamber and stared at him. What would he think of her now? Not an innocent, that was for sure, not after she'd just stood there like a stick, staring and staring. She pressed her palms against her stomach. She felt warm and soft and oddly itchy, but not like Morag's itchiness—no, this was different, and strange and quite delicious. Oh, goodness, what was all this about?

"Brandy, here I am. Ye didn't find me. I won. Now I don't have to go to bed for another fifteen minutes." Fiona suddenly emerged from a small sewing room down the hall. When Brandy didn't answer her, just looked at her as if she didn't really see her, Fiona ran to her. "I was hiding all the time in the old blue room where Marta sews. Brandy?" She edged closer. "Are ye all right? Did I give ye a fright?"

She had to get herself together, but it was difficult, very difficult. She blinked, trying to force that wonderful picture of him all naked and wet out of her brain. "Nay, poppet, ye didn't give me a fright." Damn, was that her voice? All thin and light as the sheets on her bed? How silly. "Come, Poppet, it's time for yer bath and aye, ye have fifteen extra minutes before I tuck ye in."

Ian dressed quickly and mangled his cravat into a dismal, lopsided knot, his powers of concentration apparently having deserted him. He tried first to shrug off the entire matter, thinking with a certain condescension that in England, such a thing as a young lady dashing into a gentleman's bedchamber would not be likely to happen. Well, he was in Scotland. He cursed as he ripped off the mangled cravat and fetched the last one. Evidently that meant dripping wooden tubs, undisciplined servants, and a young girl with huge amber eyes staring at him with awe and wonder. *Ye're not at all like me . . . ye're beautiful.* What a curious, strange girl she was.

He thought of Marianne, his ever modest, shy wife, and wondered if she had believed him beautiful. Absurd thought, for during their one year together, she had always blown out the bedside candle whenever he had entered her room. He had always been tender and gentle with her, but yet there was many a time when she would whimper onto his shoulder after he'd made love to her.

He looked with disgust at his cravat. It would simply have to do, since he had no others left. He very much hoped that Mabley, with his skilled hands, would arrive along with his trunks on the marrow.

He carried the branch of candles with him when he left the bedchamber. Their glowing orange light made wispy images along the dimly lit corridor. So I am beautiful, am I, Brandy? he thought, and a small smile played about his mouth.

As he neared the drawing room, he heard Lady Adella's powerful, dominating voice and then Claude's familiar cackle. Brandy would be there, of course, and he knew he had to speak to her, if for naught else to assure himself that she wasn't mortified by her behavior.

He turned the door handles, large, curved brass affairs whose knobs were griffins' heads, and entered the drawing room. Lady Adella held court from her high-backed chair, and as usual, all eyes were turned to her. She was a proud old relic, he thought, and her eccentric behavior amused him—at least it did for the moment. If it ceased to amuse him, why then, he'd deal with her. As he looked at her thick snow white hair arranged in a knot high on her head, with small sausage ringlets dangling about her narrow face, he grimaced, for such a style was suitable for a woman at least forty years her junior.

Claude sat opposite her, for all the world like a crumpled roué, looking older than his age. It was his health, Ian thought, pain could wreck a person. Bertrand and Constance shared a long settee, and Percy, a glass of sherry in his outstretched hand, leaned negligently against the mantelpiece. He searched for Brandy and saw that she was seated on a small stool just behind Lady Adella's chair. She was wearing the same gown she'd worn the evening before, and the same tartan shawl was knotted tightly between her breasts. She looked up and stared at him, like a rabbit into the barrel of a gun. He gave her a gentle, uncle-like smile. It was well done of him, he thought.

Lady Adella called to him. "Well, Ian, my lad, Bertie here has been telling us of your intoxicating pleasures today. Immersed in sheep and talk of corn. Shearing was an important topic, he told me." Snide old woman, he thought.

He saw Bertrand look down at his large hands and wished he could tell him not to pay the old meddlesome woman any heed. Ignoring her words, he strode toward her chair and said calmly, "A good evening to you, lady. I can but hope that your day was a tenth as interesting as mine." He lightly kissed her age-spotted hand.

Percy took a long drink from his sherry and set his glass upon the mantelpiece. "Tell me, yer grace, is it true that ye intend to turn us all into farmers and shepherds? That we'll all muck out stables, then try to pass ourselves off in polite society?"

The duke gave him a pleasant smile. "Bertrand and I haven't as yet decided, Percy. You must be patient. It requires time to grow a profitable corn crop, though I must admit that Penderleigh appears to have a surfeit of sheep dung in its confines right now."

Bertrand allowed himself a bit of a triumphant sneer, and Claude cackled, slapping his hand on his knees.

"Ye'll mind yer tongue now, Percy, eh?" Lady Adella chortled and thumped her cane on the floor.

"I'll mind my tongue whenever it pleases me to do so, my lady," Percy said, his eyes narrowing on the duke's impassive face.

"Aye," Lady Adella said, still malicious as a snake, all of it directed at Percival. "The duke is handy with his tongue. I like a man who doesn't lack knowing what to say. Aye, a witty man is our new Earl of Penderleigh.''

That was very low, the duke thought, watching Percy turn red with anger. But Percy couldn't tell the old woman to go throw herself off a castle turret, not if he wanted her to legitimize him. For a moment the duke felt sorry for Percy.

''Good evening, yer grace,'' Constance said in a soft woman's voice. She looked up at him through her lashes. It was well done. She held out her hand to him, just as Lady Adella had done.

She's just practicing, Ian told himself. ''Good evening, cousin, you're looking lovely tonight.'' And that was the truth. Her gowns and her sister's didn't come from the same armoire. He took her soft hand and kissed it.

Constance looked as if she wanted him to hold her hand a bit longer, but she still kept that soft smile when he released it. Then she turned and looked at Percy.

Damnation, the duke thought, the chit wants the wrong man.

He nodded to Brandy before turning toward Claude. ''I trust you all approve Bertrand's and my plans?''

''Ye make me fair loath to answer ye, me lad,'' Claude wheezed, displaying a row of blackened teeth. He turned to Percy and guffawed. ''Yer talk of sheep dung makes me think of some men's morals.''

''Ach, Uncle,'' Percy said, all suave and cold, ''ye tumbled many a wench afore yer manhood shriveled up like yer brain. Yer moralizing rings as hollow as yer head."

Lady Adella threw back her head and roared with laughter, and Constance giggled. Ian was taken aback at the crudeness. The main reason, he thought, why Brandy was so matter-of-fact about things a young girl shouldn't even know about. He should say something, surely he should, but what?

Brandy said in a voice shaking with anger, "How dare ye say such things, Percy? Such talk belongs in the stables, not in the drawing room. Ye're not a gentleman. Hold yer odious tongue, do ye hear?"

Ian grinned at her. It was well done.

"Ah, my little cousin, ye are troubled by thoughts o' tumbling with a man? Don't be. It'll come and ye'll love it, ye'll see."

The duke said, "If Brandy is troubled, Percy, it is undoubtedly because you have turned the drawing room into a stable yard."

A deep growl tore from Percy's throat, but he was called to attention by Lady Adella. "I tell ye, Percy, to leave the girl alone. She's my wee innocent, and I'll not have ye turning her ears red."

"Nay, lady," Percy said softly, ignoring the duke, "our Constance must be the wee innocent. Is not our Brandy eighteen and a woman grown?"

"It's not true, Percy," Constance said, drawing Percy's eyes to her. "I am a woman grown."

"As ye will, lassie," Percy said, "as ye will," and took a pinch of snuff.

At that moment Crabbe entered. "Dinner be served, yer grace."

Lady Adella said, as sour as a lemon, "I'll wager yer miserable flat ears were plastered against the door. Well, ye don't know a bloody bit about . . . well, never mind." She ignored the rest of them, fussing with her many shawls. Ian saw Percy straighten and make his way purposefully toward Brandy. He moved quickly, neatly cutting him off, and offered her his arm.

"Will you accompany me to dinner, Brandy?"

She gave him a grateful look, rose quickly, and slipped her hand into the crook of his arm.

As they crossed the flagstones to the dining room, he said quietly, "I would speak to you, later perhaps."

She nodded. As if aware of Percy behind them, she lengthened her stride, pulling him with her.

As he readied to seat her beside Constance, Lady Adella said loudly, "Ye'll sit over here, child." She imperiously waved Brandy to the chair held by Percy.

"Ye must get to know yer cousin, girl. He'll broaden yer view of the world. Aye, and what can he do in front of all yer relatives?"

What the devil was the old hag up to now? Ian wondered, frowning at her. Her eyes were mocking and her lips drawn into a thin line. It came as something of a shock to him that she was using her granddaughter as a cat's paw to stir up enmity between him and Percy. She wasn't only an eccentric, he thought, but also damned perverse.

Brandy sent a startled, confused look toward

114

Lady Adella, but she immediately turned back to Percy. She wasn't about to take her eyes off him. He was as good as laughing at her, knowing he'd won, knowing that Lady Adella had plucked her like a flower and tossed her to him. He said softly as Brandy hesitantly slipped herself into the chair, "Come, little cousin, as Lady Adella says, we must get to know each other better. Aye, and I'll have to mind my manners, won't I?"

"I have no desire to even see ye, Percy, much less be forced to eat my dinner in yer company. If ye don't mind yer manners, I'll stab ye with my knife."

Unperturbed, Percy continued in a low, caressing voice, meant only for her ears, "Don't ye want to become a woman, fair cousin? I can see ye now, yer thick, long hair freed and flowing, passion lighting yer virgin's eyes."

"Stop it, ye pig. Just stop it." She jabbed him in the leg with her fork, since he'd grabbed her knife and put it beside his own plate.

Lady Adella chuckled maliciously. "It appears ye've suffered a setback, my lad. Speak to her of Edinburgh and yer travels, not o' yer randy disposition."

"Yes, Percy," the duke said, "I am certain that all of us would be much amused to hear of your travels. Perhaps too, you would be so kind as to give us your opinion of the merits of Cheviot sheep?"

"One bleater speaking of other bleaters. Not much help that will be," Claude said, and laughed aloud.

"Father, please, let's eat and forget the

insults," Bertrand said, wishing only that the wretched meal would be over without coming to blows. From the look on the duke's face, he wanted to smash Percy into the floor. What did he think of all of them? Surely he must believe he'd been locked in with uncivilized oafs. He'd wanted to dislike the new Earl of Penderleigh, but after spending just a short time with him, he'd been forced to admit that the duke wasn't at all what he'd expected, what any of them had expected. For one violent instant he wished he could simply pull out a gun and shoot Percy, the damned wretch.

"Ah, our Bertrand, the peacemaker," Percy said, and forked down a bit of fish.

In the minute of silence, Ian turned to Bertrand and questioned him about the fishing along the coast. Brandy wished she could add something to this benign conversation, but could think only of her own small boat, nestled in a calm, protective cove. She started to open her mouth when Percy leaned toward her. She drew away, all thoughts of boats and fishing fleeing from her mind. She chanced to look over at Constance, and saw her green eyes resting upon her, hard and glittering.

Brandy looked down at her plate, feeling misery wash over her. Nay, Connie, she wanted to shout at her sister, Percy is a wretch and a philanderer, not worthy of yer affection.

When the interminable meal had drawn to a relatively calm close, Lady Adella made to rise. Brandy was out of her chair and standing beside her grandmother before the old lady had even planted her cane upon the floor.

"Tonight we ladies will leave yer to yer port, gentlemen," she said grandly, and sailed majestically from the room, Brandy close on her heels. Constance lagged behind as long as she dared, her eyes on Percy.

Ian wondered if Lady Adella had decided to leave the gentlemen this evening with the hope of stirring up more mischief. Probably so. He resolved to keep a firm hold on his temper.

Brandy helped to settle her grandmother close to the roaring fire. Lady Adella said softly, "Ye're a coward, child, and have no notion of how to handle a gentleman."

"I would hardly call Percy a gentleman," Brandy said softly, knowing that Constance was near.

"He'll be one soon enough, child. That shifty old eagle MacPherson prepared the papers today. Perhaps ye'll think better of her cousin when he's not a bastard anymore. He'll have a fresher look about him, don't ye think?"

"No," Brandy said. "A piece of paper won't turn him into a gentleman."

"Mayhap," Lady Adella continued, her eyes boring into Brandy's, "when he becomes a true Robertson of Penderleigh, I will see to it that the duke settles an income on him. Would ye want him then, child? Robertsons make weak husbands, lassie, and Percy would be no different. It's just a matter of knowing how to hold the reins."

Brandy realized in that moment that her grandmother not only wanted to tease her but her main goal was to tweak the duke's nose, to show him who was in control at Penderleigh. Her grandmother wasn't being very wise. In her short acquaintance with the duke, Brandy knew he was kind, he was a gentleman, and he was more stubborn than a stoat. He wouldn't let anyone control him. He could be the prince of autocrats. He wouldn't let anyone push him into doing something he didn't wish to do.

She said only, "Constance wants to wed Percy, not I." She realized even as she spoke that the duke didn't need any help from her. Not a bit.

"The eldest weds first," Lady Adella said with finality, thrusting out her pointed chin. "Our Constance will suit Bertrand."

Brandy was too surprised by this to say anything. She looked over at her sister, who was obviously bored, and watched her stroll to the windows to look at her reflection in the panes. Didn't Lady Adella realize that Constance regarded Bertrand as a brother and nothing more? She decided to hold her peace, as she was certain Lady Adella would only become more outrageous if she dared to voice an opinion contrary to her own.

Lady Adella snorted as the gentlemen filed in, a gleeful expression lighting her rheumy eyes. "I see ye didn't take long over yer port. That's odd, isn't it? Old Angus had fine port laid aside in the cellar. Ye didn't enjoy each other's company?"

"Percy has been telling us about Edinburgh," Ian said. And Percy had spun a fine story. Too bad he couldn't keep his manners when it came to Brandy.

"Aye," Bertrand said. "I enjoyed his story about how the butcher sent a sow's ear tucked in a bunch of flowers to his wife who'd made him very angry."

"That doesn't sound funny at all to me," Lady Adella said, not managing to hide her disappointment by turning to Constance and ordering her to the pianoforte.

Brandy saw Percy making toward her and whispered urgently to Lady Adella, "Let me go, Grandmama, I wish to see Fiona. She wasn't feeling well earlier. I'm worried about her."

Lady Adella eyed her speculatively but said only, "Ye're a coward, girl. Ye don't lie well either. But I'm feeling mellow. Very well, off with ye."

Brandy breathed a sigh of relief and swept a slight curtsy toward the gentlemen. "I bid ye all good night."

Ian said, "A moment, please, Brandy, I would have a word with you, if you don't mind."

Percy laughed softly. "Perhaps, little cousin, after his grace is done, I may also speak with ye."

"Not until the next century, Percy," she said, and looked like she wanted to kick him.

Percy shrugged and turned to Constance, who was tugging his sleeve. "Do come, Percy, I want ye to turn my pages."

"I will walk you to the stairs," Ian said to Brandy. "I'll be back presently, Lady Adella." He turned and followed Brandy from the drawing room.

119

Brandy stopped outside the drawing room and looked up at him. "What is it ye wanted, yer grace?"

The duke drew up to his full height and gazed down at her with his uncle-like gentle look. "I just wanted to tell you how sorry I am about Percy, my dear. His wayward tongue needs to be tamed. I shall contrive to see that he doesn't bother you in the future." He wasn't quite certain exactly how he would accomplish this, particularly in the face of Lady Adella's perverse encouragement of Percy.

"It's strange, really a mystery," she said, still pondering her grandmother's inexplicable behavior.

"What's a mystery?"

She smiled, not much of a smile, but it was an attempt. "Grandmama tells me that she intends Constance to wed Bertrand. Constance won't approve of that."

There seemed to be no end to the old harridan's plotting, Ian thought. In this instance, though, her intention was not far removed from his own. "I see," he said evenly.

He called himself back to his purpose and said gently, "I wished to speak to you, Brandy, because I wanted to apologize to you for causing you upset."

She frowned up at him, then suddenly remembered her outburst of the morning. He had meant only to be kind, offering her a trip to London, offering to polish her up, and she had behaved churlishly.

"Nay, yer grace, er, Ian. The apology comes

120

from the wrong mouth. It was I who behaved in an unseemly manner." She had believed herself angry at his offer because he seemed to view her as a gauche provincial, a Scottish girl whose manners needed mending. But after she had fled from him, she was forced to admit to herself that her outrage had more to do with the thought of living with him and his future duchess. It had galled her, and she wasn't certain precisely why. Well, actually she knew exactly why, but she refused to think about it. It would do no good. Nothing could change the future.

He thought that she'd indeed behaved outrageously, but he said firmly, "No, your behavior, although unexpected, wasn't at all unseemly. After all, how could you have known?" Although he still saw no shyness or embarrassment on her face, he couldn't bring himself to add that what she couldn't have known was that he would be standing naked and wet in his bedchamber.

"Aye, but I should have guessed. I should have known that ye'd already have a lady."

The duke blinked. "What does my being betrothed have to say to anything? That Lady Felicity would have been mortified and berated me for my carelessness?"

"Mayhap she would have, Ian. It's not likely that she would approve of me."

"I assure you, Brandy, that my future wife has nothing at all to say in this matter. Indeed, I cannot imagine a good reason for telling her."

She felt dashed to her toes with hurt. "I've offended ye. Ye don't want me now."

He blinked. Something was very wrong here.

Dammit, but this was ridiculous. There was her damned innocence again. She simply didn't realize what she was saying. "It would be most improper of me to want you, Brandy. I only spoke to you because I didn't want you to feel awkward or embarrassed around me."

She drew herself up proudly. "If ye didn't want me, then why ever did ye—" She broke off and turned away. "I'll not hold it against ye, Ian. Indeed, I'll never bring it up again."

He felt mired in confusion. "Good God, I only wanted you to understand that I harbored no base intentions toward you. Rest assured that I shall keep the bedchamber door locked after this."

Brandy had the inescapable feeling that Scottish was a far different language from the King's English. "Whatever does locking yer door have to say to anything?"

"Dammit, if I lock my door, you'll not burst in upon me again. Really, Brandy, I'm not in the habit of allowing young girls to see me naked."

"Naked. Oh, that. Well, oh goodness."

He'd never before seen someone turn red from the top of her collar to her hairline. "Oh, dear," she said in a tiny voice that sounded as if it were spun from a dream, "I thought ye were apologizing for this morning, when I was angry at ye for inviting me to London with yer wife."

Smashed into the ground and he'd not even had a single blow. Dear God, he was a conceited fellow. He threw back his head and gave way to a booming laugh. So they had been speaking at cross-purposes. "No, cousin, I wasn't speaking of this morning. What a blow you've dished up to my masculine self. You didn't give the incident a second thought."

She felt a strange tightness in her chest. She forced her eyes to his face and said, "Nay, Ian, ye're wrong."

Before he could figure that out, she'd picked up her skirts and was running up the stairs, leaving him to stare after her.

11

Ian woke with a start the next morning. He turned a bleary eye toward the weathered windowpanes to see gray drizzle streaking down the glass, then glanced at the clock at his elbow. It was barely after five o'clock in the morning. He closed his eyes. He pressed his face against the pillow. He thought about Cheviot sheep. Nothing did any good. He couldn't fall asleep again. He cursed softly as he threw back the mountain of covers.

Mindful of splinters from the wooden floor, he walked to the fireplace, and after some more full-bodied curses he managed to coax a decent flame from the wood and peat. He shrugged into his dressing gown and decided, without much enthusiasm, that he might as well pass the time until breakfast penning a letter to Felicity.

He dug out paper, quill, and ink pot and settled himself in a large wing chair close to the fire. He chewed absently on the end of his quill for some moments, forming phrases in his mind before he wrote, as was his habit.

He wrote: "My dearest Felicity." He frowned a moment and stared at nothing in particular, then wadded up the sheet of foolscap.

He began once again. "Dear Felicity . . ." The blank page stretched before him endlessly. He stroked his chin a moment, then attacked with his quill, mindful that he did, after all, owe his betrothed some account of his journey and Penderleigh.

I arrived safely at Penderleigh three days ago. Unfortunately, my poor valet, Mabley, who was riding in the luggage coach, endured a mishap near Galashiels (a town to the southwest of here), and I pray to the stars that he will arrive today. I swear I shall embrace the fellow. If he doesn't arrive, I suppose I shall be obliged to borrow a change of clothing from Bertrand Robertson, a cousin of mine. He and his father, Claude (an old curmudgeon of the first order), reside in the dower house, quite happily from what I can gather, and Bertrand has and will continue to run the estate.

For some reason I have not yet been made privy to, Claude's father, Douglass, elder brother to the last earl, was disinherited many years ago, thus altering the inheritance line. It's a pity really, for Bertrand cares for Penderleigh and would make it a fine master. Lady Adella, the late earl's widow and an unaccountable old woman to boot, may wreak some magic and reverse the disinheritance. I might add that she has already begun to legitimize Percival Robertson, a cocky young buck who hates Englishmen in general and me in particular. If you find all of these family entanglements confusing, you can well imagine how I felt until I sorted everyone out.

The "gaggle" of females, as Giles calls the three girls, also cousins, are delightful, each in her own way. The youngest, Fiona, is a scarlet-haired little vixen who leads her eldest sister, Brandy (an odd name to be sure and shortened from Brandella), a merry chase. The middle girl, Constance, all of sixteen years of age, fancies herself much the grown-up lady and flirts outrageously with Percy. Brandy, the eldest, though, is the different one.

He paused in his writing and sat back in his chair, rubbing his fingers along the line of his jaw. He found that thinking of Brandy brought words quickly to his mind.

Strangely enough, her eyes are a deep amber and match her to her nickname quite aptly. She is an unusual girl and rather vulnerable at present, for Percy, in this odd ménage, is enamored of her and makes no bones about it. She, however, wants nothing to do with him. She will be nineteen on Michaelmas Day, of marriageable age. Ah, but therein lies a problem.

Actually, he thought, she is the beauty of the family. He smiled, bemused. He decided not to mention trying to get Brandy to London. That could come later.

Everyone speaks with the soft, blurred Scottish brogue that, contrary to our snobs in England, is most pleasant to the ear. I myself find that I've slipped easily into some of their forms of speech.

He paused yet again, realizing that he had completed a full page, which normally was not at all his way. Felicity would wonder at his sudden verbosity. He cramped together the last few lines.

Bertrand and I plan to leave for the Cheviot today, if this accursed rain stops, to purchase, or at least inspect, what he informs me are the most profitable of Scottish sheep. After that we are off to several central towns to speak to local mill owners. I'm sorry, my dear, but it appears I'll be gone longer than I originally believed. There is much to be done here at Penderleigh. I trust that Giles is sufficiently entertaining you. Yours, Ian.

After writing Felicity's direction, he rose and stretched lazily, casting a dubious eye toward the sleeting rain. He refused to let the weather depress him. As he dressed quickly in yesterday's riding breeches, a frilled white shirt, and hessians, he whistled the Robert Burns ballad that Brandy had sung.

Everyone appeared to be still abed. Only Crabbe was downstairs to bid him good morning.

He opened the door to the breakfast room and, without precisely intending it, smiled broadly at the sight of Brandy, hunched over the table, dawdling listlessly over her porridge.

"Good morning, Brandy," he said, and found that the sight of her made him feel quite light-hearted.

"Yer grace—Ian. It's so early, what are you doing up?"

As he walked toward her he saw a dull flush spread over her cheeks. Why the devil was she red in the face? It was seven o'clock in the bloody morning. Oh, yes, he'd been naked and perhaps she hadn't minded, which pleased him inordinately. He coughed slightly, cleared his throat, and said, "You think I'm a lazy slug, Brandy? Actually, the rain woke me up and my eyes wouldn't close again."

She was looking at the snowy white lace at his throat and wrists. She knew he was wearing the clothes he'd worn the day before, but it didn't matter. He looked magnificent. She looked down at her lap. She was a mess, a poor relation, who was a sorry specimen.

Why was she looking him up and down? He grinned. "Do I meet with your approval?"

"Aye, I was thinking ye do quite well without yer valet."

"Thank you, Brandy, but just one more day without Mabley and I'd have to borrow some of Bertrand's clothes. Ah, porridge, I see." Damn, what he wouldn't give for just one slice of rare sirloin and a plate of eggs and kidneys.

"It's rather lumpy this morning. I think Cook must be in love again."

"In love? Cook?"

"Aye. She's got such a soft heart. Every male within fifty miles can come to the kitchen door and she'll feed him. Sometimes she falls in love and then it's our food that suffers."

She spooned a liberal amount into a bowl and placed it at the head of the table.

Ian seated himself and added some of Cook's delicious clotted cream and sugar to the brownish porridge. "Where is your wee bairn, Fiona, this morning?"

"She has the sniffles, so I ordered her to stay in bed. She hates it, so I'll have to stay close else she'll escape."

"If Mabley arrives this morning, I'll ask him to look in on her. He always carries with him a formidable array of potions, salves, and the like. Indeed, if he arrives after I leave, Brandy, do make use of his services."

"Ye're leaving?" Why had no one told her? She swallowed. "But why? Ye just got here, and it's too soon for ye to go too—"

"I'm leaving with Bertrand, not for England. We reached the decision last evening after you had gone to bed. We go to the Cheviot to look over sheep, then on to several mill towns. I fancy we shouldn't be gone so very long."

"How long?"

"A week perhaps? I'm not really certain." He wondered what she was thinking. He thought again of their cross-purpose conversation of the evening before and her bald statement before she'd fled from him. He wanted her to explain exactly what she'd meant when she'd said something about his being wrong. Wrong about what? Oh, hell, he couldn't very well bring it up again. He'd make her turn red to her toes. Again. He said, "I hope you've reconsidered and will now come to London in the fall. You will have ample time to learn your way about before being presented in the spring."

She just looked at him. He was clearly a man who never let go of a bone once he got it between his teeth, she'd give him that. Didn't he realize how much each of his words sliced into her? No, naturally not. How could he know that the thought of being with both him and his wife made her want to shrivel into one of Cook's winter apples. She looked at him steadily, shrugged just a tiny shrug, and said, "Scotland is my home, yer grace. I can't imagine why ye are so insistent at having a graceless Scot about to embarrass ye in front of all yer fine friends and yer bloody wife." She cleared her throat, hoping perhaps he hadn't heard that. "I would, yer grace, that ye would leave well enough alone, and that includes me."

"It seems to me, Brandy, that whenever you are displeased with me, I suddenly become 'yer grace.'" Ah, that stubborn chin of hers just went up a good two inches. "We'll discuss this more when I return.

"You are aware that Lady Adella is behaving outrageously, particularly where you and Percy are concerned. I want you to be careful while I'm gone. Percy shows no signs of wishing to leave Penderleigh."

Still, he'd worry. He had to do something, but what? He could break Percy's legs, he supposed. That would slow the blighter down. He brightened.

"I assure ye, yer grace—Ian, that I am well able to take care of myself. Percy's a bag of wind. He likes to bray and make me uncomfortable, but I don't worry that he'll try to kiss me."

Percy trying to kiss her didn't particularly worry him. Percy attacking her did. Yes, he would break Percy's legs—only that would raise questions, eyebrows, and all the collective Robertsons' choler. It suddenly came to him that he could protect her without her knowing of it and without breaking any part of Percy's body, though the thought was appealing. He silently examined his idea for a few moments, then nodded at his porridge bowl, satisfied. He would see to her safety and avoid making her angry at the same time. She really thought she could handle Percy if he were intent on taking her? Her innocence, he thought, always it was her innocence mixed with her faith in herself. Only this time she was wrong. She couldn't handle Percy.

She caught him off his guard when she said abruptly, "Yer future wife, what is she like? A very fine lady, I suppose, all sleek and beautiful and graceful?" *And she knows how lucky she is to have you and she adores you and touches you and kisses you all the time.*

He didn't want to talk about Felicity. Indeed, he didn't even want to remember her name at

130

that moment. He said only, "I suppose that's all true."

This was odd. He didn't want to talk about the woman who would be his wife? "What does she look like?"

Why was she so damned interested? He said, "Her hair is dark, her eyes green, and she's small. Does that satisfy you, Madame Curiosity?"

Not really. "Aye," she said. She stirred the remains of the porridge with her spoon for some moments. "What do ye think of Scotland, Ian? And the Scots?"

"I suspect that people are much the same wherever they live. As to Scotland itself, I shall be in a much better position to answer you when I return."

"Ye don't despise us?"

"Good God, Brandy, that's a ridiculous question. Why the devil would you think I'd despise you?"

"Ye're very polite. Maybe too polite, at least most of the time. And ye're kind. Bertrand thinks ye're a god. I suppose that like the rest of us, he expected another arrogant Englishman who would rob our lands and grind us under like so much dirt."

He said steadily, "And what do you think of me, Brandy?"

"As well as being polite and kind, ye're real and solid and, well, perhaps ye're exciting as well."

She was out of her chair in a flash and at the door in the next. "I wish ye good fortune on yer trip, Ian."

He called to her, "I think I would like it if you

added beautiful as you did last evening. Kind and polite are all well and good. And I shan't quibble with real and solid. Now, exciting. What does that mean, I wonder?"

He'd expected her to snarl or flee and was surprised when she said, "Since to me ye're all of those things, then ye shouldn't press for more."

Then she was gone, the door eased quietly closed after her.

To Ian's relief, Mabley arrived not an hour later, delighted to be again with his master but determined not to show it.

"A fine sight you are, your grace," he said, his voice more sour than ever as he followed the earl up to his bedchamber.

"Complain all you like, Mabley, but do pack a portmanteau, for I'm off for several days. No need to polish my hessians," he added as his valet looked near to apoplexy at the sight of his boots. He rather hoped that Mabley wouldn't make the acquaintance of Morag too quickly, for he could well imagine how the poor man's veiny nose would twitch in disgust if he got within smelling distance of her. He left him grumbling and puttering about the room and went in search of Lady Adella, determined to see her before the weather cleared and he and Bertrand left Penderleigh. Now I will spike your guns, Brandy, he said to himself as he made his way to the seaward side of the castle to Lady Adella's suite of rooms. And I won't have to break Percy's legs, though I still like the thought.

The door was open, and as he drew near, he

heard two women's raised, angry voices. One was Lady Adella's and the other, he realized after a moment, was the old servant Marta's.

"Ye're a cold and heartless old bitch."

"An old bitch I may well be," answered Lady Adella's drumming voice, "but at least I was never a plucked bag o' bones. Little ye did to warm the master's bed. He had to make do with ye and he didn't like it, I can tell ye that, kept coming back to me, and I finally had to lock my door."

"It's not true, damn ye. The master came to my bed when ye berated him and made him feel less the man. He never left me, never."

"Ye're a fool, Marta, make no mistake. I was always the master and mistress of Penderleigh. When he took to tossing up yer skirts, it was but another hold he gave me."

"I loved him, do ye hear?" Marta's voice trembled.

Lady Adella laughed rudely. "Love. You're a stupid slut. Ye got naught from the earl save his ruddy cock. And that, Marta, as ye well know, I never minded in the least. He was an animal, just wanted to rut until he was pleased, and then he snored and dreamed himself such a fine lover, the old fool. Don't ye lie to me and bleat about how he satisfied ye. He couldn't have satisfied a goat."

"But ye're nay master and mistress of Penderleigh anymore, lady. The duke isn't a weak Robertson male. It's strong he is, lady, and much used to having everything as he orders it. He speaks politely, for he's a gentleman, he is, but he's got the pride and bearing of a king, and he'll not let ye do anything he doesna want ye to do. He'll not let ye play off yer tricks wi' him."

The duke stood rooted to the spot, ethical considerations forgotten. He was rather pleased that he compared favorably to the weak Robertson males. Nor would he disagree with the kingly pride and bearing part, although George III was insane and few bothered to deny it now.

"What tricks, ye old trollop?" Lady Adella's voice grew cunning. "I do naught but make right all the wrongs of that rutting old goat. As for yer precious duke, he'll be gone from Penderleigh afore ye know it, back to where he belongs in London. And I'll thank ye to hold yer infernal tongue, ye gap-toothed hag, else I'll—"

"Else ye'll what? Set me to scouring the kitchen floors?"

Lady Adella's voice grew quiet, and the duke had to strain to hear her next words. "Ye know, I've been thinking that an heiress is not what our Percy needs. Indeed, when old MacPherson brings him to the right side o' the blanket, methinks he'll be quite suitable for our Brandy."

"So that's yer game. Ye're a witch. The girl hates him, the rutting bounder. He'd give her the French pox, he would. If ye've eyes in yer shrunken head, ye know that Percy doesna want to stay at Penderleigh. As for Brandy, he loves her not. It's her virginity that intrigues him, and aye, her aversion to him."

"Ye're a romantic fool," Lady Adella said, her voice deep with scorn. "Percy doesn't have the pox, I asked him. He said he's careful. He

134

wouldn't lie to me. Mayhap I'll encourage Percy, mayhap let him force Brandy and plant a bairn in her belly. Then I would see that he weds her. Aye, he'll dance to my tune, ye'll see, believing all the while that he is the player."

"It isna right, lady. Brandy hates him. Do ye want to see the child miserable just as ye were?"

"Shut yer mouth, damn ye. The child is too young to know her own mind, and she'll do what I tell her. And don't ye dare rant to me about love. Ye old slut, yer notion of love is a grunting, sweating male between yer legs."

"Ye're wicked, lady, more wicked than poor Angus could ever dream of being."

The duke heard the clip-clop of heavy wooden shoes and ducked back into the corridor. Damn, but the old woman was daft. If he had to drag Brandy, kicking and yelling, he wouldn't let her remain under Lady Adella's perverse thumb.

He waited a few minutes, then retraced his steps to Lady Adella's sitting room. It was time that he let her know quite clearly who was the master of Penderleigh. He found her seated, her back ramrod straight, in a high-backed chair close to the fireplace, Brandy's cushion at its place at her feet. He looked about her sitting room, hard put to imagine a more chill and forbidding place.

He seated himself opposite her and began smoothly, "I find myself faced with somewhat of a problem, Aunt, and I seek your advice."

Her faded blue eyes sharpened. "Aye, lad?"

"It concerns the girls, Brandy in particular, since she is the eldest. As I am now their legal guardian, I would like to provide them with

135

proper dowries and, indeed, a season in London."

"That makes not a whit of sense. Why?"

"I would think," he said coolly, "that you would be delighted to have the girls so well provided for."

"I can't disagree that the dowries will help the Penderleigh coffers, but as for sending the girls to London for a season, no sense in that. It's not what I have planned for them. Worry not about any of the girls, lad. I've got their futures all ticked out."

"I beg your pardon, Aunt, but I have no intention of any dowry money making its way into the Penderleigh coffers. Indeed, the money will only be released when I have formally approved the future bridegrooms."

"I told ye, lad, the girls' futures are my concern, and I'll thank ye not to meddle in what doesn't concern ye. Ye may with my blessing dower the girls, but it is I who will choose their husbands, not ye, not an Englishman who's too young to know what he's about."

"I will say this just once, Lady Adella. I will never give you that kind of control, particularly since I have remarked how you abuse it. Contrive to remember that it is I who am master of Penderleigh, and you can hold claim no longer to being its mistress. You are, in short, nothing but what I allow you to be."

She sucked in her breath, realizing that she had pushed him too far. She wasn't stupid. She quickly retrenched. "And what do ye mean by that, my lad?"

"I mean that Percy, no matter what side of the blanket he finds himself at the end of your machinations, will not wed Brandy. Indeed, as her guardian, I will no longer allow him to make a nuisance of himself where she is concerned."

"What, do ye fear that he'll overturn yer claims to Penderleigh or to Brandy?" He didn't say anything. Indeed, she knew he was angry, and keeping silent until he could gain control. She added in her best wheedling tone, "Ye've not given the lad a chance to prove himself. Percy's not bad, just ungoverned. He just needs a good wife to improve upon the raw material that's deep inside him, somewhere. Think ye, yer grace, if ye dower Brandy and she weds with Percy, then the money rests at Penderleigh. The girl doesn't know her own mind and she's just teasing him. I'll see that Percy does right by her when she's his wife."

The duke sat forward. He spoke slowly, calmly, his anger well under control. "Heed me well, lady. Percy will never touch Brandy, or Constance, for that matter. If you continue to encourage him and badger Brandy to receive his attentions, here is what I shall do. I shall have you removed from Penderleigh land, provide you with a small widow's jointure, and never again let you meddle with the lives of your family. Do I make myself quite clear, lady?"

She drew back, pressing herself as hard as she could against the back of her chair. "Ye wouldn't dare."

"You know that I would. Don't push me." He stared steadily into her rheumy old eyes. He

137

added, "No matter your crooked intentions toward Percy and Claude, just remember that it is I who hold the power. If I allow you to carry out your legitimization plans for Percy—indeed, if you choose to reinherit Claude and thus Bertrand—it is because I permit it."

Lady Adella sucked in her breath. She wished she could hit him. Aye, she wished she could stick a knife in his ribs. "Ye dare to threaten me, Duke. I much dislike threats, particularly from Englishmen."

"I don't make threats, lady. Believe me that if you go against my wishes with Brandy, I will do exactly what I have said. As to where I would move you—perhaps to Glasgow, clear across Scotland. I'd let you take Morag with you. Think well on this. I am known as a man of my word."

Although she quickly lowered her eyes to her gnarled hands, he saw that she believed him now. Good. She was showing a bit of wisdom. He said after a moment, "As you know, Bertrand and I leave this afternoon and plan to be away from Penderleigh for some days. I expect you to take immediate steps to ensure that Percy doesn't go near Brandy. After you have seen to that, Lady Adella, I want you to use your boundless influence with her and convince her that she must come to London once I am married."

Lady Adella couldn't help herself and asked in an incredulous voice, "Ye mean to tell me that Brandy already knows of yer plans and has refused ye?"

"Yes, but I expect upon my return that you

will have changed her mind. Now, lady," he said, rising, "do I have your agreement to do as I ask?"

She shot him a look of loathing from beneath halfclosed eyes and waved her veiny hand at him. "Aye, for the moment."

"You mean until you think of something else to try? Try anything I don't like, and you'll be breathing the air of Glasgow." He gave her a slight bow, turned on his heel, and left her staring after her, murder in her heart.

Shortly after luncheon, the weather cleared. Ian and Bertrand decided to take their leave before it could turn nasty again. Mabley, looking somewhat bewildered, handed his master his portmanteau. "You'll be careful, your grace."

"Yes, I'll be careful. I'll not be gone long, Mabley. My only advice to you is that you avoid a woman called Morag. That's it. Just stay clear of her and you'll go along just fine." He grinned at his valet, patted his shoulder, and took his leave.

12

"Don't get wet, poppet," Brandy called after Fiona, knowing her words just floated over her sister's bright red head. She shook her head, smiling, as she watched Fiona scramble down the path to the beach below.

She sighed and turned away, very much aware of the cause of her sudden sadness. Ian had left with Bertrand only an hour ago, and she had looked after him until she could no longer hear the clop-clop of his horse's hooves. The sun grew hot and she pulled off her shawl and rolled up her muslin sleeves to her elbows. For want of anything better to do, she sank down in the field of anemones and began absently to pull up the yellow flowers and weave them into a garland.

She felt someone near and turned to see Percy standing but a few feet away from her, legs spread, hands on his hips. He reached down and picked up her shawl, wadded it into a plaid ball, and threw it some distance from her.

She stared at him coldly. "So, the worthless sot comes out into the sunshine. Wouldn't ye rather be in a dark room drinking? Or wenching? Or braying with other sots how wonderful ye are? Ye're not at all funny, ye know. Now, throw me back my shawl and leave me be."

"Ye insult me, Brandy. Girls shouldn't toss out insults like ye just did. Ye never know how a man will react. And why do ye want yer shawl? The sun is really quite warm." His hooded green eyes wandered from her face to her breasts, to her waist. "Ye really shouldn't hide yer woman's charms, Brandy. Ye're surprised, aren't ye? Ye didn't believe anyone would see through yer disguise. I'm a man who knows women. Ye've got breasts beneath that gown that I want to see and touch and caress. Ye'll like it, I promise ye."

Her chin went higher. She was afraid, but never would she show it. "Ye are the insulting one. I don't like ye. Ye're rude and ugly. I'll tell ye just once more, leave me alone. I dislike being in the company of pigs and bastards."

She saw a dangerous glint in his eyes and instinctively drew back. She'd gone too far.

"Ye are becoming all high and mighty, lassie, what with the illustrious duke insisting that ye travel to London. Aye, don't look so surprised, Lady Adella just told me of what she called 'yer good fortune.'"

He didn't tell her that Lady Adella had also been explicit in her orders to him, the old bitch.

"Tell me, little cousin, just what did ye have to do for the duke to earn yerself a trip and a dowry?"

"Why, the duke is just like ye, Percy. He demanded that I take off my clothes and dance naked for him. Of course, I was willing to do that for a bit of coin and a trip to that barbaric London. Ye're nothing but a fool. Go away."

She rose slowly to her feet. She slowly put one foot behind the other. He was still standing there, legs spread, staring at her—no, at her breasts. He looked like a predator and she knew she couldn't win if he attacked her. She realized in that moment that Ian had gone behind her back to Lady Adella. Damn him. She would make him pay for that when he returned.

She said in what she hoped was the calm voice of a nun, "Ye aren't thinking things through, Percy. I'm yer cousin. Ye're supposed to protect me, not attack me." She didn't think that would work, but she had to try. Was there any honor in him at all? He remained silent.

"Listen to me, Percy. I have no intention of

going to London. Ye must know that Grand-mama is always meddling and plotting. As for the duke's providing all of us with dowries, well, I don't know about that." She shrugged her shoulders and took another step away from him.

"Ye're a strange lass, Brandy," Percy said finally. "Just what do ye want?"

"What do I want?" she repeated slowly, her brow furrowed, knowing what she wanted, knowing it was impossible. She looked out to sea and saw some crofters in a barely seaworthy little boat, heaving their tattered nets over the side into the water.

"I won't chase dreams, Percy. I won't try to do something that wouldn't make me happy with myself. I want what I can have, and that is what I have now—Grandmama, Fiona, and Pender-leigh." She faced him again. "Do ye intend to remain here or return to Edinburgh?"

He recalled Lady Adella's cold, mocking voice: "Ye'll leave yer hands off the girl, my randy lad. Mayhap it will be better to remove yerself from temptation. Yer heiress awaits ye, does she not?"

"Edinburgh," he said. "I believe that I will leave on the morrow. I'm off to woo my heiress. Without her father knowing just yet—until the courts have tied me up with a new ribbon."

"Is that what *ye* want, Percy?" Brandy asked, eyeing him with a bit more confidence now. There was a bitterness in his voice that made her, for the moment, feel just a bit sorry for him.

He looked at her, taking in the soft tendrils of hair that curled about her face and the full curve of her breasts he knew was beneath that gown of hers, beneath that band she probably bound herself with. "Nay, lass, it's not what I want, but I suppose it's what I must have. No, it's you I want, lassie."

Before she knew what he was about, he grabbed her shoulders and pulled her roughly against him. She cried out in surprise and fear, only to feel his mouth grinding against hers and his tongue probing wildly against her teeth. She hated his wet mouth, his violence. She began to struggle, shoving at him, trying to claw his face.

"Don't fight me, Brandy." He was gasping his words into her mouth, stifling her cries. "Ye know how long I've desired ye." Swiftly he grasped her hips, lifted her from the ground, and toppled her onto her back amid the bright yellow flowers.

She screamed once before he covered her mouth with his hand. She felt him moving on top of her, felt his weight crushing her down, and for a moment she couldn't get enough air into her lungs.

He tore at the buttons on her gown, his fingers wildly groping for her breast. My God, she thought, he was going to rape her. She twisted beneath him, pounding his shoulders with her fists, tearing his hair. His breath was hot against her mouth, and she felt his sex hard and pressing against her belly. She had seen animals mating, and knew that he would shove himself into her. She was terrified at her own helplessness.

"Brandy! Cousin Percy! Ye're playing and ye didn't invite me. Can I play the game with ye?"

Percy froze over her, his face ludicrous with shock.

"Fiona," Brandy yelled even as she was pulling her bodice together. "Get off me, ye miserable sod. Surely ye don't intend to rape me in front of Fiona, do ye? Nay, even ye couldn't be that great a villain."

She shoved Percy off her and scrambled to her feet. Percy pulled himself to a sitting position. His face was flushed with anger. Brandy heard him cursing under his breath.

"Well, can't I play? Ye were pounding on Percy and he was pretending ye hurt him, moaning and gasping like ye'd shot him." Fiona eyed first her sister, then Percy.

Oh, God, Brandy thought. She shook her head, trying to clear it. "Poppet, the game's over. Percy lost. There's no more game to play, all right?" Seeing the child's confusion, she tried, she truly did try to turn this nightmare into nothing more exciting than a tea party. "Aye, it was a new kind of wrestling Cousin Percy was teaching me. As ye can see, I beat him handily."

Brandy wanted to kick Percy, but she knew she couldn't, any more than he could attack her in front of Fiona. He looked fit to kill. She wanted to throw her arms around Fiona and thank her, for her little sister had indeed saved her. But she couldn't. She had to treat all of it lightly. A game, nothing but a silly game.

She wanted to kill him.

"There'll be another time, little cousin," Percy said as he rose to his feet. "There'll be another time and no little sister to interrupt us. Ye wanted me, Brandy, admit it, to yerself and to me. Ye're just being coy, aye, and don't ye know, so many girls act just like ye have. But we'll see, won't we?"

She took another step back. It wasn't smart to shake yer fist in the devil's face. "There won't be another time, Percy," she said, taking Fiona's small hand in hers. "Never."

Brandy left Fiona in Marta's care, avoiding the old woman's curious eyes, and made her way to Lady Adella's sitting room.

Clutching together the torn buttons on her gown, she drew a deep breath and walked into Lady Adella's line of vision.

"Ye look the perfect dowd, all rattled and tangled, yer gown not even buttoned." Lady Adella was irritated, and she was snorting after she'd given Brandy a thorough look up and down. "I swear, why can't ye take more pains with yerself, like yer sister?"

Brandy felt her cup fill to the brim, then overflow. "Listen to me, Grandmama, I would look like the queen of the May if Percy had not just tried to rape me."

Lady Adella's thin eyebrows snapped together. "He tried to rape ye? Percy?"

"He tried to rape me," Brandy repeated, the thought of his body pressing down on her making her so mad she wanted to strike out. She was breathing hard as she said, "Fiona saved me. She thought it was all a game. At least Percy didn't continue in front of her. God, I want to kill him."

"Och, so Fiona saved ye, huh? Well, that's a relief." Brandy watched as a smile deepened the lines about her grandmother's thin mouth. She

145

thought it was funny? "What are ye going to do about him, Grandmama?"

"I might have known he wouldn't keep his hands off ye, my girl. Ye tease him something fierce, and as I've told ye many times, he's just a weak Robertson male. Ye want me to do something with Percy? Really, ye silly chit, there's aught for me to do since he didn't succeed in cooling his passion for ye. Such a prissy prude ye are, child. Surely ye know what men want of women. It's only natural, particularly for Percy. He didn't succeed, so shut yer mouth. And don't ye dare kill him."

Brandy stared at her, appalled. "Ye wouldn't have cared had he succeeded?"

"Of course I would have minded. It would have changed everything. But there's no harm done. Stop yer righteous anger, child. It bores me, makes me believe ye're a Methodist. I'll see that our randy Percy takes his leave on the morrow. He'll not bother ye again, child."

"Before Percy attacked me, Grandmama, he said that ye had told him that I was going to London. Did Ian talk to ye?"

Lady Adella could nearly feel her granddaughter's anger come toward her in waves. Percy was out of her mind now. So there was passionate blood in her veins. She decided to choose her words carefully, even though she doubted the duke would ever have the gall to send her away as he'd threatened. Outrage had always worked well with Brandy, totally knocked her off her course. She said with all the hauteur of the long dead Queen Mary, "Certainly the duke spoke

146

with me, stupid girl. If ye care not about yer future, he, as yer guardian, has every right to concern himself with yer affairs."

"I'll not go, Grandmama, and I told him so. How dare he come to ye?"

She'd not distracted her. That was interesting. She smiled, splaying her gnarled hands in a display of defeat. "Very well, child, I'll not try to force ye to go to London, though I'll never ken yer mule's stubbornness. It's like old Angus ye've become, and the good Lord knows that's an abominable thing."

Brandy breathed a wary sigh of relief. "Thank ye, Grandmama. I don't want to leave Penderleigh, no matter what the duke says."

"As ye will, child. I had thought ye'd prefer having a choice of husbands, for Ian assured me that he'd put many a proper gentleman in yer path. Since it isn't to yer liking, well, I'll ensure that ye'll have yer wish and stay at Penderleigh—"

"Oh, thank ye, Grandmama."

"After what Percy tried to do to ye, I wouldn't think that ye'd want him, but—"

Brandy drew back as though she'd been struck. "Percy? What are ye talking about? What does this have to do with Percy? Oh, no, Grandmama, ye know that I loathe him. I'd never marry him, never."

"So ye want yer cream and the bowl too, lass? Well, the world doesn't turn that way. I'll have no worthless spinster at Penderleigh. Ye'll marry Percy or ye'll go to London. The choice is yers."

This couldn't be happening. Brandy tried to swallow down the lump of fear and revulsion that

147

stuck in her throat. She paced back and forth in front of Lady Adella, then spun about. "Grandmama, do ye want to make me unhappy? Why do ye hate me? What have I done to make ye treat me thus?"

"I don't hate ye, ye silly chit. Damnation, child, I want to see ye well placed afore I join yer grandfather in Hades. He had a fondness for ye, the old rutting goat, and I'll not spend eternity with him badgering me about failing in my duty toward ye."

Brandy forced calm into her voice. "If that is so, Grandmama, I can't believe that Grandfather would have wanted me to be so very unhappy. He disliked Percy, ye know."

Lady Adella realized that she had buried herself in a losing argument, and she knew that her threat was a hollow one. Never would the duke let Percy have the girl. She hastened to change her direction, gnashing her teeth impotently at the duke's orders. She resorted to a fine display of rage. She slammed her cane hard into the side of a small table and sent it crashing to the floor.

It didn't work. Brandy shook her fist. "I'll run away. Do ye hear, Grandmama? I swear that I'll run away."

Lady Adella drew up short and sucked in her breath. A cunning grin pulled up at the corners of her mouth. "Ye run away, Brandy, and I'll take Fiona away from ye." She had no idea how she could accomplish such a feat were it required of her, but she saw that she had finally won the battle. The rebellion was gone in a flash. Brandy stood there, shoulders slumped, defeated.

"Aye, that's more the thing, lass. Fiona is like yer wee bairn, isn't she? Once ye're married—after yer season in London with the duke and duchess—she'll be all yers, I promise ye."

"Ye're wicked, Grandmama, just plain wicked."

"I may be, ye silly child, but it matters naught. Now off with ye, for I wish to speak to yer Uncle Claude. He's waiting for me, he is, at the dower house."

Brandy whirled about and ran from the sitting room. She rushed from the castle, heedless of the fact that Percy could still be about, and made for a lonely stretch of beach, far away from prying eyes. She rushed to the edge of the water and gulped in the salty air. She stood staring blindly toward the empty horizon, wondering if anyone beyond that stretch of water could be as miserable as was she. Water lapped about her sandals, and she retreated beyond the reach of the rising tide to a large out-jutting rock.

She wrapped her skirts about her legs and sank her chin to her knees. She felt tears sting her eyes. She would never give up Fiona. She would do anything, even wed with Percy, not to lose her little sister. Her mind brought her back to her other choice. London with Ian—and his bride. The thought brought with it such a sense of despair that she pressed her knuckles against her eyes to keep away the damnable tears. To be in his company every day while that hated, faceless wife held his attention and his love. Unbidden, the words she had spoken to Percy rose in her mind: "I won't chase dreams."

She was a witless fool, she told herself. She couldn't have the duke, so there was the end to it. She swallowed this bitter pill and forced her thoughts to London. She had no workable notion of exactly what a Season involved. Obviously, from the way Grandmama spoke, it must involve scores of single ladies and gentlemen coming together for the purpose of deciding who would marry whom. She tried to picture these gentlemen, but only Ian's face appeared before her. She rose abruptly and kicked a stone with the toe of her sandal. I might well be a witless fool, she repeated to herself again, but I do want him, and I'll have none other. She drew herself up and stared out to sea.

She was chasing a dream, but she didn't care. Sometimes dreams were all there were.

Lady Adella leaned heavily on her cane as she followed Fraser into the small sitting room in the dower house. "Don't ye get up, Claude," she said sourly, "there's no reason for the both of us to suffer."

Fraser helped her sit down, then offered her one of his freshly baked scones.

"Strawberry jam, my lady?"

"Nay, Fraser, I like them just as they are, with the butter oozing over the sides." She gazed at him, a gleam in her faded eyes. "Morag would be a fat slut were ye still living with her. Claude, ye got the best of the bargain. Would ye like to trade Fraser for Morag?"

Claude cackled, displayed bits of buttery scone against his black front teeth. "Fraser stays right

150

where he is, lady. Besides, ye try to force him to be near Morag, and he'd take himself off to Edinburgh. Have I yer measure, Fraser?"

Fraser folded his lips into enforced silence and nodded pleasantly.

Lady Adella poked his leg with the tip of her cane. "Don't ye miss having a wench in yer bed, Fraser? I vow Morag gets scratchier by the day, seeing as how she has nay a man to tumble her."

Fraser's nostrils twitched. He said, "If ye'll allow me to say, my lady, it isn't a man Morag needs, it's a thorough scrubbing twice a day with a bar of lye soap."

Lady Adella choked on her scone, and Fraser delicately thumped her back. "I like a man who speaks his mind, Fraser. Off with ye now, for I must needs bore myself with yer master."

After Fraser had calmly bowed himself from the room, Lady Adella turned to Claude, smacking her lips free of crumbs.

"Well, nephew, now we can speak freely. Attend me well, for the subject will be closed after today."

Claude sat forward in his chair, his eyes glittering, his gout forgotten for the moment.

"Ye know that the time has come to make retribution. I suspect that old MacPherson is grinding his teeth at the tasks I've set him. But it will be done. Ye'll have yer claim to Penderleigh, as will Bertrand after ye. As to what it'll bring ye, only God and the devil know."

Claude said harshly, "Ye set me more trouble, what with yer legitimizing that scoundrel Percy before ye reinherit me. And the English duke—

151

what do ye plan to do with him, may I be so bold as to ask?"

Lady Adella raised a penciled eyebrow. "What would ye that I do—poison him like the Borgias? Come, my boy, ye know there was naught I could do whilst Angus cursed this world with his presence. After he died, I could do naught immediately, for the duke's claim carried the day. Look ye, Claude, the duke pours his English money into his estate. I have no intention of allowing the faucet to be turned off till the well is dry. Then we'll see. Ye, Bertrand, Percy—it's a fine battle we'll have if ye've any blood in yer veins."

Claude growled deep in his throat. "Ye've tied my hands, lady. And I can see that ye haven't even looked beyond the end of yer nose. If the duke's claim holds, then not one of us will ever benefit. Penderleigh will fall into the English line and be forever lost to us. Have ye any idea of how I feel to see Bertie sing the praises of that damned English duke? Why, I don't think the boy feels even now that I and then he are Penderleigh's true heirs. And ye, lady, ye are under the duke's thumb, just as am I, and ye keep yer claws sheathed."

Lady Adella leaned forward and said softly, "Aye, ye're right, Claude. But remember, the duke has no direct heirs as yet. Right now there's only a cousin—an English cousin—to succeed him. Surely, ye can't believe that a Scottish court would rule in favor of an English cousin who has no blood ties with the Robertsons." She raised her hand as Claude looked ready to protest.

"Enough, my boy. I've done all I can for ye and Bertrand, and, aye, for Percy too. It's up to ye now. I'll be saying no more on the matter."

"I want only what is my due," Claude said, his anger rising. "Ye give me the horse's saddle but not the horse." A crafty look settled into his small eyes. "What if, lady, the world were to discover the cause of my father's disinheritance? What if, lady, ye were—"

Lady Adella threw back her head and roared with laughter. "Douglass was never as doltish as ye, Claude. I'd call ye a miserable liar and hound ye as far as the Highlands. Yer father held his tongue until he reached his deathbed. His only mistake was in telling ye, my lad. If ye've a brain in yer head, ye'll not tell Bertrand, though. He seems to me a spineless creature, lapping about the duke's heels."

"I'll not let ye speak thus of Bertie. I think, lady, that ye've far more the taste for bounders like Percy than for gentlemen like my Bertie."

Lady Adella held up a conciliating hand. "Calm down, Claude, afore ye burst yer heart." She took a noisy sip of her tea and changed the topic. "I haven't told ye, but I intend our Constance for Bertrand. I'd thought we would have several years yet, but the girl has blossomed more quickly than I expected. If I don't miss my guess, yer son's hot for her."

Claude reared back his head in patent disbelief. "Wee Connie? Why, Bertie's never spared a thought for a wench in all his life, more's the pity, save that trollop in the village."

"I'm surrounded by witless fools. Open yer

eyes, my boy. Connie's not like Brandy—she thinks herself a woman grown. If Bertrand plays his gentleman's game with her, he'll soon find himself left in a ditch, with no one but himself to blame."

Claude thoughtfully stroked the stubble on his chin. "Bertie tells me that the duke plans to dower all the girls."

"Aye, but ye needn't worry about Constance trekking off to London, as the duke intends for Brandy. Lord, we'd have to wait another two years, and I tell ye, she'd have lost her maidenhead long before that."

Claude shifted painfully in his chair. Bedamned but that gouty foot was paining him today. "Very well, lady, I'll speak to Bertie. But don't expect him to ravish the chit."

Lady Adella endeavored to picture such an event but failed. "I can't even imagine Bertie without his breeches. More likely, I think, if we are to get anywhere at all, it will have to be Connie who seduces Bertie."

13

Brandy discovered during the next two weeks that the idyllic existence she had sought to cling to held less and less pleasure for her. Her thoughts centered more and more upon the duke, on what he was doing and whether his thinking ever included her. She even allowed herself the fancy of picturing herself as an elegant young lady whose Scottish accent had miraculously disappeared, whose bosom had become far less prominent, surrounded by London gentlemen, with a jealous Ian standing close by. No, she thought, the duke would never be jealous. Jealous of what? He was too certain of himself, of who and what he was to ever know doubt.

She was in the middle of seeing herself languidly waving a fan to and fro when she heard the rumble of carriage wheels and brought herself back to the present.

She walked slowly back to the castle, wondering who had come to call. MacPherson, most likely. Grandmama had mentioned that he was to visit. As she rounded the last outcropping of rhododendron bushes along the drive to the castle, she drew up dead in her tracks. There in front of the castle steps stood the duke's carriage.

She suddenly became aware that she looked like a sorry excuse for a female. Salty, damp tendrils of hair clung to her forehead, and her old gown hung about her with all the style of a crofter's wife's. She thought to skirt the front entrance and creep through the servants' door and up the back stairs when she heard her name ring out:

"Brandy!"

The duke and Bertrand stood beside the carriage, looking toward her. She ground her teeth and forced herself to wave at them. There was no way she'd get close to them. She would keep her distance.

"She always has the look of a little mermaid," she heard Bertrand say to the duke.

A porpoise more like, she told herself and forced her feet to move forward, just a little closer to Ian, each step more painful than the last.

"Yes," the duke said with a smile. He drew in a deep breath of the fresh sea air, aware that he was glad to be back at Penderliegh. The huge gray rambling castle no longer appeared to him as a crumbling old ruin and a ready drain on his purse. It was a proud symbol of Scotland's rich past.

"Come, Brandy," Bertrand called, "don't dawdle. We've much to tell, and the spice goes out of the telling if it much be repeated."

There was no hope for her. "Good afternoon, Bertrand, Ian. I trust yer trip was successful." That sounded nice and formal, elegant even. Perhaps they'd listen to her and not really look at her.

"Aye, that it was," Bertrand said. "Lord, my girl, ye smell salty as the sea itself."

In that instant Brandy hated the sea. She looked up at the duke's face to see his eyes lit with jocular good humor. She wanted to scream at him that he wasn't her damned uncle. Her pounding heart plummeted to her toes. He thought she was a ragamuffin, a dowd, a child. Damnation. She said, "I will go change now, if ye'll excuse me."

"Don't be a silly goose," Bertrand said, clapping her on the shoulder. "It matters naught if we have a mermaid in the castle."

There was no doubt about it. He did think he

156

was her uncle, she thought, as Ian added in that hideously kind voice of his, "Yes, come, Brandy, I have brought you a present from Edinburgh, and I don't want to wait in the giving of it."

A present? Had he bought her a doll? She nodded, the image of herself as that elegant young lady waving a fan to and fro gone from her mind.

As she passed beside him, Ian had the urge to wind his fingers around the salty tendrils of heavy blond hair that curled over her brow. He made no move at all. He hadn't the least idea where that urge had sprung from. He wasn't a man to give into urges, particularly ones he didn't understand.

As the three of them entered the drawing room, Ian found himself wondering just how Lady Adella would treat him. He had not, he grinned to himself, left her on exactly the best of terms.

Lady Adella, Claude, and Constance were in the drawing room having afternoon tea. It was, Ian thought, Lady Adella's only concession to her English heritage.

"Well, ye're back from mucking about in yer sheep dung," Lady Adella said, and snapped her teacup back on its saucer.

"That we are, lady," Ian said, finding he'd missed—perhaps just a bit—her sour humor. "I see you're in good health."

"Aye, no thanks to ye. Well, Bertie, yer presence relieves me. Claude's become a maudlin bore in yer absence. Better ye than I living with him."

She saw that Bertrand was in conversation with Constance, and said in a loud voice, "I can see

157

ye've missed yer cousin more than yer father. Knowing yer father as I do, I can say that I blame ye."

"Indeed I have not," Bertrand said calmly, and made his bow to Claude. "I was just telling Connie that Ian and I spent several days in Edinburgh, seeing the sights, visiting the duke's man of business and his bank."

"What sights?"

"Well, the castle, for one. And many other things as well," Bertrand said.

"I hadn't thought ye interested in brothels, Bertie," Lady Adella said slyly, fingertips tapping the arms of her chair.

Ian laughed. "Nothing so decadent, I assure you, Lady Adella. Edinburgh is a beautiful city, in fact, London's undisputed northern rival. I might add that it boasts excellent shops."

"Aye, and ye might guess that Ian insisted upon visiting them," Bertrand added, his eyes intent on Constance's face. He straightened and pointed toward Crabbe, who stood in the doorway, holding several wrapped boxes in his arms.

"Ye brought me a present," Constance yelled, leaping to her feet.

"Ye brought all the ladies presents," Ian said, looking at Lady Adella to see what she'd make of this. He wasn't disappointed.

She snorted. But she stuck out her hands fast enough when Ian handed her a prettily wrapped box.

"What is it, a shroud to cover my old bones?" she said, all indifferent.

"Nay, lady. I suggested it, but Bertrand hadn't the fortitude to visit a shroud shop. He said you wouldn't take it well, so I was forced to think of something else."

"Ye're a sly one," she said, snorted, and quickly began pulling away the layers of silver paper. "Och!" She withdrew an exquisite shawl of Norwich silk, the varying shades of blue shimmering like spun sky in her hands. "It's not fit for an old woman. It'll bring out all the wrinkles in my face. It will make me look shriveled, nearly dead." But her eyes told a different story.

"That's exactly what I told the shopkeeper," Ian said. "I told him something in plain black with no adornment." He sighed. "I suppose he went against my wishes. I will have it returned for the black."

Lady Adella gave him a sour look and clutched the shawl to her meager bosom.

The duke handed Brandy her present while Bertrand placed a wrapped box into Constance's waiting hands. He wondered how Brandy would react to a gift that was more for a fully grown woman than a girl who was a woman in years but not in other ways.

Brandy's hands trembled as she lifted out what seemed to be yard upon yard of dark blue velvet. She stood slowly and shook out the gown in front of her. She saw no sash or belt and wondered where the waist was. She looked doubtfully up at the duke.

"It's the empire style, made fashionable by Napoleon's Josephine," Ian said, smiling. He wanted to add that such a gown hugged and lifted

159

a woman's breasts and made a man want to slaver, but he held his tongue. He prayed her breasts were large enough to fill it out. God, the last thing he wanted to do was embarrass her.

"It's beautiful, utterly beautiful. It's so soft. I've never before felt anything so rich and warm. But I don't understand, Ian. It has no waist. I fear I would look quite odd in it."

"Not at all," he said, keeping his eyes on her face. "It's designed to fall in a straight line from well above your waist. The style is all the thing in London."

She looked closely at the small gathers in the bodice of the gown and realized that the small expanse of blue velvet above was meant to cover her bosom. She paled at the thought. She wanted to scream and cry at the unfairness of it. Why had nature made her a cow? Why had fashion decreed two inches of material were all that was necessary to cover a woman's breasts?

Ian was watching the myriad expressions dance across her face. She was embarrassed. She didn't like the gown. He shouldn't have bought it for her. Well, hell.

"Brandy, if the style doesn't please you, we will just have a seamstress design another gown for you. It doesn't matter, truly."

She hugged the beautiful gown against her breasts. "Oh no, it's the most wonderful gift anyone's ever given me. I thank ye, Ian, for yer kindness."

"It's nothing. I just wanted to please you." His voice was gruff, which was unusual. He turned quickly at Constance's crow of delight. He grinned to himself, for he had insisted that Bertrand choose Constance's gown. It was a deep green muslin, with row upon row of delicate lace covering what would otherwise be a most inappropriate expanse of bosom for a sixteen-year-old girl.

Brandy lovingly wrapped the gown and placed it back in the box. She looked up at Ian. "Fiona, yer grace?"

"I would never forget your wee child," he said with a smile, and pointed at a large wooden crate near the door.

She raised eyes brimming with love to his face. He shook. No, she intends it for the child, he told himself. That look is for Fiona, not me. Hell and damnation, why did that bother him?

"Let me fetch her." Brandy dipped a slight curtsy and ran from the room.

Bertrand said to Constance, "The green matches yer eyes, Connie, though the material could never be as warm and as bright."

Lady Adella shot Claude a look fraught with meaning. "I see ye have become a poet, Bertie," he said, gazing at his son with new eyes. "So ye got nothing for yer old father, eh?"

"Nay, Father, only the ladies," Bertrand said, looking quickly away from Constance, who was looking at Uncle Claude as if he'd spoken German to her.

A bright mop of red hair appeared in the open doorway, followed by a child's high squeal of delight. Fiona stood speechless in front of the large wooden crate, so overcome that her mouth was open.

"Come, poppet, I'll help ye open it," Brandy said. "Ye want to guess what it is? Ian gave it to ye, brought it all the way from Edinburgh."

"Let me help," Ian said, and pulled Fiona's small hands away from the wooden crate. He and Brandy pulled the boards until the top flew off. Brandy rocked back on her heels. "Oh, goodness," she said. "Oh, my."

"It's a horse," Fiona cried, and began to tug frantically at the lifelike mane.

"Just a moment, sweetheart," Ian said, laughing, "let me pull him out for you. Hold, now. Let go of his mane for just a moment." He pulled the horse out of the crate. "It even has a saddle and bridle," he said. "And it rocks. See?"

"Oh, goodness," Brandy said again. She was on her knees next to her sister. She looked up at him and said in a voice soft enough to melt stone, "It's the grandest present she's ever had, Ian. Ye shouldn't have spoiled the child, but I'm glad ye did. Fiona doesn't get many gifts. There's never money for that sort of thing. Thank ye."

Dear God, she looked beautiful staring up at him, her soft, lilting voice flowing over him like warm honey. Felicity, he thought, and felt a knife of guilt turn in his innards. "You're most welcome," he heard another man say to her, another man who couldn't feel anything toward her save cousinly feelings.

"I say, Ian," Bertrand said, "don't ye think it's time we informed everybody of our other purchases?"

"Yes, it's a very large and very wooly purchase, presents for Penderleigh. Seriously, we purchased sheep from a rather dour old man in the Cheviot, near to Fort David."

"A man by the name of Hesketh," Bertrand continued. "Have ye heard of him, Lady Adella? He owns a large old stone manor house that looks as time-honored as Penderleigh. He's got a long nose and he's always scratching his ear."

"Hesketh," she repeated slowly, and shook her head. She looked sourly over at Fiona, whose crows of pleasure were becoming more enthusiastic. "Brandy, remove the child and her horse before my head splits with her noise."

"Come, poppet, we can pretend he's the great wooden horse that sat before the gates of Troy."

Brandy settled Fiona and her horse near the small fireplace in her bedchamber, then pulled the exquisite velvet gown from its silver paper. She quickly stripped off her clothes, not even bothering to keep on her shift. She wanted to feel the soft, shimmering material against her skin. She slowly slipped the gown over her head and let it float down over her body. With some difficulty, she managed to fasten most of the small hooks up the back. She felt the small gathers, sewn into a stiff band of material, pushing her breasts upward and forward. Hesitantly she walked to the long, narrow mirror in the corner of her room and stared at herself. All she could do was stare, speechless, furious, red with embarrassment.

Her breasts rose from the bodice of the gown in rounded white splendor, forming a deep cleavage that seemed to start nearly at the base of her throat. Oh, my God, she was a cow, hideous and misshapen.

"Brandy, ye don't look like yerself. Ye look like a queen, a beautiful queen, and ye're all so white."

Brandy tried to cover her breasts with her hands, an impossible task.

"Aye, a queen, like that Helen who was held inside Troy that the soldiers came to save. Ian will think ye're more beautiful than any other lady in the world."

"I don't think so," Brandy said. "Nay, poppet, it's just me. Ian bought ye the horse, and for me he bought this gown. It is lovely, isn't it?"

Fiona stepped forward, looked to see that her hands were clean, then fingered the material. "It's all furry, like a rabbit. But I prefer my horse."

Absurdly, Brandy asked, "Do ye think it's a proper dress to wear downstairs to dinner?"

"If cousin Percy were here, he would be sure to like it," Fiona said with guileless candor that ripped Brandy apart. She was just telling the truth, but how could she know? She had come upon Percy on top of Brandy, but she just thought they'd been wrestling. Hadn't she? Oh, dear. No, she was too young to guess the truth.

Fiona said, "Well, I think it's stupid the way he's always looking at ye. And Connie, always batting *her* eyes at *him*."

Fiona, that precocious child, had nailed the board exactly in the right place. Brandy walked across the room toward the windows, savoring the delicious feel of the gown against her belly and legs. Her eyes were drawn to a light carriage that was pulling to a halt amid clouds of dust before the castle. She sucked in her breath as she watched Percy climb down. She quickly backed away from the windows. What in God's name was he doing here?

She walked back to the mirror and looked at herself for a long time. Then, slowly, she pulled off the velvet gown and lovingly laid it back into its box.

She thought of Ian and how she simply must do something about her appearance, else he would always think of her as a dowdy child. She quickly dressed in her waisted muslin gown, tightened the laces of her chemise over her breasts, and came to a decision. Ruthlessly she unbraided the long tresses and pulled a brush through the deep, tight waves. She fashioned a braided coronet high atop her head and drew the long masses of hair through the circle, curling the ends about her fingers. She looked in the mirror and was satisfied, at least from the neck up.

Brandy entered the drawing room rather later than usual that evening, for Fiona, still excited over her wooden horse, hadn't wanted to go to sleep. Then she wanted to have the horse sleep next to her. Brandy had to yell a bit at her. Now she prayed to be unobtrusive, but realized the moment she stepped into the room that this was not to be. Her eyes first fell upon Constance, lovely and terribly grown up in her new gown, and she choked back a stab of jealousy.

Lady Adella took one long look at her and roared, "Stupid girl, I thought we'd finally banished the ugly duckling. Ye look like a scraggly weed next to yer sister. Well, at least ye've gotten rid of yer child's braids. It's some improvement, but I'd prayed for more."

Percy said to Lady Adella, never looking away from Brandy, "As ye say, lady, our ugly duckling has changed some of her plumage, but not enough. If she'd allow me, I'd teach her how to present herself in, shall we say, a more conclusive light."

"What do ye mean by conclusive, Percy?" Constance said.

"Yer sister's a woman, Connie, but she doesn't want to present herself as one. I could help her, show her, encourage her, even."

"I don't think so, Percy," Brandy said.

Ian thought her hair looked stunning. But damn, he'd been certain that gown would be perfect for her. Brandy said to him, "The gown is quite lovely, Ian, truly it is. It is just that it did not fit quite right and I must make alterations before I can wear it."

She turned quickly to her sister. "Ye're lovely, Connie. The green matches yer eyes, just as Bertrand said, and the gown fits ye to perfection."

Constance nodded her head gracefully. Those green eyes of hers showed nothing but triumph. Aye, she thought, Brandy did look like a scraggly weed, just as Grandmama said. Tonight she'd gain what she wanted. Percy would want her, not her sister. She was pleased to the very tips of her toes that she was herself and not Brandy. She gave a pouting smile to Bertrand, since he seemed to admire her so very much. And he had bought

166

her the gown, after all. The pout made his eyes darken. She'd practiced a long time to get it just right. She felt gratified by her success. Perhaps, she thought, trying to untangle her budding woman's wiles, if she paid more attention to Bertrand, Percy would take more interest in her. She turned to Bertrand and moistened her lips with the tip of her tongue. "Do ye really like the gown on me, Bertic?"

Bertrand, more than fascinated by the pointed pink tongue, willingly allowed himself to be seduced. "Aye, Connie," he said in a voice that sounded hungry even to himself, "ye're the fairest lass in all of Scotland."

But Percy was looking at Brandy, curse him. What was she to do now? Here was Bertrand looking at her like an infatuated mule and she just didn't care. Why was Percy so interested in Brandy? Just look at her.

Percy was saying in a low voice to Brandy, "Ye don't appear sorry to see me, little cousin. Perhaps ye've changed yer mind? Perhaps ye and I can take a little stroll on the morrow? Perhaps I can teach ye all those things ye do need to learn."

"Perhaps the devil roves all about the land, like the Bible says. Perhaps the devil would like to return to Edinburgh and treat the ladies there like harlots. Isn't that what the devil does?"

Percy threw back his head and roared with laughter.

"Dinner be ready, yer grace," Crabbe shouted from the doorway.

"Ye needn't sneak in like a limpet, Crabbe,"

167

Lady Adella shouted back at his wooden face. She gave a loud creak of laughter at her own joke. "Come here, Brandy, and make yerself useful. If ye can't look like a lady, ye might as well forget yer hoity-toity manners and help me on with my shawl."

Percy whispered, "So ye've a new gown from the master, lass. I ask myself why ye must make alterations on it." He looked at her flattened breasts. He remembered her struggling beneath him. She wouldn't have fought him long, he'd told himself over and over after he'd been forced to climb off her.

Brandy arranged Lady Adella's new Norwich shawl about her thin shoulders very precisely before saying coldly, "Why did ye return to Penderleigh? Did yer heiress discover yer true nature and tell ye to take yerself to perdition?"

"What a sharp tongue sets on yer shoulders, little cousin. Nay, my heiress pleaded with me to remain with her, if ye must know."

"It's a shame ye didn't see fit to comply with her wishes. It's certain she would appreciate ye more than we do."

"I will agree with the child, Percy," Lady Adella said, "if ye don't behave yerself. No more of yer Robertson ways, Percy, else ye'll be sorry." She looked at him from beneath furrowed brows. He realized with a start that she knew of his attempted seduction of Brandy.

He felt a sudden stab of fear, for the old woman could still, he supposed, prevent him from becoming legitimate. Damn the girl, anyway, she'd wanted it, he knew she had. Coy, that was

168

what she was, and a tease. He said easily, "I shall be as meek as the Cheviot sheep the good duke has just purchased, lady."

"Percy thinks himself much in demand," Bertrand said, unable to hold his tongue and wishing he had once the words were out of his mouth, his dislike as evident as the look of surprise on Ian's face.

"Eh? Percy in demand?" Lady Adella said. "The only ones to demand ye, my boy, are the constables from debtors' prison and all those loose trollops on the east side of Edinburgh."

"Not for very much longer, as ye know, lady. Not for very much longer at all. Ye'll see. Everything will change once I'm a true Robertson." He sounded certain of himself, which he was. He even whistled all the way to the vast dining room.

14

Brandy walked quickly toward the stables, some ten minutes late, having waged an exhausting battle with an old and very snug riding habit that had belonged to her mother. She could take only short breaths because of the painfully tight lacing of her chemise.

Her step lagged as she drew near the rickety stables. She was a complete idiot for having smiled at Ian and told him how she loved to ride, and all because she just wanted him to herself for one entire morning. Now he certainly thought she must be a wonderful rider, all grace and smooth gait. Oh, God, she would be brought down, and she deserved it.

Perhaps she had a very small chance of surviving the morning with his opinion of her riding not destroyed. She would be riding Old Martha, who'd moldered happily and quite lazily in the stables for more years than Brandy could count. Surely Old Martha wouldn't mind Brandy on her back for a couple of hours, surely. She never seemed to mind anything else. She'd let Old Martha go where she liked and as slowly as she liked. Surely she could manage that. She looked at the stables, seeing them for the first time through Ian's eyes. They hadn't been mucked out for weeks, as Wee Albie avoided that task until someone found the time to yell at him until he finally did it. The loose, unpainted boards creaked at the slightest wind from the sea. There were many leaks in the roof.

"So there you are at last, Brandy. I had begun to give up hope." Ian smiled at her flushed face, wondering if she had run all the way from the castle. "You're looking lovely. I like the green velvet on you, very smart." Actually, he thought, any change from her own gowns and the tartan shawl was an improvement, but her hair, it wasn't a girl's style. She'd braided it high atop her head, like the previous evening, and set a plumed riding hat squarely over her forehead.

Brandy took several small, gulping breaths, afraid that at any minute the buttons on the fragile blouse would pop open. "Thank ye, Ian," she said, her eyes shifting to one of his huge gray stallions. "Ye look smart too," she said, and he did, in buff riding britches and a matching buff jacket and those very manly boots that came up to his knees. She thought they were called hessians.

"I thank you too. You're admiring Cantor, I see. He's one of my favorite mounts. His sire was Madras from the Kensington stud in Westerford. I'm going on and on like this because he's yours to ride this morning. I looked at that miserable old hack in the stable. She stared at me as if I were jesting when I told her she was in for a treat. I don't think she would have moved, no matter how many carrots I offered her. So, Brandy, you have Cantor. He's certainly more worthy of you since you're an accomplished horsewoman. He's a bit frisky but well mannered. Given how well you ride, you can handle him without a second thought."

Brandy had many more than just two thoughts. Cantor had wicked, shifty eyes. He was going to kill her and all because she was a braggart, all because she'd not only bragged, she'd lied without hesitation and with no regret, and now she would pay for it. She would die and it would be only her fault. Though Cantor stood quietly enough, tethered to the duke's hands, she knew he was just biding his time until he felt her own inept hands on his bridle. She gulped.

"He does look rather spirited, Ian. Perhaps he's just a bit too spirited for me. I haven't ridden such a magnificent horse in a very long time, maybe even never in my life. Perhaps it would be better if I gave Old Martha some more carrots.

She's rather greedy, and that just might get her out of her stall."

"No, I swear he's not too spirited at all. It's true he's itching for a gallop, as is my own stallion, Hercules. But Cantor is a gentleman, you'll see. I unearthed a side saddle for you." As she hesitated, he said, "You mustn't think that I can't properly girth a saddle, for I have gotten much practice in Scotland. Here, let me assist you to mount."

Brandy gulped yet again and nodded. Well, my girl, she told herself, ye must turn yer bragging into fact. If ye don't die first. She placed her booted foot on his laced fingers. Cantor sidled away just as Ian tossed her into the saddle. She hadn't even ridden a foot and it was all over for her. But no, she managed to hang on. More important, Cantor held still.

"Be polite, Cantor, you've a talented lady on your back. Show her your best side this morning." The duke patted Cantor's nose. He placed the reins into Brandy's gloved hands and turned to his own horse.

Oh, please, God, look kindly upon a fool. Then she said aloud, "Please, Cantor, don't toss me into a ditch. After you toss me onto some soft grass, please don't step on me. I promise ye carrots by the dozen if ye'll help me not to shame myself."

Ian brought Hercules prancing neatly to her side, and she knew sharp envy at his skill. "Where would you like to ride, Brandy?"

With sudden inspiration she said with a swarmy smile, "Ye lead the way, Ian, and I'll follow behind. I've covered all the land ye see, and wish to follow someone else's lead. Who knows where ye'll want to go? This will be fun."

"As you will. We'll go slowly for a bit, but then I promise you a treat. While Bertrand and I were visiting some of the crofters, I spotted a wide, flat meadow that will be perfect for a gallop." He smiled at her, and just for an instant she admired that smile of his and those beautiful white teeth. She admired that hard jaw of his, knowing he was very likely more stubborn than the most stubborn stoat.

Then reality hit and she thought of that meadow, pictured that long, long meadow in her mind, saw herself galloping across it, and nearly burst the buttons on her mother's blouse.

The duke gave Hercules a gentle dig, and the stallion broke into a smooth canter. Brandy had no time for a simple click, for no sooner did Hercules break into a slow, measured stride than Cantor, oblivious of the ineffective tug on his reins, snorted, flung his head up, nearly ripping the reins from her hands, and pranced forward.

Brandy gripped the pommel and concentrated on keeping her seat. She chanced to look down and nearly fainted. The horse was two stories high, at least. At least Ian was in the lead. She fully intended to keep him there. No way would she let him see how she was managing to keep herself in the saddle.

She forced a pathetic smile, not without some difficulty, when Ian pulled up Hercules and waited until she came alongside.

"The wooded area around Penderleigh

reminds me somewhat of the home wood at Carmichael Hall—that's my country home in Suffolk. It's a massive old place set in the middle of a huge park. I think you'd like it. There's a home wood, lots of elms and maples and oaks. And more birds than you can imagine. The only thing is, though, we don't have the sea at the back door, or any heather."

She said something about how grand it sounded, but her full attention was on Cantor and how he seemed to be doing this dance beneath her. What was a home wood? If it was where you lived, of course it would be home and the trees there would be the home wood. Well, she'd figured something new out before she died.

"No," the duke continued, looking around him and breathing in the sweet morning air, "I have nothing so awesome as the sea, but there is a long, winding lake that sits like a beautiful blue gem in the middle of the maple forest."

Cantor's ears flattened. "I should much like to see it," she said, staring at those ears that seemed sewn down to his head, so flat they were. Why? What could Cantor possibly have to be mad about? She hadn't asked him to do a single thing.

"Do you like to swim, Brandy?"

That got her attention momentarily, and a big smile. "Aye, indeed I do. I wager, Ian, that ye would have a difficult time beating me. The sea currents make one a strong swimmer, ye know. The last time Bertrand raced me, I left him swallowing water and thrashing around. I thought I'd have to go save him."

He raised a black brow, trying to picture this slip of a girl beside him stroking through the choppy waves. She'd beaten Bertrand, a man?

"Laughing at me, are ye? I see it, ye don't believe me. Well, ye'll be singing a different tune, yer grace, once I have ye in the water. I'm very strong, ye'll see. Ye can lower that sarcastic eyebrow of yers as well."

The black brow remained cocked upward and he grinned. "Bertrand called you a mermaid, but I doubt he was referring to your prowess as a swimmer."

"Nay, it's because I'm often damp and smell salty. He likes to tease me. He's done it all my life. But ye know," she added, her chin up, "I don't think he'd ever want to see Connie like me."

"Ah, so you've seen that the breeze blows in that direction. Bertrand is besotted with your sister. Actually, it took hardly any encouragement from me during our trip for him to praise your sister in the most revoltingly glowing terms. He nearly put me to sleep, he kept going on for so long about her beautiful hair, her magnificent eyes, her straight nose—good God, he just wouldn't stop. It's too bad that Constance doesn't as yet return his regard. But she's young. Time will tell."

"Ye ending in a platitude, yer grace? Time has nothing to do with it. You know as well as I do that it's that damned Percy again, curse his blighter's eyes."

He laughed aloud.

175

"Oh, dear, I keep forgetting that I shouldn't curse in proper company."

"I'm not feeling particularly proper at the moment. Damn away, Brandy. And you're right, I did spout a platitude. Not, well done of me. Now you've got me on my toes."

She sighed. "If only Connie would see him for what he really is—a vain, strutting villain. Goodness, I pity that poor heiress of his."

"Perhaps," the duke said quietly, looking straight at her, "just perhaps once he has the Robertson name and his heiress, he will forget about all that he can't possess."

"It isn't important, truly, it just doesn't matter. Grandmama was encouraging him one minute, and scolding him, telling him to keep away from me in the next. I had hoped to be rid of him. It's strange that he came back just after ye did yesterday. Did he tell you why he'd come back to Penderleigh?"

He shook his head. "I wouldn't worry about it. Since I'm about, he'll keep his distance. Remember, Percy is a lot like Lady Adella. He likes to make mischief. He likes to mock and to sneer. I suspect he became that way to protect himself from slights. I can't imagine that being a bastard would be a very pleasant way to face life, people being the way they are. I suppose that he heard of Bertrand and me being in Edinburgh and thought it safe to return. But who knows? To be honest, I really don't care at the moment."

With those words he dropped her right back on Cantor's back. How could she have forgotten that death was so very close for even five minutes?

She'd been talking about swimming. And Percy. She was a bloody fool.

Ian drew up suddenly. "Here we are, Madame Excellence. The meadow. You're dying to grind me beneath your heel, aren't you? All right, then, a race. Our first race will be by land and, if you're willing, and I can see that you are, our second will be by sea."

"Men are all big talk. You'll eat our dirt. Then what will ye say? 'Aye, Lady Adella, I hate to admit it, but I was trounced by a mere female.' And she'll laugh louder than Uncle Claude and thwack her knee, and you'll be so humiliated, you'll slink away to your bedchamber and hide for a full week."

"All that? My, but we're cocky, aren't we? As for this race, Brandy, Cantor has all the speed of Hercules, so you get no beginning start. The last one to the trees must pay a forfeit."

Brandy looked across the long stretch of meadow and knew she would die a fool. And she would die soon, even though the trees on the far side of the meadow seemed at least five miles distant. She opened her mouth to confess that she was a shiftless liar, but she couldn't get the words out. She looked at the duke, saw that beautiful smile of his, the challenge in his eyes. Her head nodded. She hadn't told it to, but it had, just nodded and nodded. She heard a voice come out of her mouth: "I have all the advantage I need, Ian. Prepare to lose, yer grace. A forfeit, ye say?" In that instant she dug in her heels and slapped the reins against Cantor's neck.

She heard Ian's shout of laughter behind her.

For a brief moment she forgot her fear, so smoothly did Cantor race across the meadow. She felt her riding hat loosen in the wind and slapped her hand down on it, pressing her body close to Cantor's neck. She saw Ian close rapidly beside her, and she lost what little sense of self-preservation she had left. She dug in her heels. She actually encouraged Cantor to go faster, as fast as the wind.

The once faraway trees loomed closer and closer. She would run into those trees and not just kill herself but also Ian's horse as well. She had to do something. How the devil did one pull up the ton of horseflesh beneath her? She heard Ian's deep laughter as he pulled ahead of her. She watched him draw Hercules to a smooth stop at the very edge of the trees and whirl him about to face her.

She told her riding hat to fend for itself, and with both gloved hands she pulled back on Cantor's reins with all her strength. Not only didn't he slacken his speed, Cantor ignored her. She tugged frantically, then just gave it up and closed her eyes as Cantor headed full tilt toward Ian.

15

She heard a shout of laughter. How she loved his laugh. It would be the last thing she would hear before she died.

Cantor reared up on his hind legs. Brandy dropped the reins and grasped the pommel with all her strength. It was over in a flash. Cantor had pulled to a panting stop, Brandy still miraculously in the saddle, and Ian held her horse's reins, those beautiful dark eyes of his alight with amusement.

She was so relieved to still be on the horse's back, to still be breathing, she hardly heard him when he said, "What is this, Brandy? Did you think to run me out of the way and thus claim you beat me? Is this what you did to poor Bertrand when you raced in the sea? You just ran over him? You scared the very devil out of me. You have not an ounce of fear, do you?"

She yelled out, "Cantor is the faster, Ian. It wasn't your superior horsemanship at all. I demand another race, yes, but not today, perhaps tomorrow or next year. Perhaps the turn of the next century."

He was laughing and didn't hear her last words. "You're not a good loser, Brandy. You know I'm the better rider. Come now, just admit it. You won't, will you? Stubborn girl. Very well, we'll race again, just name the date."

The day pigs flew, she thought.

"Next week," she said. "Aye, next Wednesday."

"Wednesday it is. Now, what forfeit can I claim?"

Forfeit. She'd forgotten all about a forfeit. Just so long as he forgot about a race next Wednesday, she'd give him anything he wanted. She slipped her foot free of the stirrup and slid to the ground.

Ah, sweet earth. It was solid. It didn't move or snort. She said, looking up at him, "Whatever ye wish, Ian. Anything."

He dismounted and tethered the horses to a yew bush. "Whatever I wish, eh?" He grinned and walked over to her.

She looked up at him. She looked at that beautiful mouth of his.

"Brandy," he said.

She took a half step toward him, her lips slightly parted.

He stood stiffly before her, his arms at his sides. Before he had time to applaud his strength of character, she stood on her tiptoes and locked her hands around his neck, drawing him down to her. She wasn't all that certain what to do, but it didn't matter. She kissed him, with all the warmth in her heart. She felt the strength of him, the heat of his mouth, and sighed softly. She wanted this never to end. She could stand on her tiptoes forever. She loved the taste of him, the smell of him, the feel of him against her.

His control nearly deserted him for the first time in his adult life. No, he couldn't do this. She was innocent. She didn't have any idea what she was doing, certainly what she was doing to him, a man, who was harder than a stone. He didn't part his lips, though he wanted to taste her more than he could even begin to imagine himself. He wanted his tongue in her mouth. He wanted to stroke his hands down her back, cup her buttocks and lift her against him, caress her, slip his fingers—no, he couldn't, he wouldn't. He was shuddering at the thoughts and raw sensations pulsing through him. No, he couldn't. It was the hardest thing he'd ever done in his life, but he pulled her hands from around his neck.

"No, Brandy, we can't, we mustn't."

She backed away from him then, surprised she could even walk since she just wanted to sink down to the ground and stretch out on her back. She just wanted him to hold her and kiss her and come over her—"Yer forfeit, Ian," she said, and her voice was as raw as the feelings that were tearing up her insides.

She was so damned vulnerable. She was innocent. He had to protect her from himself. "That isn't exactly the forfeit I'd intended," he said, and thought himself a dolt for saying such a stupid thing.

"But it was the forfeit I wanted to give to ye. And after all, I did lose the race though I'm the better rider, as ye'll see next Wednesday."

Straight talking, he thought, and wanted to grab her and kiss her until they were both so needy they wouldn't stop and he would know her and teach her and—

He groaned and ran his hand through his hair. He had to stop this. He had no choice. "Brandy, listen to me. Dammit, I'm your guardian. I'm engaged to another lady. You're an innocent child—no, well, girl—very well, woman—and I would be the most despicable of men to take advantage of you. Do you understand—"

"Child? Girl? Ah, and that woman was just a lame sop, wasn't it? Damn ye, yer stupid grace, I am a woman, not just a sop woman. I'm nearly nineteen. Ye call me a child and a girl so ye won't

181

have to think of me as someone who could be more to you than—ah, never mind."

He drew up and stared at her.

She was so furious she didn't want to see if he had anything more to say, just rushed on, "I knew exactly what I was doing, and I'll not allow ye denying it with yer nonsensical words of taking advantage. Damn that other woman. I'll not go to London to live in the same house with her, do ye understand me? I'll not let her kiss ye in front of me and caress ye, and then look at me like I'm some sort of rodent from a ditch. And ye know she will. She's a fine lady, isn't she? All right and proper and knows her own worth. And she'll hate me, but not as much as I'll hate her. I don't even know her, and I hate her to her toes.

"I won't go and ye can't force me to go. I'll not live in the same house with that hateful woman. I'll have Percy first, do ye understand me?"

She didn't think, just rushed to Cantor. She jerked his reins free of the bush, and, without a thought to her fear of him, managed to climb into the saddle.

"Brandy, wait, I must talk to you about this, explain to you—"

"Nay, go to the devil, yer grace," she yelled at him. She dug in her heels. Cantor knew that the graceless bundle on his back had absolutely no control over herself, much less over him. With a happy snort he dove forward, back across the meadow.

Ian stared after her a moment, his own anger rising. Damn her for not allowing him to explain.

God, how very simple everything had been before he came to this outlandish place. Before he met her. Before he realized what beautiful hair she had. Before he realized that he loved to be with her, to hear her talk, to see this world through her eyes. Damnation.

He jumped on Hercules's back, loosed his full strength, and galloped after her. He drew alongside just as Cantor broke through the trees back to the main road. He was leaning over to grab the reins from her hands when she jerked back on the bridle and tried to wheel Cantor away. Cantor, recognizing the hand of his master, reared back on his hind legs, tore the reins from her hands, and planted himself in a stubborn halt.

"Ye wretched beast." She lunged forward to grab the reins from Ian's hands, but he pulled them from her reach. They stared at each other a moment silently. Brandy, her anger having melted, wished for oblivion. They continued to stare at each other. Ian was thinking of how she'd look with her hair free of her braids, all spread out on a pillow and he was over her and—

He said finally, every word firm and correct and so painful he'd thought he'd die, "Now, if you would not mind, Brandy, I would like to continue our ride. I don't want you racing back to the stable, looking as if you'd been escaping the devil. The last thing I want is for your family to wonder if anything improper is going on."

She gazed at him, baffled at this calm, possessed speech. Then she merely nodded, not trusting herself to speak. He placed Cantor's reins back into her hands, and they proceeded back along the path, away from the castle. Ian was cursing himself silently for sounding the pompous ass—like a pompous English ass, all straightlaced and stiff in the collar.

He chose a much traveled path that forked off the road, past crofters' huts, away from the sea. He became aware that the sky was darkening dangerously, but he kept riding, telling himself that he didn't care if she got soaked. After some time, he thought he'd found a quite correct and proper string of phrases to present to her, and drew to a halt in a quiet wooded area, a few feet from the path.

"Would you like to dismount here, Brandy?" As he spoke, he began to dismount. No sooner were the words out of his mouth than the darkened sky was split by a dazzling bolt of lightning. A crashing boom of thunder followed quickly in its wake.

Brandy's voice caught in a scream as Cantor, frightened and blinded by the jagged flash of lightning, reared up with a wild snort, tore the reins from her hands, and plunged forward. She made a mad grab for the reins, but they were beyond her reach. She screamed, "Ian, help me. I can't stop him. The reins, I can't reach them." She felt hollow with fear. She'd believed she'd die through her own stupidity, not through a ridiculous accident that shouldn't even be happening. A low-hanging branch tore her riding hat from her head. Any moment now she would follow her hat and be smashed beneath Cantor's hooves.

Then there was another loud clap of thunder,

sharp and white, and she smelled burning wood. Cantor lengthened his stride and crashed all the faster through the dense undergrowth. A silver of hope flashed through her mind as she heard Ian closing fast behind her. She had jerked around in the saddle to measure his distance from her when the reins, hanging loose, tangled themselves under one of Cantor's hooves, and inevitably, he stumbled.

Ian had nearly reached her when he saw Cantor fall to one knee and Brandy fly over his head. Her name died in his throat as he watched her fall to the ground amid masses of tangled ivy.

He drew up Hercules and leaped from his back. His first instinct was to gather her up into his arms, but he didn't. He knelt down beside her and placed two fingers against the pulse in the hollow of her throat. The beat was steady, if somewhat rapid. Gently he felt each of her arms for broken bones, then her legs. Damn, it didn't matter. She could be hurt internally, and that could easily kill her. He'd never been so scared in his life.

"Brandy," he said, leaning close to her still face. He gently slapped her cheeks, but she didn't awaken. He rocked back on his heels, wondering what to do. As if the heavens had already not done enough with the accursed lightning and thunder, several large raindrops suddenly splashed on Brandy's face.

"Well, damn," he said under his breath. He had to find shelter, anything. He pulled off his riding jacket and covered her. He gazed a moment grimly down at her still face, then rose and strode into the woods. He hadn't gone too far when he spotted a crofter's hut. He would take Brandy there and send one of the children back to Penderleigh for help.

The rain was coming down in a thick gray sheet when he lifted her into his arms and carried her to Hercules.

Holding her in the crook of one arm, he grasped Cantor's reins in the other hand and slowly moved the small cavalcade toward the hut.

As he drew nearer, he saw that the hut had long been abandoned, its thatched roof sagging precariously over the stone walls. The thatch was supported in the front of the hut by two skinny poles and would afford, at least, some shelter for the horses.

He dismounted slowly, shifted Brandy's weight to his right arm, and tied the horses. With the toe of his boot he kicked open the narrow front door. It creaked ominously on rusted hinges, and he prayed that it wouldn't collapse on him.

When his eyes adjusted to the dim inside, he realized there was just one small room, its floor still covered with rotting boards. He stepped gingerly toward a crudely wrought fireplace and gently laid Brandy beside it, smoothing his coat under her.

Another booming crash of thunder brought him to his feet. Cantor whinnied, but he didn't tear away, thank God. Ian spotted a pile of peat clumps in one corner and thanked the Lord for at least something of use.

The beauty of peat was that it needed very little coaxing to burn. Though a goodly amount of smoke gushed into the room, it was something. He pulled out his handkerchief and wiped the rain from Brandy's face. He stared at her firm chin, her very straight nose, and her thick brows that flared ever so slightly toward her temples. He felt damnably helpless. A memory he had thought long buried rose suddenly in his mind. Vividly he remembered the wrenching helplessness he'd felt when, at last, he had realized that there was nothing he could do to save Marianne. Even when he'd managed to reach Paris, stealing into that revolution-racked city under the cover of night, he'd known that he was too late. He'd known it in his gut.

He wouldn't let it be too late for Brandy.

16

"Dammit, Brandy, wake up," he shouted at her. "Ye don't have to yell at me, Ian," Brandy whispered, forcing her eyes to open. His sigh of relief was audible, and her mouth moved to a painful smile.

As much as he wanted her to talk, to reassure him that she was all right, he said, "Don't talk if it hurts you. Where does it hurt? No, that's all right, just rest. You can tell me later, or now, whatever you wish."

Brandy gulped down bile in her throat. The nausea was twisting her belly. She wouldn't vomit, she wouldn't. She tried to raise her hand to her head.

"For God's sake, Brandy, hold still." He forced her hand back to her side.

"I hit my head. It hurts."

"Yes, I'll just imagine it does. You've a lump growing here the size of an egg beneath this damned braid."

She cried softly and turned her face away. She wanted to vomit and she wanted to die. She didn't want him to see her doing either one.

"I don't know why the devil you must needs braid your hair so tightly. Not only does it make you look like a bloody little girl, it's got to be uncomfortable."

"It hurts," she said, knowing tears were filling her eyes, wishing she hadn't spoken.

"Then be quiet and I'll do something about it. I'll try not to hurt you more." Her single thick braid had long since come free of their pins. He picked up the end of the rope and began to pull it free. Damp, springy waves fell over his hands, and he smoothed down the deep ripples. Finally he finished his task, and Brandy breathed a small sigh as pressure from the heavy braid was eased away.

"Is that better? Yes, I can see that it is. Stop braiding your hair, Brandy. I don't like it braided except when you put it on top of your head." He turned away then and tossed several more clumps of peat into the smoking fire. Why had he said all that? It couldn't matter what she did with her damned hair.

The duke's words had floated gently over

Brandy's head, for she felt so near to retching that it required all her will not to succumb. Another wave of nausea passed and she could at last think a bit more clearly. She'd lied to him. She was a fraud, a sham. She had to tell him the truth before she died. "I lied to ye, Ian." She just looked at him, waiting for retribution.

"What did you say? You lied? Are you delirious, Brandy? Can you see me clearly? Tell me how many fingers I'm holding up."

"Ye needn't be a gentleman about it. It's my wretched pride, ye see, and now I have paid the full price. I'm going to die, but I didn't want to die with this on my conscience."

He frowned and unconsciously gathered a mass of her dark honey blond hair in his hand and smoothed it next to her face, off the filthy floor. "My mind isn't working properly. I promise I'll yell this poor roof down if you'll just tell me what you're talking about. Now, what is this about pride? Oh, yes, I'm not about to let you die, so you can stop harping on that."

"Ye don't know? What do ye mean ye don't know?" Surely something was wrong here. Surely he couldn't be blind to what she'd done. No, he was just being a gentleman, being kind to a miserable female.

He nodded slowly then, finally realizing what she must be talking about. He felt her mouth against his, then heard her angry words. She regretted it now, regretted kissing him, regretted pulling him down to her. He should have been relieved that she regretted it all, but instead he felt sorry at what could not be.

189

She gave a sigh, thinking that with Ian, confession was quite an easy matter. And she had been such a braggart. "Ye don't think less of me? Ye don't think I'm a bad person? Could you possibly forgive me?"

Dammit, why did she persist in pushing the matter? He said shortly, not looking at her, "Of course I don't think less of you. There's nothing at all to forgive." His conscience forced him to add, "You must know, Brandy, that it was as much my fault as it was yours. More my fault since I'm a man and, well, I'm older than you are, and more experienced in these matters. I should have exercised greater control."

"Nay, Ian, ye mustn't shoulder any of the blame. It was all my fault, for I didn't wish ye to know of my cowardice. I'm paying right now for my sin. But I might have hurt ye too, and that was unforgivable." If only he would rant, if just a little. Could he not shout at her just once, like Grandmama?

It dawned on him suddenly that their conversation was suspiciously like another held that long ago evening. At least this time it wasn't a matter of his standing in front of his leaking wooden tub stark naked. He laughed and lightly touched his hand to her cheek.

"I fear, little one, that we are again speaking at cross-purposes. We'll begin at the beginning. Now, what exactly do you mean with all this cowardice talk?"

"Oh," she said, remembering as well, "ye mean when ye were naked and I thought ye were talking about the London trip?" She looked up at him with such intensity that he felt himself quite naked once again.

"Stop thinking what you are thinking, Brandy. Just stop it."

"Very well, but I learned a lot that evening. I never before knew that a man could be so beautiful." She sighed.

"Cowardice?"

"Oh, all right. If ye must know, I've always been afraid of them. I think perhaps that one of the nasty beasts bit me when I was an infant. Cantor is a lovely horse, truly. It's just that horses make me want to back away from them, ever so slowly and quietly. They scare me to my toes."

"You're afraid of horses," he said, looking as blank as the poor walls of the hut. "Here I thought you a bruising rider. You didn't show a lick of fear when you ran Cantor right into me. My God, you rode him faster than the wind across that meadow. All that bravado, and that marvelous challenge of yours. That trick of nearly running me down—in truth, you couldn't stop Cantor?"

"Aye, I didn't want ye to think me just a silly twit. You're so *perfect* at everything, whilst I am—"

"Me, perfect? What utter rubbish. I have more than my share of failings. As to your so-called cowardice, I think rather you were quite brave, mayhap foolishly so." He paused a moment, drumming his fingertips on his knee. "I would never think any less of you just because you didn't like horses. Another thing, you don't have to prove your worth to anyone, do you understand?"

"Ye truly don't mind? Ye're not lying to me because ye feel sorry for me?"

"No, I don't feel sorry for you. I feel sorry that your head hurts. As for the other, forget it. If you never ride a horse again, it doesn't matter. Or perhaps if you'd allow me, I could teach you how to handle them. Horses can be dealt with, you know. You can talk to them, scold them, yell at them. They're usually good-natured. But you just think about it. I don't suppose you're going to confess to me now that you can't swim a stroke?"

"Nay, I'm certain to beat ye at that. Maybe. Well, I did beat Bertrand. It's true that he'd just recovered from a nasty fever, but I still beat him fair and square. You're only used to swimming in that measly lake of yours in Suffolk. What do you know of tides and currents and getting shoved into rocks?"

"Not much, but I'm a quick study."

She shivered suddenly and closed her eyes. She didn't look good. Rain was dripping in not three feet away from them. What the hell was he to do? He wasn't about to leave her.

"Is it your head, Brandy?"

"Aye, it hurts."

"I'm afraid to move you just yet. Just lie still and keep any more confessions to yourself. Besides, I don't think I'm up to any more of them."

She managed a slight smile. It made him feel better. She had guts. He hadn't realized until just this moment that he'd never been drawn to any female who had guts. He was used to softness and helplessness. He was used to gentle smiles

192

and gentle requests. He was used to being the strong one, the one who gave and supported. But here she was, lying in the middle of a rotted floor, looking as pathetic as a person could look, but she wasn't whining or crying.

"Well, the least I can do is get that wet jacket of yours off. Hopefully, your blouse will dry out closer to the fire."

When he gently drew her up into his arms to slip off her riding jacket, she went stiff as a board. "Hold still," he said, wondering what the devil was wrong with her. "Surely you're not afraid of me, not you. I have no intention of offending your modesty."

She sucked in her breath and thought she'd pass out. Please, God, she prayed, don't let him notice my bosom, please. She thought of the gaping buttons across her chest and felt near to tears. It was too much. He'd never admire her if he saw those cow breasts of hers.

He pulled off her jacket and frowned at the frayed white blouse. It was so very tight on her—she must have worn the riding habit since she was ten years old.

"There, is that better, Brandy? No, don't pull away. Just let me hold you. It'll keep you warm. I don't want you taking a chill."

"Ye're wet too, Ian." But she didn't move. Evidently he hadn't noticed anything, bless the saints. She shivered again, not with cold, and was rewarded when he drew her more tightly against him.

Quite unintentionally he dropped a light kiss on her hair. Brandy raised her hand and touched his cheek. Once again, quite unintentionally, he leaned down and kissed her soft mouth. She forgot her aching head, her blouse that gaped apart, and unhesitatingly parted her lips.

The gentleman made a last protest, only to lose to masses of silky, thick hair tangled in his hand and a warm mouth that kissed his chin, his cheek, his ear. He in turn kissed her forehead, her straight nose, and finally, God, finally, he found her mouth. He felt her fingers run through his damp hair, and heard her say his name. Just the way she said his name made him shudder with need.

He caressed her shoulder and throat before moving slowly to her breasts. He was thwarted by the layers of clothing. Damnation, so many clothes. He began to pull open the buttons on her blouse.

Oh, no, he wanted to touch her breasts. She pulled away from him, so embarrassed she forgot her aching head. She wanted to sink through the rotted floor. How could she tell him that he really didn't want to see her because if he did, he'd be repulsed?

Damn, he'd frightened her. Innocent—he kept forgetting how very innocent she was. He dropped his hand and drew a deep breath. He'd come very close to dishonoring her. He turned away from her, angry at himself for his loss of control. He was a rutting bounder, just like Percy.

She felt him withdraw from her. He didn't want her but rather that faceless lady who was to be his duchess. She pulled away from him and came up onto her knees. Her head hurt, but not so badly now. The nausea she could control. She smoothed down her hair and rose slowly to her feet. He made no move to hold her back.

He rose then and faced her. He felt like a prig, but he couldn't help himself as he said, "You must forgive me for being overly affectionate with you." Affectionate? Ha. "I didn't intend this. I suppose it's that we're here alone and I'm very worried about you." Yes, that was it, but he knew it wasn't, and he was a bigger blighter than Percy.

"Aye," she said. "Certainly. Of course. I'd like to return to Penderleigh. The rain has lessened."

"Very well. I'll lead Cantor. I want you to concentrate on keeping yourself in the saddle. No, I think I'll carry you back. I don't want to take any chances that you'll fall off."

That sounded wonderful to her. To be close to him for just a little while longer. She watched him stoop and pick up both of their damp jackets.

She turned her back to him as she shrugged hers back on. If he was surprised by that, she was grateful that he didn't say anything.

The ride back to Penderleigh wasn't as wonderful as she'd imagined it would be. He held her close, so close she could feel his heart beat, but every step Hercules took sent a shaft of pain through her brain.

Once back at Penderleigh, all the pandemonium handled smoothly by the duke, she was tucked into her bed by Marta, who scolded her, patted her, gave her small drinks of tea that had drops of laudanum in it, ordered undoubtedly by the duke.

It was kind of him, she thought even as she fell

into sleep, that he'd just told everyone she'd met with an unavoidable accident. Her last thought was that she never wanted to be on another horse's back for as long as she lived.

17

Brandy awoke early the next morning with a slight headache, ravenous hunger, and an urgent desire to speak to the duke. Crabbe raised a surprised face as she crossed the front hall and hurried toward the breakfast room.

"Surely ye shouldn't be out of yer bed, miss," he called after her. "Why, ye were as white as a mullet's craw yesterday."

"I'm fit as a new penny this morning, Crabbe. Is the duke about yet?"

"Nay, miss. He was up even earlier this morning. Off with Master Bertrand to Clackmannanshire, I believe. The Cheviot sheep, ye know. Aye, Penderleigh will be rich once again with the duke at the helm. Sheep—beautiful, woolly sheep that will bring more groats than we've dreamed about fer years. Rich, what a lovely thought."

Brandy couldn't remember a time when Penderleigh had been rich. The duke hadn't told her he was leaving today. She tried to hide her disappointment and walked ahead of Crabbe into the breakfast room. She served herself a large bowl of porridge, as Crabbe hovered like a clucking mother hen next to her.

"Master Percy also took his leave early this morning," he said, pouring another spoon of porridge into her bowl. "Honey, miss? Aye, surely ye want honey. It'll put the bloom back in yer young cheeks. Aye, Master Percy is gone, a good thing, I said."

"A good thing indeed," she said. "That's enough honey, thank ye. I wonder why he came in the first place. Just to cause mischief, I'll wager. But now he's gone again, so I won't think of him anymore."

"I know why he left, miss," Crabbe said, and she knew he was nearly frothing at the mouth to tell her. She was probably the only one who didn't know, since she'd been in her bed, deeply asleep with the laudanum Morag had given her.

She leaned close. "Can ye tell me, Crabbe? Is it all right?"

"Aye, I can tell ye, miss. Lady Adella ordered him to be gone last evening. Told him that she didn't want to see him again until he was no longer a bastard." Crabbe actually smirked as he added, "Leastwise as regards his name, she said. He didn't like that, I can tell ye, but he had no choice but to take himself off. I myself saw him out the front door."

"Then we've peace for a while. Did the duke say how long he would be gone?"

"Not long, Master Bertrand said. Indeed, they may even return today if all is in readiness for them. Master Bertrand said he didn't mind riding, even if it didn't gain them anything, since it was such a beautiful day."

He might return today, she thought, and

wanted to sing and smile at the same time. She ate her porridge instead.

Crabbe watched her eat for three minutes, then, satisfied, she supposed, that she wouldn't expire from her riding accident, he nodded and left the room. Brandy finished her porridge at a leisurely pace, her thoughts turning to Ian.

With the sheep purchased and on their way to Penderleigh, it wouldn't be long now before he went home to England. After what had happened yesterday, she knew that he would have to leave the complications that she had piled on his head. Well, he'd done some piling too, but she'd been the one to start it, and she knew it. She hadn't thought about any consequences, she'd just reacted to him, a man, the only man she'd ever known that she admired. More than that, she loved him.

It was that clear, that simple. It was also just as clear and just as simple that he was betrothed, and a gentleman didn't break an engagement to a lady. The other lady would have him. There was simply no hope for it. She was the interloper, the outsider. She was the one who'd behaved badly. The other lady was doubtless in London thinking fond thoughts of the duke, knowing that he would be her husband, trusting him, thinking of him just as Brandy was. She was right to love the duke, for Brandy knew that he would return to London and he would marry that lady.

She had to accept it. The only man she wanted she could never have. And rightfully so. She was nothing, a poor Scottish female with nothing to her name, not beauty, not money. While he was magnificent, everything she was not and would never be. She stared silently at her empty porridge bowl. Then, forcing a smile, she went to the nursery to fetch Fiona. She wanted to get away from the castle, with all of its prying eyes. She bundled up Fiona and took her to the small cove where her boat was moored.

It was late in the afternoon when she bore Fiona back to the castle, both of them damp with salt spray and windblown. There was a strange carriage standing at the front of the castle. Another one, older, the horses blown, drawn up behind it.

"Perhaps it is one of Grandmama's friends," she said to Fiona, and drew the child with her into the front entrance hall. Her feet suddenly froze to the ground at the sight of the most beautiful lady she had ever seen in her life. She was standing beside that first carriage, looking at Penderleigh. She was small, with a gloriously slender figure that made Brandy so jealous she wanted to howl. She was wearing a golden traveling gown that fit snugly under her normal-sized bosom and fell in straight lines to her delicately shod toes. This was how the gown Ian had bought her from Edinburgh should look. This lady's bosom wasn't falling out of the gown, not at all. She looked elegant, very confident, and well she should. Her black curls framed her face under a bonnet of matching gold straw with bunches of darker gold ribbons, glossy as a raven's wing. Her eyes were slightly slanted and a deep leaf green, fringed by thick black lashes.

Then to Brandy's surprise, she saw Ian come

around the side of the carriage. The lady held out both her hands to him. Brandy watched as he strode to her, took her hands, raised them, and kissed her fingers. Then the lady was speaking to Ian, laughing up at him, and he was smiling down at her. Brandy knew that the lady was the duke's betrothed. Actually, she'd known the first instant who she was. She'd felt it. The two of them looked like they belonged together, both elegant, both confident, both with a natural arrogance that seemed right. Suddenly the lady turned, as if sensing her presence, and gave a light trill of laughter.

She said in a loud, very clear voice, "Why, your grace, Scotland is indeed a strange country. But look, you allow your servants to enter through the front door. These are the front doors, are they not? It's difficult to tell since it all looks like a rather dismal pile of gray stones. That one turret over there is crumbling. I trust I won't have to go near it."

Why, that malicious bitch. She just lost some of her beauty and elegance in Brandy's eyes. Indeed, Brandy, who'd wanted for an instant to change places with that exquisite piece of womanhood, now wanted to smack her. Brandy's eyes flew to Ian's face. He was standing perfectly still. There was no expression on his face.

"Careful, my dear, you are sailing in uncharted water," another gentleman said in a silky smooth, almost mocking voice. He'd just stepped out of the carriage. He shook the duke's hand as he spoke. At any other time Brandy would have been sorely tempted to laugh at his outlandish costume, so many gold buttons and fobs were there on his coat and waistcoat. But instead she stood in wretched silence, her hand tightening painfully about Fiona's fingers, wanting to yell at the lady and knowing she couldn't. She was learning quickly that life could be the very devil.

"Brandy, ye're hurting me," Fiona cried, and tugged Brandy's arm. She released Fiona's hand as Ian stepped resolutely forward. Fiona ran to Ian and grinned shamelessly up at him, holding up her arms. Ian laughed and picked her up, lifting her over his head, shaking her and making her shriek with laughter.

"I must put you down now, Fiona. Ah, Brandy, I'm glad you're here. You're feeling better, aren't you?"

"Aye, I'm fine," she said shortly, not moving an inch toward him.

"I would like you to meet Lady Felicity Trammerley. Felicity, this is Brandy, the eldest of my female cousins. And this delightful bundle of enthusiasm is Fiona, my youngest cousin."

"Your cousins?" Felicity said blankly. "Both of these persons are your cousins?"

"That is what he said, Felicity," the other gentleman said.

"Well, then. How very delighted I am, to be sure," Lady Felicity said, only slightly inclining her graceful neck. So Brandy is the *different one*, she thought. Those were the duke's strange words in his letter to her. And she'd known, she'd known immediately, that there was danger here. Ah, but she'd been dead wrong. Different indeed. To think that she, an earl's daughter and an acclaimed beauty, could ever have imagined that the Duke of Portmaine could possibly be interested in such a disheveled, frowzy brat who dressed like a peasant and smelled like a fish. And he was holding that other little urchin as if he enjoyed it. It made her toes curl. How could he have forgotten so quickly who and what he was, and particularly what he owed to her, his future wife?

Brandy blurted out, "Fiona and I have been fishing."

"Aye," Fiona said as Ian set her back on her feet, "but we didn't catch anything because Brandy's head ached and she just wanted to sit in the boat and do nothing."

Contempt was plain in Lady Felicity's slanted eyes. She turned back to the duke. "All of this is very odd. My mother would never have allowed me to be out all day in a boat. So brown one becomes. It isn't healthy. It isn't proper. One becomes quite ugly."

Brandy's hands were fists at her sides. She was very close to damning everything to the devil and leaping on this miserable lady who was such a pain in the arse, as Uncle Claude would say, then cackle. How dare she act like she'd just come into a savage land and look at all the inhabitants as if they weren't fit to polish her boots?

The gentleman with all the fobs stepped forward. He said with faint amusement, "Brandy, is it? A quaint name, my dear, and charming. I am Giles Braidston, you know. Ian's *English* cousin."

Brandy didn't want to, but she dipped a curtsy.

He seemed nice, much more like Ian, but still, he'd come with this Felicity and she didn't trust him an inch. There were many ways to throw out insults.

"Are those buttons real gold?" Fiona demanded, a dirty hand already reaching out. "Ye look like one of those beautiful peacocks I saw once before Grandmama got angry with it and had Cook bake it for dinner."

"An accolade indeed. I hope I won't end up in Cook's baking pot like that poor peacock. You like these buttons, do you? Yes, they are real gold, and when you have clean hands you may touch them, all right?"

"I'll do it right now. Nice and clean, ye'll see." Fiona dashed away from them toward the stairs. "I'll be back in but a moment, sir. Ye'll not forget yer promise, will ye?"

He laughed and waved Fiona way. "I never forget anything," he called after her.

"Have you taken leave of your senses, Giles?" Lady Felicity said, a dark brow arched upward. "Given half a chance, she will probably tear them off your coat and chew on them. Goodness, she'll lose them."

Ian frowned. How could Felicity show such a want of manners? It was on the tip of his tongue to tell her to mind her tongue when he suddenly remembered his own first impressions of Penderleigh and Scotland. It was certainly not what Felicity was used to, and he admitted that it must all be quite a shock to her. She gazed up at him at that moment with melting eyes—Marianne's eyes—and he forced a smile.

Brandy saw that look and wanted to stuff her in that old rusted cannon and fire it and her off into oblivion. "Excuse me," she said to no one in particular, and walked quickly toward the stairs, trying as best she could to keep her back straighter than Grandmama's cane and her chin proudly in the air.

"So this is Penderleigh Castle, eh, Ian?" Giles said, breaking the brief tension. "At least you're not wearing kilts yet, old boy. No, still that severe style you insist upon. Ah, but it's a grand old pile, isn't it? When was it built, I wonder. It must be at least four hundred years old. Look at those turrets. Felicity's right. That one is about ready to crumble to the ground. Too bad it's not a seaward one; then it could just fall into the sea and not trouble anyone overly."

"Nay, Giles, no kilts for me just yet. I haven't the nerve, truth be told. But Bertrand, another cousin, informs me that I have the legs for the kilt."

"*Nay* and *kilts,* dear sir?" Lady Felicity said in a sweet voice that made Ian's belly turn sour. "I fear that if you do not speak English, I shall have difficulty understanding you."

The duke wished for many things at that moment, but uppermost was his desire to wave his hand and have Felicity and Giles magically gone, back in London. But it wasn't to be. He was their host. He thought of Lady Adella and winced. Oh, Lord, that was going to be something. "Do forgive me, my dear. I have told Crabbe—he's the Penderleigh butler—to inform Lady Adella of your coming. Come, let's go inside, although the day is glorious. Shall we go into the drawing room?"

Felicity said not another word. She followed Ian through the great old hall, eyeing those rusted suits of armor with some disbelief. She followed him finally into the drawing room. She said nothing until she allowed the duke to seat her in a faded old chair that was, she thought, a relic worthy of a servant's room.

"There, now we're all settled."

"We are?" Felicity said, then shut her mouth because Ian wasn't even looking at her. He was saying to Giles, "Now tell me, whatever are you doing here in Scotland? Surely such a journey has been very uncomfortable for Felicity. Good God, it's a six-day trip."

"Your betrothed missed you sadly, cousin," Giles said, and only Ian saw him roll his eyes heavenward. "Yes, very sadly. You know what I mean, surely. Well, perhaps you don't, but you will soon enough. I've enjoyed a rare treat for the past week. Soon it will be your turn. For the remainder of your days."

"I have been gone from London longer than I had originally anticipated," the duke said, waving away his words. He knew all the while that he could count on his left hand the number of times he'd even thought of London. "There has been much to occupy my attention. Bertrand and I have been to the Cheviot to purchase sheep, and, of course, there have been several trips to visit the various mills, you know." He ground to a halt, seeing that Felicity was staring at him in utter horror.

"What did you say, Ian? Cheviot sheep?"

"Good God, Ian, what a bore. My condolences, poor fellow. You see, dear Felicity, I was right in assuring you that Ian had not forgotten his obligations, that he just placed them elsewhere for the time being. What do you think of Cheviot sheep, my dear?"

18

Lady Felicity went rigid with anger. "You don't mean to tell me that you, a duke and a peer of the realm, have been playing at being a shepherd? You've actually bought sheep? Visited tradesmen? Toured mills?"

"Yes, certainly, and none of it was boring in the least," Ian said coolly. "You see, it's my intention to make Penderleigh self-sufficient. All the raw materials are here in abundance, all the labor we need, everything. All that was needed was capital."

"Indeed, I have to agree that there are certainly *raw* materials in abundance here," Felicity said sharply. She felt tired, dirty, totally put upon and frankly wished she could tell the duke what she thought of his absurd activities. Then she saw the duke's eyes narrow briefly in what she recognized as his autocratic, stubborn look, and quickly retrenched. God, she hated that look. Ah, but once they were wed, she'd see all those dreadful traits of his overcome. She'd smash them. She'd grind them beneath her slipper.

But now she had to soften her words, though it galled her to do so. "What I mean to say, my dear, is that I have missed you sorely and begrudge all the time you have spent away from me. Am I not allowed to miss the man I will marry?"

She was rewarded for her pretty speech with a smile. Ian didn't even hesitate. He said, "It's been difficult for me also, Felicity." He said nothing more. He wasn't stupid. He didn't want to dig a hole so deep he wouldn't be able to climb out of it.

Giles cleared his throat, then coughed ever so gently behind his hand. Ian turned to see Lady Adella walk in a most stately manner into the drawing room.

He rose quickly to his feet. "Lady Adella, I would like you to meet my cousin, Mr. Giles Braidston, and my betrothed, Lady Felicity Trammerley. They've come to pay us a visit."

Lady Adella gazed upon the dashing Giles and instantly liked what she saw. Now, this was a true gentleman. No grubbing about an estate for this one. She took in every elegant line of Lady Felicity's apparel and her well-bred countenance, and decided that Brandy could well learn style from living in the same house as this girl.

She nodded welcome down her long nose and allowed Giles to kiss her veined hand. "Most charmed, my lady," he said at his smoothest, which was very smooth indeed.

As she sailed past Lady Felicity, the girl gave

her a tight-lipped smile. What a ridiculous old relic, Felicity was thinking, lowering her eyes. That black gown was at least thirty years out of style, and the way she was wearing her hair. The abundant sausage curls made her look like she was wearing a wig that was very old and not well styled. Her fingers itched to pull on those sausages and see if it was a wig.

"So when do ye wed Ian?" Lady Adella asked Felicity without preamble.

"In August. At St. George's in Hanover Square."

"Ah. All hoity-toity. I approve. I'll allow ye some time for yer wedding trip afore I send Brandy to ye. How about October, Ian? Ye'll be back from yer wedding trip by then and ready to receive Brandy?"

Felicity's mouth fell open. She tried to speak, but no words came out. She just stared at her betrothed, wanting to scream at him. The duke at this particular moment appeared to find his cravat rather snug. Finally, Ian said, "Actually, Lady Adella, since Felicity has just arrived, I haven't yet had time to discuss the matter with her."

Giles said softly, "I can't imagine why in the world not, Ian. Felicity has been here for the better part of fifteen minutes, and has, old boy, made Brandy's acquaintance. Why the delay? It does give one cause to wonder."

Ian ignored Giles and rose. "Lady Adella, which bedchamber may Miss Trammerley use? She is fatigued from the journey and should rest before dinner."

Lady Adella nodded and bellowed, "Crabbe! Get yer stiff bones in here, ye old sot. We've guests and there's work for ye to see to."

Felicity shuddered. Her nostrils flared, a habit Ian had admired before but now he didn't like it a bit. She felt contempt for Lady Adella, for Penderleigh, and she was taking no pains to hide it.

"Aye, my lady?" Crabbe looked inquiringly at his mistress—ah, but he wanted to look at that glorious female creature who looked to be suffering the pain of the damned. As for the gentleman, he was a fop, along Master Percy's line, but perhaps more depth to him. Time would tell. Who were these people? Friends of the duke's doubtless. They looked all stiff in the lip.

"Have Marta prepare two bedchambers— mind ye, not Morag. We don't want our guests to wake up itching from that licy old trollop. Wait, Ian, put Lady Felicity in that lovely blue room just down the hall from yer master bedchamber. It'll suit her just fine. Crabbe, you pick a bedchamber for our pretty gentleman here, some-thing gay, something to keep his spirits lifted."

Ian swallowed a smile, nodded to Crabbe, and offered Felicity his arm. "Crabbe will see to you, Giles," he said over his shoulder as he escorted his betrothed from the drawing room.

Ian led a very silent Felicity to a guest chamber of an indeterminate shade of blue, down the corridor from his own bedchamber. Upon his initial inspection of all the rooms some time ago, he had thought the room rather plain in its furnishings, but not inferior. The paint wasn't peeling off the walls. It did look old and worn and there was charm, surely there was charm in that quaint old window seat, even more charm in that ancient armoire with its brass handles. He quickly told himself he'd been blind. He now saw it through Felicity's eyes. It wasn't a pretty sight. It was old and threadbare and shabby.

He chose to ignore her sharp intake of breath and asked, "Would you like a bath, my dear?" It immediately occurred to him that he must ensure that she was not beset by either Wee Albie or the leaking wooden tub.

She nodded, tight-lipped. "That would be fine, Ian. It has indeed been a long trip and quite fatiguing." She added smoothly, "You mustn't worry about the proprieties, my dear duke, for my abigail was with me."

"I wish you'd written me of your intent to come here. How many servants did you bring?"

"Only Maria and Pelham, Giles's valet. Surely there is room in this beastly castle for them."

"Certainly," he said, and that word came out a sharp snap. He pulled out his watch and consulted it. "Dinner is served at six o'clock, my dear. The family meets in the drawing room shortly before that time."

"That's much too early, Ian. Why, at home we don't dine until eight. Surely—"

"You're not at home. You're in Scotland. You're at Penderleigh. Lady Adella has been the mistress here for more years than your mother has been on this earth. This is what she wishes. Thus, this is what is done. Now, I will see to your bath." He turned to leave, looking toward the door with great fondness.

"Ian, whatever did that wretched old woman mean about Brandy coming to London? Surely you don't intend for me to take that dowdy child about in *English* society?"

"Brandy is not a child. She will be nineteen in the fall. As to her appearance, why, she spends a great deal of time out of doors. She loves to fish and to swim and to be in her boat."

"You expect me to turn that one into a lady?"

She was incredulous. Ian wanted to shake her. His voice was as cold as his father's used to be when he was angered. "She is already a lady, Felicity. Contrive to remember that she's an earl's granddaughter. As to her appearance, I daresay that a proper wardrobe will solve that problem."

"I suppose that I shall have to watch her boating about in the Thames, or perhaps she can go to Astley's Circus and ride on the backs of those show horses."

"I have said all that is important," he said, and he knew he sounded cold as a fish on ice. "Now, if you're finally through criticizing everything and everyone, I will have your bath fetched."

Felicity raged silently until he was out of her bedchamber. Then she smashed her fist against the counterpane on the bed. A cloud of dust rose up. She sneezed. Dear God, what kind of horrible place was this? She paced the length of the bedchamber. How dare he dismiss her feelings? How dare he treat her as one of no importance at all? She tore off the stylish bonnet set atop her black curls and hurled it into a faded brocade chair. She paced the length of the dismal little room again and again until her anger calmed. There was not, after all, any reason for her to be so upset. What did it matter that the duke was being particularly obnoxious? She could deal with him. She would pretend and cajole and he would smile and she would win. Oh, yes, she would win in the end.

Ah, but what to do about that utterly disgusting girl? Nearly nineteen, was she? Well, she didn't look it, thank God.

After the duke had asked Crabbe for Felicity's bath water, he made his way back downstairs to the drawing room. He drew up at the open doorway to see Giles sitting close to Lady Adella. That lady, it appeared to him, was captivated by his cousin. He heard Lady Adella give a creak of delighted laughter. "Aye, indeed, my boy, old Charles had quite a reputation in those days. Ye'll not believe what he did to the minister's wife. What was her name? Oh, aye, it was Clorinda. That's it. Clorinda, and he stripped her to her naked hide right in the stable and pinned her next to her mare. Everyone spoke of it. She came away with straw in some very uncomfortable places. Aye, old Charles was an out-and-out rotter. A fine piece of man he was." She cackled just like Claude. So that was where Claude had gotten that irritating habit of his.

Ian walked forward. "You must excuse me, Lady Adella, but I must take Giles upstairs. Else he will never achieve his exquisite appearance by dinnertime."

She gave a grunt of disappointment. "Very

well, lad, if ye must. We've plenty of time, I suppose." She waved a bony hand toward Giles. "Sharpen yer wits, my boy. It's fifty years worth of gossip I'll want from ye. Ah, to have ye here is gratifying."

"I shall do my pitiful best, my lady, to gratify you completely," Giles said in that smooth voice of his that always held just a hint of laughter, and followed Ian from the room.

"Fancy that," Giles said as they climbed the stairs. "She knew old Lord Covenporth. Killed himself with womanizing and drink, you know. His grandson, Aldous, is treading much the same path, I fear. He'll run out of his pleasures soon enough, for Coven Manor is heavily mortgaged and the better part of it is entailed. Ah, well, up until a year ago he was quite a good sport. Now he whines even though his misfortunes are his own fault."

The duke grunted, wondering to himself why Giles seemed to prefer such a set of rakehell men.

Giles drew to a halt at the top of the landing to look back down at the old hall. "Dear me, Ian, what an outlandish place, to be sure. There isn't much here to remind one of Carmichael Hall, is there?"

Ian thought of his huge, sprawling estate in Suffolk, with its forty bedrooms and indecently large ballroom, and shook his head. "I should have to say, perhaps, that Penderleigh is more quaint. It's alive with history and tradition, Giles, and I think even you will admit that the view toward the sea is breathtaking. Certainly there is none of the filth and smut of London here, none of the cutthroats, none of the gaming hells, none of the excesses that fill everyone's craw."

Giles cocked an incredulous brow but said only, "I'm certain you are right in your opinion. Well, I'm not really certain at all, but it's what you want to see, thus that's what it is. You're the duke, after all, and everything should order itself up to your wishes."

"You're fuller of nonsense than Morag is of lice. Or maybe it's ticks. I'm not certain."

"Oh, God, that's a hideous thought. Ticks? Lice? Please, Ian, I'll do anything you wish, just keep that woman away from me."

The duke laughed. As Ian shepherded Giles to his bedchamber, in the opposite direction from his own, he asked, "Now, Giles, just what the devil do you mean by escorting Felicity here? You know I wanted her to remain in London. This is no place for her. She doesn't like it, and I don't imagine that she will ever come to like it. Why, damn you? Why?"

"Don't blame me, Ian, I beg of you. It was your damned letter that quite set her mind to it. Actually, I had little choice in the matter. You told me to be her escort. What the hell was I to do?"

"My what?"

Giles shook his head, a ghost of a smile playing about his mouth. "Your letter, Ian. Lord, never have I seen you set so many glowing words on paper. That chit Brandy found herself the subject of much too many sentences. Jealousy fairly dripped from dear Felicity's lovely eyes. Indeed"—he paused, casting a warning look at his cousin—"were I you, Ian, I would think twice, even three or four times, about leg-shackling myself to such a termagant. She isn't what you think she is, Ian."

"I trust, Giles, that you didn't encourage Felicity in such an outrageous opinion. You, of all people, should know that I would never turn my back on my obligations. As for Brandy, I am the girl's guardian, and as such I intend to do what is best for her. When she comes to London, Felicity will treat her with kindness. She will do all that is suitable. There is nothing more to be said."

"Rest assured, old boy, that I in no way encouraged Felicity's thinking. Indeed, I found myself forced to be an unwilling recipient of her venom all the way to Scotland." He drew to an alarmed halt as Ian opened the door to his bedchamber.

"Good God, I do hope that you will tell me that this is where you expect my valet to sleep."

"Dammit, Giles, I simply haven't had the time to see to the refurbishment of the castle. This room is perfectly adequate, and I've already suffered similar observations from Felicity. You are snobs, the both of you. Since you're here, though, I would be quite happy to allow your artist's talents full rein. Not that I'll listen to you, necessarily, but it will give you something to do other than pander to Lady Adella's lascivious side."

"I would be hard pressed to know just where to begin," Giles said, dusting off a chair top with the tail of his coat. "This place needs more than just my excellent taste, not that my taste isn't an excellent place to begin. It needs an army of carpenters, an army of furniture warehouses, a battalion of—"

"Shut up, Giles, and stop your jabs. I don't care what you do. Order that valet of yours—old stiffnecked Pelham—to turn your room into proper form. If you must know, my Mabley is quite enjoying himself now, after his initial shock."

Giles sighed in gentle suffering and walked to the window. "No wonder it's so devilish damp. The place is very nearly hanging into the sea. To think that I let that ice maiden talk me into coming here. I wanted to say no, I begged her to reconsider, but do you know what she said?"

19

"No, what did she say?"

"She went on and on about wishing to see your new estate, how you must miss her dreadfully, and that she wanted very much to make you happy and the only way to do that was to present herself in front of you." He shook his head. "I don't believe that, of course. It all had to do with Brandy, as I told you. Believe me, Ian, she's an ice maiden."

"Ice maiden? I thought she was a termagant."

"Unfortunately, I believe that dear Felicity is both. If I do not miss my guess, she will be all ice and coldness at night and a termagant boiling

216

with acrimony during the day." He brushed a speck of dust from his coat sleeve and added softly, "Poor Ian, she is not at all like Marianne, you know." He ignored the tightening of his cousin's lips and the rush of color to his cheeks. "Much the same looks and appearance, I grant you. Of course, if you wish to make a marriage of convenience—"

"You go too far, Giles," the duke said, his hands fisted at his sides. "Marianne has been dead these six years. She has nothing to do with anything. As to Felicity's character, either during the night or the day, I think you must grant that I am in a much better position to judge than are you."

"Don't call me out at dawn, Ian. Undoubtedly you are quite right, but then, you have never spent the better part of a week with her."

"Giles, you're goading me to the point of planting my fist in that beautiful face of yours. Not another word. Just believe me. All Felicity needs is a firm hand, and, as I have told you before, she will do my bidding."

"You make her sound like some sort of filly to break to bridle." He looked as if he would say more, but only shrugged. "Have you been much in the company of Felicity's brother, Lord Sayer?"

"He's a gambler, something of a womanizer, I hear, but an excellent horseman. I don't dislike him. He strips well in the ring and shows a good account of himself. Like your friend Aldous, he doesn't whine. Why?"

Giles shivered delicately and regarded his

beautifully manicured nails. "I find him rather indelicate, rather outspoken, mayhap vulgar."

"Why? Because he doesn't wear gold buttons the size of saucers?"

"I don't think it's particularly smart of you, Ian, to draw attention to your own lack of style," Giles said, and the laughter was clear in his eyes and in his voice.

The duke threw up his hands. "Damn you, Giles, stop tossing around those damned barbs of yours. Lord, but you and Percy will have a fine time of it."

"Percy? Who is this? Another Scottish relative?"

"He's a bastard," Ian said, and grinned like a fool. At Giles's arched brow, he added, "His father, now dead, was one of Lady Adella's two sons. Percy was born on the wrong side of the blanket but is in the midst of becoming legitimate at this very moment."

"Good Lord," Giles said, rubbing his hands together, "and here I thought I was going to be bored down to my toenails."

"Ah, here's Pelham. I'll see that Wee Albie sends up your bath." The duke laughed again. Why the devil was that so funny? Giles wondered as he stared after his departing cousin.

When the duke finally reached his own bedchamber, he looked about the large, gloomy room. He doubted it had ever looked inviting or warm or cozy. It was quite different from his magnificent suite of rooms at Carmichael Hall, but in his opinion, even in its current dilapidated condition, it wasn't all that bad. He caught himself wondering idly what Brandy would think about his ducal residence—and in the next moment walked over to a wooden chair and kicked it violently toward the fireplace.

Mabley came bustling into the room, saying, "We mustn't dawdle, your grace. You know how particular Lady Adella is about gathering in the drawing room before dinner. Crabbe told me that once a visitor was only twelve minutes late and Lady Adella had Crabbe dump his plate over his head at the dining table."

"No," Ian said, "we don't want haggis dripping down our necks." He eyed the bald head and cherubic face, and found himself smiling at how Mabley seemed to have settled in.

"Do with me what you will, Mabley. I'm in your hands. The only favor I ask is that you please not make me as grand as Giles."

"I should think not, your grace. My, my, whatever happened to this chair, I wonder?"

Brandy shook her fist toward Felicity's bedchamber as she paced the threadbare carpet in her room. How dare that fine English lady call her a servant? Damnable twit, aye, that's what she was, a twit. How could Ian ever bear her? No, she didn't want to think about that. Call her a servant, would she?

She halted in front of her mirror and felt all her anger collapse in on itself. She looked like a crofter, no doubt about it. Her hair was knotted and wind-whipped all about her face, face and hands sticky with salty seawater. She smelled a strong whiff of her own fishy scent. Oh, dear, it was too much.

Constance chose that moment to dance into her room in a state of nearly incoherent excitement. "Brandy, I got a glimpse of her. Did ye see her gown and that gorgeous bonnet? And so small she is. I felt the perfect clodpole just being near her. Why, she can't possibly even reach Ian's shoulder. And her hair, it's even a purer black than mine, and those green eyes of hers, as pure as the moss down at Slanaker's forest."

"I didn't see anything so very special about her," Brandy said.

It wouldn't have mattered if Brandy had compared this new goddess to a rut in the road, for Constance took no notice at all. "Ah, and that gentleman—Giles Braidston. He's so elegant, so very fashionable, far more so than the duke. Grandmama told me that he's Ian's cousin, and even though she called him a gossiping fellow in that sour way of hers, I could tell she was impressed. Ugh—fish. Brandy, do ye wish to disgust our guests? Ye look and smell like a fishmonger's wife. Goodness, do take a bath. I do wonder if my new gown—the green one—is stylish enough for Lady Felicity's taste."

She dashed to Brandy's mirror and peered closely at her black curls. For the first time she noticed that her sister was very quiet, just standing there, her fists at her sides, staring at nothing in particular. Constance frowned, her brows drawing together. "Ah," she said. "Her coming here distresses ye, doesn't it, Brandy?"

"Why should I care where she goes? But I will

tell you something, Connie. She's a rude bitch. You think she'll be polite to you? I doubt it. She thinks she's above all of us. She thinks we're crude and savage."

"Perhaps all that is true," Connie said slowly, studying her sister's face. "But she's also going to marry the duke. Even if she dripped charm, even if she called you the prettiest lass alive, I can't imagine ye liking her."

"That's drivel and ye know it, Connie. It will always be drivel. I'll thank ye to forget what ye just said. No one would like to hear it."

Constance shrugged. "As ye will. It doesn't make any difference to me. Ah, Brandy, ye might try wearing the new gown Ian bought for ye." Brandy didn't say a word. "I must go. I think I'll have Marta do something special with my hair." She was humming an English ballad as she left Brandy's bedchamber.

After Constance left her, Brandy thought a moment about the beautiful velvet gown and dismissed it with a sigh that bordered on fatalism. Ian would be sure to think her a perfect cow, with her bosom sticking out as it would in that dress. She was so unlike the petite, exquisitely slender Felicity, damn her eyebrows. She gazed toward the closed door. Had she been so obvious in her feelings that even Connie had seen them? Evidently so. She would have to be much more careful.

After biding her time for a good hour until a tub was free for her use, she managed to convince herself that the famed Robertson pride—at least it was famed according to Lady Adella—must see her through this evening. She arranged her long hair in the Grecian style, pointedly ignored the lovely velvet gown, and yanked down a waisted green muslin. She added the crowning touch of her mother's faded shawl, drawing it closely over her breasts, and forced her feet downstairs.

Felicity, after driving her maid to distraction with conflicting orders and demands, finally achieved a result that pleased her, and walked down the wretchedly dim corridor downstairs to the drawing room. She knew that she was some minutes late, but she didn't care, for she was determined not to let Ian dictate to her. It was best to begin as she meant to go on. She would bow to his wishes when it seemed to be in her best interest to do so. This wasn't one of those wishes. She would have preferred eating in her bedchamber, but she doubted there was any such thing as a tray in this pile of stone.

Ian gave her a slight nod, his look not particularly loving, and made brief introductions to Claude, Bertrand, and Constance. Felicity looked closely at Constance, for this girl, unlike her sister, gave the impression of budding beauty, with her carefully coiffed black hair and her green dress. Yes, she was lovely and just might be beautiful in a couple of years. Why that dowd Brandy? It made no sense to Felicity. Then she got the shock of her short life.

"Ye're late," Lady Adella said, not mincing matters, guest or not, "and I, for one, don't like my haggis cold. Ye'll not do this again, or ye won't like the consequences. Give me yer arm, my boy," she said to Giles and stuck out an arthritic hand.

Felicity wanted to shriek at the crude old lady, but she knew it wouldn't serve her well. She merely nodded, saying nothing. When the duke drew her arm through his, she looked up at him from beneath her lashes. Surely he would condemn the old lady's rudeness and believe Felicity the epitome of tolerance. No, there was no smile for her, curse him. He was angry with her for being late. Well, he would get over it soon enough. She would smile at him, perhaps tease him a bit. But he did look stern, withdrawn even, and so very severe in those black, even clothes of his.

She'd spent a week with the laughing, stylish Giles. Ian was nothing like his cousin. A pity. She shuddered delicately, her eyes drawn to his large hands, to the long fingers, blunted at the tips. She thought of him touching her. She shuddered again.

As Ian seated her at the long dining table, he said mildly, "You must see that it's important to Lady Adella that everyone is punctual for dinner. I trust you will pay more attention to the clock in the future, if for no other reason than to avoid her sharp tongue. And also those vague consequences she threatened you with. Though if it's boiling oil, I'll try to make her select a milder punishment." He'd meant it as a mild jest, to lessen the tension between them, but she didn't even look at him. Would she be in a snit all night? He drew a deep breath and waited.

He waited a few more moments, just stood there, but Felicity said nothing at all.

No smiles for him just yet, she was thinking, and so she ignored him and turned her attention to Lady Adella, who was saying to Giles, "Tell me more about Dudley, my lad. Ye know I fancied myself in love with his grandfather once, the old scoundrel. I heard that he ran aground against Fox—one never went against Fox and came away unscathed—and was forced to burrow away for two years in his country estate in Kent."

Giles willingly cudgeled his memory, but as the event described happened before his entrance into the world, he was forced to dwell upon the grandson. "A dull sort of chap, my lady, turned squire in a corner of Kent, and has quite half a dozen brats hanging onto his coattails. No wickedness of the grandfather in him, it would seem, just dull, mundane life for him."

He sent a wicked look toward Ian and added, "Much like our Ian here, I fear, perfectly content to ignore his ducal advantages and consequence, and trudge over his acres. Admit it, Ian, you scorn town life, and if you have your way"—this said with a pointed look toward Felicity—"you'll want closer to a dozen brats. From the size of him, Lady Adella, I'll bet he'll breed giants, all just as sturdy as those oak trees on his property. Yes, at least a dozen, more's the pity for his wife."

"You know I can't pick you up and throw you into the haggis, Giles," the duke said. "But I just might sneak into your bedchamber and toss you out the window onto that cannon below." He grinned as he spoke, then turned quite serious, looking at Felicity. "Though I must admit that I do prefer country life. I love to fish in Carmichael Lake and give Cook the trout to bake for my supper. I enjoy racing my horses across the eastern meadows and shooting pheasant in the maple forest. There are Roman ruins to explore and an old abbey that Henry VIII destroyed in the sixteenth century. There is peace and quiet there and history that won't fall into meaningless rubble it would in the filth and destruction of London. And if I could be assured of half a dozen little Fionas, I would most willingly populate Suffolk with my offspring."

Felicity dropped her fork into the mess of unnameable food that was on her plate. She stared at Ian. She shook her head. She said, "Ian, surely you are joking, yes, you must be. The country is wonderful when it is snowing and Christmastime. It's most satisfying to ride out in a sleigh to find the best yule log. But who cares about those silly ruins? About that spider-filled old pile of rocks that was once an abbey? Ah, and the most important thing. I can't imagine anything more vulgar and common than redheaded children."

She sat back in her chair and smiled at every-one.

20

Brandy clutched her wineglass and said in the coldest voice Ian had ever heard from her, "My little sister is not vulgar, Lady Felicity. Vulgarity, I think, is that quality in people that makes them quick to hurt others' feelings. It is that quality that shows they have no manners, probably little breeding as well, and not enough brain to hide their meanness in honeyed words."

Felicity forced a laugh that held no mirth. "Miss Robertson, I meant no insult. After all, your dear little sister is your fishing companion, isn't she?"

Ian said sharply, "Fiona is many things, Felicity. I think, though, that Brandy regards her more as her own child rather than her sister— her wee bairn, as we would say in Scotland."

"Wee bairn, your grace? All these strange words *ye* for *you* and *wee* for *small,* I vow I'm in a foreign country. Do contrive to speak English, I beg of you."

"You are in a foreign country," Brandy said. "We speak Scottish here. Shouldn't you contrive to speak our language instead of us trying to speak yers?"

Claude, who hadn't bothered to attune himself to any unpleasant undercurrents, said with his grating cackle, "I daresay ye're quite right, Lady Felicity. For a lady such as yerself, we must all mind our speaking and treat ye in the manner in which ye're accustomed. It's Scotland, aye, but ye're our guest."

Felicity searched for sarcasm in this speech, found none, and decided that perhaps this one Robertson—old and toothless though he was—saw true worth when he saw it. She nodded graciously to Claude. How dared that brat accuse her of not having a brain?

Lady Adella, however, kept the pot boiling. "So ye don't like the distraction of town life, eh, Ian? I hope I can count on ye for one season to launch my Brandy into the *ton*."

Lady Felicity said coldly, "I fear, Lady Adella, that his grace and I intend a rather extended wedding trip. Have you no suitable relatives in, say, Edinburgh? Surely, such society as Edinburgh offers would be more to her liking and more suited to her abilities."

Giles looked sharply at Felicity, saw the mulish set of her mouth, and shrugged. He looked beneath his lids at Brandy. Surely Felicity couldn't have noticed those ridiculously huge amber eyes. At least he thought the color was amber. In this dim light they looked amber. Actually, it was a romantic light, he thought, all the shadows in the huge room soft and vague, all the harsh lines smoothed out.

No, Felicity hadn't really looked beyond Brandy's clothes to what she really was, and that was a beauty and a girl with a tongue in her mouth that wasn't as poisonous as a snake's, except when one she loved was attacked. So Felicity didn't have enough brain to hide her meanness.

227

Brandy was right about that, at least some of the time. At other times, Giles had to admit that Felicity could charm the bagpipes off a poor musician. And that's what she managed to do—usually—to Ian.

"Nay, I won't want Edinburgh for Brandy," Lady Adella continued serenely, seemingly oblivious of Felicity's insult. "What with Ian providing the girl with a proper dowry, and she being, after all, part English, I wish her to find a suitable husband in London. She's an earl's granddaughter. She'll have money. She can look as high as she wishes."

"What about me, Grandmama?" Constance said, leaning forward, looking ready to go into battle.

Claude grinned widely and poked Bertrand in the ribs. "We have other plans for ye, my lass. Ye need have no worry about yer future. Be that not right, Bertie?"

"There is a proper time and place for most things, Father," Bertrand said, his voice as stiff as his back had just become. "I find that ye have missed on both counts. I'll thank both ye and Lady Adella to let me mind my own affairs."

He avoided Constance's look of sheer confusion and gave his attention to his haggis, which didn't taste quite as good as it had. Connie had no idea about how he felt about her. Well, she was young. She was skittish. She was just learning how to be a female. He loved to watch her try out her tricks, except on Percy, the bloody sod. The good Lord knew too that he loved to watch her change and grow, say silly things, then look thoughtful and say something that made him very proud of her. She needed time. She didn't need any prodding from Lady Adella or his damned father, curse the two of them.

"Just see that the hair on yer head isn't gray by the time ye make up yer mind, lad," Lady Adella said, and waved her fork at him.

Ian said in a lovely, soothing voice that spread calm on the raging waters, "I find that Bertrand always shows remarkable good sense." The duke added quickly, seeing Cook's attempt at trifle nearing the table, "It's been an excellent dinner, but Cook outdid herself. It's my wish that we save dessert for later and adjourn to the drawing room."

Brandy gave him a small wicked smile that curled his toes. "But, Ian, trifle is such an English dish. Are ye certain ye have no wish to try it? Didn't ye tell me how much ye loved it the other time Cook prepared it just for ye?"

His toes uncurled. He smiled, a smile that promised retribution. "I doubtless said everything you've attributed to me. Now, why don't you assist Lady Adella to the drawing room?"

"Aye, commander," she said under her voice, but not under enough. He received unexpected assistance from Giles, who rose and began solicitous removal of Lady Adella. "Why don't we all go, Ian? The sooner we retire to the drawing room the better, old boy. I don't think the gentlemen have anything worthwhile to say by ourselves. Your cane, my lady. Now, where were we? Ah, yes . . . Dwyer. Do you remember that old curmudgeon, Viscount Dwyer, my lady?"

229

"Dwyer, Dwyer," Lady Adella repeated slowly. "Can't say that I do, my boy," she finally admitted, the furrows in her brow deepening in disappointment.

"It doesn't matter, my lady," Giles said smoothly, "he really isn't worth the bother." Actually, to the best of Giles's knowledge, there was no Viscount Dwyer. Ian caught his eyes, his own holding a warning, but Giles ignored him. He was having a jolly time.

"I say, my boy," Lady Adella said, once she was settled in her chair in the drawing room, "why don't ye tell me about yer own family, and the duke's? I know my sister's daughter married a regular sawed-off little creeper, and I'd like to know how Ian gained his giant's body."

"Mayhap your sister's daughter played the little creeper false, my lady."

Lady Adella chortled, and Brandy was relieved that her grandmother's mouth wasn't full of food. It was a chortle in Claude's best tradition. She turned and gave Giles a light buffet on his immaculate shoulder.

Brandy, who couldn't bear to see Ian assist Felicity into a chair—as though she were some sort of helpless baby, she thought with a silent snort—inched closer to Giles and her grandmother and asked, "Seriously, Giles, we know so little of yer family. Ian hasn't ever spoken of them—"

"What? He doesn't speak of his splendid antecedents? What gall."

Brandy saw that his eyes were mocking, even though he was smiling widely at his cousin. "Our

230

illustrious head of the family hasn't even bothered to tout his proud lineage a little bit? I say, Ian," he called to his cousin, "you leave it to me to puff up your consequence. Very well, I'll do it if I must."

"Puff away, Giles," the duke said, "but don't bore the ladies until they fall into their teacups."

Felicity didn't like the fact that the duke—he was a duke, for God's sake—joked about his famous family. It wasn't proper. It was nearly sacreligious. "Really, your grace, how can you make light of your noble ancestors? They fill the pages of our history books. They've won battles, they were ministers to kings, they were in politics, they bought beautiful properties and—"

"Yes, and bought boroughs too, doubtless," Ian said. "Yes, they wouldn't flinch at buying votes for those toadies who licked their collective boots. Of course, most of them were in the House of Lords, and so they didn't have to spend any groats. They simply bored everyone to death with their speeches."

Brandy said in the sweetest, falsest voice he'd ever heard, "Aye, Ian, to be such a vaunted peer of the realm is no mean thing. I swear I wouldn't be bored hearing a speech from one of your grand ancestors. And I'm quite ready to be suitably impressed, that is, as soon as Giles has seen to Grandmama's creature comforts."

Felicity snapped to like a lieutenant. "I would have you know, Miss Robertson, that the Carmichael family has a noble and proud lineage. Pure *English*, mind you, not tainted with any foreign blood."

"How quickly you forget the Comte and Comtesse de Vaux, my dear," Giles said in a voice of pure silk that slid over his listeners.

"Giles!" The duke was furious.

Brandy stared at him. Still, she couldn't help herself. "Who were the de Vaux, Giles?"

"I've been silenced. That's for our dear duke to answer, Brandy, not I."

Felicity said with finality, "I for one, Giles, don't see what difference the de Vaux made. After all, they added no French blood to the Portmaine line."

"Quite so, my dear," Giles agreed, and withdrew his snuff box from his flora waistcoat pocket.

"Brandy," the duke said suddenly in his commander's voice, "go and play for us. I want to hear a Scottish ballad."

Her eyes flew to his face only to see that he was looking at Giles, and he wasn't pleased. She was too startled at this odd turn of events to refuse.

She sang a sad Robert Burns ballad, but earned at the end of her endeavors only Miss Trammerley's sniffing comment: "How difficult it is to enjoy a song when one can't understand the words."

Brandy was thwarted in discovering more of Ian's family and the mysterious de Vaux, for Felicity rose with a delicate yawn and prettily begged the duke to escort her to her room. "The corridor is so very dark, your grace, I fear I will lose my way. I might even trip over one of those uneven boards. There are probably rusty nails sticking up. The carpet is so frayed that a body

232

has to be very careful. Yes, please come with me."

"I wish she would break her ankle," Constance whispered to Brandy with a goodly dose of malice.

"Oh, no, Connie," Brandy whispered back. "If she broke her ankle, just think how long she'd stay. We'd probably have to wait on her."

Claude rose painfully on his gouty foot and gallantly kissed Lady Felicity's hand.

"Don't be an old fool, Claude." Lady Adella snorted, a low, deep sound that everyone but Giles and Felicity were used to. Both of them jumped and stared, but Lady Adella didn't notice. "Lady Felicity certainly has no wish for yer arthritic attentions."

Lady Felicity evidently didn't agree, for she smiled as graciously as a queen whose subject had just pleased her at Claude, who then preened like a peacock. She bade vague good nights to the company in general and left, her slender white hand through Ian's arm.

The duke was annoyed. He didn't like being annoyed, and so when he spoke to Lady Felicity, he didn't soften his voice as he normally would have with her.

"As much as it must please me to see you," he began as he escorted his betrothed up the stairs, "your manners have been sorely wanting this evening."

Lady Felicity felt every bit as annoyed as the duke. She sucked in her breath and gritted her teeth against unladylike curses. It was hard, but she kept her tongue behind her teeth. He was in one of those moods of his.

The duke continued, "I realize all this must be very strange to you, but you must make a push to be pleasant. It won't kill you to just be nice to everyone, not to complain, not to criticize everything and everyone. You'll only be here a short time. Surely that isn't too much to ask."

It was too much. She forgot everything her mother had taught her and screeched, "Pleasant!" She turned on the huge, altogether too dark man who was to be her husband, and said with sarcasm dripping off her tongue, "How very *easy* it is to be pleasant in this moth-eaten household. And how very *pleasant* you make it, your grace, with your talk of populating Suffolk with a dozen brats like that hideously vulgar child Fiona. Indeed, what a *pleasant* thought it is picturing myself as some sort of breeding mare locked away in that huge mausoleum, Carmichael Hall. If you ever believe I would give up London life, you sorely mistake the matter, your grace."

"Are you saying, Felicity, that you don't wish to bear my children?" Her eyes unconsciously flitted over him, and he sensed her distaste of him. He was a large man, but surely she must know that he wouldn't hurt her, particularly in bed. He'd been so gentle with Marianne. Surely she must know—perhaps she didn't. Perhaps she was just frightened, as a virgin should be.

"You've said quite a lot there," he said, not knowing whether he wanted to throw her down the stairs or reassure her that he would go easily with her. No, he had to have an answer. "Don't you want to have my children, Felicity?"

She wasn't a fool. She splayed her hands in front of her and drew a measured breath. "What a ridiculous question. I'm overtired, yes, that's it. It was a long trip. I need a good night's sleep."

"Yes, certainly," he said, and opened the door to her bedchamber, calling on the same tolerance he had always given to Marianne. He'd been too harsh with her this evening, and now he regretted it. It wasn't well done of him. All that she'd said during the evening, well, it was simply that she was very tired. Surely he had to understand that. He smiled down at her, but didn't touch her.

"I will see you in the morning," he said, and left her.

21

The nursery overlooked the front drive at Penderleigh. It was from this vantage point that Brandy watched the duke toss Felicity, dressed in an exquisite blue velvet riding habit, onto Cantor's back. She felt close to choking with jealousy, for Felicity sat tall and straight in the saddle, quite at her ease, the perfect horsewoman who would never flinch or fall off. Aye, she was very elegant and self-assured, the perfect mate for the duke, the *English* duke, not some ragtag Scottish excuse for a peer's granddaughter. She knew she had to stop this. But Felicity was riding Cantor,

Brandy's horse, her precious horse that she could have been killed riding. The chapters in this book were clearly written, the last scene not to be changed. She had to give it up. Brandy turned away to resume Fiona's lessons.

This morning Brandy laid aside the ponderous tome of Brandenstone's history of Scotland and instead unearthed a crinkled map of England and set Fiona to the task of locating Suffolk. She enjoyed torturing herself. That was her only explanation.

"Suffolk," Fiona said, rendering the word magically Scottish. "Where is Suffolk, Brandy?"

"It's a country in England, poppet, where Ian lives when he's not in London. He has a country estate there, called Carmichael Hall. There's a lake on his land. He swims in that lake." She pictured him coming out of that lake not wearing a stitch of clothes, wet and shaking himself, just as he'd been that evening she'd burst into his bedchamber and seen him wet and naked from his bath. Oh, dear, she had to stop this.

"Och," Fiona said, "that's his ducal residence." Fiona ran a stubby finger down the eastern side of England.

"Good heavens, poppet, wherever did ye hear that?"

"Grandmama," Fiona said, her concentration still on that map of England. "Brandy," she said, looking up. "What's a ducal?"

Brandy threw back her head and laughed aloud. "Oh, poppet," she said merrily, "ye make it sound something like a porpoise. Or perhaps a drink Fraser would make for Bertrand or Uncle

Claude. *Ducal,* my, love describes what Ian is, since he's a duke. The two words go together." It wasn't the best definition in the world, but Fiona appeared satisfied, nodding.

Fiona finally laid her forefinger upon Suffolk, then raised her eyes to look at her sister. "When is that nasty lady going to leave?"

Brandy sighed. "I don't know, poppet. She's the lady who's going to marry Ian."

"Why would he want to marry her? He laughs a lot now here with us, even when Percy's here. I bet he won't laugh much if he has to live with her. Maybe you can talk him out of it, Brandy."

"I, poppet? I can't do anything. I'm sorry, but that's just the way it is."

"Why did she come here anyway? She doesn't like any of us. Why?"

"That's a good question. I don't think I have an answer to anything, Fiona."

"Well, I hope she doesn't drag Ian away with her. Maybe if I put a toad in her bed—"

Brandy caught Fiona up in a tight hug. "I don't think so, poppet. But ye know, I'd like to see her face if ye did. One of those big toads that hop around down at the Perranporth swamp. No, we can't. Ian wouldn't approve, and she is going to be his wife. We have to be nice, although it makes my stomach hurt." And she wondered what he was doing, what he was saying to Felicity, at that moment.

Ian was riding beside Felicity at an easy canter along the road that lay parallel to the cliff. It occurred to him to wonder just why he persisted

237

in remaining in Penderleigh. Getting the Cheviot sheep settled and all the accounts straight leaped to the fore as plausible reasons, but he realized that if he said those words aloud, he just might be struck down for lying through his teeth. No, it was Brandy who held him here, and he couldn't deny it to himself any longer. Ah, but it didn't matter, dammit. He thought of how she looked up at him as though he were the only important person on the face of the earth to her.

He thought again of the hour he had spent with Brandy at the hut. Her beautiful, soft mouth and the innocent, little gasps of pleasure that she'd breathed into his mouth when he'd kissed her.

"Ian, do slow down, if you please. I have no inclination for a gallop, particularly on this rutted path. It's a good fifty feet down to that beach. There appear to be no decent roads in this accursed country."

Ian drew in his horse as he did his breath and turned to Felicity. "Sorry, my dear. I wasn't paying attention."

"Ian, whatever is the matter with you? You aren't behaving at all like yourself. You've changed and I can't say that I approve. It's as if you're enjoying wallowing with these vulgar people. I'm sorry, but it's true. They're only remotely related to you. Surely you don't have to enjoy yourself with them, do you? Wouldn't you prefer to be back among your own sort?"

"Felicity," he said, reining in Hercules beside Cantor, "why did you come to Penderleigh? I did write you explaining my delay here. As to enjoying my wallowing, why, yes, I do enjoy my kinsmen very much. They're really quite genuine, even Uncle Claude, who cackles through his remaining teeth, and Lady Adella, who's as sour as Cook's strawberry jam. Come now, why did you come to Penderleigh?"

She wasn't about to tell him that her mother had encouraged her to keep an eye on him, that her mother had been perfectly aghast when he'd upped and left England and Felicity.

"He's too far away from you, my love," her mother had said, patting her cheek. "Men who aren't carefully watched over can get into trouble. Yes, my love, perhaps you'd best go to that wretched place and fetch him home, where he belongs. Men's characters are not steady. Better for his character to be unsteady around you than away from you." No, Felicity wouldn't tell him that.

She gave a light laugh, charm in her voice, bloom in her cheeks. "I told you, Ian, that I missed you. Surely that is enough reason to pay my betrothed a visit."

A black brow arched upward a good inch. "Come, Felicity, all the way to Scotland? Carmichael Hall, perhaps, I can credit."

Felicity smoothed the wrinkles from her gloves, an activity that helped her to control her anger at him. "It would appear," she said finally, her voice cool, cooler than it should be, but she couldn't help it, "that you will cross-examine me. I find you changed, your grace, just as I said before."

"Changed, my dear? It's just that you haven't seen me away from London acquaintances

239

before. Further, I admit to being somewhat surprised that you would forgo your pleasures in the middle of the Season to come to a place that you obviously despise. Your trip was really a waste of time, you know. There was no reason for you to come, no reason at all.''

Did he believe her stupid and blind? The pot that had been boiling ever closer to the edge finally bubbled over. "Is it so unbelievable that I wished to see you? Or perhaps it is that you are uncomfortable, your grace, that I have dared to interrupt *your* pleasures? Are you really so blindly arrogant that you didn't believe I would see clearly enough that Brandy, that wretched little slut, is trying to make you forget what you owe to your rank, what you owe to me?

"She doesn't fool me with her ridiculous dowdy clothes and those childish braids. I saw the way she looked at you, all those drippy, absurd little smiles, her attempts at banter with you that weren't at all amusing. Did you really believe that I wouldn't notice how very fondly you wrote of her in your letter? Or didn't you even care?"

He stared at her, not believing that such bile, such venom, could come out of that beautiful mouth, a mouth he'd believed was soft and gentle. He pulled back on Hercules reins and his stallion reared. He calmed his horse and that in turned helped him to calm himself. What did she want him to say? To agree with her that Brandy was a slut? She'd asked him if he'd even cared. He wondered if she wasn't right. Did he care?

He said finally, his voice low and calm, "What is it you mean to say, Felicity?" He knew he was a fool to ask for more of her fury, but for the first time since he'd known her, he didn't understand her. He knew now, of course, that he'd never really understood her, curse Giles for being right. Curse him for not listening to his cousin. But he wanted her to finish it. He said again, "What do you really mean to say, Felicity?"

She turned her face away, forcing herself to remember that she was, after all, the eldest daughter of the Earl of Braecourt, and not some flyaway little ragamuffin in the wilds of Scotland. She shrugged. "I suppose it's quite natural for you to wish to take your pleasure, even in this hateful, uncivilized place. I understand that mistresses and whores are a common diversion among the gentlemen of our class even if they are betrothed to a lady. I would ask that you not bring your whore to London after we are married. And if you do sometime in the future bring her to London that you don't parade her under my nose and in front of all our friends."

"Ah, so since I'm a duke, then it only stands to reason that I would have mistresses and visit whores. It stands to reason that I wouldn't understand or respect any vow of fidelity or honor?"

"That isn't the point, your grace. As I understand it, gentlemen's mistresses and whores have nothing to do with honor or vows. It is simply the way things are."

"Things aren't like that with me. If I make a promise or a vow, I keep it. I don't care about anyone else. I daresay your brother, Lord Sayer, has told you all this, hasn't he?"

"He has told me you will probably treat me as

well as you would treat your favored mistress and that you will leave me alone as soon as I've bred you an heir. He said this is the way of gentlemen. But it's not just my brother. I'm not blind, your grace. I see married couples. Perhaps they appear close for a while, but then he finds a mistress and she finds a lover."

"It's a depressing truth," the duke said, "but again I will tell you I'm not like that. Many gentlemen of my acquaintance are happily married and faithful to their wives. I might add that their wives are also faithful to them. But to get back to the point of all this. You traveled all the way to Penderleigh—because I wrote of Brandy and you, Felicity, you assumed that she must be my mistress? I think that I begin to understand you."

And perhaps he did. All of it was pique and jealousy of her position, or rather of what her position would be when she became duchess of Portmaine.

"I trust that you do, Ian. You will not then bring her to London? You won't shame me in front of all our friends? You will wait until after we're married and then be discreet about it?"

"I will never bring Brandy to London to be my mistress, married or not. Brandy refuses to come to London, though, of course, it is my wish that she to so. I wish her to have a Season to enjoy herself, to meet a gentleman she might come to admire, a gentleman she might wish to wed. But as I said, she refuses to come."

He said abruptly before she could comment on that, "I asked you last night, Felicity, if you wished to bear my children. Now, I believe, I must require an answer from you."

22

She lowered her eyes, the picture of the shy maiden, but she couldn't keep her voice quite level. "I will, of course, do my duty."

"Your duty," he repeated, his voice as level as the beach below them. Jesus, how could he have been so blind? So utterly unknowing of who and what she was?

"You must have an heir. Even my mother agrees with that. Every lord must have a son to carry on his name and title. There is Giles, your nominal heir, but since he's only two years younger than you are, it isn't likely that he would be alive to step into your title. Doubt me not, your grace. I will do what is expected of me."

"Do you love me, Felicity?"

She was so surprised that she jerked too sharply on her horse's reins and it took an unmeasured step off the narrow cliff path. Ian quickly drew him back. She laughed. She settled herself again in the saddle and fanned her lovely gloved hands. "How perfectly quaint, your grace. My dear duke, I begin to believe that your wits have become muddled in this backward country. I certainly have a great *regard* for you and your family, as I trust you would expect in the future Duchess of Portmaine. Surely you haven't succumbed to notions suitable for the lower classes and silly females who read novels filled with romantic drivel."

"A duke and duchess are so different from everyone else, then?"

She gave him a strange look that he realized held tolerance and a dollop of contempt. "A duke and duchess should set the example for those of lesser birth. Maudlin sentiment, of a certainty, has no place in circles such as ours. I can't imagine that you would want the Duchess of Portmaine to enact ill-bred clinging scenes, fit only for the stage. It isn't the way I was raised. I would never do something so tasteless."

He gazed at her, saddened. Perhaps he'd agreed with her at one time. But not now. He realized now that she was right—he had somehow changed, had become a man he wasn't certain that he understood anymore. Maybe he'd always been that man and been blind to himself. He just didn't know. He sighed. Even if he was not a duke, he was still a gentleman, and a gentleman did not break an engagement formally announced, though the good Lord knew he couldn't begin to see himself spending the rest of his life with this woman. Well, it was his own fault. He'd seen in her what he'd wanted to see. He'd made his own decisions. Now he'd pay for those decisions, dearly. She was what she was, and there would be no changing her. Quite simply, there was nothing more to say.

"I think it's time we returned to Penderleigh," he said shortly, and wheeled Hercules about.

Felicity smiled and gave him a gracious nod, and followed his lead.

Percy's arrival later in the day did little to lift Ian's mood. He was surprised, however, to see the armor of cynicism that Percy habitually draped over himself replaced by open cheerfulness. He was smiling. He appeared happy.

It would take some getting used to. Percy announced that he was now a true Robertson and no longer a bastard, the Scottish court, under obdurate pressure from MacPherson, having legitimized him the afternoon before in Edinburgh.

Ian saw Bertrand pale visibly at the news. As for Claude, he snorted angrily, fastening his rheumy eyes upon Lady Adella. She appeared vastly amused and clapped Percy smartly on the back before turning to Claude. "Yer turn will come, don't fret yerself," she said, her voice snide. "What's another week—or month, for that matter? One thing at a time, old MacPherson's not capable of more."

But it was Felicity's reaction to Percy that surprised Ian the most. He had fully expected that she would elevate her patrician nose, repulsed at being in the same house with a bastard, a *former* bastard. He was wrong, quite wrong. Percy possessed himself of one of her small hands, whispered some doubtlessly flattering words, and planted a light kiss upon her wrist. She blushed faintly. Ian couldn't believe it. He'd always been so circumspect with her, so careful not to abuse her innocence in any way or shock her, but Percy, it appeared, could have kissed her on the mouth and she would have kissed him back, and thanked him.

Giles, as was his way, accepted Percy's acquaintance with his usual urbanity, and remarked to Ian in pensive undertones that regardless of the fellow's antecedents, he was possessed of a rare way with the ladies.

With the exception of one lady, Ian thought, looking at Brandy.

At dinner that evening, Percy recounted with relish his brief visit after his legitimization with Joanna's father, Conan MacDonald. "Ye should have seen the look on the old codger's face when I told him I'd kept to his wishes and not returned until my name was fixed up right and tight. He turned positively purple, but he knew he couldn't turn me away from that pugfaced daughter of his. I'm a true Robertson, and that name goes a long way."

"Why, sir," Felicity said in her most charming voice, "do you court a lady you don't admire?"

"I would venture to say," Giles remarked, a knowing gleam in his eyes, "that our mistress Joanna is an heiress."

"Indeed," Percy agreed with a satisfied laugh. "And a plump little pigeon who believes the world revolves around me. Of course, for all his wealth, Conan MacDonald still carries the smell of the shop, but I think I can easily bear the odor."

"And the adoration," Giles said.

"For a while, at least," Percy agreed.

How odd, Ian thought, that Felicity didn't have

any problem at all understanding Percy's thick Scottish brogue. He was still smarting from how blind he'd been to her, how completely and utterly blind. He'd been a fool. He forked down a bite of haggis. It sat well on his belly now.

"MacDonald will have ye, then, my boy?" Lady Adella asked.

"Can ye doubt it, lady? Old Angus, may he rot in hell, still exercises a powerful influence amongst the Scottish gentry. Ye may well guess too that I wasn't at all backward in extolling the rank and virtue of our current earl of Penderleigh. The old man's mean eyes bulged but good when I made it know that it is an English duke who now holds the title."

Lady Adella waggled an arthritic finger at him. "Ye didn't tell MacDonald that ye were the duke's heir, did ye, ye rascal?"

That was it, Ian thought, nearly crushing his wineglass before he set it down. "The duke's heir is yet to be born. I trust that he will make his appearance in the next year or so."

Giles murmured close to Felicity, "Ah, you'll be well occupied, my dear. The master has given his orders. A brood mare. Well, you'll make a lovely one, for a while at least."

Brandy heard his soft words and wanted to howl at the moon, only there was only just a sliver of a moon this night.

"Hold your tongue, Giles," Ian said, and there was cold anger in his voice.

But Giles just gave the duke a crooked grin. He raised his wineglass. "I propose a toast, Ian. May you have better luck this time."

Brandy's head jerked up. Ian had paled beneath his tan. Whatever did Giles mean, "this time"?

Constance, to this point seated very quietly beside her, suddenly tossed her napkin unceremoniously on the table and rushed from the dining room.

"Whatever ails the chit?" Lady Adella demanded of no one in particular. "Damned girls. They can cry one minute and laugh the next. It's vexing on my nerves. Surely I never did that when I was her age."

"No one would remember," Claude said and chuckled. "It was so many decades in the past."

"I'll take care of her," Bertrand said, and left the room.

He was drawn by the sound of angry hiccuping sobs coming from a small parlor just beyond the drawing room. The door stood ajar and he drew up, seeing Constance flung facedown upon a sofa, sobbing wildly.

She looked so lovely with her black hair streaming over her bare shoulders that he wanted more than anything to gather her up in his arms and kiss her until she was no longer crying but kissing him back. Instead he sat down beside her and said softly, "Nay, lass, don't cry. There's no reason for ye to cry."

"It's ye, Bertrand," she said without enthusiasm, and wiped her hand across her eyes.

"Aye, it's I," he said, wishing she could see him differently, wishing she could see him like he saw her.

"Did Grandmama or Uncle Claude send ye after me?" She hiccupped and he smiled.

"Nay, I came because I'm concerned about ye." He pulled a handkerchief from his waistcoat pocket. "Here, Connie, dry your eyes and tell me what troubles ye."

She dabbed her eyes and cheeks and looked away from him, twisting the handkerchief between her fingers.

"Come, lassie, ye know ye can trust me. Haven't I always been yer friend?" Aye, he thought, always her damned friend.

Constance saw no disapproval in his eyes, only kindness. She blurted out, "Percy will wed that dreadful Joanna, he now makes no bones about it. Ye know he doesn't love her, it's only her money he wants. He's despicable. I can't believe I admired him, wanted him."

Bertrand blessed Percy silently. "Perhaps, Connie, but ye surely must understand Percy's position. He loves his gay life in Edinburgh. Without the money to maintain his pleasures, he would assuredly be miserable. He has chosen what he wants, and if it must needs be a marriage to a lady he doesn't cherish, then, in a way, I can only pity him."

"But I thought him more noble," she said, and hiccuped again. "And ye, Bertrand, ye defend him. Ye've never defended him before. You've always said he was no good and not worthy of anyone's notice."

That was true enough, but now he could afford to be fair about Percy, even to try a mite of generosity. "Nay, lass, ye must know that I could never

249

approve of what he does. It's just that I under-stand his motives. Ye must forget him, Connie, he has never been worthy of yer affection."

She was silent a moment. Was Percy now out of the picture? He surely hoped so.

"It's still not fair," she said.

"Life does not always bring us what we think to be just. Ye know that well enough. Ye've lived here all yer sixteen years. All of us had a devil of a time living with Angus. Perhaps it's not much better now with Lady Adella, just different."

"But, Brandy, why should she go to London while I have never even been to Edinburgh?"

He didn't blame her in the least for this griev-ance. It was a valid one. "Brandy is the eldest, Connie, although," he added with what could be a dash of brilliant insight, "some think her less the woman than ye are."

"Aye, that's true enough."

"I don't think, though, that she will go to London. It is the duke who desires it, not Brandy. Can ye believe that Lady Felicity would wish either of ye in her home after she's married to the duke?"

"No, it's not very likely. She's a witch, Bertrand. Poor Ian. Why is he marrying her? He certainly doesn't need any money. Why?"

"I don't know. Maybe all the ladies in London are like her and she was the best of the lot. I can't see ye having much enjoyment in her company. Edinburgh, though, is quite another matter. It's a beautiful city, Connie, and before long I am certain ye will pay a long visit there. Ian told me that London boasts no finer shops and attractions than our own Scottish capital."

She didn't appear entirely convinced of this, but she didn't say anything more. She rose and straightened her gown. "Ye're kind, Bertie." She lifted her face to his. "Can ye see that I've been crying?"

He took the handkerchief from her hand and rubbed away the tears from those luscious soft cheeks of hers. "Nay, ye're as lovely as ever. If anyone asks, we shall simply say that ye had the headache."

"Thank ye, Bertie."

When they returned to the dining room, no one made comment about Constance's sudden flight, though Ian saw Lady Adella give a sly wink to Claude.

Brandy looked at her sister, knowing that Percy was responsible. At last, she hoped, she'd seen him for what he really was. She looked lovely and very calm. What had Bertrand said to her?

After dinner, Brandy managed to work up the courage to speak to Giles. Her opportunity came when Felicity, prettily entreated by Percy, sat down at the pianoforte and played a Mozart sonata with a good deal of skill. Brandy's question made Giles shake his head. "My poor Brandy, you didn't know about Marianne?"

"Nay."

"When I wished Ian better luck this time, I referred to his first wife. She died under the guillotine, you know. He couldn't save her, and he tried."

"Marianne was French—a de Vaux?"

"You've an excellent memory, my dear. Yes, she was a lovely, fragile little creature, utterly adored by her parents and by her husband, Ian."

"I see."

Giles gave a start at the misery he read in those beautiful eyes of hers. Damn, it appeared that Ian had unleashed a woman's emotions in the girl's breast. He shrugged rather philosophically. She was young, and young hearts didn't break, they only bruised a bit.

He remembered his last bruise. It was more than two years ago. He couldn't remember her name anymore.

23

After spending his morning with Bertrand and the crofters herding together the scores of Cheviot sheep into their enclosures, Ian felt he smelled rank enough to baa. Since he didn't want to foist himself on the family or on Giles and Felicity, in particular, smelling as foul as he did, he walked quickly toward the small, protected cove. The salt water should take care of the worst of it.

He looked for Fiona building a sand castle but didn't see anything but driftwood, huge black boulders, and scattered pebbles. He stripped off his clothes and dropped them on a dry, sunny rock.

His skin tingled as the cold seawater lapped

about his legs. He ignored this shock of it, waded in waist deep, then struck out with long, firm strokes into deeper water. He'd imagined he'd become used to the water, but it wasn't true. It remained cold. He swam until he imagined his mouth was turning blue. A porpoise swam so close he could almost reach out and touch it. Fiona's porpoise. Still, he didn't want to get out of the water. He flipped onto his back and floated, looked up at the cloudless blue sky. What a glorious place, he thought. If he were never to return to London, he fancied that it would be no great loss to him. London, with all of its unremitting social demands, and Felicity, the woman he would marry, the woman who didn't love him, just esteemed him—either him or his wealth and title—and would begrudgingly bear his children. Well, damn. He'd made a mistake for which he'd pay the rest of his days on this earth. How could he have been so obtuse?

He sighed and closed his eyes against the sun's glare, willing himself not to think about anything at all.

Brandy walked along the promontory, too depressed to notice that her tartan shawl was making her gown sweat into her back. She thought of poor Fiona, trapped this one afternoon each week with Lady Adella, who insisted that she spend three hours with her to learn the manners of a lady born. Brandy had wanted to point out that customs and mores had changed quite a bit in the past fifty years, but she didn't want her grandmother's tongue to sharpen on her. Fiona was made to sit on the old red brocade cushion at Lady Adella's feet, setting crooked stitches into a swatch of embroidery and listening to fifty-year-old stories of Grandmama's long ago conquests.

She made her way carefully down the steep path to the beach. She didn't at first notice the neat pile of men's clothing laid on a rock. She shaded her eyes with her hand and gazed out over the water.

She knew it was Ian, even before he stood and walked toward shore. She stared at him—there was no way in God's green earth she could look away. Surely there could be no man to compare with him. His thick black hair was plastered about his head, making him look rather boyish. But that was all that looked remotely boyish. She looked at the thick black hair on his chest. As he waded into shallow water, she saw his flat belly, the line of black hair that spread down into the bush of hair at his groin. She stared at him, just as she had that long ago evening she'd run into his bedchamber. Ah, but he was beautiful. Thick strong legs. She hadn't seen his feet. She'd wager her tartan shawl that they were beautiful too. Then he stepped from the water and stood a moment on the rocky beach, stretching his arms above his head.

She thought she was going to swallow her tongue. He could have no idea what that movement was doing to her innards. Ah, but she wasn't the one who would have him. He was further out of her reach than he'd ever been. He was also naked and she supposed it was the best treat she could expect from this wretched day.

She'd had a brief tiff with Felicity over London and how she was certain that Edinburgh couldn't begin to compare to England's capital. Who cared? She'd been so depressed to even give her the edge of her sharp tongue. She'd just looked at her, turned on her heel, and left her standing there alone in the drawing room.

She just couldn't look away from him. She knew she shouldn't be staring at him like a ninny, but she wasn't about to turn around and walk away. No, she'd take what she could get. She drank in all of him, acutely aware of the warmth low in her belly that felt urgent and, truth be told, rather wild and intriguing. She remembered their afternoon in the abandoned crofter's hut. He'd kissed her, his arms holding her close to his chest. The thought of being naked against him, feeling that crinkly black hair against her flesh, having his hands stroking down her back and, well, even lower, made her wonder what it was all about. And there was no doubt about it, after seeing Ian naked, Brandy wanted to know about this mating between men and women. She would have shot Percy if he'd tried again to stroke his hands anywhere on her body, but Ian, well, she supposed she'd let him do anything he wished.

Ian finished buttoning his white shirt, that garment still, unfortunately, reeking of sheep, and shoved it into his black knit britches. He threw his rumpled cravat over his arm and pulled on his boots. It was a bright patch of color that brought his eyes slewing in Brandy's direction. It took him but an instant to recognize her faded tartan shawl.

"Brandy!" Good God, not again. He yelled, "You little witch, come out here at once. I mean it, now. I want you to tell me you just arrived, not more than ten seconds ago. Tell me the sun is sharp in your eyes and you haven't been looking at me."

Brandy didn't move an inch. She'd been standing back, hoping he wouldn't see her. She didn't want to embarrass him, but now she had. Yet again.

He sighed. "All right. Just how long have you been standing there?"

"Well, rather a long time if you would know the truth. Remember when you were on your back floating and that porpoise came toward you? Then you waded out of the water. It was a long wade."

He felt a raw push of lust and that would never do. He yelled at her, "Brandy, dammit, this is the second time you've placed me in an altogether ridiculous position. Don't you realize you shouldn't stare at naked men? Don't you realize you should have turned right around and gone straight back to the castle?"

He was right, of course, but not at all to the point. She moistened her lower lip with her tongue. She was thirsty. She wanted very much to kiss him. He sounded angry, but what could she do? There was just one way to get out of this with a dab of pride left. She turned on her heel and ran back toward the cliff path.

"Wait, dammit," he yelled after her, and broke into a run. He wanted to get his hands on her. When his hands were on her, as they wanted to be, he didn't know what he would do, but he had to find out.

Ian heard a loud report that didn't penetrate his brain. Then he felt as though someone had shoved a knife in his back. The force of it hurtled him forward, facedown, onto the beach. He couldn't seem to move. He tried to rise, but felt a blaze of agony freeze his breath in his lungs. He fell forward, blackness closing over him.

Brandy froze in her tracks, the sound of the shot stunning her. She stared at Ian, who lay motionless, his blood beginning to ooze through his white shirt, forming a spreading stain of deep red. It couldn't be real, it just couldn't, but it was. Someone had shot him. God, he could be dead. No! She screamed his name and ran as fast as she could. As she fell onto her knees beside him, she looked back to see if there were anyone in the direction the shot had come from.

Another shot rang out, and she felt its hiss as it whizzed harmlessly past her head. She threw herself down over Ian, covering his body as best she could with her own. Dear God, someone was trying to kill him. It had been no accident. There was another shot. This one kicked up the sand not a foot from her head.

She opened her mouth and screamed as loud as she could, screamed until her voice was raw and deep. And still she screamed. There was nothing else she could do. Surely someone would hear her, someone had to. She didn't want to think about the person who'd fired three times at Ian, how that person could at this very moment be coming toward them, his gun pointed at them.

Time was her enemy, an eternity of minutes that held her motionless with Ian bleeding beneath her. She didn't realize she was crying until she saw Bertrand and Fraser through a haze of tears, running down the snaking path toward her.

"Bertie," she screamed. "Thank God ye've come. Please, God, hurry. Someone has shot him." She quickly rolled off Ian and ripped open his shirt to bare the wound.

She pulled off her shawl, rolled it into a ball, and pressed it with all her strength against the bloody wound in his back.

"Good God, Brandy. Was that you screaming? What the devil?"

Bertrand pulled her from Ian's side and shouted to Fraser, "Hurry, man, fetch the others. Send someone for Wee Robert. Don't waste an instant. Good God, he's been shot in the back." He pressed his fingers over the wound to slow the bleeding. "We heard shots, then your screams. Who was it, Brandy? Did you see him?"

"I didn't see anyone. Bertrand, oh God, will he be all right?"

"I don't know, Brandy, the wound is deep, but I don't know if the ball hit a vital organ. We'll have to wait for Wee Robert before we know anything. Come, lass, you've got to help me now."

Percy and Giles came running down the path. Giles said nothing until he had examined his cousin. "Surely you must have seen who it was," he said sharply, staring up at Brandy's white face.

She shook her head, mute.

Giles said, "Well, it doesn't matter now. Come, Bertrand, Percy, we must get him back to the castle." The three men lifted him carefully. It took what seemed like an eternity to gain the top of the cliff.

"Damn, but he's pale as a sheet," Bertrand said. "Who the devil could have done this?"

"It must have been an accident," Percy said. "There's no other explanation. An accident."

"It's just as well that he's unconscious," Giles said as he shifted Ian's weight. "Damn, he's heavy."

They finally reached the castle. Brandy dogged their heels, past a shrieking Morag and a gaping Constance, staying as close to Ian as the men would allow, until they had reached the duke's bedchamber.

Bertrand turned to her and said gently, "Ye did well, lass, but now ye must go. We must undress him and put him to bed. When Wee Robert arrives, please bring him up, all right?"

She was staring up at him, mute, her face white. He shook her shoulders. "Listen to me, he'll live, I promise ye. There's naught more ye can do. Go now, ye must speak with the others."

She didn't want to leave him, but she knew she had to. Yes, she'd go downstairs and tell everyone what had happened. Then she'd wait for Wee Robert. She looked at Percy because he was helping lift Ian onto the huge bed. His eyes appeared to her more hooded than usual, his mouth drawn in a cold, tight line. She turned frantic eyes to Bertrand.

"Ye'll not leave him alone, Bertrand, promise

me. It wasn't an accident. Someone tried to kill him. Someone fired three times at him. Promise me ye'll not leave him."

"I promise, lass. Go now."

Brandy didn't take the time to strip off her bloodied clothing, but instead made her way downstairs to the drawing room.

"Take this, child," Lady Adella ordered, handing her a glass of brandy.

She gulped down the brandy, coughing until she believed her lungs must surely burst through her body. But then the blazing warmth reached her belly. It calmed her. She set the empty glass on the sideboard.

"What did you do to the duke?" Felicity yelled as she ran into the drawing room. "By God, you're covered with blood, his blood. What did you do to him, you filthy little trollop?"

"Someone tried to kill him, on the beach in the protected cove. There were three shots. One bullet went into his back."

Felicity looked at Brandy's bloody gown. Her mouth worked. Then she screamed and fainted onto the carpet. A small puff of dust wafted up.

"Useless creature," Lady Adella said, and snorted.

Brandy and Constance each took one of Felicity's arms and dragged her up onto a sofa.

"That's Ian's blood on yer gown, Brandy?" Constance said in a small, scared voice.

"Hush, Constance. The girl doesn't need ye to state the obvious." Lady Adella turned to Brandy. "Ye must get a hold of yerself, child. Fraser's gone to fetch the magistrate, Trevor.

Now, tell me before ye go and change ye gown, did ye see who did this terrible thing?"

"Nay, Grandmama, I looked all around, but I didn't see anyone. Whoever shot him must have been hiding in the rocks atop the cliff."

Lady Adella looked away from Brandy's pale, drawn face and stared thoughtfully down at her gnarled fingers.

"A poacher, it must have been a poacher," Constance said.

"No one's poached here for years," Lady Adella said. "There's nothing to poach. People aren't that stupid. Nay, someone tried to kill the duke."

Still, Constance repeated her belief to Mr. Trevor, the magistrate, some while later.

"There aren't any poachers within fifty miles of here," Brandy said, her voice harsh and cold. "It's just as Grandmama said, what's here to poach? Nothing at all."

"Still," Mr. Trevor began, but Brandy heard Wee Robert's familiar voice and raced out to see him. He let her talk, just nodding, knowing shock when he saw it. He let her walk beside him to the duke's bedchamber and patted her hand before closing the bedchamber door in her face.

Time seemed to have stopped. Brandy came back into the drawing room. Mr. Trevor was speaking in a low voice to Lady Adella.

He looked up at Brandy's entrance. "We can decide upon that matter, Lady Adella, after I've heard Brandella's story." He frowned. His frown deepened after Brandy told him the few facts. "It would appear to me that ye saved the duke's life, lass." He turned to Lady Adella. "I understand, my lady, that Mr. Percival Robertson no longer stands in, shall we say, an ambiguous position."

"Aye, that's true enough," she said slowly, eyeing him as a fox would a pheasant. She then drew herself upright and added in her most imperious voice, "Ye'll stop yer nonsensical thinking, Trevor. I'll thank ye not to involve any of the family in this affair. I suppose ye'll be asking me next if Claude Robertson's gout is nothing but a wily trick and he pulled the trigger. A lawless tinker must be the culprit, and it's time for ye to go find the wretch. Bedamned to ye, I've known ye all yer blessed life, even knew yer mama, weak-kneed woman that she was. I'll see that ye're unblessed if ye don't mind yer manners. Catch that bloody tinker and stop thinking what ye're thinking."

The lines about Mr. Trevor's mouth deepened, but he remained calm, which was an accomplishment, Brandy thought, in near awe, after being subjected to one of Grandmama's harangues.

He said now, "It's a serious matter, my lady, and I'm only trying to do my duty. I ask ye to forget, at least for the moment, any tinker, for there aren't any about to the best of my knowledge, and tell me who in yer judgment would wish the English duke dead. Nay, don't rave at me any more about the loyal, honest Robertsons. That isn't the point now. A man's life is at stake, yer kinsman's life."

Percy's name stood starkly in Brandy's mind. She wanted to shriek his name aloud. He'd come running down the cliff path so very soon, as if he'd just been waiting. But she held herself silent. Every Robertson, each in his own way, would gain by Ian's death.

Lady Adella thwacked her cane hard against the floor and snorted with disgust. "Damn ye, Trevor, why does any villain show his true colors? I'll tell ye again, ye are sniffing in the wrong foxhole. No Robertson would have done such a cowardly deed."

Mr. Trevor held his peace. He wanted to say that old Angus would have shot anyone in the back in an instant of displeasure, but he was dead, and he didn't want to risk Lady Adella toppling over with apoplexy. It also seemed to him that Mr. Percival Robertson was the likeliest suspect, as his becoming legitimate had made him next in line to the title. Ah, but what about Claude and his son, Bertrand? Wasn't the devious old lady undoing the infamous disinheritance? No, he had no intention of dismissing other members of the family. What an altogether wretched situation. Why an English duke? And in his part of the county too. It wasn't fair. It was more than a sober man could bear.

He rose slowly to take his leave. "Let us trust, Lady Adella, that his grace will be able to provide me more information on the morrow. I will be back to speak with him, God grant that he's still alive."

Lady Adella snorted and waved him away. "Of course he'll be alive, ye fool. He's of my blood. He'll not be brought low by a coward's bullet."

When Crabbe had escorted Mr. Trevor out, Lady Adella turned a contemptuous eye toward

Felicity, who was sitting on the sofa, still looking dazed. She looked very helpless, fragile, and Lady Adella admired such ability. "Brandy, call for Lady Felicity's maid. She'll do better in her own room."

Brandy did as she was bidden, thankful for any activity that would keep her mind occupied.

24

As the morning lengthened into afternoon, Wee Robert still hadn't come downstairs.

"Tearing yer shawl to shreds won't make him come down any faster, child," Lady Adella said. "It was a shock, I'll give ye that, hearing that shot, watching him fall. I'll not even reprimand ye for falling on him. Ye saved him and that must stand by itself. Try to ease yerself, Brandy. That's a good girl."

"Aye, Grandmama." But she continued fretting mercilessly at the fringe. It occurred to her that her grandmother was acting uncommonly gentle with her. That would have made her nervous had she not been so scared for Ian.

Crabbe entered the drawing room a step in front of the doctor. "Elgin Robert, milady."

"I've eyes in my head, Crabbe. Well, Wee Robert, how fares the duke?"

Elgin Robert took no offense at this nickname, having grown quite used to it over the past fifteen years, and walked wearily into the room. He was a man whose body had betrayed him, rendering him a mere five feet tall in his stocking feet. He rubbed a chubby hand over his brow and advanced toward Lady Adella.

"His grace will, I think, recover, my lady," he said in a gentle, almost girlishly soft voice. "The ball entered his back just below his left shoulder. I might add that yer kinsman was a stoic to the point of causing me concern. Not one sound did he make when I drew out the bullet. White and blown he is now, to be sure, but resting more comfortably. There's only fever and infection to concern us now."

Wee Robert gratefully accepted a cup of tea from Constance and took a long drink. "The duke is young and quite strong. He'll pull through quite nicely, quite nicely. Nasty business, though. Did Trevor have any notion of who shot him? Brandy?"

"Nasty, indeed," Lady Adella said. "That fool Trevor left here as stupid as he was when he came. I vow that man is only good for catching urchins who steal apples. He believes it's one of us who shot the duke. And, no, Brandy doesn't know a bloody thing, more's the pity."

"Is his grace awake?" Brandy asked.

"Nay, lass, I gave him a hefty dose of laudanum. Sleep is the best healer, ye know."

Percy, Giles, and Bertrand entered the drawing room together, each man's face white and drawn.

Wee Robert turned to them. "I thank all of ye gentleman for yer help." He turned away abruptly, realizing that possibly one of them had

265

brought the duke to his present condition. It was a hell of a mess.

Bertrand nodded and asked, "Trevor came, Lady Adella?"

"Aye, I was just telling Wee Robert that the man brays like an ass. It's his idea to lay the blame at a Robertson's door. Of course, it must be one of those damned tinkers responsible. No Robertson could have done such a thing. Actually, no Robertson would be such a bad shot. The killer had three tries and botched all of them except that first one."

Giles raised a brow and gazed at Percy and Bertrand.

"Where is Uncle Claude?" Brandy blurted out.

Bertrand stared at her. "Good God, Brandy, surely ye don't think that my father could be capable of such a despicable act?"

"For that matter," Percy said, interrupting, "do any of us know where the other was when Ian was shot? For all we know, it could have even been Brandy who brought him low."

"We might begin with where you were, Percy," Bertrand said coldly.

"Ah, dear cousin, do I detect a note of suspicion in yer voice? If ye must know, I was endeavoring to avoid the filthy stench of yer precious sheep, difficult since their odor carries itself in the breeze."

"I don't think that such haggling will get us to the truth," Giles said, "nor will it aid in cementing trust or friendship. Incidentally, where is Lady Felicity?"

"She went into hysterics, then fainted," Constance said, a good deal of contempt in her voice.

"A stupid question," Giles said and sighed. "I should have guessed as much. Some things never change, do they?"

Wee Robert, who was hunched down with his teacup, embarrassed and uncomfortable, rose and bowed to Lady Adella. He couldn't wait to leave. He felt sorry for those who had to stay. He said, "I can see that my presence is no longer needed. I will pay the duke a visit tomorrow morning. Brandy, don't look so scared. He should be fine. Don't worry."

"But what if he worsens during the night?" Brandy asked in a panic.

"I'm but fifteen minutes away, lass."

After Crabbe led Wee Robert out, Bertrand turned to Brandy. "It was lucky for Ian that ye were on the beach, lass. But ye put yerself in grave danger, ye know, and that scares us all to our toes."

Percy said, "Just why were ye there on the beach, Brandy?"

"I was merely avoiding the stench, like ye, Percy." She found herself looking about from one face to another, searching for any sign that might betray the owner's guilt. But she saw nothing, and as she had no wish to hear any further pointless bickering, she slipped quietly from the room, her destination the duke's bedchamber. His valet, Mabley, had to be with him, and it was this gentleman that she wanted to see.

She walked quietly past Felicity's room,

wanting to raise her fist and shake it, but of course she didn't, just kept walking, wishing that lady would just somehow disappear. She quietly opened the duke's door and slipped into the darkened room. She didn't see Mabley and cursed him silently for leaving his master alone. She heard Ian's deep, even breathing and walked quietly to his bedside. He appeared so natural in his sleep, the strain of his ordeal not evident on his face.

"Miss Brandy. What are you doing here?"

She spun about, automatically placing a finger to her lips.

He lowered his voice as he walked toward her. "You shouldn't be here, really you shouldn't," Mabley said. He looked at her closely and saw such fear in her eyes, fear and pain. Damnation, he was too old for this kind of thing. His hands were still shaking from wiping the sweat from the duke's brow while Wee Robert had probed for the bullet.

She shushed him again with her finger on her lips. "His grace is resting. He's sleeping. Didn't the doctor tell you he would be all right? No, we don't have to whisper. He's got enough laudanum in him to keep a battalion of troops asleep."

Still she said nothing, just motioned for him to follow her. He trailed after her, wishing he could have a mug of ale. Yes, that would make his old bones settle nicely.

She said without preamble, "We mustn't leave his grace alone, not even for a moment, Mabley."

"It weren't my intention to leave him take care

of himself, Miss Brandy. You needn't worry your-self about the duke, not with me here."

"Nay, ye don't understand. Ye know that someone tried to kill him. We can't trust anyone, do ye hear? He's helpless as a babe now, he can't defend himself."

"It makes no difference. I'm here. I'll take good care of him."

Brandy used her grandmother's imperious tone: "If ye'll stay with him during the day, I'll not leave him at night." There, she'd said it.

"That would be most unseemly, Miss Brandy. Surely Mr. Giles or Mr. Bertrand or—"

"Can you promise me that none of those men shot the duke? No, of course you can't. I don't want any one of them ever to be alone with him, ever. Don't ye see, Mabley, we can't afford to take any risks. He could die."

Mabley rubbed his sagging jaw, trying to gather together his weary wits. "If it could be dangerous, like you say, then I'll not allow you, a small female, begging your pardon—"

Time for more of Lady Adella's imperious voice. "See here, Mabley, Grandfather Angus had a remarkable gun collection. I'll have one of his pistols with me. I'll keep the outer doors locked. Does that make ye rest easy?"

Mabley was very much of the belief that guns and females were not fit company for each other, but he could tell she wasn't about to back down. At least he could be certain that she hadn't shot the duke. One of those blighters had, but not Miss Brandy. What was he to do?

He gave her a sour look. "You'll wear yourself

269

out, miss, and then what will your grandmother say to me?"

"Nonsense. Now, promise me ye'll not leave him. I'll bring ye yer dinner later and then ye may take yerself to bed." Brandy turned away before he could come out with another argument. She smiled as she heard his defeated sigh behind her.

The small clock on the mantel rang out a faint ten strokes. Brandy rose from the hob, where a pot of broth lay hot and ready, and walked quietly to the bed. She laid the palm of her hand on the duke's forehead. He was still cool to the touch, thank God. Still, Wee Robert had warned that a fever could strike at any time during the next few days.

"I'll not let anyone hurt ye again," she said, leaned over and kissed his mouth. "Ye'll sleep now and heal. I'll watch over ye." She straightened and walked back to the warmth of the fire. Quickly she stripped off her clothing and pulled on her cotton nightgown over her head, tying the drawstring at her neck. It took her longer to unbraid her hair and brush out the masses of ripples. Finally she fastened her shawl about her shoulders and walked back to the bedside.

He lay motionless, breathing deeply and evenly. She settled into the large chair she had drawn up and tucked her feet under her. Before allowing herself to relax, Brandy looked one last time at the locked door, then at the small pistol that lay on the nightstand beside her. Mabley was sound asleep in the adjoining room. That door was also locked, Brandy having insisted that he comply with her instructions. Her only concern was the corridor door to Mabley's room, for which there was no lock.

Only Lady Adella and Mabley knew of her vigil. To Brandy's surprise, Lady Adella had heard her out, regarding her in a rather peculiar manner, but didn't gainsay her.

"Humph, it's just as well that we don't tell anyone else, child," she had said, looking away. "I have no desire for that milk-and-honey Felicity to be raising a ruckus and ruining what little peace I have left."

Brandy heard no ruckus from anyone that night. She was surprised when Mabley shook her shoulder the next morning.

"Oh, Mabley, it's morning already? I'm sorry. I'd thought to be dressed and wake ye up."

Mabley grunted, then looked down at his sleeping master. "Hie yourself off now, Miss Brandy, I'll see to him now."

Later that morning, Mr. Trevor arrived and asked to see the duke. Wee Robert gave his consent, and while both men shared a cup of coffee with Lady Adella downstairs, Mabley gently awakened his master.

Ian awoke somewhat reluctantly, still dazed from the laudanum and with an intense pain in his shoulder.

"Ah, your grace. I'm glad to see your eyes open again."

Ian wanted to sit up and he did try, but the pain in his shoulder brought him low. He cursed and closed his eyes, trying to gain control of the godawful pain. He forced himself to breathe deeply and slowly. In and out.

"You just lie still, your grace," Mabley said in his most soothing voice. "I'll fetch you some broth that Miss Brandy has kept warm for you."

In a voice that didn't sound at all like his, Ian said, "How long have I been asleep?"

"Since yesterday afternoon, your grace. Wee Robert gave you a powerful dose of laudanum, if your grace recalls."

"Wee Robert," the duke repeated slowly. "Why does that name seem familiar to me?"

"The doctor, your grace. A tiny little Scotsman, but fair good with his hands. He dug the ball out of your back."

Ian winced at the now sharp memory of lying in exquisite agony as someone dug out that bullet. Other memories tugged at his mind, and he felt himself go pale.

"Mabley, is Brandy all right? She was with me on the beach, just before I was shot. Jesus, she's all right, isn't she?"

"Your grace mustn't upset yourself. Miss Brandy escaped injury. Indeed, the young lady, from what I can glean, your grace, saved your life." He didn't think it wise to mention that the young lady was also the duke's self-appointed guardian during the night. No, the duke would have a fit if he knew that. He had very set notions about ladies and where they belonged.

"Mr. Trevor, the Scottish magistrate, wishes to see you, your grace. Do you feel well enough to speak with him?"

Ian nodded and tried to clear his mind. After

he'd eaten the soup Brandy had made for him, and relieved himself, a bushy-browed gentleman dressed in somber black came to stand beside the bed.

"It's just a few minutes I need to talk with ye, yer grace."

Ian nodded again, and tried to focus his wits away from the pain in his back. Mabley hadn't lied to him, had he? Brandy was all right, wasn't she?

"It appears to me that yer grace is a lucky man."

"Mabley told me that Brandy saved my life," the duke said, trying desperately to remember anything that would identify who had shot him.

"That she did, yer grace." Mr. Trevor saw that his grace looked distracted. He was in pain, Trevor could tell that easily enough. Well, let him talk about Brandy, then. He said, "Evidently, yer grace, when ye fell, she threw herself over ye, two more shots barely missing her. Yelled like a banshee, she did, scaring off the killer. Her screaming and the gunshots brought the family running."

"You swear to me she's all right?"

"Quite all right, just scared for ye."

"She could have been killed. What made her pull such a stupid stunt?"

"Aye, but she wasn't hurt. It's very worried all the family is, yer grace. Is there naught ye can tell me? Take yer time. Think back to what ye were doing, what ye were thinking about."

"I'd been swimming," the duke said. "All those sheep, they stink like the devil. I wanted to

273

wash the odor away as best I could before returning to the castle. I came out of the water. I spoke with Brandy and then she, ah, then she left. I remember vaguely hearing something, it must have been the shot, then I don't remember anything else."

Mr. Trevor saw the duke's brow was furrowed in pain. He rose. "I'll fetch Wee Robert, yer grace. Ye need him now, not me. We'll talk more of this later. Perhaps ye'll think of more details. Anything would help."

Ian barely heard him. He blinked several times in an effort to clear away the blur of his bedchamber. He saw Brandy clearly again, her face red, staring at him on a beach. Staring at him pointedly. Again. Staring at all of him. And quite admiring him.

Then someone was standing beside him and he felt the cool rim of a glass pressed against his mouth. He opened his mouth from habit, took several long drinks of a cool liquid, and closed his eyes and let the quiet darkness close over him.

"The wound is healing nicely, no infection there. But his grace has got the fever." Wee Robert sat on his black coattails in the drawing room, facing the assembled family. As he spoke, he eyed Lady Felicity, the duke's betrothed. A more weak-kneed, swooning lady he had yet to meet. He couldn't quite imagine her as a fitting matc for the duke, a strong man, a tough man, a man used to command. She looked used to fainting and crying. She grew rather pale at his words, but she didn't faint again, thank the good Lord.

Brandy asked quietly, "How long do ye expect the fever to last, sir?"

Wee Robert said, "I won't mince matters with ye, lass. There be some who never recover from the fever. But like I told ye yesterday, his grace is young and a stronger man I've yet to meet. He'll pull through it, I'll wager."

"But he's a *duke!*" Felicity shouted.

Wee Robert said with a touch of humor, "Aye, miss, that he is. Undoubtedly the title will assist him greatly to get well."

"I believe what Lady Felicity is saying," Giles said smoothly, with a gentle smile toward Felicity, "is that it is rather incredible that one of his grace's rank should find himself in such a situation."

Wee Robert rose. "That is a matter for Mr. Trevor, I think. There is naught more I can do for his grace, Lady Adella. I've given Mabley instructions for his care. I wish ye all a good day."

Bertrand walked with Wee Robert to the door.

"What a damned mess," Claude said irritably. "I swear my gout has pained me more in this past day than in the last year. Damned shooting."

"I think I would prefer a little gout to a ball in the back," Percy said with such contempt that Claude nearly jumped on him.

"No, don't, Claude," Lady Adella said, but nothing more. She just sat there, staring at all of them, one at a time.

Bertrand returned to the group. "Ye all know,

I presume, that Ian could tell Trevor nothing save the obvious. Nothing more than Brandy knew."

"I agree with Lady Adella," Claude broke in. "It must have been one of those filthy tinkers. They're a damnable lot, ye know."

Brandy sighed and rose. "If ye'll excuse me, Grandmama, I must give Fiona her lessons. Then I wish to see how the duke fares."

"Don't cast such a long face, child, else ye'll give the child nightmares." Lady Adella waved Brandy from the room, then eyed each of the assembled company in turn, her gaze speculative. "I dislike mysteries and I dislike scoundrels, having lived with one for over fifty years. That a man could be such a villain and on Penderleigh land makes my stomach turn."

"I don't think, Lady Adella," Percy said softly, "that Trevor counts only men among his suspects."

"Come, Percy," Bertrand said, so angry with his cousin he wanted to hit him, "do ye believe that Lady Adella balanced a gun on her cane?"

"I merely speculate, dear cousin. If Trevor is going to continue poking about, asking us all sorts of ridiculous questions, I see no reason why the ladies should be excluded from such fine sport."

Felicity rose and said in a trembling voice to Giles, "I feel dreadful. Maria must bathe my temples with lavender water. Why did the duke ever insist upon coming to this wretched place? Look what it has brought him—to death's door by some scheming Scottish barbarian. Oh, how I wish none of us had come here."

"Then why don't ye leave?" Constance asked

sweetly. "All ye do is complain and faint and call us names. Yer're not worth a thing. Aye, just leave."

Felicity turned on her. "You spiteful little Scottish brat. You can't even speak English properly. And just why is that dowd of a sister of yours going to see the duke? She's nothing to do with him, nothing. I'm his betrothed. I should see him if anyone should, and I'm just not strong enough right now. Ah, I hate this wretched place."

"I have seen Ian," Giles said. "He's got the fever just as Wee Robert said. Mabley is staying close. He'll call us if Ian worsens."

"Aye, Mabley says he's becoming delirious. Damn." Bertrand suddenly smashed his fist against his thigh.

"Are ye damning the fact that the duke is ill or that the killer missed his mark?" Percy inquired in a goading voice.

"What a despicable thing to say," Constance said, rising, her hands fisted at her sides.

Giles broke in. "Mabley tells me that his grace won't be left alone for a single minute. I think that should cool our would-be killer's zeal. Now, I think, Lady Adella—that is, if you do not mind— that we should have our afternoon tea."

25

"Ye'll not let anything else happen to Ian, will ye, Brandy?" Fiona looked worried and frightened. It wasn't that she didn't know about death. Grandfather Angus had died. But he had been so old she couldn't begin to imagine how he could still be alive. Brandy tucked in the bedcovers about her little sister's neck, leaned down, and kissed her forehead. "Nay, poppet, I'll let none hurt him again. Ye're not to worry now. He's big and strong. He'll get well, I swear it to ye."

She left Fiona and went to her own room. She just wasn't up for all the snipping that would be going on in the drawing room and at the dinner table.

It was a pale, drawn figure that Mabley admitted to Ian's bedchamber as the evening advanced toward ten o'clock. Brandy's eyes went immediately to the bed. "He's quiet, Mabley. Has the fever broken?"

Her voice was so hopeful that Mabley disliked having to dash her down. "Well, not exactly, Miss Brandy. He's been delirious, tossing about and muttering about this and that. Six years it's been, yet it's her name that he cries out, over and over. What a horrible time that was. I worried greatly for him then." Mabley shook his head wearily.

Brandy was staring at him. She said, "Ye mean Marianne?"

"Yes, Miss Brandy. I think he's reliving that terrible time all over again." Mabley's old bones were so weary that he plumped himself down in a chair and closed his eyes. He could still picture the duke's white face the day he'd returned alone from France. Aloud, he said, "His friends feared for his reason. Even the king sent his condolences,

278

I remember. It was a sad time, yes, a sad time indeed."

Brandy took a tight hold on herself. Marianne was long dead and she, Brandy, was very much alive. Ian needed her care. If she had to share him with a ghost, she would do so. Felicity she refused to even admit into her thinking. "Go to bed, Mabley, ye're near to dropping."

Mabley turned at the adjoining door. "You'll call me, miss, if his grace becomes too restless for you to handle?"

"Aye. Be certain to lock the door, Mabley. His grace is in enough danger with the wound. I don't want to have to worry about the man who was scoundrel enough to shoot him."

Mabley withdrew, locking the narrow door after him. He stood for a moment in the middle of the small dressing room and eyed the lumpy truckle bed that had been his nightly companion for so many weeks now. Just knowing that Morag had changed the linen this very morning made him itch. Like Lady Felicity, he wished they'd never come to Scotland. He prayed that His Grace would soon be on the mend and, once mended, would consent to leaving this land with all its strange foods, funny speech, and salty sea air.

As he slowly removed his black coat, he glanced toward the closed door. His thin brows drew together over narrowed eyes. It wasn't right that Miss Brandy should be protecting his grace—better one of the men, Mr. Giles, for example. A stubborn young lady she was, and more than just fond of his grace, he guessed. She was in for a bruised heart, he knew, for although he himself had no liking for the haughty Lady Felicity, he knew the ways of the Quality. His grace was as good as leg-shackled, what with the formal announcement and all the settlements agreed upon. If asked, he would have gladly enlightened his grace as to the differences between Lady Felicity and the duke's poor first duchess. A pity, he thought, yes, it was a pity, but nothing could be done about it, nothing at all.

Brandy stood quietly beside the duke's bedside, looking down at him. His face was hot and red from the fever. She wiped his face with a cool, damp cloth. As she rubbed the cool cloth over his neck and shoulders and arms, he muttered something she didn't understand and turned his face away on the pillow. She wiped his face again. He tried to strike her hand away, but he didn't have the strength.

"Hush," she whispered. She pulled the heavy goosedown cover up over his bare chest, mindful of his fever, even though the room was warm. The white strips of linen bound about his chest and under his back stood out starkly against the curling black hair. She lightly stroked the cloth above and below the bandage.

His breathing became less raw. He didn't move around all that much, but the fever was still on him.

She was ready to drop where she stood. If only the fever would break. She spent another half hour wiping him down. Then she stretched and went to build up the fire, which had fallen into thick layers of orange embers. After she undressed and changed into her nightgown, she fastened her tartan shawl once more firmly about her shoulders and sank into her chair, pulling a rough wool blanket up to her chin for warmth.

She was pulled from her sleep by the sound of garbled words and curses. In an instant she was beside him, looking down into his face. She felt tears sting the back of her eyes at the pain she heard in his voice:

"Marianne, Marianne. If only you had trusted me . . . told me, Marianne. I would have tried to save them. . . . Marianne, why did you doubt me? Too late . . . I was too late."

"Oh, no, Ian, it wasn't yer fault. No, don't blamc yerself for her death. Hush, my love, hush. I love ye more than she could have, Ian. I would never have left ye. Why didn't she trust ye?"

He began to twist about, arms flailing, and Brandy, fearing the wound would opcn, rcsolutely blinked back tears and sat down beside him, holding down his shoulders as best she could.

"Lie still, Ian, ye must lic still."

His voice rose, and she saw his visions of the guillotine, its blade whooshing down to sever Marianne's head. And she realized that Marianne had gone to France to try to save her parents. Why hadn't she told him? Why hadn't she asked for his help? He'd been her husband. Why? It made no sense at all.

"It wasn't yer fault, Ian," she said again and again, willing him to listen to her, to believe her.

She touched her fingertips to his lips and pressed her cheek against his, holding him tightly to her.

Through her fingertips, he whispered yet again Marianne's name, and in her misery Brandy closed her mouth over his, willing him to forget his ghost. He responded to her, and she was surprised at the sheer want she felt when his tongue explored her mouth—at least she believed it was want. Maybe it was lust, a word she'd heard enough from the mouths of the Robertson males. She knew she wanted more of these feelings he was bringing to her body, knew she wanted to touch him, hold him to her. His arms went around her, his large hands sweeping down her back to her hips.

She knew she must pull away from him. He didn't know what he was doing. He believed she was his first wife. He believed she was Marianne. She did try to pull away from him, but he tightened his hold on her and she couldn't move.

"Ian, no, ye mustn't." But she wanted him to continue what he was doing and she knew it. She knew she was lying to him and to herself.

His lips were suddenly slack. He was staring at her, his eyes bright, penetrating.

"My love," he whispered, "my little love." He pulled her down to him and kissed her. She tasted his urgency, felt the urgency in him, accepted his tongue when she opened her mouth to him.

He thinks I'm Marianne, she thought dully, hopelessly, and then she didn't care at all. She accepted him, accepted what he would do to her. He would be hers tonight and that would be enough. Just tonight.

With sudden strength Ian pulled her on top of him, and she felt his sex hard against her belly through the down cover. She buried her face against his neck as his hands caressed her hips, tugging her nightgown. She helped him eagerly, with no pretense, with no virginal terror. The thought of him naked against her made her nearly frantic. She herself ripped her nightgown in her urgency to get it off her. She pulled back the blankets. She stared down at him, at all of him, at his swelled sex in the mat of black hair. Oh, God, she knew what he would do, and she couldn't imagine that he would fit inside her. She felt a shaft of fear, then shook it off. He wanted her—rather, he wanted a ghost, and she was willing to be that ghost for him tonight.

"I love ye," she said to him, knowing he couldn't hear her, and even if he did, they wouldn't be her words, they'd be Marianne's words.

His hands were kneading her hips, more gently now, and she was eased once again atop him, her belly and legs naked and pressed hard against him.

He clasped his arms tightly about her back and rolled over on top of her. His fingers were on her breasts, then her belly, and lower, finding her, and she was shocked at the pleasure it brought her. Ah, it was wonderful, these feelings. She didn't want him to stop. She didn't want the feelings to stop. She could feel them building and building. She didn't know what would happen, she just knew she wanted all of it. She pressed her hips upward against his fingers.

She felt his fingers part her, probe into her, and felt his sex coming into her. She knew it wouldn't work, it simply couldn't. He was too big. All excitement was gone. She wrapped her arms tightly about his neck and arched upward. She lurched upward with pain as he pressed inside her. She was terrified now that he would rip her, that she would die here in his bed.

Still, she wasn't prepared for the pain when he tore through her maidenhead. It was deep and ripping. She knew she mustn't scream, that it could wake Mabley and bring him running into the bedchamber.

He suddenly pulled back until he was nearly out of her, then drove with all his strength again into her. He was fully inside her now, lying against her, breathing hard.

He was moving now, speaking words to her she didn't understand. French words, sex words. No, she wouldn't cry out, she couldn't. He was kissing her chin, her nose, her mouth. It hurt so badly that she sank her teeth into the hollow of his neck and let her tears streak along his cheek. She felt a tremendous tautness in him as he drove back and forth in her, his arms tight about her. Suddenly he shuddered and tensed over her. A cry she couldn't hold in came out, but she'd buried her face in his neck, muffling the sound. She felt him heave then, heard the low moans tearing from his throat. She felt his seed deep inside her body. He collapsed on top of her, burying her beneath him. His breath came in deep, sighing gasps as his face fell beside hers on the pillow.

Brandy lay very still. He was heavy, but for the moment she didn't care. For the moment he was hers, all hers. His breathing calmed, and she felt the warmth of his mouth against her cheek. He gave a deep moan and was quiet. She believed that he slept.

I am part of him now, she thought, and tightened her arms about his waist. She lay quietly until she could bear his weight no longer. As gently as she could, she eased herself from under him and lay against his side. She gazed at his face in the dim candlelight and let her fingers trace along the firm line of his jaw, feather light.

For tonight, at least, he was hers, and she wouldn't allow Marianne's ghost or Felicity's claim on him to ruin her happiness. She pulled the covers over both of them and carefully rested her face against his shoulder, cherishing the moments until she would have to leave him.

Ian awoke with a start, feeling as though his mind had been gone from his body for a lifetime. Perhaps two lifetimes. For a moment he was disoriented and gazed with some confusion at the bright shaft of sunlight that streamed through the windows. He planted his mind firmly back into his body and tentatively raised himself to his elbow.

"Your grace."

"Mabley, good God, man, what is the day and the time? I feel like I've been away for a very long time."

"Your grace is clear-headed?"

"I have my wits restored, I believe." He carefully flexed his back, and winced at the pain. "My shoulder is on the mend, Mabley."

"It's Thursday, your grace, and near to ten o'clock in the morning."

"You mean that I've been unconscious since yesterday?"

The deep lines in Mabley's old face smoothed out as he smiled at his master. "Yes, your grace, that, and you were out of your head for some time with the fever. Your Grace had all of us mightily worried."

"Out of my head? You mean I was delirious?" He frowned, trying to piece memories together.

"Yes, your grace." Mabley approached his master and added softly, "You remembered it all again, your grace."

There was no need for him to explain further.

To Mabley's surprise, the duke didn't dwell on that. He said, "It would appear, Mabley, that someone had taken me into profound dislike. I recall very little of it. Has the culprit been caught?"

Mabley shook his head. "No, your grace. A Mr. Trevor, the Scottish magistrate, is looking into the matter. I will send Mr. Giles to you if you wish. I haven't been with the family."

"Yes, I would speak with Giles. Damn, but I'm hungry and much in need of a shave and a bath. See to that first, before you send up Giles, will you, Mabley?" He paused a moment, looking hard at his old retainer. "You look like you're ready to fall on your ass, Mabley. Don't tell me you were my only nurse."

"No, your grace. Miss Brandy took care of

you during the nights. Now, don't get yourself lathered. You must know that Lady Brandy is very strong-willed. You just rest easy, your grace, and I'll be back shortly." He continued at the uncertain look on his master's face, "The bell cord is broken, your grace. I'll fetch Wee Albie."

"It appears that there are a lot of wee people about. I seem to recall vaguely someone named Wee Robert."

"The Scots doctor. He'll be here to see you this morning, no doubt."

After Mabley closed the door quietly behind him, the duke slowly swung his legs over the side of the bed and tried to rise. He hated his helplessness, and cursed silently as his legs refused to hold his weight. He sank back down, rubbing the growth of beard on his face. Be damned if he was going to be an invalid. He flung back the covers.

Two splotches of dried blood stood out starkly on the white sheet. He froze when jagged pieces of memory began to fit themselves together. He gazed down at himself and saw more blood, as well as his own seed. He dashed his hand across his brow. He remembered. Oh, God, no. Surely he couldn't have done that to her. He felt a nagging soreness and raised his hand to touch his neck. He could feel teeth marks. He touched his fingers to his cheek, remembering her tears as he'd thrust himself deeply into her, not letting her ease, just heaving himself over her and into her, just taking and taking more until he'd found his release. He'd given her nothing except pain. And she'd endured him.

Mabley returned shortly to find the duke sitting up, staring vacantly ahead of him. He imagined his master must be in a good deal of pain. Strong he was, and proud, and he viewed illness as something to be overcome as quickly as possible. It hadn't been two days since someone had shot him, yet here he was sitting on the side of his bed. "Your grace, this will never do. You're weak. It's to be expected. We don't want the fever to come back. Here, let me help you back under the covers. Mr. Giles wants to speak to you. Perhaps you wish to eat this broth while you see him? You need to build your strength."

Ian nodded silently. "Yes, Mabley, the bath can wait. Give me the soup and send in Giles."

Ten minutes later, Giles came into the bedchamber, paused in the doorway as he looked his cousin over, and said, "Ian, old fellow. If you've got your appetite, you must be on the mend." Giles crossed to the bed and looked closely at his cousin. "You are feeling better?"

"Yes, Giles, much better. Do sit down while I eat this soup. You might know they're calling it chicken soup, but I swear there's not a shred of chicken to be found. Just this broth that doesn't taste like anything."

"Be grateful that it doesn't. Would you prefer the taste of Cook's trifle?" Giles grinned at the duke as he sat down on the leather chair at the bedside. He began to tap his fingertips together in a thoughtful way.

"Do you remember anything, Ian, other than the obvious? Did you see any strange shadows that didn't belong on the beach? Perhaps you heard something odd that didn't quite fit?"

"I remember far too much," the duke said slowly. "Unfortunately, none of it concerns the identity of my would-be killer. Mabley tells me there's a fellow by the name of Trevor poking about."

"Yes, an old fool, Lady Adella tells us. He is, I think, a well-meaning fellow, but there are woefully few facts to aid him. As you can well imagine, all the Robertsons are at each other's throats. Accusations and suspicions are rife. I mean to get you away from this place, Ian, as soon as you are well enough to travel."

The duke lowered his soup spoon, silent for some moments. He said finally, "No, I think not, Giles. It isn't that I'm much concerned about appearing the coward by returning to England, no, not that. It's just that there's something I must still do here. No, I don't intend to try to find out who killed me. It would probably be a waste of time. I doubt that the bastard would in any way bring himself to my notice."

"Do you refer to Percy?"

"If he's a bastard in character as he was in name, then yes. What does Lady Adella have to say about the matter? Come, I know she'd say quite a lot, it's her way."

"She made a sour comment about disliking scoundrels and mysteries. Other than that, she has joined in the fray with the rest of the family. Felicity, as you can imagine, has been somewhat of a trial."

The duke said abruptly, "Did you know, Giles,

that Brandy has stood guard over me at night? A stupid thing to do and so I'll tell her."

"No, I didn't know. I don't think Felicity would like that, though. No, I daresay she'd screech the rafters down from the ceiling and topple the armor from the walls. Brandy is a very unusual girl."

"Indeed, I would have to agree with you, cousin."

"After you were shot, she demanded of Claude exactly where *he* had been. She was like a little terrier. But you know, Ian, it doesn't set right with me, your wanting to remain here, for whatever reason. I tell you, no one, including myself, can venture other than suspicious guesses as to the identity of the person who tried to kill you. Can't you see how foolhardy it is for you to remain, possibly giving the fellow another chance at you?"

"I assure you, Giles, that I shall be very much on my guard. And if I keep myself surrounded by Robertsons, what chance would the scoundrel have?"

Giles didn't appear happy with the duke's decision, but he kept his mouth shut. The duke had a reputation for holding to a course once he'd set it.

"You know, old boy, Felicity isn't going to be happy about your decision. She's spared no pains telling everyone what a detestable, horrid place this is and how she plans to see us all gone from here the moment you are better. Once I thought Lady Adella would throw her cane at Felicity, but the old bird managed to hold onto her control. In her place, to be honest, I don't know what I would have done. Your sweet Brandy didn't say a word, just got up and left the room. For a while there I thought she'd gone to get a gun. If she had, that would have proved interesting."

"I will have to speak to Felicity. After Mabley's shaved me and drowned me in my bath, send her to me, will you, Giles?"

Oh, yes, he wanted to speak to Felicity. He wanted to speak to her very much.

26

"You're a much braver man than I, cousin." Giles patted the duke's arm and took himself from the room.

The duke tried to concentrate upon the possible identity of his would-be killer, but found that it wasn't a killer in his mind, it was Brandy. "What a damned mess," he said to himself.

Giles found Felicity sitting alone in the drawing room downstairs. He imagined that there had been other people in the room and that she'd driven them out. She said in a voice sharp with boredom, "Well, Giles, what of his grace? Is he coming down today?"

Giles eyed her petulant mouth and the narrowed, quite beautiful eyes. There was just a dab of amusement in his voice as he said, "I found Ian much improved, my dear. Indeed, I left him in Mabley's capable hands, getting a shave if you must know, and a bath."

"Yes, he is so terribly dark," she said, more to herself than to him.

"There is that," he said. "Now, Ian has asked to speak to you, my dear, after he has had his bath. I will take you up in a while. You mustn't act shocked, for the fever and pain from the wound have changed him a bit."

"I wish we knew which one of these ghastly men is responsible. No one will say anything, you know. Even while they insult each other in the most vulgar manner imaginable, they are protecting each other, I am certain of it. And that boorish doctor—goodness, he's so very short. How can a doctor be so short? Well, you saw how he insulted me, Giles."

Giles vaguely recalled that Wee Robert hadn't shown what Felicity undoubtedly considered due concern for her nerves. "He was, most understandably, I thought, very worried about the duke, my dear." He pulled out a small, elegant snuffbox, flipped it expertly open with one finger, and helped himself to a generous pinch. He sneezed delicately and removed a fleck of snuff from his sleeve. "Poor old Mabley looked worn to the bone, what with him having the full care of Ian during the day. Thank God it is Brandy who—"

"He's another one who shows no proper respect for his betters. I shall see that shriveled old turnip is soon out of my house. What do you mean, he's taken care of the duke during the day? What about Brandy? What has that rude girl have to say to anything? Surely she hasn't now decided to come to London? I tell you, Giles, I won't have it. That miserable little slut won't be in my house once I'm the Duchess of Portmaine."

"Did I mention Brandy? I don't remember." He looked away to gaze a moment at the dusty bagpipes hanging limply over the huge mantel-piece. Beside them hung the crested Robertson coat of arms.

But Felicity had caught the scent. "You of all people mustn't try to keep things from me. It is *she* who has been with him at night, isn't that true, Giles?"

"Yes, but I can see no reason for you to be upset about it. You didn't volunteer to stay with him, did you? Undoubtedly she did a fine job of nursing him."

"Hah. I can just imagine how well the little slut *nursed* him."

"If you'll recall, Felicity, the duke was seriously wounded. I don't think he's had the strength to even feed himself, much less dawdle with another female. Also, I don't think Ian would appreciate you calling his ward a slut. Ah, look at the time. I must warn you, my dear, that Ian is set upon staying here. I tried to convince him to leave, but he has no intention of doing so. He says he has more work to get done before he returns to England. No, I don't think he's going to budge."

Felicity jumped to her feet. "This is ridiculous. Surely he's in no fit state to make such a decision. I hope you told him so."

"You know as well as I do that when Ian makes a decision, he sticks to it. I tried to talk him around, but it didn't work. You must have learned by now that your betrothed is a very determined, stubborn man. Once he sets a course, it takes more than mere mortals to change him from it."

"Determined is he," Felicity said, her white teeth clenched. "And just what does he think I am—a weak, simpering little fool like his first wife, Marianne? I will tell him, you may be certain, that I have no intention of lying down on the floor like a rug and let him tread upon me. Determined? We'll see about that."

"Oh, Lord," Giles said as Felicity picked up her skirts and nearly ran out of the room. He didn't think he'd ever seen her move so quickly. She ran rather gracefully.

Within minutes, she was knocking sharply on the duke's bedchamber door.

Mabley opened it and stared. She was out of breath. She looked fit to kill. "Lady Felicity?"

"Well, it isn't Lady Adella," she snapped at him. "Pray tell the duke that I wish to see him, Mabley. The corridor is drafty, so don't keep me waiting."

"His grace is expecting you, Lady Felicity," Mabley said, and quickly backed out of her way.

"Do come in, Felicity," Ian called from the bed. He said to Mabley under his breath, "Make yourself scarce. Have a mug of ale, then come back."

Mabley slipped past her out of the room.

Felicity gazed across the room, her eyes flickering briefly toward the mammoth fireplace, then to the huge bed. It was a man's bedchamber, stark, with no delicate hangings or furnishings to soften its lines. The room suited him. Ian lay in the center of the bed, his black head in stark relief against the white pillow.

"Giles tells me you're feeling better, Your Grace," she said, trying to sound conciliatory. Her mother had always told her that bending just a bit to get what she wanted wouldn't hurt her pride overmuch. But it did hurt.

"Aye," he said in the Scottish vernacular that she loathed. "Thank you for coming, Felicity," he added, his voice ironic. "I think it important that we talk."

"Giles has already informed me that you don't wish to leave Penderleigh. I can't imagine that it would bode well for your health to remain here. Tell me Giles was mistaken. Tell me you want to leave here as soon as you're well enough."

He said easily, "As I explained to Giles, I still have something that requires my attention here. Thus I have no intention of turning tail and dashing back to England. I'm disappointed, Felicity, that you don't appear to understand my reasons."

She drew back at the harshness in his voice. What did he have to be angry about? She was just trying to make him see reason, nothing more. Her fingers itched to hit him, but a lady couldn't do that. Ah, but she could sharpen herself a bit. "*I've* disappointed *you,* your grace? What about *my* wishes in this matter? Surely you cannot imagine that I enjoy being surrounded by vulgar, rude barbarians? Do you know they all yell at each other and accuse each other? You know as well as I do that one of them is obviously a murderer."

He was looking at her with even newer eyes than he'd had before he'd been shot. And before he'd been shot, his eyes had been quite new when they'd looked at her. He saw now that she was sharp and spiteful. He saw no generosity in her, no caring for another, just malice and contempt. He wasn't about to draw back, to measure his tone or his words.

He was nearly smiling as he said, his voice low and cold, "I still live, as you see. As to your calling the Robertsons vulgar and rude, madam, it appears to me that you should examine your own behavior. Not one conciliatory word have I heard you utter since you have come to Penderleigh. You pride yourself on being the daughter of an earl, but I will tell you that your manners have been as low as the lowest fishwife's."

"Fishwife? How dare you call *my* manners into question, Ian? Ah, I see what it is now. I suppose you feel that little slut Brandy behaves in a manner better to your liking?"

"I hardly think Brandy comes into this conversation, Felicity," he said matter-of-factly. Ah, but his voice was still wonderfully cold, filled with his dislike for her. "Brandy a slut? How odd that you'd think such a thing. I wonder what she thinks of you?"

"She counts for nothing. It doesn't matter what she thinks about anything. And she is a slut, nothing more than that." Her dislike continued to overflow. She couldn't have stemmed it unless her mouth had been sewn shut. She realized she was shaking with anger, but she didn't care. "Let me tell you, Ian, that Giles let it slip that your precious Brandy has most obligingly nursed you during the nights. Did you much enjoy her care, your grace?"

"Brandy is generous, at times overly so," he said, and knew guilt in equal measure to the pain in his back.

"I suppose you believe I should emulate that little trollop? Or perhaps you would prefer that I docilely hang my head like your saintly Marianne and bow to your every ridiculous whim?"

"You go too far, madam." And she was going even further than he'd prayed she'd go. He wanted to applaud her show of meanness. He wanted to fan it to outrage.

"Do I, your grace? Oh, yes, you refused to ever discuss Marianne with me, did you not? Did you believe me such a witless fool that I would not quickly discover that I bear a marked resemblance to her? I even know that all your mistresses have black hair and green eyes. You've gained quite a reputation with your requirements. Well, listen to me, Ian, I'm not your damned Marianne."

"You state an irrevocable fact, Felicity. What is your point?"

His coldness sent her over the edge. "My point is, your grace, that I shan't play the role of a second Marianne. I once believed that you knew what you owed to me and to your own name, but I begin to see that I was sadly mistaken in your character. You behave more in the manner of one of these beastly Scots than an English peer."

"*Your* behavior is very enlightening as well. And you're quite right. I see I have little to nothing in common with you, Felicity. Give me the Scots anyday."

"There are some, my dear duke, who do not find me as repugnant as you seem to do. Indeed, there is the Marquess of Hardcastle, a noble, refined gentleman whose suit my father discouraged because of your attentions." She smote her forehead, a very effective ploy. "To think I paid him no attention because of you."

"Undoubtedly Horace would slobber with joy to hear you say that. Indeed, I would wager that you would believe him the most spectacular male human in the world until he dared to disagree with you. Ah, I grow weary of arguing with you, Felicity. I have told you my plans, and I repeat to you, I have no intention of changing my mind. None. But if you wish to continue with your malice, pray do. A clean spleen is a healthy spleen, my mother always said to my father."

"I suppose that little fool Brandy fairly drips honey about you, pandering to your every whim? I suppose you have but to nod and she comes running to do whatever it is you want? That is what you prefer, is it not, your grace? An ignorant, sniveling little—"

But this was going too far. He said sharply, "Hold your tongue, madam. You expose your own character more than even the Marquess of Hardcastle could take."

"Oh, how very wrong I was about you. To think that I let myself be drawn in just because of your rank and position."

"Felicity," he said with deadly calm, "you begin to bore me. Actually, you really began to

298

bore me when you walked into the room a good ten minutes ago. Now you're deadening me. Perhaps Giles will listen to your shrill raving, but I won't. No more."

She drew up to her full height and squared her shoulders. "You are insulting, and I shan't stand for it." Her voice became as formal and cold as the queen's. "I demand that you return with me to London as soon as you are able. If you refuse, your grace, I beg to inform you that our engagement is off."

He wanted to dance. He wanted to sing. He felt not one single bit of guilt. Just immense relief. He said very softly, "I refuse."

She stared at him in some astonishment, turned away, and marched, head held high, to the door.

She said over her shoulder, her voice heavy with sarcasm, "I wish you luck, your grace, with all of your Scottish relatives. You will not object, I am certain, if I send a retraction of our engagement to the *Gazette*."

"Not at all. Say all that is proper to your parents. Oh, yes, Felicity, don't despise a marquess, even Horace, who has a marginal brain, because it's but one rank less than a duke."

"Go to the devil," she screamed at him, then slammed the door behind her as loud as she could.

When Giles entered the duke's bedchamber not many minutes later to see how he had fared in his battle, he drew up short, his look of concern falling to the floor. "Well, I'll be damned. You've the look of the cat who has swallowed all the cream. What the devil have you done?"

"Congratulate me, Giles, I'm no longer a betrothed man. Felicity broke our engagement. I believe the estimable Horace, Marquess of Hardcastle, will shortly be bowled over by her."

Giles sucked in his breath. "I never thought she'd go that far. Oh, dear, Ian, I'm sorry. Wait. You're laughing."

"My dear fellow, you've always told me she wasn't at all like Marianne, that she wasn't malleable, that she wasn't particularly kind or gentle. So now I believe you. I should have believed you long ago. Aren't you pleased that I've been rescued from a life of domestic horror? Damn, I was such a blind ass. One must never try to recreate the past, it's folly, particularly—" He paused, a deep smile lighting his eyes.

"Particularly when, Ian?"

"Ah, nothing, Giles. I was just thinking out loud. Now, if you would grant me a huge favor. Please take Felicity back to London."

"Very well," Giles said, and he was smiling. How he could actually smile at the thought of spending six days in Felicity's company amazed the duke.

"Your medicine, your grace."

"Ah, Mabley. See, Giles, he refuses to leave my side. As long as I remain abed, I am protected better than the king. Don't worry." He stretched out a large hand toward his cousin, who grasped it firmly. "I thank you, Giles. Do take care. No doubt I shall see you in London in the not too distant future."

"Very well, Ian, I'll get Felicity out of here in the morning."

"I just hope she doesn't carry you kicking and screaming from Penderleigh this very afternoon."

Giles gave his cousin one long last look. "You look like the devil, Ian. You must rest now. No more excitement. No more broken engagements. Take good care of your master, Mabley," he added, and took his leave.

The duke gave Mabley a big smile. "You know, Mabley, I'm much more in the mood for a celebration. Fetch some claret, man. Surely there must be some in the wine cellars."

The duke thought he saw a decided sparkle in Mabley's rheumy old eyes as he turned to leave the room.

27

The duke caused a stir when he came into the drawing room late the following afternoon.

"Good God, Ian." Bertrand rushed to his side, ready to give him an arm. "Surely this is too soon for ye to be up and about. Shouldn't ye still be in yer bed? What did Wee Robert say?"

"I have slept nearly the entire day," the duke said, grinning at Bertrand, though it was just a bit forced, "and have grown quite tired of my bedchamber as well as my own company." He turned from Bertrand and bade the assembled company an easy greeting, though his eyes were hooded. He looked at Brandy, but all she did was stick up her chin. He couldn't very well walk up to her and kiss her, so he just nodded at her.

"Well, lad," Lady Adella said from her high-backed chair by the fireplace, "Bertie told us ye were rather white about the ears this morning. How is this ye appear nearly fit again this afternoon?"

"Lady Felicity is long gone," Constance said. "Seeing the back of her would make anyone feel better."

She received a sharp look from Lady Adella, but then the old lady laughed and thumped her cane. Constance looked to be quite pleased with herself.

"Yes, I know," the duke said, his eyes again going to Brandy's face. "I must agree with Constance. There is a new lightness about the place now, an easing of tension, don't you think so, Brandy?"

"It's true my fingers aren't itching to slap any faces," Brandy said, grinning at her sister. "Och, and she was trying, she truly was."

"Ye don't appear too terribly cast down to me, Your Grace," Claude said. "Is it as ye say? Ye are pleased the lady's gone?"

"More than you can imagine, Claude."

"I beg ye to sit down," Percy said, making room for the duke on the sofa. "I have no wish to bear yer weight again. It's powerful big ye are, Ian."

Crabbe appeared in the doorway to announce dinner. Ian turned to Brandy and held out his arm. He said nothing, merely waited. He quirked an eyebrow at her. He wanted to wink, but knew that if he did, she just might bolt.

She gave a quick little nod and placed her hand in the crook of his arm.

Amid the usual confusion that attended Lady Adella's preparation to quit the drawing room, Ian leaned down and said quietly to Brandy, "You know, do you not, that Lady Felicity has broken off our engagement?"

"Aye, I know. She was delighted to tell us all what she thought of us. She went on for a good ten minutes. Constance was a brat, Fiona remained vulgar with her red hair. On and on until she got to me. I thought she would pop her stays. I escaped with just a simple slut, and that was even a bit garbled, so if she'd been called on it, she could have denied it. I think she was afraid that if she truly went after me that I would leap on her and smash her. I was tempted, but she did draw herself in. She has some control, at least when it comes to her own survival."

"She saw the blood in your eye."

"I think so because it was surely there, blood and my hands were good fists."

"I never believed Felicity was stupid. She was herself and that, unfortunately, was a different woman than I believed. I've had more luck than a single man deserves." He raised his eyes to heaven, then said to her in a very quiet voice, "I would speak to you, Brandy."

She looked up at him and frowned. "Are ye certain ye're feeling all right?"

"I'm tired, but that's to be expected. My

shoulder hurts, but it's bearable. I just hope I won't fall asleep over my soup."

If the duke thought he'd detect guilt on a Robertson face during dinner, he was doomed to disappointment. Although each Robertson, with the exception of Claude, had paid a short visit to his sickroom, full of clucking outrage and concern, none had in any way betrayed himself. And if he had believed that dinner would be a subdued affair, with the pall of mystery hanging heavily in the air, he had to grin to himself, for the Robertsons showed no hesitation in discussing the affair.

"I tell ye, my boy," Lady Adella said over a fork of boiled salmon, "I'm convinced it was a worthless tinker who shot ye."

"In which case, lady," the duke said lightly, "the fellow would be long away from Penderleigh. We must trust that he was not also eyeing our sheep."

"I see ye've still yer sense of humor about ye," Claude said, smacking his lips over a mouthful of bannocks. "I can't say I'd be up to much wit if someone had shot me."

"What would ye, Claude," Percy said with that patented sneer of his, "that the duke accused ye of being a bloody killer, albeit a poor shot?"

Claude choked on his bannocks, and Bertrand thwacked him soundly on the back. "Ye'll hold yer tongue, Percy," Bertrand said, furious now. "I'm tired of yer snide barbs that do nothing except make others feel miserable and angry. Keep yer trap shut, else I'll take ye outside and turn that pretty face of yers into pounded meat."

304

"It's all a piece of nonsense, Percy," Constance said, "and well ye know it. Poor Uncle Claude can scarce get about with his gouty foot. Do be quiet, else I'd be tempted to help Bertie pound ye into the ground."

"Ye see what a good lass she is, Bertie?" Claude said to his son.

"I see," Bertrand said, gazing briefly at Constance's red face.

"This is all quite interesting," Percy said. "I'll hold my peace. I don't want Constance upset."

Bertrand turned to Ian. "Ye must know that Trevor is leaving no stone unturned. Though what stones there are appear to have nothing at all under them. It's a puzzle, a mystery that none of us like."

"Aye," Lady Adella said, "that ass Trevor has turned every stone over except the one that hides the scoundrel. Maybe it's a boulder and that's the problem. Trevor hasn't the ability to turn it over."

"It's possible," the duke said. What else could he say? That one of them was a bloody liar?

"What do ye intend to do, yer grace?" Percy asked, his voice for once perfectly serious, with not a single hint of a sneer.

Ian paused a moment, then said, "That depends upon several things. I should know my plans by tomorrow."

Lady Adella said, "At least ye're free of that whining little chit. What a pain in the arse that one was. She complained and whined that no one cared about her and her overset nerves. She wouldn't have made ye a good wife, Ian, not at

305

all. Good riddance, I say." Lady Adella added somewhat wistfully, "Though I don't conscience to tell ye that I shall sorely miss Mr. Giles Braidston. A dandy lad that one is. He knew all about Lord Brainley. Fancy that, Adolphus died some thirty years ago, I heard, but his wickedness lives on in the minds of young men. Aye, I wish I'd known Adolphus." Lady Adella fell silent then. Brandy was glad she didn't know what her grandmother was thinking about.

"Lord Brainley was one of the founders of the Hell Fire Club," Ian said to Brandy.

She looked at him blankly, cocking her head to one side in question.

"No, I don't think I'll answer that," he said, wishing he'd kept his mouth shut. He saw that she wouldn't let it go and said with a shrug, "Let's just say it was a group of wicked young men with too much money who delighted in hurting others."

It was with some relief that Ian greeted the end of the meal, for his wound was beginning to pain him beyond what he could control. He wanted his bed and the oblivion the laudanum would bring.

"Ye're not looking at all the thing, Ian," Bertrand said when they rose to follow the ladies to the drawing room. Ian nodded briefly, and Bertrand continued in a low voice, "I know this is a nasty business and that there is no one that ye feel ye can really trust. For so long as ye remain here at Penderleigh, be it a day or a month, I think it wise to let everyone be told that ye will never be alone."

Ian said, "Really, Bertrand, I do appreciate your concern, but I have Mabley—"

"A tired old man, Ian. None of us want to take chances and nor should ye. When ye leave the castle, I want at least two of us to be near ye all the time. It's a wise precaution, and I'll not argue with ye more."

"Aye," Ian said with a tired smile. "If you fancy to be Saint George, I'll not quibble with you. It would appear that, like Trevor, I will also fail to discover the identity of the fellow. No, Bertrand, say no more. Like you, I also have my suspicions, but they are only that, suspicions, not tangible proof."

When Ian looked around again to find Brandy, she was gone. He'd not believed her to be a coward. On the other hand, he wouldn't have believed either that she would have given her virginity to a man whose mind was raging with fever. Why had she done it? He said brief good-nights to the family and walked thoughtfully to his room.

The duke rose early the following morning, felt deep pain in his shoulder, chose to ignore it, and walked down that interminable corridor to the main staircase, Mabley arguing with him the whole way.

"Give it a rest, Mabley," he said finally when he reached the huge Robertson entrance hall. "When I'm tired, I'll come up and lie down. Go drink a strong cup of tea."

He didn't see Brandy, and he'd expected to. He ate his breakfast, then went in search of her.

He didn't find her in the drawing room or in Fiona's nursery. She wasn't outside lurking behind the rhododendron bushes.

He left the castle and walked quickly to the beach, aware that Bertrand and Mabley, his morning protectors, were trailing not far behind him. He saw her standing on the beach, staring out over the water. He was relieved that Fiona was some distance away, squatting on her haunches, playing with some driftwood and sand. Bertrand and Mabley remained at the top of the cliff. He didn't give a good damn what either of them thought when they would see him speaking to Brandy.

He made his way quietly down the cliff path. He called out, "Don't run away from me. It wouldn't be fair since you know I can't catch you. That's right, just stay put and let me talk to you. At least you owe me that much, don't you? You had your way with me and left me without a word of reassurance. You don't like the sound of that? Now you're looking hunted. That's all right. I can deal with hunted. Just don't move."

She didn't move but she wanted to. She wasn't embarrassed. No, it went much deeper than that. She was frightened, it was that simple. He didn't realize he had the power to smash her into the ground. No, she had to hear him out, endure his words, his excuses, his apologies, his attempts to make things right—she knew he'd try to make things right—and then she could escape him. Then she could hide and will herself to forget. He came right up to her, not a foot away, and he looked down at her with a strange smile.

He was pale beneath his Scottish tan. Immediately she raised her hand to his face and lightly touched his chin with her fingers. "Surely ye shouldn't be up so early. Isn't your shoulder paining ye? Shall I call Wee Robert? Ye shouldn't have climbed down the cliff path." Oh, God, what was she doing, touching him, acting like he was hers? She slowly drew her hand back to her side.

"Anything else? No? All right, I will see Wee Robert this afternoon. If you take one step backward, I'll believe you a coward. Now, don't move, Brandy."

"Ye're giving me orders, and I've never liked orders. Just ask Lady Adella. When I was younger she'd bellow out that I was a stubborn stoat." Chatter was good for the soul, but, oh, it was harder than she'd begun to imagine. She made a harsh sound in her throat, whirled about, and ran toward the rock path back up the cliff. She'd gotten no more than three steps when a strong arm closed around her waist and she was lifted and tucked like some sort of package under the duke's right arm.

Her anger gave way immediately to fear. "Don't, Ian. You might make the wound start bleeding again. Please, I swear I won't run again. Please, put me down so you won't hurt yerself." But he paid her no heed, just tightened his arm about her waist.

"I'll survive, but I have serious doubts about you, in my current mood. You'll obey me now and I'll hear no more about it." He dropped her on the wet, sandy beach, very near the lapping waves. "Now, do you wish me to tie you down, Brandy? I will, you know, if you don't face up to what we've done. You're acting like a girl, not a woman. And I know now that you are a woman. So act like one."

She looked up at him standing over her, his hands on his hips. "Did ye hurt yer back?"

"Not yet, but if I do, it will be your fault." He looked down at her, on her back, up on her elbows, her face flushed. From embarrassment? From anger at him? He didn't know, but he fancied he was going to find out soon enough. Ah, and that splendid thick blond hair of hers, all pulled back slick into those boring fat braids, fit only for a schoolgirl. A memory stirred. Masses of thick, soft hair swirled over his face. Damn, just as he caught the memory, just as he knew he could breathe in the scent of her and her hair, it was gone, leaving an elusive scent just beyond his senses. So much of that night was gone, but he hoped someday he would remember it again, every single moment. He'd held her hard against him, he'd been inside her—oh, God, he had to stop it. At least for now.

He stuck out his hand and pulled her to her feet. "First things first, Brandy. Let me tell you that both Mabley and Wee Robert sang your praises. What you did scared ten years off my life, but I thank you. You saved my life. Can you tell me why you did it? Not that I'm stupid enough to preach that a lady should have cried out delicately and swooned so that the bastard would have finished me off. No, I'm grateful to you, beyond grateful. You gave me my life. Why, Brandy?"

She could deal with this. But she wondered at his question. It was so obvious, it had to be, even to one of Wee Albie's brain size. She just shrugged and kicked a pebble with her scuffed boot. "You make me sound like a heroine, but I'm not. Everything happened so quickly. You were on your face, unconscious, blood pouring out of the bullet wound in your back. I didn't think, truth be told. I couldn't let anyone hurt you. I just acted." She shrugged again.

"You know, I wouldn't let anyone hurt you either."

"Perhaps gentlemen are like that."

"Just what the devil does that mean?"

"That you would save any Robertson if such a situation arose."

"And you wouldn't?"

She gave him an evil grin, splaying her hands in front of her. "I just might run the other direction if Percy had been the Robertson shot."

"Good point. Mabley also told me—all stiff he was and sniffing—that you were my guardian for two nights. He said I was helpless, that it could be someone in the castle who'd shot me, that you wouldn't leave me alone. He even said you fetched a gun from Grandfather Angus's collection. Does it even work?"

"Aye, I loaded it myself. And I'm sure Marta or Mabley also told you that I even kept my bedroom door open last night and the night before, and a lighted candle just outside in the corridor."

"You what? Oh, I see. No, but thank you for telling me of yet another plan executed to protect me. You couldn't stay in my bedchamber since I had my wits again. You didn't want to take the chance I'd look at you and want to haul you into my bed. Again."

She looked straight at him. She felt tendrils of salty, damp hair blowing over her face. She swiped the hair away. "Truth be told, ye didn't do any hauling at all."

28

"I see. So that's the line you're going to take, is it?"

He looked at her closely, noting the dark smudges under her eyes. "You've not slept well. I don't like that. I understand it, but I don't like it. Now, I will thank you again for protecting me. Now let's talk about you in my bed and me attacking you."

"I told ye that ye didn't do any hauling or any attacking."

"Brandy, look at me. Lady Felicity is long gone. Bless Giles, he deserves a longer life for being the sacrificial goat to escort her back to London. I think I'll have to buy him a startling new waistcoat, perhaps one in puce and mauve. What do you think?"

"I'm very glad she's gone. She wasn't a nice

lady, Ian. But perhaps you're thinking now that you miss her, that—"

He broke into deep, full laughter. "Miss her? Felicity? No, you must be speaking of someone else, aren't you, Brandy? It has been quite some time now that I realized my mistake. I thank providence that I was made Earl of Penderleigh. It gave me an excuse to leave London and come here. I'm deeply grateful that Felicity became jealous of the way I wrote of you in my one and only letter to her and followed me here. If she hadn't come the good Lord knows I would never have seen her true colors until it was too late.

"I think too, to be honest about it, that Felicity also came to the same conclusion. I daresay she now looks upon me as some vile, selfish beast she's well rid of. No, Brandy, I don't miss her at all. If my shoulder didn't hurt, I'd fall on my knees and kiss the ground in thanksgiving for my rescue."

"Oh."

"Oh? That's all you can say? Come now, please stop this game you're playing with me. No, don't punch me. I just might fall over in a swoon and then where would you be? Listen to me, we really must talk. You can't avoid it any longer. We made love, Brandy. I took your virginity. I realized that when I was sitting on the edge of my bed the following morning and saw your blood and my seed on the sheets and on my sex."

She turned away and sat down on a large rock, tucking her legs beneath her, smoothing her skirts over her scuffed boots. He had another memory—ah, so very vivid—of the feel of her hips and thighs. His fingers twitched. He felt a stab of lust so sharp he had to turn away from her. And she couldn't begin to understand a man's lust. Well, she knew from her one experience with him, but it had been just one night. And she'd been a virgin.

"Yes, you were a virgin and I took you without a by-your-leave. And you, Brandy, you didn't yell the house down. You didn't hit me, which would have gotten my attention as well. Why didn't you?"

She was silent as the stone she was sitting on.

"I've never known you to be so silent before." He reached out and grasped one of her hands. Her hand was cold. He found himself warming that hand between his two large ones, just rubbing, holding her hand.

"Brandy, I'm sorry for many things. But mainly I'm sorry I hurt you. If I'd had my wits about me, well, then nothing would have happened. Given that I was out of my head with fever, I wasn't easy with you. I hurt you and I regret it. A woman's first experience with a man shouldn't be painful."

She was staring out to sea. "Ye didn't hurt me," she said only. Oh, God, the memories. The painful ones were there, but they meant nothing. He'd held her and stroked her and kissed her. No, the pain had been nothing. She didn't even know she'd bled. She was still a bit tender between her thighs, but that she accepted, for he was large. That thought made her turn as red as her nose did on a very sunny day.

"No," she said again, still not looking at him.

"Ye didn't hurt me. Not much anyway, less than much. Don't worry about it."

He frowned at her, then let go of her hand. She turned to him and watched him untie his cravat and bare his neck. "All right, if I didn't hurt you, then why did you do this?"

"Oh," she said, staring at her teeth marks on his neck, pale against his skin but still distinct. "I'd forgotten about that. I couldn't scream and I wanted to, so to keep myself quiet I guess I bit you. I'm sorry if that hurt you."

He rolled his eyes. "Yes, you hurt the hell out of me. You've probably scarred me. How can I ever forgive you? It's a pity I can't show you the trail of tears you left on my cheek, though I tasted the salt from them the next morning. As to the blood stains on the sheets, I only hope that Morag's mental perceptions are as lacking as her personal hygiene."

"This has nothing to do with anything. Why are you saying all these things? For God's sake, put your cravat back over your neck. No, don't move, I'll do it. I don't want you to stain your shoulder." She very gently eased his cravat back into place.

"Of course that night has to do with a lot of things. I took your virginity. You're a lady, not a mistress who knows exactly what she's doing. You came to me, I'll accept that, but I mean to understand you and I'm not about to let you leave this beach until I do."

She looked up at him then, a mistake, she knew, because he was so beautiful and she wanted him so desperately.

"There's nothing to understand," she said, wanting to touch him. "What happened was my choice. Aye, I came to you because I wanted to. I wanted to know what it was like between a man and a woman, but just with ye, only with ye. I wanted that one night and I knew I'd never have another chance. It was all my decision, ye had nothing to do with any of it."

"All your choice? That's leniency with the truth if ever I heard it. Not my choice?"

"Ye didn't even know who I was. I seduced ye, Ian, and ye didn't have a say in it. I know ye're a gentleman and thus ye have to feel guilty, particularly since I was a virgin. But don't. Again, it was my decision and I did what I wanted to."

"So I'm not to feel guilty. I'm really not in the habit of bedding virgins, you know." He paused a moment, remembering all of her words. "You wanted me?"

"Aye," she said baldly. "I wanted ye."

"Well, you had me, but it wasn't much fun for you, was it?"

"It was good enough. Ye'll forget soon enough, Ian, and I want ye to. I absolve ye of any ridiculous guilt you wish to bear."

"But I have no wish to forget, little one," he said and tugged her hand until she was leaning against him. He reached out his hand and lightly stroked his fingertip over her eyebrows. "You're beautiful, you know that?"

She just looked at him, at his mouth. He swallowed. He couldn't help himself. He leaned to her and lightly kissed her mouth. Her lips were salty. He smiled even as he licked them. She jumped. He retreated.

He said, his voice now brisk, "I'm now blessedly free of any marriage entanglements. I'm now in a position for you to make an honest man of me. Will you marry me, Brandy? Will you be my duchess?"

She'd known he'd ask. He was a gentleman, after all. Even though she'd taken all responsibility, which was only right, he'd still done it.

She said only, "No."

He stared at her, not believing that one single, devastating word. "What did you say?"

"I said I won't marry ye." She tried to pull her hand away, but he wouldn't let her go.

"This isn't at all what I expected. Really, Brandy, I don't see that you have much choice in the matter. We made love. I spilled my seed inside you."

"So? Why, Ian, why have I no choice? Is it because I'm no longer a virgin and thus damaged goods? Why do I care? I have no intention of marrying. It doesn't matter."

"That's one of the stupidest things I've ever heard you say. And believe me, in the past half hour I've heard a good deal of stupidity come from that beautiful mouth of yours. Oh, damn." He leaned over and kissed her again. He felt her mouth open and thought he'd die. He had to stop this. He wasn't about to take her again, this time on a beach.

He said against her warm mouth, "We shall both do what is right and appropriate. I've asked you to marry me. You will now tell me you would be happy to marry me. No more arguments. Is that clear?" He kissed her again. "Tell me that's clear and that you'll say yes. Either that or you can just nod." He kissed her again and then again. He wanted to touch more of her, but he didn't dare allow himself to.

She leaned back. She smiled at him. "You taste good. You taste like dark wickedness, all sweet and hot, just like I'd expect you to taste."

"Stop it, at least for the moment. Assure me that you'll marry me and I'll kiss you until you can't breathe. I'll kiss you until the tide comes in and tries to wash us out to sea."

She pulled back in the circle of his arms. She raised her hand and lightly touched his cheek. She felt immeasurably older than he. She felt ancient and sick at heart. "Ian, listen to me a moment. Would ye still wish to be free of Lady Felicity if what happened between us hadn't happened?"

"Another stupidity. You know I'm beyond grateful that she broke off our engagement. She has nothing to do with anything." He actually shuddered.

Brandy looked down at a broken fingernail, anything to look at except him and his mouth and his beautiful man's face. She said slowly, "If I hadn't come to yer bed, would ye have ever thought to ask me to be yer wife?"

That was a kick he hadn't expected. He had to deal with this just right. Everything hung in the balance here.

He said in a deep, calm voice, "I have never thought that my perceptions were overly lacking.

I even continue to believe myself a rather acceptable judge of character. I know you're not indifferent to me—indeed, that fact was fairly obvious from the first evening when you burst into my room. I can't deny that I tried to ignore you, treat you as a child, but it was because I was still betrothed to Lady Felicity. I had to see you as someone I couldn't have. Remember that afternoon at the crofter's hut? I kissed you and you kissed me back. I wanted you desperately and I know you cared for me. You've said now that you wanted to come to me that night I was fevered. You said you wanted to have that one night with me. Now I'm offering to give you every night for the rest of our lives. It's true you came to me freely. It's also obvious that you aren't now or ever will be a wanton woman. Doesn't it seem a reasonable thing for me to conclude that your heart, as well as your body, now belong to me? Of course I care for you, how could I not? You're bright, you're loving, you've a wicked wit, and I know we'll suit. Forgive me if I could do all of this better, but it seems to me that the last thing you'd want to do is turn down my marriage proposal."

He was forcing her to say it. She supposed she owed it to him, but still, it hurt so much, hurt so very much. She stared at him mutely, wishing life could be different, that his past could have been different, but it was not to be.

She said, "It isn't my feelings I question, Ian. Never my feelings."

"What the devil do you mean by that?"

"Very well. I'm young and inexperienced, but

I'm not a fool. I would never wed where there's no love. Or if the love is all on one side. Nay, don't interrupt me, for I would say what I feel. To be an *English* duchess would require you show me a great deal of patience and tolerance. I'm ignorant of yer ways. I don't mean I'd use the wrong fork or bellow something disrespectful to the queen, but ye were raised from your cradle to be a duke, a peer of the realm, the English realm. I was raised by Lady Adella. Aye, that would make anyone groan. I've never been away from Penderleigh. All I know is what's here. The only people I've ever dealt with are here. They're all Scottish. Don't ye understand, Ian?"

"All that you're talking about—it's nothing. I'll show you how to go along. There won't be any grand problems. They're all in your mind."

"All right, then, that's really just the prelude. Ye force me to strip the bark off the tree. Ye don't love *me,* ye love *her.* I can't marry ye, not knowing that."

He wanted to shake her. Then kiss her, then yell at her perhaps. "I don't love Felicity. I never loved her. Why the hell won't you believe me and stop this idiocy?"

"Aye, I know you never loved Felicity."

"Then what are you talking—" His voice fell like a rock off a cliff. He could but stare at her, no words in his brain or on his tongue.

She tried to smile at him, to reassure him, but she couldn't manage it. God, the pain was nearly unendurable. "Aye, ye can't say ye don't love Marianne. Of course ye didn't really care for Felicity, for she was naught but a blurred copy of yer first wife. Oh, Ian, I can't win ye from a woman six years dead. Whenever ye would look at me and see my gracelessness, ye'd but think of *her* and hate me for it. Love her if ye must, but don't force me into rivalry with a ghost."

He jumped off the rock and stood in front of her, his eyes dark and narrowed. He yelled, "Why are you playing this game with me? Do you wish me to feel more the scoundrel than I already do? I can't and won't accept what you have said. Don't you see, Brandy, I must set things aright. I must. I have no choice."

She rose also, and stood tall and proud. "I'll say it again. Ye're absolved, yer grace, of any dishonor. I refuse to allow ye to sacrifice yerself. Ye need have no concern that anyone will ever know that I shared yer bed, for I have no intention of telling anyone."

He slashed his hand through the air. He was so frustrated he wanted to howl with it. But still—she'd known, she'd known. He drew a deep breath. "Forget Marianne. She's dead, long dead. You're alive. I'm alive. We will wed. We will live together and it will be good between us. I admire you and you love me. I want you more than I've wanted any woman in a very long time."

"But ye can't say ye love me, can ye, Ian? Not like ye loved Marianne."

He went perfectly rigid. "Brandy," he said finally, his voice low and urgent, "I want you to wed me, to come back to England with me. You must realize that it is foolhardy for me to stay. Indeed, I can no longer be blind to the fact that the man who shot me will continue to evade me as he is everyone else. There is really naught to hold me here save you. Even the Cheviot sheep are all penned and happy. Marry me. Come back to England with me."

"I can't," she said. "I'm sorry, Ian, but I can't." She forced herself to turn away from him. "As for the villain, whoever he is, aye, I think ye should return to England. I can't bear ye being hurt again. Go home, Ian. Ye've saved Penderleigh. Ye're more generous than any of us could have expected. Ye've given Bertrand pride and responsibility. You've given him the means to see us well into this new century. We'll survive now, thanks to ye. We even have sheep, and ye're right. They're all settled. Our people are happier than gypsies with handfuls of gold coins. Go home."

He stared down at her. He could think of nothing more to say.

She gave him a brisk nod. Without another word she walked away from him down the beach, toward Fiona, who was still trying to make the sand turrets of her castle stay upright.

29

Ian and Bertrand stood on the front steps of Penderleigh in quiet conversation, while Crabbe and Mabley directed the loading of the carriage. The duke's curricle stood just beyond, Wee Albic holding nervously onto the horses' reins. It was very early, scarce past seven in the morning, a bright, sunny day it would be, the warmth of spring in the air.

If everyone believed the duke was leaving because he was afraid for his life, no one said anything, which he appreciated. He was in no mood to discuss anything with anybody, particularly the identity of the bloody bastard who'd tried to kill him.

"As much as I'd like ye to stay, Ian, getting ye out of Scotland does make me easier in the mind. I'll write ye, naturally, to tell ye how we progress with the Cheviot sheep."

"See that you do, Bertrand. I'll like to hear how happy the crofters are. Write me about the family too, if you wouldn't mind. Since I'm to be an absent owner and an absent relative, I do want to know how everyone is going along." As he'd told everyone good-bye the previous evening, he'd looked closely at each one's face, including Lady Adella's, wondering and wondering which one of them wished him dead. Brandy hadn't been there, curse her hide.

She'd excused herself shortly after dinner, so that he'd had no opportunity to speak privately to her. Not that he had anything more to say to her. Both of them had said everything. He would never understand her, never.

Marianne was dead, long dead. Why would his second wife care if he occasionally dreamed about his first wife? If he sometimes felt the sharp pain of her death yet again? If he chanced sometimes to relive that terrible nightmare in Paris, or remember the more tender times? Surely a wife would understand that, surely a wife would adjust.

He'd told her he was very fond of her. She'd told him that she loved him. Well, she was very young.

"I'll continue to keep a fire lit beneath Trevor. There must be something more the fellow can do."

"I wish you luck on that one, Bertrand."

"Excuse me, yer grace. May I speak with ye before ye leave?"

Ian turned sharply away from Bertrand at the sound of her voice. He felt something deep within him lurch at the sight of her, something warm and really quite satisfying. He also wanted to strangle her. She was standing some feet away from him. She looked nervous and uncertain. Well, she should. Perhaps she'd changed her mind. Perhaps she would plead with him to forgive her, to marry her. Yes, that had to be it. He took a quick step toward her. He wanted to pull that damned braid apart and untangle her hair with his fingers. He wanted to bury his face in her hair and smell the lavender scent. Lavender? How'd he know that? From that night she'd come to him. The scent, strong for a moment, now faded away.

"I'll see how Mabley and Crabbe are faring," Bertrand said, knowing well when to lose himself, and walked to the carriage.

"I didn't know ye meant to leave so early. May I have but a moment of yer time, please?"

What was going on here? She didn't sound like a woman who was ready to give over, a woman who was ready to plead to become his duchess. He nodded and followed her back into the castle, to the drawing room.

She saw that he wanted to speak, and fore-stalled him. "I need money," she said baldly.

"You what?"

"Perhaps a hundred pounds, if that isn't too much for ye." She saw his dark eyes narrow. She couldn't let him turn her down. She said quickly as she reached her hand out to touch his sleeve, "Ye said that ye meant to dower both Fiona and me. I need the money now. Couldn't ye please just deduct it from my dowry?"

"Would I be too common to ask why the hell you need one hundred pounds?" God, he sounded like a cold bastard, but he couldn't help it. He got another elusive scent of lavender.

Up went her chin. She stared at him straight in the face. "I need it for clothes, yer grace."

Like hell, he thought. Why was she lying to him? What the devil was going on here? He started to pin back her ears, when he looked closely at her. She looked scared and determined, an illogical combination, but that's what was showing on her expressive face. And she was pleading, not her tone of voice, but those eyes of hers, pleading with him for one hundred damned pounds. Her fingers, with their short, blunt nails, wildly plucked the fringe of her shawl. He wished she would put her hand back on his sleeve. God, she was warm and soft. He loved her hands on him.

What else could he do? He folded his tent. "Very well. Fetch me paper and ink." At the tilt of her head, he said, "It would be foolish to give you a hundred pound note. I'll write you a draft, and MacPherson will handle the transfer of funds for you."

She was out of the room in a flash. As if she expects me to change my mind, he thought. When she returned but a few minutes later, he still couldn't think of a likely reason why she should want the money. Why one hundred pounds?

He took the paper and ink from her outstretched hand and wrote out instructions to MacPherson. He paused a moment before writing in the amount. He thought she could have very little idea of the value of a hundred pounds. Whatever her reasons for wishing the money, he wanted her to have enough. He entered the sum of two hundred pounds, signed his name, and handed her the paper.

She sputtered and very nearly dropped the paper when she read the amount.

He said smoothly, "I've found that clothes are far more expensive than I believe they will be. Even clothes in Edinburgh. Clothes are important. You always want to look your best."

"That's very true. I thank ye, yer grace. Ye'll take care, won't ye?"

"Brandy—" He took a step toward her.

She quickly splayed her hands in front of her and backed away from him.

Damn her. His voice was hard as he said, "Very well. Since I am returning to London, it's doubtful that anyone will ever have to do any worrying about me again. You've made yourself very clear. I can see there's nothing more I can say to you to change your mind. I wish you good-bye, Brandy. I trust you will achieve what it is you're after. Some virginal knight on a white horse, no doubt, with no past, no painful memories."

He gave her a mock bow and strode from the drawing room, not looking back. A man had his pride, after all.

She walked slowly to the window. She saw Ian and Bertrand shake hands. Just behind the closed carriage, burdened with luggage strapped firmly to the boot, Mabley stuck his head out of the window to speak to Crabbe. In but a few moments Ian stepped gracefully into the curricle. With a final wave to Bertrand, he flicked Hercules's reins. The small entourage jerked into motion and was soon lost to sight among the thick rhododendron bushes.

He was gone. He was well and truly gone. She could have gone with him. She could have married him. Ah, but the price was too great. She looked down at the paper he'd written for her. The price was much greater than two hundred pounds.

Brandy detested tears. They never helped anything, just made her eyes puffy and red. They'd never made her feel any better for crying them in her eighteen years. But in this instance she didn't even realize they were running down her cheeks until she tasted salt. She dashed her hand across her mouth. There was no time for this. She had too much to do. MacPherson lived in Berwick and it would take her at least two hours to walk there.

She straightened her shoulders and walked back up the stairs to her room to change her sandals for a pair of stout walking boots.

Five days later, the Duke of Portmaine pulled Hercules and Canter to a stop in front of the huge columned entrance of the Portmaine town house, a giant edifice that dominated the eastern corner of York Square. It was a bright April afternoon, the sky was cloudless, the air sweet, though not as sweet as in Scotland. His mood was not happy. It would have been better had it been raining. Rain or fog, either one. Anything but this bloody nice weather.

He dined alone that evening, sorting through the huge pile of invitations and correspondence that had accumulated in his absence.

As it was the height of the Season, he found that his presence was requested at a seemingly endless number of routs and assemblies. He was on the point of tossing the myriad gilt-edged invitations into the fire when it occurred to him that the last thing he needed was to entomb himself in this barn of a house. He had left Scotland behind, and now it was time for him to become an Englishman again. He had no intention of going to ground, like a mole. No, he would live life to the fullest. He would enjoy himself. He would have every woman who even aroused his male interest. He would sate himself on females.

During the next several weeks, the Duke of Portmaine, jokingly referred to as the Scottish

328

earl by his friends, was seen at a dozen social functions, dancing with even those young ladies who weren't all that toothsome. If some chose to assume that the duke was trying to forget Lady Felicity's jilting of him, well, there wasn't anybody around to disagree. The duke certainly never mentioned a single word about Lady Felicity. It made all society talk about how noble he was not to call her the heartless chit she indeed was. Society was even more aghast when Lady Felicity was seen in the constant company of the Marquess of Hardcastle. The gentleman in question got stouter as her attentions increased. They were seen everywhere.

The gossips were kept well supplied, as it appeared that the duke passed an equal amount of time in various gaming hells, a different woman on his arm each time, each one lovelier than the last.

The duke was also becoming fond of opera. He was seen in his box several nights in a row. Of course, the incredibly beautiful leading lady, whose lungs were covered by truly remarkable breasts, was seen a good deal of time in his company. He was seen coming out of her apartment, apparently not caring who saw him, yawning, straightening his waistcoat or his cravat, all in all, thumbing his nose at everyone.

It was obvious that the Duke of Portmaine was going to the devil. No one was surprised, when the Season drew to a close in the beginning of June, that none of the young ladies who'd dared to flirt with his grace had received an offer of marriage. Lady Felicity's announcement, however, appeared in the *Gazette*. It appeared that she was marrying the Marquess of Hardcastle in the fall, the fickle witch. No one blamed the duke for a single thing. The more wicked he was, the more everyone forgave him. He was noble, he was good, it was fine for him to be wild as a young buck, at least until, say, the fall.

The duke shook his head when he read the announcement. James, his butler, however, was the only one to see the amused smile that played about his grace's stern mouth. "Poor blind ass," he heard the duke say to himself. "He'll learn, but it will be too late."

One morning toward the middle of June, the duke didn't come out of his bedchamber until the clock stroked twelve times. It was noon. When he came down, he had the most terrible hangover he'd ever had in his life, which was saying something, since his years at Oxford hadn't been particularly sober. He thought of his opera singer, of the four other courtesans who'd warmed his body and his bed. It was too much. It was time to stop.

He was drinking a cup of very strong coffee prepared by his compassionate cook when James soundlessly appeared at his elbow, bearing a silver salver that held his grace's mail.

"Good God, hasn't everyone yet had the good sense to leave town and go to Brighton? More damned invitations. I'm tired of all these wretched parties. I'm even more tired of myself."

James didn't bother to reply to these comments. They were private, just between his master and himself. But he agreed with the duke.

Every servant in the duke's household would agree with what he'd just said. He stood quietly behind his master as the duke leafed through the various-sized envelopes. He saw with some surprise that his grace singled out a letter, one that had come all the way from Scotland. How odd, his grace's hand was shaking a bit as he slit open the envelope.

The duke read the letter, then read it again. He smiled grimly as he said, "Well, James, it seems that Percy has achieved at least one of his goals."

"Yes, your grace?"

"One of my Robertson kinsmen, James. Percy, the former bastard. He's to marry Miss Joanna MacDonald in two weeks' time at Penderleigh Castle. My presence is graciously requested. I imagine her father wants to be reassured that the new master of Penderleigh is indeed an English duke and not some sham invented by Percy."

"Ah," said James.

The duke was silent for several minutes. James watched as the duke tapped his fingertips together, his dark eyes focused on a delicate Dresden figure atop the Buhl cabinet in the corner of the breakfast room.

"Will your grace be returning to Scotland?" James asked finally, so curious he was itching with it. Something had happened there, something that had to do with His Grace's broken engagement to Lady Felicity. It must have been something both good and bad, the good being that he wasn't going to marry that harpy. The bad being that he'd been wretchedly unhappy and off his moderate course since he'd returned to London. James waited.

The duke turned slowly in his chair, and James was more astounded than relieved to see that the grim lines had disappeared and his master was actually smiling. A big, fat smile, a real smile.

"I think, James, that there's nothing more worthless than a stupid man. God, am I ever the stupidest man ever planted on earth. Talk about blind, I've taken the cake. All I can hope now is that I'm not too late. Scotland must be beautiful in the summer with all the heather in bloom. Fetch me writing materials, I must write to Giles and cancel our evening. Oh, and James, inform Mabley that we'll be leaving within the hour. I wish the carriage and my curricle brought around and ready for a journey by eleven o'clock. No later now. I want to be at Penderleigh in five days."

"Will your grace be gone long?" James asked.

"Well, there's to be a wedding, you know," the duke said and actually rubbed his hands together. "I'll keep you informed, never fear."

Not many minutes later, the duke was shrugging himself into a light tan riding coat. He looked quickly at the clock on the mantel, then consulted his own watch. He had turned to leave his bedchamber when his eyes fell upon the small painted miniature of Marianne set in its place of honor atop his dresser. He looked into the leaf green eyes rendered so lifelike by the artist, at the glossy black hair pulled back from her forehead, at her tender, sweet mouth. He remembered how that soft mouth could tremble. It didn't move him a jot, that memory.

He clasped the miniature in his hand and strode downstairs. "James," he called out to his butler, "while I'm gone, see to the placement of this painting in the picture gallery, where it belongs." He tossed the miniature into James's outstretched hands, pulled on his gloves, and walked away, his stride firm. He was whistling as he climbed into his curricle.

30

Brandy lay on her back amid a field of blooming anemones, her arms pillowing her head, staring up at the cloud-strewn sky. Darkening clouds were jostling about for the upper hand, swept in by a building squall coming off the sea. A sharp wind tugged tendrils of hair loose from her braids and whipped them into her eyes.

She sat up, feeling as listless and dull as she'd felt for more days than she cared to count now. She brushed away the tangles with the back of her hand. She gazed toward the castle, its aged gray stone etched in stark relief against the dying afternoon light. She rose slowly to her feet and smoothed her gown, knowing that she must return and force herself to smile. Percy and Joanna MacDonald were due to arrive on the morrow. Or was it the day after? She couldn't remember. She didn't care.

To everyone's utter consternation, even Morag had bathed in honor of the pending wedding.

How strange it was, she thought, moving slowly along the cliff path, that the pain hadn't lessened over the past two months. She'd not been so foolish as to believe that she could forget him. She wondered if he occasionally thought of her, and if so, what his thoughts were. Probably they were angry thoughts. He'd been so angry that last morning. Yet he'd given her two hundred pounds.

She heard the rumble of wheels in the distance and sighed. Evidently Joanna and Percy had come a day early. She looked up to see a mud-spattered curricle pull gracefully around the bend and draw to a halt on the gravel drive in front of the castle.

"Here we are, not a second beyond five days. Excellent job. We've even beaten the storm." Ian jumped down to the ground and patted his horses' steaming necks. He gazed toward the castle and wondered for perhaps the twentieth time how he would approach Brandy. He'd rehearsed a goodly number of speeches given several possible encounters, the most extreme as seeing her as impossibly difficult, at which point he'd throw her over his shoulder and haul her away. He tried to picture her crying and pleading with him to marry him. Well, truth be told, he hadn't imagined that scene more than once, and that in a mood of particularly profound optimism.

Perhaps it was the streaking dark clouds whirling in over the sea that made him turn for a moment toward the cliff, or simply the clean smell of the sea air. He saw Brandy standing not far from him, her skirts billowing about her in the rising wind, standing so still that he wouldn't have noticed her otherwise.

All the practiced eloquent phrases disappeared from his mind as though they'd never lived there. He called her name aloud and took a quick step toward her, his arms outstretched.

Brandy only saw his mouth form her name, for the wind whipped away the sound. He was home. He'd come back to her. She grasped her skirts and ran full tilt toward him. She flew into his open arms and would have toppled them both had Ian not leaned forward to catch her. She wrapped her arms tightly around his neck and buried her face against his cheek.

"Ye're here," she whispered against his neck. "Ye're here. Ye came back."

He felt her lashes against his face and held her more tightly against him, one arm across her back and the other curved beneath her hips. He felt a tremendous shudder pass through her body, and he gave a shaking laugh. "Come, my little love, you'll strangle me," he said against her temple.

She laughed, leaned back, and began kissing him, his ear, his neck, his chin. Then he was kissing her warm mouth, feeling the utter acceptance in her, the utter giving. He wanted to caress her, all of her, but he knew he couldn't, not here in the front of Penderleigh Castle. He didn't want to, but he forced himself to let her slide down his body. He continued to hold her even when her feet were finally on the ground.

She threw back her head and looked up at him. "Ye're here," she said again. "I'm so very glad."

He sighed, pulled her against him, and kissed her some more. "Ah, but you're sweet. I love the taste of you. I've dreamed about tasting you."

"Will you kiss me like this forever?"

"Until I cock up my toes," he said, laughing into her mouth, then kissing her again and again.

"Oh, dear, ye're not just here for Percy's wedding, are ye?"

"No." He breathed in the fresh salty smell of her hair. "No, I'm here because of you. Only you. You will have me now, won't you, Brandy?" She hesitated only a moment. He kissed her again, saying, "I'm a stupid man. It took me much too long to come to my senses. My only concern now is that I shall be the one with the surfeit of love in our marriage."

"Marianne?"

"In a bittersweet past, Brandy, where she belongs. I no longer desire Marianne or someone like her. What I want is a stubborn Scottish lass with thick blond hair and amber eyes. A Scottish lass with a good deal of common sense, wit that will keep me on my toes, and loyalty that runs deeper than the North Sea. Answer me now, will you have me? Will you be my duchess?"

"I think ye're beautiful, Ian. Ye're kind. I love the way ye make me feel when ye kiss me. But know, Ian, ye're that Lady Adella calls a household tyrant, at least that's what she called Grandpapa Angus on better days. She said he interfered in everything, ordered everybody around, and stuck his oar even into her business."

"If ever I near the tyranny of Grandpapa Angus, you can boot me out of Carmichael Hall to sleep with the goats. I don't want to order you around. I want to love you and make you smile and give you more pleasure than you can begin to imagine even exists."

"All that?"

"Yes, I want to give you all that. I'm sure to think of more things."

"Are ye certain? Ye know that I can't speak proper English. Ye know ye'll have to teach me. Ye'll have to be patient with me."

"Aye, but seeing that I can't live without ye, I'll bring in my dear mother to instruct ye in everything."

"Yer mother?"

He laughed. "No, Brandy, I wouldn't wish my parent on any sentient person, even an enemy. Well, perhaps an enemy but certainly not my wife. Perhaps Percy. Yes, she'd do wonders with Percy. We'll manage, you'll see. All my people will love you."

"If they don't, then ye'll pound them into the ground?"

"Exactly."

Hercules chose that moment to nudge his master in the back. "You see, even my horse agrees with me. You must say yes before he humiliates me by trampling me in the back."

"Aye—yes."

He leaned over and kissed her again, lightly this time, though he wanted more, so much more and he knew she did too. "Come, Brandy, I want

337

to tell Lady Adella, Bertrand—even scratchy Morag."

"She bathed for Percy's wedding."

"Good God, that must have made everyone speechless. What did Fraser think?"

"He just walked around shaking his head. Who will ye tell after Morag?"

"I fancy I'll climb up to the turrets and yell it to all the Cheviot sheep. Perhaps MacPherson will hear me and come personally to congratulate us."

"Oh, dear," she said.

He frowned down at her. "You don't want me climbing the turrets? What's the matter? You've already changed your mind?"

"Oh, no, ye're mine now, Ian. It's just that, well, I don't want either of us to say anything this evening. I want to wait until tomorrow. Please, Ian, it's very important to me."

She placed her fingers on his mouth. "Nay, please, just trust me in this. Tomorrow ye can tell my family—if ye still wish to."

"What the devil do you mean, if I'll still wish to? What game is it you're playing, my girl? You somehow think I'm going to change my mind between now and tomorrow morning when the clock strikes eight o'clock?"

"No game, I promise. Please allow me this." She was pleading with him. He didn't understand. But he didn't want her ever to beg him for anything.

"Very well." he said and kissed her again. "But know this, Brandy, if I don't like your reasons, I'm going to beat you."

She hugged her arms tightly around his back. She smiled up at him. "It will be exactly as ye wish, yer grace."

He groaned. "I see bad times ahead for me. I see myself doing anything and everything just to win a smile from you, just to win a kind word."

She laughed and poked his arm.

As no stable boy appeared, Ian and Brandy led Hercules and Canter to the stables. She watched him silently as he removed the harness and rubbed down his horse with handfuls of fresh hay. He looked up at her, and a frown furrowed his forehead. "You've grown thin."

"Perhaps a bit. I've not been terribly hungry."

"There are dark circles under your eyes. I don't like that."

"I haven't slept well. But that's all yer fault."

"I'll give you two months to put meat back on your bones, no longer. If you don't, I'll be forced to take drastic action."

"And just what sort of drastic action are ye talking about, yer grace?"

"We'll just have to see, won't we?" He kissed her again, the smells of horse and hay and linseed oil filling the air.

Brandy excused herself the moment Crabbe, with a wide grin on his cadaverous face, ceremoniously swept the duke into the drawing room. She ordered Morag to tell Wee Albie to bring the tub that didn't leak to her room.

Some two hours later, her hair still damp from its washing, Brandy smiled shyly at Ian from across the expanse of dining table, but his attention was claimed by a chattering Constance.

339

"Just fancy yer coming back for Percy's wedding. None of us thought ye would, what with ye not really liking Percy and Percy acting the way he did and maybe trying to, well, never mind that. No Robertson would try to kill ye, Ian. Ye've got to believe that."

"Hold yer runaway tongue, girl," Lady Adella said, her voice as sour as the lentil soup that was growing cold and untouched on Ian's plate. "There not a mite of proof, and I'll thank ye not to mention the dreadful business. It has been two months, yer grace, and it's to be hoped that ye've no more bloodletting to fear."

There was a good deal of sudden eating at the table. Lady Adella broke the silence with a crude laugh. "Oh, no, it will be poor Joanna Mac-Donald who'll have the bloodletting. Robertson men only want to marry virgins, ye know. Aye, poor Joanna will have quite a shock on her wedding night."

Brandy choked on her wine, then laughed.

Lady Adella turned her sour look on her granddaughter. "Ye used to be such a prude, child, but look at ye now. How can ye laugh about wedding nights? Ye know nothing about anything. Just barely the basics of what goes on between a man and a woman. Why, even that time Percy tried to force ye, well, he didn't get very far, did he?"

"No," Ian said. "If he had I would have killed him. The blighter was lucky. Let's hope he doesn't need much more luck because I wouldn't think he'd have much left available to him." He said to Bertrand, "Now, tell me how are the crofters faring with the Cheviot sheep?"

"There are smiles on their faces because they already see more food on their tables. Even those who thought sheep were only good to eat have taken them to heart. I fear many of them are becoming pets."

"Those damned sheep eat everything in sight," Claude said, waving his fork at his son. "They're everywhere."

"They smell," Constance said. "If the wind's from the land they fill your nostrils, sometimes even at night."

"Aye, Bertie," Lady Adella said in a crafty voice. "Ye need to take care, else Constance won't have ye and ye'll be fit only for Morag."

"Oh, Grandmama," Constance wailed, her eyes on Bertrand's face. He seemed not at all put out, she thought, and wondered at it. She was dreadfully embarrassed, but she didn't know what to do about it.

Bertrand said with a hint of amusement, "I assure you, Lady Adella, that Fraser has the most sensitive nose of all of us. Never does he allow me into the dining room until he's sniffed about me at least twice. As for Constance," he added, smiling toward her, "I trust she hasn't noticed anything amiss since the sheep have arrived."

"One sheep died," Brandy said to Ian. "We asked Prickly Ben to look at him. We were afraid, of course, that it could be some sort of disease that would spread to the rest of the flock, but Prickly Ben said no, the sheep had eaten some gangle weed and it bloated its belly."

"I routed out all the gangle weed," Bertrand said. "Actually, Constance and I together."

"That's about the only time ye've seen each other, Bertie," Claude said. He said to the duke, "He spends all his time with his damned account books. Never has time for his father or his family."

Brandy looked up. "Oh, but I thought ye took Bertrand his lunch sometimes, Connie."

Constance shifted uncomfortably in her chair. Ian smiled to himself. It appeared that Bertrand had made some headway with the girl during the past two months. He certainly seemed more certain of himself. He gazed fondly down the table at Brandy, wondering if she realized that she'd embarrassed the devil out of her sister.

Lady Adella seemed unusually mellow to him this evening, but then again, money had continued to flow freely up to Penderleigh. He could well imagine that the old lady would keep her ire in check so long as he made it worth her while.

"How is yer cousin Mr. Braidston?" Lady Adella asked, her sour look and sour tone gone for the moment. "Such a natty fellow he is."

"Giles goes along very well, Lady Adella. As my decision to come up to Scotland was rather sudden, I was forced to write him a note. I'm sure he would have wished you a fond greeting."

"Too much of a dapper dog for my tastes," Claude said. "It isn't healthy to know so much about so many people. It can come home to roost."

It was hard, but Ian managed not to be too blatant in the direction of his eyes and his conversation to Brandy. Jesus, how he wanted her. He wanted to shout to everyone that she would marry him. Why had she insisted on waiting until tomorrow? He'd thought and thought, but couldn't figure out what her reason could possibly be. He decided that he would personally burn the muslin gown she was wearing, along with the tartan shawl.

In the middle of a bite of fish, he was suddenly reminded of the two hundred pounds—for clothes, she had told him. Well, she was a bad liar. He'd see to it that she told him soon enough what she'd really done with the money.

He looked up as Lady Adella said, "Ye look burned to a socket, my boy. Because dinner was so delicious and I'm feeling particularly mellow, I'll spare ye the torture of the girls' singing. Crabbe, ye old sot, pour all of us a glass of port. Then our duke can take himself off to bed."

So he was "our" duke, was he? Times had changed.

Shortly thereafter, Lady Adella led Constance and Brandy from the dining room, exhorting Bertrand not to bore Ian on his first evening back with estate affairs. "I told him he could take himself to bed, but here ye are, wanting to pelt him with yer sheep talk. He'll have plenty of time to poke around yer sheep, after all. And ye, Claude, don't whine too much to him either. At least not yet. Give him a day or two to settle in."

Claude didn't whine, but Bertrand's enthusiasm was difficult to stem. It was a good twenty minutes before Claude thwacked his cane on the floor and demanded to join the ladies.

Brandy wasn't in the drawing room. Ian took the excuse Lady Adella had given him and made his way up the winding staircase, down the long, dim corridor toward the earl's bedchamber. He paused momentarily outside Brandy's room. He raised his hand to knock. He wanted to see her. Hell, he wanted to kiss her and caress her until he felt like he would die if he had to stop. Well, damn, he couldn't do it. He went on down the hallway to his room.

The summer storm had blown in. A pounding rain streaked down the windowpanes in the earl's bed-chamber. Ian pulled the faded curtains and moved toward the sputtering fire. He added more clumps of peat and stirred the crackling embers with the toe of his boot. As with his first visit to Penderleigh, he was without the assistance of Mabley, whose carriage rumbled along a good day behind him.

He slipped a small pistol from his portmanteau and laid it atop the table beside his bed before he stripped off his clothes and changed into a dressing gown. He poured himself a glass of claret and sank into a deep leather armchair, stretching his feet toward the fire.

The claret was smooth and warm in his belly. Soon the flames were fanning outward in blurred patterns.

He was suddenly jerked awake by a soft, insistent knocking on the door. He quickly rose, grasped the small pistol, and called, "Enter." He couldn't believe his eyes. "Brandy, what the hell are you doing here?"

31

She stepped slowly into his bedchamber, closing the door quietly behind her. She was dressed from neck to toe in a flowing white cotton nightgown that made her look absurdly young. He caught his breath at her hair. It hung in long, thick waves nearly to her waist. She was pale. She looked scared to death. What was going on here?

He took a step forward. "Love, you know that you shouldn't come to my room. No, forget that nonsense. What's wrong? What's happened to upset you?" He reached her, wanting desperately to bring her against him, but he forced himself to hold back. He just took her hands in his.

"Brandy? Come, what is it? Whatever is wrong?" He couldn't help himself. He rested his hands on her shoulders. "Good God, you're shaking. And here I am holding this ridiculous pistol." He quickly laid it on the bedside table and returned to her. "Come to the fire and warm yourself. Then we can talk."

That ridiculous nightgown. She must have had it for years. It left only her bare feet showing. She wouldn't look at him. What the devil was wrong?

"Sit here."

He pulled up a chair near the fire and pulled his own over to face hers.

She didn't sit down. She took a very deep

breath and plowed forward, knowing what she must do. "Ye wondered why I didn't want to announce our engagement this evening. I do have a good reason."

"Let's hear this very good reason," he said. "But I won't believe it when you tell me, I warn you now."

"It's an excellent reason. Please be patient and don't ye dare laugh at me. Now, listen. Ian, it was Marianne ye shared yer passion with that first time."

"Not just the first time, it was the only time."

"Don't quibble and don't interrupt. I must be certain, don't ye see? I've got to know that it's me ye love, for myself—that it's me ye desire now, not Marianne."

This was a kicker. For a moment he could only stare at her. He said finally, very slowly, "So you wish to stay with me tonight? Share my bed? Do I take it that on the morrow you will tell me if I have passed muster? Really, Brandy, I've always believed you very creative, but this strikes out into new territory."

"Mayhap that part of marriage isn't important to ye, Ian, but it is to me. That is, it's important, I know. Don't ye dare grin at me like that, ye miserable man. I am perfectly serious. Please, Ian, let me stay with ye tonight."

"I do hope that I don't fail your test, Brandy. What if I murmur my mother's name in my sleep? All right, I'm not laughing at you. But I didn't lie to you. Marianne is in the past where she belongs. She's no longer a part of my life, just there in my distant memories, some painful, some nice, but all vague and blurry now. She's got nothing to do with us. I do think she would be pleased that I've finally seen the light and moved on in the right direction with my life, namely in your direction, Brandy.

"There's more to this, you know. What a comedown it would be for me were you to refuse to marry me because you think me a poor lover."

"Ye know very well it's not about that at all."

"Very well, Brandy, I now consider myself irrevocably compromised."

She wanted to hit him for twisting about her reasons, but the opportunity slipped by unnoticed. He came to her and pulled her to her feet, all the while smiling down at her in a way that made her bare toes curl. "Little idiot," he whispered, and lowered his mouth to hers. He pulled her tightly against him, winding one hand through the masses of hair and allowing the other hand to sweep down her back to her hips.

He released her after a moment, grinning down at her.

"That's very nicely done. Please, give me some more, Ian."

"You mean you don't remember what else is to come? Perhaps it's better that you don't, since it wasn't very pleasant for you. But this time, Brandy, this time I swear to you that you're going to have quite a fine time with me." He began to kiss her. Ah, she enjoyed kissing and now she was opening her mouth to him. He thought he'd died and gone to heaven. He felt her pressing hard against him. He knew she felt his sex hard against her belly. At least his body wouldn't come as a surprise to her. No, she admired his body, and that made him feel very good.

She moaned into his mouth and jumped at the sound she'd made. "Give me more," he said, and his tongue was in her mouth. Gently he eased his hands to the tie string at the neck of her nightgown and began to draw it open. To his surprise, she stiffened and tried to pull away from him.

"What is this, my love? How can you seduce me if you won't let me get this nightgown off you?"

It had come down to it. There was no going back now, but, oh, it was difficult. What if he looked at her and winced? She'd guess even if he didn't change expressions, she'd know he found her repellent.

"Brandy?"

She straightened, shoulders squared. "Nay, I must face up to it. I must do this myself. Please, Ian." She took a step back from him. She said nothing when he cocked his head to one side in question. "Just a moment." She drew a deep breath. There was no going back now. She pulled the ribbons open on the nightgown. She took another very deep breath and slipped her arms from the sleeves and let the nightgown fall to her waist. She squared her shoulders. She waited. She looked at him closely.

The duke very nearly swallowed his tongue. He sucked in his breath. He couldn't believe his eyes. Surely there could be nothing more amazing in this world. To think he had believed her a slender, almost thin young girl, still immature.

He stared at the most glorious breasts he had ever seen in his life. They were incredibly white and rounded, the nipples a soft, pale pink, blending with an artist's touch into the creamy ivory. They had to be the most beautiful breasts in all of England.

"*Good God!*"

Perhaps she'd expected him to pale a bit, and he had. Oh, God, all her worst nightmares had come true. She turned away, wishing she could die.

"Brandy," he said, utterly baffled.

She tried to cover herself with her hands, but it was impossible. She gulped, not wanting to do anything except run, but she managed to say, "I understand, Ian, truly I do. I've hidden my ugliness from ye, and it wasn't right. I should have told you about it before I accepted your marriage proposal. I wasn't fair to you. If you can't bear me, then I will release you. No one will ever know."

"What ugliness?" He searched for a disfiguring mole, perhaps a birthmark on her shoulder that bothered her, but all the gorgeous flesh he could see was smooth and white and looked so soft he thought he'd spill his seed. He wished she'd move her hands.

She did, her arms now at her sides. "I'm sorry. I'm a cow, ye can see that well enough. I just wouldn't stop growing and had to bind myself so no one would know how awful I'd gotten." She couldn't stand his staring at her any longer. She clutched her nightgown against her breasts.

She looked as if she would burst into tears at any moment.

What had she said? Her breasts were ugly? He could only shake his head. He had to feel his way carefully through this war zone.

He said slowly, "Let me see if I've got this right. You're telling me that you think your breasts are ugly? You think you're deformed?"

She nodded, looking more miserable and pathetic than before. He couldn't hold it in. He threw back his head and laughed.

"I hadn't believed ye'd be so unkind."

He gulped in air and controlled his amusement. God, she really believed it. "Listen to me, Brandy, I'm not laughing at you. I'm laughing at this ridiculous situation. Tell me, who the hell gave you the notion that you were a cow? That you were somehow misformed? Did someone actually tell you that you were ugly?"

"Aye, Morag did. When I was fourteen my dresses wouldn't button across my chest. She laughed at me and said I was in a fair way of growing two fine melons for the market. She said I'd be a laughingstock if anyone ever guessed what this earl's granddaughter was hiding under her clothes. She said all the men would stare at me and think I was loose because I was so big."

"Damnation, let me at that woman. I'll kill her. At least, if I kill her now, she'll go to her grave clean."

"But she was right. I tried as best I could to bind myself, but Percy knew, even though I always wore my shawl. He was always staring at me like I was some sort of freak. I didn't understand it. If I was such a freak, then why did he want me?"

"He didn't think you were a freak, Brandy, do you remember when we were alone in the crofter's hut? I wanted you then and you pulled away from me?"

"I thought it was ye who pulled away from me. But it's true. I didn't want ye to see me. I was ashamed. I didn't want to see ye stare at me and look revolted."

"Do I look at all revolted to you?"

"Well, I've got them covered right now."

He reached out and yanked the nightgown out of her hands and let it sink back to her waist. "I'm still not revolted. You know something? I think we've spent much of our time together being confused as to the other's motives. And the blue velvet gown I brought for you from Edinburgh? It was quite low-cut if I remember correctly."

"It's a beautiful gown. I felt like a queen when I put it on. But, Ian, I couldn't wear it. I looked like two huge breasts. My cleavage starts at my throat."

He smiled. He didn't laugh, not now. He said, "Brandy, have I ever lied to you, or done anything to make you mistrust my words?"

"Nay."

"Give me both of your hands and drop the nightgown. That's right, let it fall to the floor."

For a long moment she couldn't move. She just stared up at him. "This is very difficult."

"Come, give me your hands."

"Oh, dear," she said, and thrust out one hand

toward him, still clutching the nightgown at her waist with the other.

"Both hands, if you please."

She closed her eyes tightly and blindly thrust out her other hand. The nightgown rested an instant on her hips, then fell with a soft rustle to the floor.

He nearly swallowed his tongue. Dear God, she didn't realize how beautiful she was? How utterly exquisite? His hands itched to touch her, to caress all that white flesh. He wanted to taste her, he wanted to wallow in her. The fullness of her breasts was emphasized even further by a narrow waist that curved into very nice hips. Her belly was flat, her creamy skin covered lower down by a triangle of curling dark blond hair. Her legs were long and sleek, firm with muscle. She was without a doubt the loveliest female he'd ever seen in his life. Well, he loved her. Of course she'd be the loveliest.

Ah, those breasts of hers. He'd never tire of looking at them.

"Open your eyes, Brandy. Now, come with me."

He helped her step out of the nightgown and led her by the hand to a long, narrow mirror that hung next to an old armoire. He held her in front of the mirror, his hands on her shoulders. "You're a beautiful woman. Look at yourself and tell me if you can possibly doubt my words."

His hands tightened on her shoulders. She forced herself to look in the mirror. Her breasts stared back at her. "Oh, God," she said, "this is horrible." She tried to pull away from him.

"I won't have you calling your husband-to-be a liar. Dammit, Brandy, look at yourself. You're incredible and it makes my knees knock together to think that you're all mine."

She opened her eyes and looked again at herself in the mirror. She saw that he was standing behind her, his hands on her bare shoulders. His eyes met hers in the mirror, and very slowly he pulled her hair back from her face and shoulders. He brought his hand around and cupped her chin in his palm.

"Do you have any dislike for your face? No? Excellent. Let's move down a bit."

Control, he thought. He had to keep himself controlled. It was the hardest thing he'd ever done in his adult life. He drew a deep breath, and sent his hands downward. He let his fingers caress her, until each hand cupped a breast. He swallowed convulsively.

Her eyelashes fluttered. Her lips parted. He leaned down and planted a light kiss on her temple. He was a man, not a boy. He could deal with this, he had to deal with this. He heard himself say in a deep voice, "Your breasts are exquisite. Contrive to remember that Morag is quite scrawny. Jealousy and sheer stupidity made her say what she did."

He forced his hands to leave her breasts and move down to encircle her waist. As his fingers roved to her belly, he felt her shudder. He hoped it was lust on her part and not embarrassment at what he was doing. Ah, yes, her breathing had quickened. It would be close, but he would finish this. She would believe him, trust him, and then he would wallow in her.

"Remember you once told me that I was the beautiful one? Such a fool you are, Brandy."

She turned in his arms and wrapped her own about his neck. "Ye promise, Ian?"

"Aye, I promise."

She pulled open the sash of his dressing gown, and he felt her hand move from his bare chest downward to his belly. All his control vanished. "You're a witch," he said and flung off his dressing gown. He heard a rip and couldn't begin to care. He swung her up into his arms and carried her to the bed. "I swear I'll not hurt you this time. You're going to enjoy yourself."

She wanted to tell him how very magnificent he was, but his lips closed over her breast and she couldn't believe the delicious sensation that rippled through her, all the way to her belly. He wound his hands in the thick masses of blond hair and sought out her mouth, teasing her with his tongue until she opened her lips to him. She felt his hands sweep down her back to caress her hips and stroke her between her thighs.

"Oh, my, are you truly supposed to do that, Ian?"

"What about you? Your hands are all over me." He'd loved her hands closing over his sex, but that could wait. They had all their lives and he prayed it would be many, many nights. "Don't move now, just enjoy what I'm doing to you."

"Well," she began, then squeaked when his mouth closed over her. "Oh, Ian, I don't know about this."

"Just be quiet, relax, and enjoy it."

His hands lifted her to his mouth and he was hot and needy, his tongue all over her, and when she cried out, it shocked her. "Oh, goodness, I didn't mean—" She felt the most incredible urgency building, building deep in her belly. It wouldn't stop. It couldn't stop. If it did, she'd die, she knew it. She pressed her hips to his mouth, giving herself completely, and when she reached the first climax of her life, she thought if she died, it wouldn't be a bad thing at all.

He caressed her with his hands and with his mouth until her release was easing. Then he entered her, slowly, very slowly. She pressed her hands against his back, drawing him deeper into her. She waited for the pain, for she felt herself stretching to hold him, but there was no pain, only an exquisite fullness. Deeper and deeper he went, and soon she wondered if either of them would know where one began and the other left off. She moved beneath him naturally, and clutched him tightly to her. When he gasped aloud, arching over her, she looked at him and knew she'd love him until she left this earth.

She felt a lazy feeling of contentment that made her wonder if anything could exist outside this room, outside of them. She rather hoped it didn't. She didn't want this moment or the next one after this one to end. She wanted him lying on top of her, his face beside hers on the pillow, his breathing still harsh and deep, his heart still pounding furiously against her breasts. He was still deep inside her. It felt wonderful.

"I love ye," she said into his shoulder. "I didn't bite ye this time."

He laughed and brought himself up on his elbows. "Well, Brandy, do you think my desire for you is sufficient? Do you think I pictured Marianne or any other woman in my mind when I was inside you? Will you accept me both as your husband and your lover?"

She gazed up at him, her eyes hooded, and nodded, unable to find the words to tell him how she felt. So she said again, "I love ye. I'll love ye forever."

"And I you. Count on it. And your breasts as well." He leaned down and kissed them. He moaned and kissed them again. "The most beautiful breasts I've ever seen. Let me kill Morag."

"No," she said with great seriousness, "let me kill her. She's a nitwit."

He laughed, a deep, rumbling sound, full of pleasure. "I wasted two months, Brandy. But never again will I willingly let you out of my sight."

"Or yer bed?"

"You can't begin to imagine what I'm going to do to you once we're married. Perhaps you can. But know this, Brandy, your pleasure will be my lifetime goal." Then he squeezed her so tightly she yelped. He kissed her ear. "Thank you for not biting my neck."

"Ye're welcome. Ian, may I ask ye something?"

At the seriousness in her voice, he drew back slightly so that he could see her full face. "Aye?"

"Do ye truly want children? I remember ye joked about having a half dozen little Fionas.

Did ye truly mean it, or were ye just jesting with Giles?"

"Indeed I do. But I'm not wanting a brood mare. We'll have as many children as you wish. There are ways to prevent conception, and we'll use them if you wish to."

She sighed with contentment. "I'm relieved ye want children. However, I didn't know ye could prevent conception."

"It's not completely reliable, but if you wish, we'll try them."

"Perhaps. Someday. When do ye wish to marry, Ian?"

"Soon, very soon. How about tomorrow or the next day? How about in thirty minutes? How about just after I make love to you again? That would be about fifteen minutes from now."

"Nay, I don't think it would be wise to wait."

He saw a small smile playing over her mouth. What game was she playing with him? "What wouldn't be wise?"

"Waiting too long to wed. Perhaps we could wait a day or two, though."

"Are we again talking at cross-purposes? No, I am, but you're not. You're stringing me along like a trout on your line."

"Not I. It's just that I want to be slender when we wed."

"Slender? You're skinny. Well, skinny in places it's all right to be skinny. Are you planning to gorge yourself on Cook's haggis?"

"Nay, in fact, it makes me quite ill."

"Brandy, that's quite enough. No more games.

357

No more twitting me. What the devil are you talking about?"

"Very well, yer grace," she said in the falsest docile voice he'd ever heard. "I'm pleased that ye want children, for in truth, we'll have a wee bairn by Christmas."

32

He stared down at her. She was pregnant? Oh, God. The vagaries of fate plowed through his brain. "You're pregnant," he said, his brain as blank as a man who'd drunk too much brandy. "You're going to have a babe."

"Aye."

"And you didn't see fit to tell me? You didn't see fit to write me?"

"I'm telling ye now, Ian."

His brain was working. It terrified him. "Would you like to tell me what you would have done if I hadn't come back?" He wanted to shake her hard. He also wanted to crow in satisfaction. He'd made love to her just once, took her virginity, and she was pregnant with his child. She couldn't begin to imagine what that made him feel. But what if she hadn't told him? He rolled off her and lay on his back, staring up at the shadowed ceiling. "Tell me, Brandy."

"I don't know what I could have done. I didn't even realize it until just a few days ago. I was just getting used to the idea. I was just beginning to be afraid. There, I've told ye the truth, so stop that dark, cold voice of yers."

He groaned in exasperation. Only a few days, well, perhaps she would have written to him. What would he have done? He would have raced back here like a man on his way to a feast. He would have married her in a flash. But, dear God, what if he hadn't come to his senses? Well, he had. What would it matter if the child were born two months early? It could hardly matter, for he would remove her soon to Carmichael Hall.

He turned and pulled her roughly into his arms. "Did I ever tell you that you're more stubborn than I am? No, don't shake your head. I'm a saint of docility compared to you. If ever you keep anything from me again, I swear I'll thrash you."

"Not until after Christmas, I hope."

He spoke with sudden decision, "No big wedding in Hanover Square for you, my girl. You won't mind missing out on a big wedding, will you?"

"Bah, it's nothing to me. I don't want to be surrounded by people I don't know who would likely expect me to stumble over my wedding gown."

"Excellent. I shall have Bertrand help with the arrangements. Will you wed me on Saturday, Brandy?"

She was silent for a very long time. He was close to shaking with impatience when she said, leaning against his shoulder, "All right. But only because I want to be skinny."

He couldn't believe how relieved he was. But his mind was already leaping ahead. He said,

"At least I don't have to worry about your care. Edward Mulhouse, a doctor and an excellent friend of mine in Suffolk, will attend you."

"He's a man?" She sounded utterly appalled.

"All doctors are. Certainly he's a man. Come, Brandy, Edward is young, but you won't find a finer doctor anywhere. What is this? You're embarrassed because a doctor will examine you, and yet you come to my bedchamber and seduce me—twice—without a by-your-leave?"

She poked him in the ribs. He felt her magnificent breasts against his side. He closed his eyes and swallowed hard.

"It wasn't exactly like that," she said, and pressed harder against him. She felt his hands rove over her belly. "Our babe is in there," she whispered.

"It's incredible," he said. His fingers moved lower.

"Damn ye, Ian," she said at last, "if ye're going to dally with me, I'll just have to seduce ye again."

"Yes," he said. "That's a fine idea."

He remembered to ask her before she fell contentedly asleep, her cheek against his chest, "Brandy, whatever did you want the two hundred pounds for?"

She was silent for some moments, and he felt her breasts quicken their upward and downward movement against him. He wanted her again. No, he couldn't. They were both very tired. She was probably very sore.

"I told ye, the money was for clothes."

"Don't lie to me, Brandy. Come, out with it."

"Why are ye so interested? I can't imagine that

a mere two hundred pounds could mean much of anything to ye." Then she turned and buried her face against his shoulder and said in a muffled voice, "Please, Ian, don't ask me for a reckoning, for I can't tell ye."

"You *refuse* to tell me?"

"Aye, I refuse. Don't give me that kingly look of yers. I'll thank ye to remember that ye can't threaten me until after our babe is born."

"Oh, I can threaten all I like, it's just that I can't do anything more. I'll just have to use my superior wit and reasoning power on you. We will speak more of this later, Brandy."

He wouldn't drop it, she knew that. But at least she wouldn't have to come up with another lie just yet. She curled close to him, kissed his shoulder, and burrowed her face against his chest.

Ian awoke near dawn the next morning, realized Mabley would surely succumb to apoplexy were he to arrive at Penderleigh and open the door upon the two of them. It was difficult, but he managed to slip Brandy back into her nightgown. He disliked disturbing her peaceful sleep almost as much as covering those beautiful breasts of hers. God, and all the rest of her. It was almost too much for a man to bear.

He carried her to her room, on the watch for any early rising servants. He kissed her gently on the forehead and returned to his bed for several more hours' sleep.

Brandy wasn't at the breakfast table. Ian smiled to himself, picturing her lying in her bed, smiling, satisfied, and anticipating being with him again. Men, he thought, their minds were very basic.

Bertrand, though, was soon shown into the breakfast room by Crabbe, and Ian grimaced slightly at the sight of the heavy account ledger he carried under his arm.

"Good morning, Ian," he said, all hearty and revoltingly well rested. Ah, but who cared? "I trust ye slept well last night. Nay, I see ye still look a bit weary. A pity, but perhaps ye've just enough energy to take a small look at the accounts."

"I'm fine, Bertrand," the duke said, and smiled at the rusted cannon in view outside the window. "You're going to let me eat my breakfast first, aren't you?"

"Certainly. Where is Crabbe? Where's the porridge? Now, while ye're waiting, I'll just summarize all we've done in the last two months. Listen carefully now, Ian."

"I'd thought you'd done that last evening."

"Oh, nay, that was just the barest titillation."

"Devil seize you, Bertrand. Very well, go ahead, addle my wits."

If Bertrand thought the duke's attention to be wandering during his recital, he made no mention of the fact until, at the end of a half hour, he paused, seeing that the duke was looking thoughtfully out the window. "I daresay that Napoleon will much appreciate my services."

"What's this? Napoleon? What the devil are you talking about, Bertrand?"

"Nonsense, nothing but nonsense. I just wanted to assure myself that yer thoughts were indeed many miles away from here, and they are."

"No, not miles away at all." The duke grinned. "I beg your pardon, Bertrand. If you must know, I've got much too much on my mind at the moment."

"Ye're worried that yer attacker still awaits ye here?"

"Not really. Well, now that you mention it, perhaps I shouldn't forget it entirely."

"Then what are ye plotting, Ian?"

The duke gave him an expansive smile. "That, my friend, you'll discover soon enough. I meant to tell you, after watching you and Constance last night at the dinner table, that you've made rather impressive headway since I last saw you."

Bertrand was concentrating hard on his knuckles. "Dammit," he said suddenly, "she's so very young, and skittish, despite all her bravado about looking and acting older than Brandy. Ye must know that Lady Adella and my father are forever twitting the both of us, and that doesn't help matters." He sighed and said somewhat in the matter of a stoic, "I really haven't all that much to offer her either. Living in the dower house with my father and me? Although Percy is no longer a problem—thank God—she naturally dreams of fine clothes, carriages, servants of her own, not to mention rubbing shoulders in fine society. What can I offer her here at Penderleigh? Just a bunch of bloody sheep."

"You've become melodramatic, Bertrand. This isn't a problem. I'll tell you what I think, that is, if you don't mind my meddling in your affairs."

"I don't see why the hell I should mind,"

Bertrand said. "Lady Adella and my father show no hesitation at all. When one of them shuts up, the other begins."

"What I think," the duke said, "is that your hands are much too light on the reins. It's quite clear to me, after last evening, that Constance isn't at all indifferent to you. Quite the contrary, in fact, she needs but a firm hand—your firm hand—to ring down the curtain. You must know that Constance is a very romantic girl. I think what she needs is a rather masterful approach. Surely you've thought along those lines?"

Bertrand ran his fingers through the shock of red hair on his forehead. He was silent, but he looked like he was thinking harder than he'd ever thought in his life. Suddenly he struck the palm of his hand against his knee.

"Damned if ye're not right. Ye really think it requires naught but a firm push to topple her over the edge?"

"Precisely. I'm assuming you can handle that, Bertrand. If you can't become the master, I wash my hands of you."

Bertrand rose, his ledger book forgotten. "Aye," he said more to himself than to the duke, "I'll do it. Not just at this precise moment. I must think about this and plot my strategy. That was why the English knocked us out of our kilts in '45. There wasn't enough strategy. I'm good at strategy. I'll figure out exactly what is to be done and how much of it to do."

"Good luck," the duke called after him as Bertrand strode from the breakfast room, never raising his head, never looking back.

Bertrand rehearsed many such masterful scenes in his mind as he went about his duties during the day, grunting when he found one not to his liking, and grinning broadly at another that caught his fancy. He was on the point of returning to the dower house to scrub himself down when he saw Constance approaching him. A gentle breeze had ruffled her soft black curls, and he thought she appeared utterly delectable. He squared his shoulders and waited for her to draw near.

"Och, ye smell like a sheep, Bertie."

It wasn't perhaps the best of beginnings, but he didn't care. He seized the opportunity. He had a strategy. "Aye, Connie. I fear, though, that it's not to be helped—at least during the day."

Those green eyes of her widened. She had gorgeous thick black lashes. She knew it well, but who cared? "What do ye mean, at least during the day?"

She looked mightily interested. "What I mean, Connie, is that at night ye'll never have cause to take me into dislike."

"Oh." She studied the toe of her shoe.

"Would ye like to walk with me?" he asked, realizing that they were standing opposite each other like two statues. A master would walk and be fluent in his speech as he walked. He would be more eloquent than was even necessary to win her.

"Aye," she said, and when he put out his hand, she didn't hesitate to lace her fingers into his.

He said abruptly, "Connie, when will ye be seventeen?"

"In August, Bertie."

"I should have remembered. I'm sorry, but I've other more important things on my mind. Isn't it strange? I've known ye all yer life."

Constance thought of the plump, wild-haired little girl that she had once been and paled. Then a memory of Bertrand when he was all of fourteen years old popped into her mind, and she giggled. "Ye were so tall and gangly. And all that red hair, I swear it was like looking at a sunset just before a storm."

"Do ye think that our children would have my mop of red hair or lovely silk black hair like yers, Connie?"

Her fingers tightened in his. She laughed nervously. She scuffed the toes of her shoes. "What a question, Bertie. I fear ye've been in the sun too long. Haven't ye?" She looked up at him from beneath her lashes.

"Nay, it's ye whom I've let rove about in the sun overlong. And ye can forget all yer childish nonsense about Percy, or any other man, for that matter. Ye can forget all of them except me."

She tossed her black curls. "And what if I don't, Master Bertrand?"

Ah, she said it herself, *Master*. It sounded wonderful. He said with a small smile, "Why, lass, I'll beat ye." He then took her shoulders and shook her lightly until she looked up at him.

"Ye'd beat me?" She was suddenly breathless. "Really, Bertie? Ye'd beat me?" It was amazing to him. He felt his confidence soar. This was all he'd needed to do? If he'd been alone he would have kicked himself for being so blind. Thank God the duke had stuck his oar in.

"Aye, black and blue, if ever ye dare look at another man."

"But surely, I'd not look pretty if ye beat me."

He managed to maintain a fierce look and at the same time he lowered his voice to an intimate whisper. "Never would I harm yer beauty, Connie, but I would, mayhap, take my hand to yer lovely bottom. Aye, I'd pull ye over my thighs and pull up all yer petticoats and then, well, don't tempt me." He watched her wet her lower lip with her tongue. He added quickly, "Perhaps I'll pull ye over my thighs and pull up yer petticoats just because I want to. Just because it would give me pleasure to do it. Just because I'd want to see how beautiful and white ye are, how soft ye feel beneath my fingers."

She'd turned a delicious shade of pink. Her lips were parted. She was staring up at him as if she'd never really seen him before. He was a genius.

"I think, Connie, that ye'll wed with me—in August, the day after ye turn seventeen. I have no intention of waiting for ye longer."

She gave him a sloe-eyed look that made him want to strip off her clothes and throw her onto the moss-covered ground. She lightly touched her fingertips to his cheek. She nodded.

He promptly pulled her tightly against his chest and kissed her. Ah, he thought as her lips parted for him, he was indeed a master. And it was only his first try at it.

33

The duke looked about the crowded drawing room. Brandy wasn't here. Where the devil was she? He hadn't seen her all day. What game was she playing now? He found that he was looking forward to seeing what she'd do. He liked being surprised, he realized, and she was good at surprising him. Ian forgot her games for a moment when Bertrand entered, his face a picture of satisfaction.

"My dear fellow," the duke said with a grin, "can I assume from the jubilant expression on your face that you've won the damsel?"

"Aye, that ye can. But please don't say anything just yet. I want to announce our engagement right and proper at the dinner table."

Ian realized suddenly that Bertrand was looking past him, toward the door, his mouth agape. "Good God," he said, sounding utterly nonplussed.

Ian turned about to see Brandy gracefully entering the drawing room. Jesus, he thought, sucking in his breath, staring at her like a benighted fool. She wore the blue velvet gown he had bought for her in Edinburgh. She was walking straight and tall, her shoulders back. Her glorious breasts blossomed above the bodice. She had fashioned her hair high atop her head, threaded with a matching blue velvet ribbon.

Two long curls rested provocatively over her bare shoulders. He was delighted at her transformation. Actually, he couldn't quite believe it. Where there'd been the girl, now there was the woman, and surely there could be no lovelier a woman than she. She'd been right, her cleavage started nearly at her neck. He grinned, picturing her outrage when he would agree with her later this night.

He saw, with some amusement, that like Bertrand, the rest of the family were held for a moment in speechless silence.

Brandy searched out his eyes and drew herself up even straighter at the wicked approval she read there.

Constance found her tongue and blurted out, "Brandy, what have ye done to yerself? How did ye manage to arrange yer hair like that? I thought ye knew only how to plait braids. And yer—well, yer bosom. I didn't know ye had such, well, never mind. It's amazing. Ye're beautiful and so very different than ye were just yesterday."

Lady Adella gave a sudden roar of laughter. "Shut your mouth, all of ye, and that means ye as well, Claude. Pull yer tongue back in yer mouth and yer popping eyes back into yer head. Well, child, ye're no longer pretending to be a scraggly weed. Come here and let me get a closer look at ye. Goodness gracious, don't ye look just like I did when I was yer age."

"Surely not," the duke said. "Never could she aspire to such heights."

Bertrand, who had long held the belief that his Constance was, at least in the physical sense, far

369

more mature than Brandy, managed to say, "Ye look lovely, Brandy. The dress Ian bought ye becomes ye perfectly, as does everything else."

"It's damned unsettling," Claude said. "She was a little girl and now she looks like a damned queen. It makes my poor gout flare. It makes my heart beat erratically staring at those other parts of her that she's always kept covered until this evening."

Brandy just nodded and sat down, not at Lady Adella's feet but in the chair next to hers. She knew she'd caused a stir. She'd been scared to death, truth be told, but when she'd walked into the drawing room and seen Ian, that had been all she needed. She was beautiful. All of her was beautiful. Even her breasts. So Uncle Claude's heart was beating erratically. That was interesting. She smiled at Ian. The look in his eyes was worth all of it. Wicked, wicked man.

"Now if ye'll only stop chewing yer fingernails, miss," Lady Adella said. "Even when I was yer age and looking even more beautiful than ye do now, I didn't chew on my fingernails."

Only Crabbe displayed no outward emotion upon seeing Brandy. "Dinner, yer grace."

The duke rose and crossed to Brandy. "May I have the honor, Miss Robertson, of escorting you to dinner?"

"Since ye've asked me with proper respect and deference, yer grace, I suppose it would be very small of me to say nay to ye."

"Never *small,*" he whispered close to her ear, "and I'll thank you never to say nay to me either."

370

Wicked, she thought. Utterly wicked. She loved him dearly.

He said pensively as they walked across the entrance hall toward the dining room, "Did you think me so unwilling last night that you decided you had to take special pains with your outward plumage? Aren't I fortunate to have you both in your glorious gown and in your equally enticing natural state?"

"I was thinking just the same thing about ye, Ian. Ah, that first night when I ran into yer bedchamber and there ye were, standing there for me to admire and even study, aye, now that I really think about it, ye were absolutely preening for me, just like a peacock. Then I saw you in yer evening clothes. Such a contrast, and yet now that I can have you both ways, I will consider myself as fortunate as ye consider yerself."

"Have I just been outwitted?"

She gave him a beatific smile.

Ian seated Brandy, then walked to the head of the table. He said in a low voice to Crabbe, who stood at his elbow, "Be so good as to unearth several bottles of champagne, will you, Crabbe?"

Bertrand found that he could contain himself only until Morag and Crabbe took themselves out of the dining room. At a wink from the duke, he cleared his throat and sent Constance a quick, reassuring smile.

"I would like to say, Father, Lady Adella, that in spite of yer infernal meddling and yer crass attempts at matchmaking, Constance has finally convinced me that it is my filial duty to comply with yer wishes and wed with her. In short, she'll be my wife in August after she turns seventeen. Aye, I'm a dutiful son, willing to go to almost any lengths to please my sire."

"Bertie," Constance cried. "Ye think yerself so amusing, do ye?"

"Let him crow, Connie," Brandy said. "Men need to crow and bray. It makes them puff up, like peacocks. I'm so happy for ye."

"I told ye, Claude," Lady Adella said with a huge grin, "that it would be more likely that our Connie would seduce Bertie. But it's odd. It doesn't seem to have happened that way at all. What, Bertrand, have you done to my granddaughter?"

"It's what he will do to her," Claude said, and laughed. "From the look in his eyes, it'll be a long time before the girl will be able to walk properly. It's to be hoped now that our little lass here can keep ye from that trollop in the village."

Bertrand almost groaned. Damn his father and his loose mouth. He looked at Constance. To his surprise, she was preening, tossing that lovely black hair of hers, obviously pleased with the utterly outrageous remark from his sire.

"He'll nay look at another woman, Uncle Claude, I promise ye," Constance said, and Bertrand nearly swallowed his tongue. Oh, God, he had to wait until August?

"So ye'll wed in August," Lady Adella said. She frowned. Then she primly pursed her lips and remarked with her own unique perversity. "I think, Claude, that the child is much too young for marriage. What with Bertie's pleasures in the village, believe ye not that he can wait to wed with her for two or three years?"

"Grandmama, I'll be seventeen."

"Lady Adella," Bertrand said smoothly, wondering what the old relic was up to now, "wasn't Constance's mother but sixteen when she wedded yer son?"

"Hoisted on your own petard, ma'am," the duke said.

Claude looked confused. He looked as if he'd just come into a room and thus didn't understand what people were talking about. "What is this, lady, ye want to butter yer bread on both sides?"

"Aye, and in the middle too," Brandy said.

"Ye can shut yer mouth, my fine little lady. At least our Constance has secured herself a husband, while ye, ye silly child, will probably hang on my sleeve till ye've got gray hair." To her surprise, Brandy just grinned shamelessly at her. She turned to Bertrand for better bait. "So, my bucky lad, ye've tied up everything right and tight? May I ask why ye didn't ask my permission or yer father's afore ye approached my little Connie? After all, what can a young girl like Connie know about the ways of men? Aye, my boy, ye didn't do the right thing at all."

The duke, who was vastly enjoying himself, said, "Surely, Lady Adella, you could never think Bertrand so remiss? Let me reassure you completely. Bertrand was very proper. Before he approached Constance, he asked my permission."

"Yer permission," Lady Adella roared. "Who

gives a sheep's offal for yer permission, my fine duke?"

"Why, I'm her guardian, ma'am."

"Look ye, duke or no duke, ye're impertinent and I don't like it." She drew up, her expression suddenly wily. "Ah, then as her guardian, my dear duke, may I ask what ye intend to do for her? I'll nay let her go empty-handed to her husband."

"No," the duke said, his voice calm as the North Sea this evening, "of course, I have no intention of doing so." He paused and looked first at Claude, then at Bertrand. "I want you all to listen to me. You remember, of course, that someone wants me dead. Indeed, that person may still want me dead. It only makes sense that what was true two months ago is still true today, whatever that something may be. However, I am as certain in my own mind as I can be that you, Bertrand, were in no way responsible, or you, Claude."

He was silent for a moment, looking at the sea of questioning faces around the table.

"I'm of the further belief that an Englishman, despite the fact that he holds circuitous blood ties to Scotland, shouldn't hold a Scottish estate or title. I think that I have come to better understand Scotland, its people, and its traditions. A Scottish earldom must have a Scottish master, it's only right and just. Therefore, as soon as Claude and Bertrand have been reinherited under Scottish law, I intend that both the earldom and Penderleigh revert to them, just as it would have if the old earl had not cut Douglass, Claude's father, out of what was rightfully his. That, Lady

Adella, is, I suppose, in part my dowry to Constance. She will someday become the Countess of Penderleigh."

"That's what ye were so intent upon this morning when I tried to talk to ye," Bertrand said, so startled that he could think of nothing else to say.

"Yes, in part."

"I'll be damned," Claude said, staring at the duke as if he'd never seen him before. "I'll be damned and damned yet again. This makes my heart beat more erratically than looking at Brandy's bos—than looking at the lasses. I'll be damned."

"Explain yerself, yer grace," Lady Adella screeched. The duke thought for a moment that she'd hurl her fork at him. Why the devil was she angry?

The duke raised a quieting hand to still the babble of voices. "There's really nothing more to explain, lady, save that, as I said, a Scottish earldom belongs to the Scots, just as it is appropriate that as an Englishman I hold English lands."

"The English are rapacious bastards, greedy and vicious," Lady Adella said. "The English don't just turn over property and titles."

The duke just grinned at her. "Perhaps I have tainted blood that makes me unnatural."

"But ye've poured *English* money into Penderleigh," Bertrand said.

"Yes, it was needed. Now that all the raw materials have been fine-tuned, so to speak,

Penderleigh will turn a fine profit, particularly, Bertrand, under your fine management."

"I'll be the earl of Penderleigh," Claude announced suddenly. "I'll be damned and damned again. I'll be the Earl of Penderleigh."

"And ye, Connie," Bertrand said with a quiet smile, "will some day soon have yer fine clothes and carriages and mayhap even a house in Edinburgh."

"I shall be a countess," Constance said. "I'll be damned."

"Well done, yer grace," Brandy said. She felt as if her heart would burst, it was so full.

"Yer mother must have played yer father false, Ian," Lady Adella said, "for never could ye have gotten such an idea from that little creeper she married."

"Little creeper, ma'am? The fourth Duke of Portmaine a little creeper? I'll have to ask my mother if such a thing was true. However, I remember my father very well, since he only died when I was nineteen. No, ma'am, he was many things, but never a creeper."

"And what if," Lady Adella continued slyly, "the Scottish courts do not choose to reverse the disinheritance?"

The duke just smiled at her. "I have the utmost confidence in your abilities, Lady Adella. But, of course, if you appear to be not up to the task, I will be forced to step in and see that the thing is done."

Did she never give up? She amused him as much as she enraged him. His plucking the power from her hands had to be quite a blow to her.

He was on the point of concluding that she had thrown in her hand, finally, when she said so acidly it would burn the polish off the silverware, "And just what, my fine *English* duke, do ye intend to do about my Brandy and Fiona? Now that ye've broken with Lady Felicity, ye've quite ruined Brandy's chances. Poor little girl, she'll be here forever now, attending me, taking care of all my needs, being my little drudge."

"Now, that boggles the mind," Bertrand said.

"Shut yer trap, Bertie," Lady Adella said. "Well, my fine English duke, who's so damned generous? What about my other girls? What about Brandy, who's so old she's nearly a spinster now?"

Brandy, who knew every one of her grandmother's vagaries in all their infinite variety, said, "Am I really almost a spinster, ma'am?"

"Hush yer smart mouth, girl. Well, yer grace, what brilliant scheme have ye concocted for them?"

"I think," the duke said slowly, frowning down at the parten bree on his plate that now looked very unappetizing, "that there's just one thing I can do."

"Aye? What the devil is it?" Lady Adella said, leaning forward so far that the beautiful Norwich shawl Ian had given her was nearly in the gravy.

The duke sighed. "I suppose," he said, "that I'll just have to marry the spinster. At least since I'm her guardian, I won't have to worry about being turned away. Yes, that's what I'll do. I'll sacrifice myself and marry the spinster. It will be difficult, but it's just, it's right. I'll do it to please you, Lady Adella."

"Marry Brandy?" she screeched. The tips of the shawl were in the gravy. "Ye can't marry her. Damn ye, it isn't funny, and I'm not at all amused. Ye marry my granddaughter?"

"Ian, are you—" Bertrand stalled.

"Oh, Brandy, ye a duchess and I'll be a countess. We'll be famous for our salons. Everyone will want to meet us. All the ladies will copy our style. Just imagine."

"I'll be doubly damned," Claude said. "But perhaps his grace is jesting?"

"Oh, no," the duke said. He continued, "As to Fiona, I think we'll give her a few years yet before we find her a husband. Ah, here is Crabbe with the champagne. Perfect timing, Crabbe."

"I've never been tipsy before," Constance said. "But tonight just might be my first time."

Although Lady Adella dutifully toasted the repeated announcement of each happy event, it was obvious that she wasn't happy. When Claude chanced to say again, "I'll be damned. I shall be the Earl of Penderleigh," she turned on him, thumping her champagne glass down so hard the delicate stem broke.

"Shut up, ye bloody fool. Ye're just like old Angus, forever boasting that *he* was the lord of the castle, when nothing could be further from the truth. Ye know well that I was always both master and mistress, and will continue to be so after the duke has left us. I'll continue to play the bagpipes, and ye'll dance to my tune."

Ah, so that was it, the duke thought, and looked

378

toward Claude. This should prove interesting. He also hoped that he wouldn't be disappointed in Claude. He watched as Claude drew back his shoulders, looking positively dignified. He said with devastating calm, "Ye've always been a power-mongering old witch, lady. Aye, Old Angus allowed ye to play off yer tricks, holding us all on a tight rein, making us dance or cower as the mood struck ye. Ye're nothing now except the *dowager* countess of Penderleigh, and as such, why, I think the best place for ye is in the dower house.

"However, lady, if ye make a push to mind yer tongue and grant me the proper respect and deference due to the Earl of Penderleigh and the head of the household, I suppose that I'll let ye stay in the castle."

Lady Adella's face was purple with rage. Ian would have applauded Claude's speech except he was afraid Lady Adella would expire on the spot.

"Ye said to me yerself, lady," Claude continued in a low voice, "that it was time for ye to make retribution. The duke has done yer work for ye. And don't get him wrong, lady, if ye don't do as ye should, he'll take it out of yer hands and do it for ye."

Bertrand sat forward in his chair, his eyes on Lady Adella. "Will ye tell us now about my grandfather Douglass, Lady Adella? Will ye tell us why the old earl suddenly disinherited him?"

"Aye, lady," Claude said. "It's time ye made a clean breast of it. I've hated the secrets. They've festered in the castle walls themselves as well as in my heart. Go ahead, for if ye don't, I shall. After all, if it hadn't been for ye and yer uncontrolled, hotblooded ways—"

"Shut yer mouth, Claude." Lady Adella sank into her chair. She closed her rheumy old eyes. "Ye're a whiner, Claude, always have been. I told Douglass never to tell ye, that it wouldn't end well if he did. Ye see now that I was right."

"I think it's ended very well," Bertrand said. "Everything will be as it should have been in the first place. The line has been reestablished. Tell me, Father, tell me why we were disinherited. I don't wish to wait until ye're on yer deathbed."

"Aye," Brandy said, sitting forward, her elbows on the table, "tell us, Uncle Claude. After all, ye could be struck by lightning and then none of us would ever know."

Lady Adella clutched her broken champagne glass and stared down at it. "Nay, Claude, close yer mouth. Ye'll not get it right. I'll tell everyone now. As ye know, being the eldest son, Douglass should have inherited the title and ye, Claude, should have followed neatly after him. I was much younger then, ye know, and Douglass was a man, unlike that weak, rutting Angus, his younger brother. Aye, we became lovers and none were the wiser for it until the old earl caught us in the hayloft. A terrible temper the old earl had, and he beat Douglass until he was nearly senseless. He severed the line on that day, disinherited his firstborn son and all his descendants. Angus never knew the reason, the gloating prig. His father decided I'd learned my lesson. He didn't want poor Angus to be hurt that his wife had played him false.''

''My father, Douglass, told me this on his death-bed,'' Claude said. ''By that time ye were old, Lady Adella, and I could scarce believe him. I looked at ye and I just couldn't believe that any man would have ever wanted to make love to ye. But it was true.''

The duke, now worried about Lady Adella, said, ''Perhaps I should more closely inquire into Brandy's antecedents. All these secrets, all this intrigue, why, who knows from whose seed she sprang?''

He achieved the result he'd hoped for. Lady Adella whipped up her head and looked at him with fire in her eyes. ''I'll thank ye to watch yer tongue, my fine duke. It's possible that there's dirty linen somewhere in yer closet as well.''

''I'll thank ye not to say anything about dirty linen, lady,'' Claude said sharply. ''Douglass married and I was born in wedlock.''

''Yer grace,'' Brandy said, ''perhaps we could go to the drawing room. Connie can play the pianoforte for ye. Everyone can become calm again. Everyone can regain his balance.''

"I'll be damned," Claude was heard to say several more times that evening.

Lady Adella recovered herself by bedtime. Ian heard her say as she rubbed her gnarled hands together, "A countess and a duchess. Aye, I've done well by the both of the girls. And I'll do well by Fiona, too."

It was with a good deal of regret that Ian kissed Brandy outside her bedchamber door, then opened the door and shoved her inside. "Saturday," he said, sounding to be in extreme pain. "I can wait until Saturday."

"Don't I have a say in this?"

"No. Go to bed. By yourself. Be quiet. Kiss me again."

"If I may congratulate yer grace," Fraser said after saluting the duke in his usual manner with his garden trowel, his round face split with a smile.

"Thank you, Fraser. Is Bertrand about? Or is he mooning over his future wife?"

"He's having his lunch, yer grace. Mooning as well, I imagine. He just holds up a fork and looks off into space and grins like a madman. As to Master Claude—well, yer grace, ye can well imagine that he slept very little last night. Master Bertrand said that all he could do was sit in front of the fireplace, mutter to himself that he was going to be the Earl of Penderleigh, slap his hand on his knee, and talk about fate."

Ian laughed. He followed Fraser to the parlor, where Bertrand was indeed sitting motionlessly, not eating, his food untouched, just staring out the window into Fraser's beautiful garden. He looked up at the duke and gave him a fat grin.

"Ian, come in, come in. Fraser, bring his grace some of yer excellent scones and strawberry jam. Like me, his grace must keep up his strength—trying times ahead for the both of us."

The duke sat himself across from Bertrand at the small circular table and said after Fraser had left the parlor, "More trying than you imagine, Bertrand. And that is why I am here. Just how does one procure a special license in Scotland?"

Bertrand raised a startled eyebrow. "I had no idea that ye wished to move forward so quickly."

"I don't wish to give Brandy any time to change her mind. There's also the matter of a parson."

"Yer scones, yer grace," Fraser said, moving quietly to his elbow. The duke nodded and said no more until Fraser had once again taken his leave.

"Well, ye know that Percy and Joanna are to arrive today. Do ye wish to avail yerself of their parson?" He shook his head. "Lord, I can't wait to see the look on Percy's face."

"Actually, I'm expecting him to be well behaved, at least in front of his betrothed. This is important to him. Yes, he'll be polite and suave."

"Aye? What is it, Fraser?" Bertrand asked, turning in his chair.

Fraser was frowning. "I don't rightly know, Master Bertrand. Wee Albie came with a message fer his grace." He extended a folded sheet of paper toward the duke.

"What the devil?" Ian took the paper from Fraser and spread it out on the table before him.

He read the large, scrawled words once, then yet again, unable to believe what he was seeing.

". . . if ye wish to see Brandy alive again, ye will come unarmed and *alone* to the abandoned wooden barn that lies just to the west of the high cliff road. . . ."

"Fraser, fetch Wee Albie. At once."
"Aye, yer grace."
"Good God, Ian, what's the matter? What is that letter?"

35

Giles suddenly rose and cocked his ear toward the barn door. "Ah, our hero now, come to rescue his damsel."

Brandy twisted about, pulling herself to a sitting position, and looked wildly toward the barn door. She screamed, "Ian! Go back! Don't come in. Giles will kill you." She stared in mute misery as Ian kicked in the rickety wooden door and hurtled inward, rolling onto his side in the shadowy corner of the barn to come up on his hands and knees. He blinked rapidly to accustom his eyes. It was so bloody dark in here. Giles yelled, "No, Duke, I know you've got that damned pistol of yours palmed in your right hand. You try using it and I'll kill Brandy. See,

I've got a pistol against her temple. Throw that gun toward me, Ian, now!"

He felt the weight of failure. He'd literally been blinded by the gloom in the old barn. He stared toward his cousin. Giles, he thought, Giles. All the time it had been his cousin. Not a Robertson, but his English cousin, the man who was his nominal heir. He threw the gun toward Giles. "I've done as you asked. Get that gun away from her head."

Giles lowered the pistol from Brandy's temple.

Ian called, "Brandy, are you all right?" She lay propped up against a moldering pile of hay. Giles was standing near her now, the pistol lax in his outstretched hand.

"Aye. Oh, Ian, ye shouldn't have come."

"Don't be a fool, Brandy. Clever of you, Giles, with your Scottish spelling—you had me quite convinced that I would find Percy here to kill me so I couldn't reinherit Claude and Bertrand."

"Yes," Giles concurred with a brief bow, "I thought it was a good touch. You would have saved me much trouble, Ian, had you died that first time."

"Why, Giles?"

"I do so dislike that blunt manner of yours, Duke, but since you will know the truth, I must plead guilty of greed. A plain *Mister* Giles Braidston has never been to my liking, you know. I believe I've hated you since I came wailing from my mother's womb. I think I must have sensed even then that you'd won and I'd lost. You would be the Duke of Portmaine. I wouldn't be much of anything."

Ian said slowly, instinctively sparring for time, "There are only two years between us, Giles. You have known all your life that I was to hold the title. You hated me? Surely I gave you no reason to. No one ever turned up their nose at you. Your income is handsome. You can have nearly anything you wish. You certainly lead your life as a gentleman of leisure."

"Paltry, Ian, paltry. I can't remember the day when I wasn't heavily in debt. Being your nominal heir has, indeed, been the only bar to my more pressing creditors. No, Ian, I'm the natural Duke of Portmaine, not you. I hear you gave away Penderleigh and the title. I will reverse that, naturally. Even if Lady Adella tries to reinherit that old fool Claude, why, your vast wealth will be in my hands and any of their machinations won't come to anything. A duke doesn't give away his birthright. You're a fool."

Ian forced himself to keep his voice steady, not to show incredulity or anger. "You made no attempts on my life when I married Marianne, Giles. There could quite easily have been an heir born within another year had she not died."

Giles said, his voice almost gentle, "My dear cousin, do you not recall how very much time I spent with your young wife? We were much the same age, you know, and it required little effort on my part to gain her confidence, for she held you in tremendous awe. You always wondered, did you not, what prompted her to be so bold as to take herself off to France, supposedly to save her parents? You cursed yourself because you

386

hadn't gained her trust, because you failed to save her from the guillotine.

"One afternoon while you were at your club, I paid her a visit and found to my surprise that Sir William Dacre had just told her that she was pregnant. Within hours, cousin, I presented her with a letter, again supposedly written in great haste, from her esteemed parents, the Comte and Comtesse de Vaux, begging her to come to France and plead their case before Robes-pierre's tribunal. I was eloquent, I assure you, and finally convinced her that if you knew she was carrying your precious heir, you would never let her travel to France. She pleaded with me to help her. I had gotten her to Paris when she tearfully told me that she'd left you a letter. I thought myself quite done in until she told me that she had dared not mention my name for fear that you would blame *me*.

"I did then what I had to do. I sent Marianne's direction to the citizen's committee, and was on a packet back to London within the hour. I only discovered later that her parents had fallen under the guillotine nearly a week before. I thought it all rather ironic. Then, of course, she was guillotined."

The duke simply couldn't take it in, not at first. Giles had seen to it that Marianne had been killed. He as good as released the hook on the guillotine himself. He'd murdered her. He wanted to fling himself on Giles, to choke the life out of him. He couldn't keep his rage to himself even though there was still a cool, logical part of his brain that was clamoring for him to keep his

control. "You filthy bastard. Marianne was innocent. She'd never harmed anyone in her life. You
murdered her. God, I'm going to kill you."

"I can imagine that you want to, Duke. Don't
move or I swear I'll kill Brandy. Come now and
think. You must realize there wasn't anything else
to be done. If she'd borne you a son, I could have
no longer nourished hope of becoming the Duke
of Portmaine. Nor could my creditors. Nor could
my friends. In short, I would have been treated
as a simple Mr. with nothing to impress anyone."

Brandy saw Ian's rage, the trembling of his
hands. She had to buy time to gain control. She
said to Giles, drawing his attention from the duke,
"But Lady Felicity—she was to marry Ian, yet
ye didn't kill her. Ian was yer target."

Giles did look at her, but only for a moment.
"As I told you, Brandy, Scotland was a blessed
opportunity and one I couldn't afford to pass by.
Everyone was sure to suspect one of the Robertsons. And I must admit that Felicity was a very
different kettle of fish from Marianne. Such a
greedy, cold lady, Ian. How lucky you were to
be rid of her. I must admit that she taxed my
ingenuity, for her mind was so much set upon
being the Duchess of Portmaine."

The duke said slowly, "All those barbs to her
as well as to me—I thought it merely your way
of warning me, protecting me. But it wasn't. You
wanted her to be appalled at the thought that I
wanted children. You wanted her to be so
revolted that she'd break off our engagement."

"Yes, Duke. I had nearly given up hope of
routing the lady when your autocratic, stubborn

temper combined with her hatred of the Robertsons, Brandy, and Scotland finally won the day.
I quite enjoyed escorting her back to London.
Your money was paying all the bills, and I didn't
have to worry about the bitch any longer."

"You encouraged her in her jealousy of
Brandy, didn't you, Giles? It was you who pushed
her to come to Scotland, you who made her question my honor."

"Naturally. I even spoke ever so solicitously to
her dear mother, another bitch. The note you
wrote me the day you left London—that came
as quite a shock to me. You planned to marry
Brandy. I hadn't guessed, but I should have. How
did it feel, Ian, to have your betrothed and your
mistress under the same roof?"

"Ian, don't." She held out her hand. Ian
stopped dead in his tracks. Giles took a hasty
step backward, only a few feet in front of Brandy.
She found herself growing almost morbidly calm,
for she knew that Giles would kill them both
when he had finished his bragging. She barely
heard Giles's voice as she frantically searched
about for something, anything she could use as
a weapon. She had almost decided to hurl herself
at him when she saw a long wooden-handled
haying fork half buried under clumps of moldering hay. She inched toward it until the toe of
her shoe reached the haying fork.

"Surely you must realize, Ian," Giles said,
"that I cannot allow you to wed Brandy. I regret
what I must do, but there is simply no other way.
My plan is distasteful, I admit, for I don't really

want to kill her. But there's no hope for it. Once I sent you the note, her fate was decided."

Ian saw Brandy moving slowly behind Giles. If only somehow she could distract him, if but for an instant.

"I believe I've explained myself to you. Now, I have a long ride ahead of me. I will be well ensconced in London when the news of your tragic death at the hand of a Scottish Robertson comes to my ears. Ah, what a stir I'll cause. I'll shout and scream in the House of Lords that you, my noble cousin, was murdered by a savage Scot. Who knows what will happen? Maybe this ridiculous pile of a castle and all the Robertsons will be transported."

From the corner of his eye, Ian saw that Brandy was easing the haying fork into her hands. If Giles saw her movement, all would be lost. He rushed into speech. "I believe you now, Giles. You do hate me. I've been blind. Have you laughed at me when I had my secretary pay your bills? Or did me paying you make you hate me more?"

"Of course I hated it. Wouldn't you?"

"Did you conceive your plan when you first heard of my Scottish inheritance?"

"No, not at first. But enough, Ian. I'm not without feeling and assume that you would wish to die first. I am truly sorry, cousin, but I must now bid you a final good-bye."

"No!" Brandy shrieked as she heaved up the haying fork. She swung it wildly, with all her strength against Giles's back.

Giles whirled on her, striking the side of her face with the butt of his pistol, sending her sprawling to the ground. Ian hurled himself toward Giles, grabbing furiously at his arm. They grappled in panting silence, Giles struggling to turn the pistol inward to the duke's chest. He felt himself weakening in his cousin's powerful grasp and tried desperately to pull himself free. He stumbled backward, jerking the duke with him. Ian stepped on the pronged blades of the haying fork, and the wooden handle whipped up, striking his arm. Giles drove his fist into Ian's stomach and leaped back, shakily aiming the pistol at the duke's head.

"Hold, Mr. Braidston!"

Giles only dimly heard the sharp command. As he tightened his finger on the trigger, he heard a crashing sound explode in his ears.

Ian watched in amazement as Giles, his face distorted in ghastly surprise, weaved above him, then fell heavily to the ground.

"Are you all right, y'grace?"

Ian gazed up into the leathery face above him, for an instant too stunned to speak. "You saved our lives, man. Who the devil are you?"

"Me name's Scroggins, y'grace." He dropped the smoking pistol to help Ian to his feet. "The young lady hired me two months ago to protect you. You've led me a fine chase, y'grace, what with all your gallivanting about in London, then your trip back here to Scotland. Always fancied visiting Scotland, I did, and just look what happened. All the action was here, not back home."

The two hundred pounds.

Brandy was struggling up on her elbows, her

vision blurred from the blow Giles had given her. She smiled up at him. "No, I'm all right, Ian, truly, I'm quite all right now. Thank you, Mr. Scroggins. You've done all I could have wished for. Thank you for our lives."

Ian dropped to his knees beside her and cupped her chin in his hand. Gently his fingers explored the line of her jaw. He smiled at her. "Your jaw isn't broken, thank God. But you'll be black and blue for your wedding." He turned briefly toward Giles's fallen body. "He's dead?"

"Yes, indeed, y'grace. I couldn't take the chance of only winging 'im, for he still might have shot you. And you were me client."

"My thanks, Scroggins."

Scroggins chuckled. "I don't mind telling you, y'grace, I was beginning to wonder if the young lady weren't a bit screwy in her thinking. But a job's as you finds it, even though you have to trek all over the countryside." He frowned down at Giles's body. "Mighty wily cove, your cousin was. Very nearly fooled I was. Aye, I'll admit it and I'm the best. But I knowed something was in the wind when you flew off on that mighty brute's back, your eyes blazing murder."

Ian looked a last time at Giles. Brandy placed her hand upon his arm. "Let's leave this place, yer grace."

"I'll take care of 'im, y'grace. You take care of the young lady."

"There's a local magistrate. His name's Trevor. I'll send someone from the castle to assist you." Ian cupped Brandy's elbow with his hand for support and walked beside her from the barn.

The bright afternoon sun blazed down from a cloudless blue sky. Ian drew a deep breath. Never had life seemed more precious and, at the same time, more fragile.

"I owe you much, Brandy, including my life. I can't remember when the expenditure of two hundred pounds bought me so very much."

"I never knew who the man was. You see, Mr. MacPherson arranged it all. He proudly informed me that he had hired the services of a former Bow Street Runner." She paused a moment, gazing up at his profile. "I'm sorry for deceiving ye, Ian, but I thought if I told ye the truth about the money, ye would be touchy, thinking yerself inviolable. Ye're a proud man, Ian, that's why I kept it to myself. Ye would have sent him packing, wouldn't ye have?"

He thought grimly that this might very likely have been the case. Because he was too damned proud to admit that he could be killed. It chilled his blood. "Perhaps," he said. A man could only admit to so much, after all. "How do you feel?" He kissed her mouth, then hugged her tightly against him.

"Like I've been knocked in the head too many times. Surely marriage can't be any tougher than this was."

"I sure the hell hope not. However, now that I see you in the sunlight, I know you're going to be black and blue on Saturday. Everyone will call me a brute and not worthy of you."

"Ian, I'm so sorry about Marianne."

For a moment he couldn't speak. Giles had paid with his life. Ian didn't think it was enough.

So much loss all because of a single man's greed. "Thank you, Brandy," he said. He lifted her into his arms and swung up upon Hercules's back. "Let's go home."

36

Danvers, the Carmichael butler for more than thirty-five summers, looked out from the long parlor windows over the front lawn of Carmichael Hall at the two squawking peacocks—one male and one female, a disaster, he'd said from the very beginning. The male simply wouldn't leave the female alone. At the moment his tail feathers were spread in riotous color. He was chasing the peahen, his brand of charm, Davers thought. The peahen ducked back behind one of the elm trees that bordered the perimeter of the home wood.

Danvers had heard her grace call the male Percy. His grace had said pensively that he wasn't sure what to call the female, but he had at least one excellent idea. Her grace had punched his arm. Regardless, Davers would like to see the Percy peacock in Cook's baking pan, the bloody bleater.

"Never a moment's peace," he said to Mrs. Osmington, the duke's admirably efficient house-keeper. "I wouldn't be a bit surprised if Dr. Mulhouse, jokester that he is, gave them those wretched birds as a wedding present only because her grace said that England lacked the color of

394

Scotland. It's my belief that those puffed-up noise boxes will scare away the deer."

"Well, you must know, Mr. Danvers," said Mrs. Osmington, her fingers unconsciously fiddling with the huge circle of keys at her waist, "I heard her grace laugh in that good-natured way of hers and admit to his grace that she'd really been thinking about heather, not peacocks."

Danvers grunted and turned away from the windows. He withdrew a large round watch from his black coat pocket. "Dr. Mulhouse has been upstairs for over an hour with her grace. It is hoped that all is well with the heir."

Mrs. Osmington nodded her head in a peculiarly birdlike movement. "At least her grace, most sensibly in my opinion, is very conscious of her delicate condition, not galloping about the countryside like Lady Dorrington, who I'm convinced suffered complications because—" She drew to a disconcerted halt. "How right you are, Mr. Danvers. Such a long time it's been and nearly lunchtime it is. I must inform Cook it's likely we'll have another place at the table."

Dr. Edward Mulhouse was at that moment frantically searching his brain to come up with something that would make the duke's wife relax. She was stiff as a board, her eyes were tightly closed, her hands were fisted at her sides. It was obvious she was embarrassed, miserably uncomfortable, and that if the duke hadn't insisted she be examined, she would never have let him come within two rooms of her.

He adopted his most soothing voice. "Come

now, it's all right, Brandy. I've attended more than two hundred births. Please don't be embarrassed. Won't you relax?"

Nothing changed. Edward looked up at the duke. He was beginning to feel as inept as she was embarrassed.

The duke said, with all the flavor of the autocrat in his deep voice and a wicked grin on his face, "Brandy, if you don't ease, I'm going to force brandy down your throat until you're giggling and carrying on like you did with me just last Wednesday night. Don't you remember how—"

"Ian, don't you dare." Her eyes flew open, her fists tightened. She looked ready to jump up and hit him.

He grinned like a sinner at her. "Come, let poor Edward do his job. I'm watching him carefully. You needn't worry that he'll do anything untoward. If he does, he knows I'll pound him into the ground. He knows that after I've pounded him, I'd plant him in the petunia bed. Then I'll send goats over to eat the petunias."

She laughed. "You're not funny, Ian. I'm just laughing because, well, never mind. I'll make you very sorry you said all that in front of Edward."

"Let him do his job," the duke said again. He pulled a chair to the bedside and took his wife's hand. "Onward, Edward, do what you have to do."

"Brandy, please relax your stomach muscles. There, that's better. Ah, the babe kicked me." He smiled as his hand carefully pressed against her growing belly. "Lively little fellow, feels like he's turning cartwheels."

"The babe's a little brute," Ian said. "I was simply showing my wife a bit of affection just this morning, and he walloped me with a big foot. I know it was a foot even though Brandy swore it was his head. No, I told her, all the Dukes of Portmaine have big feet." Ah, he thought, she was distracted. In fact, if she didn't shoot him after this was over, he'd be surprised. "Yes," he said, "in that respect, he'll be just like his father. Big feet and a great lover."

"Don't forget born diplomats," Edward said.

He watched Edward's hands disappear beneath the sheets. He didn't like it, but he imagined that Brandy was ready to expire. Edward was fast, Ian would give him that.

In just another moment Edward rose, smoothed down the covers, and said, "Everything is just fine. You're small, Brandy, but that's just as well. We don't want you to become over-large, given the size of your husband. Yes, all will be well. Now, if you could just speak to your husband about his constant conceit at beating me at chess. I hear you play. Beat him, Brandy, bring him down."

"I'll try," she said. "I promise."

"Seriously," Edward said, "you're the picture of health, Brandy, and so is the babe. You've nothing to worry about, save, of course, Ian driving you to bedlam. I swear if he demands one more detail of the birthing process, I'm going to let him do it."

"God, no, thank you," the duke said. He actually turned pale. "You've got to be here, Edward, you must."

"I think you've got him, Edward. Play a game of chess with him after lunch. Just perhaps you'll win this time."

The duke smiled. "We'll go down now, Brandy. I'll send Lucy to you, though I'll bet you she's pacing the outside corridor like a mother hen. You'll have luncheon with us, won't you, Edward?"

"I will."

Ian patted Brandy's hand and accompanied Edward from the bedchamber.

Edward said as they walked down the great staircase, past the second footman, into the hunting room, "If you hadn't been present, I believe she would have refused even to admit me."

"Perhaps, but in spite of her grumbling, she did keep to the bargain. She promised when the babe kicked, she'd let you examine her. Now, Edward, is everything truly as excellent as you told Brandy?"

"Indeed, yes," Edward said, accepting a glass of sherry. "As I said, the babe's smaller than I expected, and that's a good thing. I think the less weight she gains the better. It should make the birthing easier for her. At least that's the modern view of many of your London *accoucheurs*."

Edward swirled his sherry about in its beautiful crystal glass, which was at least three hundred years old. "She's also carrying the baby very high, which in my experience indicates a boy. But I refuse to lay a wager with you."

"I believe Brandy is thinking of a daughter—

a pert, redheaded little girl like her sister Fiona. The child will come to live with us next month."

"Good Lord, Ian, what a staid, virtuous family man you're becoming. Within a year of your marriage, you'll have two children. What is this Brandy was telling me the other day—you've struck some sort of Persephone arrangement?"

"Nothing quite so mythological. I wouldn't ever expect Brandy to give up all she knew and spend all her time in England. We'll spend some months every year at Penderleigh. You'll have to come and visit, Edward. It's a grand old place— moth-eaten in many places and a romantic crumbling turret—and a servant, Morag, who never bathes, except for that one time in honor of Percy's marriage.

"Ah, Edward, I can just imagine you seated across from Lady Adella, listening to her tell you exactly what to do and how to do it and when to do it. I'll wager she'll even come up with some physical complaints you've never heard of just to test you. Yes, I'd like to see you swallow your tongue. We'll travel to Scotland early next spring."

"It sounds like a trial, Ian. I'd never heard a Scots accent before. Most folk love to hear Brandy speak. That beautiful lilting accent of hers. I hope she never loses it."

"I won't allow her to. I imagine when we go to London some will want to turn their noses up at her, but since she is a duchess, I doubt anyone would dare try it. She's doing very well here. She was so worried that she'd blunder and embarrass herself and me." He grinned. "No chance of that.

The servants would kill for her. All except for that one maid, Liza, who thought she was an usurper. She's no longer at Carmichael Hall, naturally."

"After you dismissed her she said some pretty bad things about the duchess in the village, but no one paid her any heed." Edward slapped his hands to his arms. "Lord, but the cold weather is upon us early this year."

"I hope those bloody peacocks take a chill and fold down their feathers," the duke said.

"Unkind, Ian. What is a poor man to give to a duke for his wedding gift?" He looked about the large, dark-paneled room, the gun collections sufficient, he thought, without a smidgeon of envy, to outfit an entire regiment. He remembered the toy soldiers and guns he and Ian had shared when they'd been eight years old. "The fellow who sold me the birds told me they were sound sleepers. They do sleep at night, don't they?"

"Most of the time. Ah, here's Danvers with the mail." Edward watched the duke quickly pull out the very foreign, very dirty envelope and hold it up. "A letter from Lady Adella. It's sure to make Brandy forget her embarrassment with you. I only hope that she won't go into convulsions when the old lady rants on about the new earl's—that's Claude, you know—repulsive conduct. Poor Claude, he's only held the title for little more than a month now. I dread to hear what she'll be calling him when we go there in the spring."

Although Brandy didn't quite fall into convulsions at the outrageous recital of Lady Adella's woes, she did choke with laughter over her soup. The duke thwacked her back, telling her to have a care with his babe.

"Poor Grandmama," Brandy said. "She sounds miserable. Can you believe that Uncle Claude had the courage to order her to turn the keys of the castle over to Constance? Not, of course, that Grandmama ever much concerned herself with housekeeping matters, but to call her naught but a—ah, where is it?—aye, 'a meddlesome, interfering old woman and *only* the dowager countess'—she must have been teetering on the edge of apoplexy."

"That or we'll get word that she shot him."

"Or struck his gouty foot with her cane," Brandy said, grinning.

"I have a great aunt Millie who sounds remarkably like Lady Adella," Edward said. "She's known to shrivel the local vicar to his knees with her vitriol. Her sisters and brothers live in terror of her."

"Perhaps the two of them could live together. What a competition that would be." The duke added, "Ah, Brandy, listen to this: Lady Adella says that Percy has been hot off the mark and 'planted a bairn in Joanna's belly.' It appears that Percy is showing himself quite the model husband, a circumstance, she adds, that will last only as long as Joanna's extreme strength of character."

"We must write," Brandy said, "and congratulate them. I think if anyone can curb Percy's more undesirable tendencies, it is Joanna."

"Since she holds the purse strings," the duke said, "there's hope. Lady Adella's last line, if I can make it out—yes, it appears that Fiona begs her to tell you that she had nearly tamed the porridge—no, papou—"

"Porpoise, Ian, porpoise. How delightful for her."

The duke just shook his head. He said to Edward, "Another cousin, Bertrand, calls Brandy a mermaid since she loves the sea so much. I look at her now and think about that and it makes me laugh so hard I nearly choke. Can you begin to imagine a pregnant mermaid?"

"I wonder how a mermaid could birth a baby," Edward said, saw that Brandy was staring at him appalled, and quickly cleared his throat. "Just a ridiculous question. No, Ian, don't say anything. I don't want the duchess to throw me out with the peacocks."

"Not you, Edward," she said. "I want you to tell my husband that I'm going to have twins. That will give him his just deserts, to have a fat and lumpy wife."

Edward laughed. "I've already told him it's just one babe this time, Brandy. You'll have to find another way to bring him down."

"She finds ways daily," the duke remarked, and took a bite of very thin-sliced ham, one of Cook's specialties. He looked down at the letter again, saying, "Your esteemed grandmother appears to have spent all her excess bile. She even wishes you well. I wonder if it caused her pain to do that? Now, Edward, that you're in possession of some juicy family skeletons, I trust you'll not resort to blackmail."

"I won't do that until after I've finally beaten you at chess." He consulted his watch. "I must be going. Luncheon was delicious, as usual. I've got to visit Rigby Hall. Lady Eleanor is breeding again. This is her tenth child. She isn't happy with Sir Egbert."

"I wouldn't be happy either," Brandy said. "Goodness. Tenth?"

As they rose from the table, Ian said, "I remember you complaining about nothing to do. Not even a boil, you told me. Now, if the gentlemen of our acquaintance continue the way they are going, you will find yourself boot-deep in babes."

They stood on the front steps and waved Edward on his way. Brandy turned her face up to her husband. He kissed her and kissed her again. His hand lay lightly on her belly. "I love you," he said, and she touched her fingers to his beloved face. "And I ye, Ian."

He kissed her again, his hand moving up to lightly touch her breast. He groaned in her mouth. "Just the feel of you," he said, his breath hot against her lips, "I love to feel you."

The duke heard Danvers coming close. He cursed under his breath. He removed his hands from his wife's breast. He looked at her mouth and nearly cried. Then, as Danvers grew close to them, the duke turned to look out over the front lawn.

Brandy said in great seriousness, even though her hands itched to touch him, "Ye know, Ian,

England simply doesn't have the smell of Scotland."

"No, there aren't any sheep within miles of here."

Danvers was nearly upon them. Brandy forced herself to take a step away from her husband, for his hand was hovering near her belly again. "That," she said, "isn't what I meant."

Danvers cleared his throat just at the duke's right elbow. The duke said, "That's true, but hear me, Brandy, we do have peacocks, if Danvers allows them to live outside Cook's baking pot. What do you think, Danvers? Do we let the squawkers live another week?"

"It will be close, your grace. Very close."

Brandy laughed, drawing close to her husband again. He hugged her against his side.

"Life is very nice," she said. "I'm so glad I decided to marry you."

"Very nice indeed," the duke agreed. "If you hadn't married me, I would have thrown you over my saddle and carried you off to some distant island. You didn't have a chance."

"That's a very nice thought."

The duke then kissed his wife in front of the Portmaine butler, who didn't bat an eye and who, in fact, had forgotten what it was he'd meant to tell the duke.

IF YOU HAVE ENJOYED READING
THIS LARGE PRINT BOOK AND
YOU WOULD LIKE MORE
INFORMATION ON HOW TO
ORDER A WHEELER LARGE PRINT
BOOK, PLEASE WRITE TO:

WHEELER PUBLISHING, INC.
P.O. BOX 531
ACCORD, MA 02018-0531